THE WARMTH OF HER AFFECTION

ELSIE FULBROOK

Quills & Quartos
PUBLISHING

Edited by Jo Abbott and Regina McCaughey-Silvia

Cover by Evelyne Labelle, Carpe Librum Book Design

ISBN 978-1-956613-53-7 (ebook) and 978-1-956613-54-4 (paperback)

For R

CHAPTER ONE

Hertfordshire April 1815

There are few things more interesting to confined country society than the arrival of a young gentleman of means. Unfortunately, however, although Netherfield Park had stood for almost five years in want of a tenant, it showed no sign of being occupied, whether by a young gentleman or anyone else. The people of Meryton therefore had to be content with the news that, after standing only two years empty, the smaller, more isolated Purvis Lodge had been taken by a young widow.

Gossip flew around the drawing rooms and parlours of the Hertfordshire matrons as to this new arrival. Her name, it appeared, was Mrs Wilson, and she was universally agreed to be youthful, although no one seemed to have yet met her. It was a mark against her name that she had not employed any of her servants from the local area, having instead brought a small number with her. They were viewed with some suspicion when encountered shopping or running errands in the town, for they kept to themselves and exchanged only minimal pleasantries with their peers.

Purvis Lodge stood just beyond the confines of the Meryton parish boundary, so any hopes that Mrs Wilson would be displayed for the good people of the town to scrutinise were disappointed. One or two of the more enterprising matrons, however, recalled they had for some time wished to hear a sermon from the rector of St Michael's, who had been in post for only four years, and thus made their way to the neighbouring church one Sunday morning. They returned from their venture with very little to report on the sermon but a great deal to report on the lady.

"She certainly *is* a lady," Mrs Long confided to her particular set in Mrs Philips's drawing room. "Bears herself very proud, and her mourning dress must have cost a pretty penny."

"Indeed," Mrs Philips agreed. "Such deep mourning. She must have been most attached to her husband. And so young to have lost him!" She cast her eyes up in a mournful attitude that had the assembled women nodding and murmuring their sympathy.

"Is she so very young?" asked Mrs Bennet with some interest. With five unmarried daughters, ranging in age from eighteen to twenty-five—and even the youngest having been out for three full years—news of a wealthy young widow moving into the neighbourhood was not entirely welcome.

"Very young indeed," Mrs Long confirmed. "It is hard to place her precise age, with her black garb and sober features, but she is certainly not as old as your Lizzy. Perhaps as young as Kitty, or even Lydia."

"Not more than twenty and already a widow!" Mrs Philips was inclined to see the romance in the young woman's mysterious history. "And with those poor boys of hers, too."

This interested the group all over again, and Mrs Philips preened at being the first to bring the news of the children. Mrs Long was quick to add her own comment. "Oh yes, two small lads, they cannot be more than three years old. Twins, I imagine. Could not be more different, however. One with hair as gold as the sun—much like his mother's, from what I could make of it, although his face bore no resemblance. The other takes more from her in features but with an unruly mop of dark curls."

This new piece of information kept the women discussing the matter for some time, until reluctantly Mrs Bennet stood up to leave. "Well, I must be returning. No doubt this young widow will bring little change to our society, although Lord knows we could do with more variety!" She made her good-byes and called her youngest daughters to her side from where they had been seated with other younger ladies of the town.

As soon as they were in the carriage, Mrs Bennet burst out, "Well! If I never hear another word about Mrs Wilson, I shall not be sorry! Why she interests everyone so, I cannot fathom. Anyone listening to their conversation would think our society was limited! I shall think no more about her."

Lydia, sprawling on the seat opposite, rolled her eyes. "It was all the other girls could speak of, too. So dull! Why can't something interesting happen in Meryton?" Kitty agreed with her, then complained about Lydia taking up too much of the seat. The journey back to Longbourn continued in much the same manner for the entire ride, each taking it in turns to complain of the other's particular wrongs.

Having determined to think no more of the new inhabitant of Purvis Lodge, Mrs Bennet naturally spoke of little else for the remainder of the afternoon. Her youngest daughters, soon growing tired of the conversation, made little pretence at attending and would interrupt her with questions or arguments about their ribbons and gewgaws. Her middle daughter, Mary, attended somewhat more closely, and observed more than once that Mrs Wilson was to be commended for retiring to spend her period of mourning away from the temptations of society; although having made this original observation, she could add nothing to it and fell silent. Only the two eldest, Jane and Elizabeth, listened with anything akin to compassion, reflecting on what it must be like for the young woman to find herself alone in an unknown society with two small children, and wondering that she had no family to go to.

"When do you intend to call on Mrs Wilson, Mama?" Jane interjected after Mrs Bennet ran out of breath from one of her longer speeches. Mrs Bennet looked astounded.

"Visit her? And why would I do that, pray?"

"Because she is new to the neighbourhood and might be in want of good society," Jane replied mildly.

"I am sure Lady Lucas will be calling on her this week," added Elizabeth with an innocent air.

"Oh, well, Lady Lucas may do as she pleases," Mrs Bennet sniffed. Nevertheless, she looked thoughtful.

It did not surprise either Jane or Elizabeth when, at breakfast the next morning, Mrs Bennet announced her intention to call on the newcomer. Genuinely curious, and also wanting to protect the stranger from their mother's effusions, they both agreed to accompany her, although the younger girls declined. Privately, Elizabeth was grateful because this meant the widow need not be afflicted by her youngest sisters' exuberance or Mary's moralising.

Purvis Lodge was around a mile and a half from Longbourn, taking the road from the front drive. Elizabeth would have much preferred to walk there across the fields which, cutting across part of the Netherfield grounds, would be under a mile, but her mother insisted it looked as though it might rain, and that the carriage was required. The three women therefore arrived in some state at Purvis Lodge.

They were greeted by a woman some ten years older than Mrs Bennet, who showed them into the drawing room where the young mistress was sitting. Elizabeth's first impression was that she was indeed young, for she could certainly not be more than twenty years of age. Her second impression was that she was timid, for as she stood to make her curtsey, she kept her eyes largely downcast, and only a brief, nervous smile crossed her lips. Her third impression was that her eyes, when she lifted them briefly, were pitifully sad. Had her mother not been present, Elizabeth might have immediately gone and taken the younger woman's hand and begged to be her friend, but this was a polite call, and decorum demanded that she remain at her mother's side.

They offered the gifts in their baskets, which were accepted with quiet, undemonstrative thanks, and made conversation regarding the house and the local area for the duration of their call. As the time came to depart, Mrs Wilson softly said, "Forgive me. I do not expect to be much in company. You have been very kind to call, and I shall return your civility, but I beg you please do not importune me with many invitations to larger gatherings. I find I am not yet ready to be in society."

Mrs Bennet was inclined to take this as something of a slight, and in the carriage began with a characteristic, "Well!"

Jane, however, wishing to think the best of the newcomer as she did of everyone, cut in gently. "I thought Mrs Wilson seemed very amiable. She must have been sorely grieved to have lost her husband so young. She did seem appreciative of your kindness in visiting, Mama. Did you not hear her say, Lizzy, that we were the first to call on her at home?"

"Indeed I did," said Elizabeth with a laughing smile at Jane's subtlety. "And I believe I liked her very well, although she was so timid. Perhaps in time, as her mourning passes, she might be persuaded more into society."

CHAPTER TWO

M rs Wilson, it seemed, was firm in her intention not to be drawn into many visits or social events. She returned calls to Longbourn and to the other women who called on her, but declined all evening invitations and absented herself from wider social events.

When she called at Longbourn, she spoke little, facing the arrayed Bennet women with an alarmed eye. Mrs Bennet kept up a constant stream of empty chatter about local affairs, Lydia and Kitty occasionally interjecting, and Mrs Wilson nodded politely. Jane smiled benignly from her seat; when opportunity allowed, she attempted to steer the conversation away from gossip to the interests and pastimes of their visitor, but Mrs Wilson would not be drawn on the topic. She rebuffed Jane so gently, however, that even Elizabeth could not take offence on her sister's behalf. She thought, at one time, that Mrs Wilson was glancing across at the pianoforte, and was almost persuaded she was about to ask whether any of them played. As Mrs Bennet chose this moment to inform Mrs

Wilson of the recent scandal caused by one of the women of the town having been seen with new French lace on her dress, for all that it was so difficult to obtain, however, she had no way of proving her suspicion. When the time came to leave, she gave her thanks and departed as quietly as she had arrived.

Slightly against her will, Elizabeth found herself being drawn into the mystery of the young widow. She had such poise, coupled with such reserve, that Elizabeth could not prevent her heart weaving romances around the sadness in the lady's eyes, although her mind fought against the impulse. She felt there was a story to be told, somewhere, and longed to know what it could be, but felt equally strongly that Mrs Wilson had made her preference for privacy clear. Elizabeth intended to respect such a preference, particularly since it was not accompanied by any outright slights to her family or the people of Meryton, but she could not help but think over some of the many possibilities.

A few days after Mrs Wilson's call, Elizabeth decided on a whim to take a walk in the direction of Purvis Lodge. She persuaded Jane to join her, and the two set out together across the fields, which were thankfully dry. They did not intend to call on the occupant, but curiosity drew them in that direction, and they did not resist its pull.

They were just within sight of the lodge when they caught a glimpse of a small blond head looking at them with red eyes from a dip alongside the path. The child was perhaps two or three years old, and Jane, always drawn to children, smiled at him. He hid his head from her before peeping out again.

He whispered something that sounded a great deal like "No tell Tommy."

"Not one word," Jane agreed solemnly, as Elizabeth

smiled and winked at him. He nodded seriously at their acquiescence.

With a last smile, they passed the boy and continued on, intending to make a circuit back on a different path. As they neared the house, however, they encountered another person in the form of a flustered-looking maid running out of the gate, skirts lifted and twisting in every direction with frantic haste. "Master Joey!" she called in evident distress, before noticing the two young women and dropping an anxious curtsey. "Oh, beg pardon, I did not see you."

Jane smiled kindly at the worried girl. "I believe you may find what you seek back along this path. There is a small dip in the road."

The maid gave her thanks with wide eyes and scurried past them, where she gathered up the small charge despite vehement protests and much wriggling. "Master Joey, you know you are not to leave the grounds without your mama's say-so." She carried him back towards the house, offering the briefest of nods in lieu of a curtsey to the two young ladies, who had stopped a short distance away. "Thank you, miss," she said quietly to Jane, turning in at the gate. Joey's eyes peered over her shoulder at them until Elizabeth lifted a hand to wave, when he quickly hid his face.

Although they had not technically been introduced, their new acquaintance remained much in their minds, and not many days after this, Jane was again persuaded to join Elizabeth for a walk along the path leading to the interesting widow and her young family. They did not tell their mother the direction they intended to walk; Mrs Bennet had decided, in concert with the other women of Meryton, that whilst Mrs Wilson was clearly respectable, she could bring no great variation to their days. They would respect her privacy by not seeking her out any more than was strictly necessary, but instead would gossip freely behind her back about the cut of her clothes and the style of her hair.

"At least," Mrs Bennet said to Mrs Philips during one morning call, "she is not likely to take any suitors from our girls if she goes so little into society. Not that there are many suitable young men to be found," she bemoaned. "Poor Jane will have to go to London for another Season at this rate, or she will never be married! I only hope our brother Gardiner will take her to the theatre more when she goes, for I do not think she went above twice the last time she was in town."

Once free of the house, Elizabeth skipped, breathing in the morning air and smiling at her sister. "I am glad you joined me today, Jane. I could not bear to think I was off to be curious by myself, even if it is just walking past the lady's home."

Jane smiled. "I do take pleasure in a walk, Lizzy, although not as far or as frequently as you. Besides, my curiosity extends so far that I hope to see the mysterious Tommy sitting in a dip by the path on this walk."

Elizabeth laughed aloud. "Do not let my mother hear you say so. She would misunderstand you entirely and imagine all manner of things on your behalf without waiting to discover that it is your love of children, rather than any other reason, that draws you out of doors."

Jane smiled indulgently at her sister. "Lizzy!"

They walked on in silence until they reached the house. By unspoken agreement, they slowed, although they made sure not to stare. Elizabeth smiled at Jane's attempt to conceal her mild disappointment that no children were visible, but said nothing. They had passed the house and were beginning to pick up their pace when they heard a voice behind them.

"Excuse me, miss."

The sisters turned to see the same young girl as they had encountered on their previous visit bobbing a small curtsey.

"If you please, the mistress noticed you were passing and wondered whether you might call on her this morning?"

Elizabeth's broad smile was met by a nervous return from the maid. "That is very kind of her," she replied, and with a quick look at Jane, who nodded her affirmation, continued, "we would be delighted."

They were shown into the drawing room as before, but on this occasion, to their delight, the mistress was accompanied by Master Joey and another small boy. Their young mother smiled at the two ladies and came forward to meet them.

"Thank you for stepping inside to join me," she said quietly. "I heard you passed by not so long ago, and I was hoping you might walk this way again. I had hoped to know you both better."

"And we you," Elizabeth replied with merry eyes. "Although I must confess, we were drawn this way not only for that purpose, but also to make the more formal acquaintance of a young gentleman present."

Said gentleman had placed himself close by his mother's skirts but was looking out at them with large eyes. Jane smiled at him, and he hid his eyes for a moment before looking back with a small smile of his own.

Mrs Wilson put her hand fondly to his head. "Ah yes, you have met Joey already. Come out and meet the ladies, my love." The boy stepped out and made a comical attempt at a bow as his mother introduced them, which Jane and Elizabeth acknowledged gravely. She then turned to her other son, who was playing with tin soldiers in a corner of the room. "Tommy, come and meet our new friends."

Tommy did not look up. The battle he was fighting

between two of his soldiers continued with greater fervour. "Tommy!" his brother hissed at him, but to no avail.

Only when Mrs Wilson said more sharply, "Thomas!" did he look up, a small frown on his face, and make his way to her side.

He endured the introduction but returned immediately to his toys. Jane, unperturbed by this, took a seat close to him, allowing Elizabeth to lead the conversation. She watched Tommy play, and after a while, leant across to him and asked whether the soldiers had names. He looked at her again with a furrowed brow and nodded. She looked at him expectantly, and, pointing to them in turn, he gave them each their names. Jane proceeded to ask who was the bravest, whether any of them thought the uniform was rather itchy, and whether any of them had a sweetheart at home. This last question drew another wrinkled frown from the boy, but his brother, who had been drawn in by the conversation, pointed to one of the soldiers that had a slightly misshapen hat. "Gon' marry her soon," he whispered. "Got fightin' first."

Whilst this important conversation was taking place, Elizabeth was talking to the boys' mother. To begin with, they kept to safe topics: the state of the weather and locations of particular beauty or interest in the neighbourhood that Elizabeth could eulogise at length, although Mrs Wilson confessed she had not yet ventured far from her home. After a while, Mrs Wilson asked about the local society, and Elizabeth, in response, drew affectionately teasing caricatures of some of their neighbours. This produced a wide-eyed smile from the younger woman, who, for all her widow's weeds, appeared to Elizabeth to have little worldly experience. She decided to chance a question of her own. "Have you no similar characters from your own home?" she asked.

Mrs Wilson's expression, which had been open and

engaged, even if a little surprised at Elizabeth's freedom, closed upon itself. She hesitated before replying. "I was not long out of school when I was married. I regret I have not spent long in any society in recent years."

"Well, we are glad to have you in ours." Every trace of humour had disappeared from Elizabeth's tone, although she stored up the interesting fact of the lady's education, and she spoke only in gentle earnestness as she tentatively reached out and lightly touched the younger woman's sleeve. "I do hope we might be friends, Mrs Wilson."

The widow looked across at her sons, by now playing happily with Jane, and then back at Elizabeth. Her eyes were sad, but a timid smile played at the corner of her mouth as she replied, "And I, also."

After this mutual statement of intent, Elizabeth felt the call had taken enough of Mrs Wilson's obviously limited social energy. Catching Jane's eye, the sisters rose together and bade their new friends goodbye. Mrs Wilson looked on benignly as both young boys followed Jane to the door, and Tommy earnestly tugged at her sleeve. "Come 'gain, Miss B'nnet?"

Jane looked at Elizabeth and then at Mrs Wilson, who nodded. "Yes, I do hope to do so, Master Tommy. I shall see you again soon."

After this encounter, a friendship quickly sprung up between the three young women. Elizabeth and Jane began to call on Mrs Wilson regularly, when the weather permitted. Occasionally, she would return the call, although she never stayed at Longbourn for long and was always quieter in the presence of the assembled Bennets than when she was in her own home. Lydia and Kitty clearly unnerved her with their exuberance, although she made some tentative overtures to Mary, particularly once she discovered that she played the pianoforte and could be pressed to perform. Although Mary's skill was more in technical perfection—the result of long hours of imperfect rehearsals—than in expression, Mrs Wilson appeared as enraptured as though she had witnessed a first-rate display of talent.

Whilst friendship blossomed, Elizabeth made little headway with discovering Mrs Wilson's history. Occasionally, she would unthinkingly let slip something about her childhood, which sounded lonely to Elizabeth, for she confessed she had few friends her own age. About her marriage and recent past, however, she would say nothing, clumsily turning the conversation whenever it came up. Elizabeth did not press her for more details than she was willing to give. As her affection for her new friend increased, she found in the enjoyment of her company that it became easier to fight her curiosity on the subject of the lady's past.

Even her Christian name was something of a mystery, for although Elizabeth and Jane after some weeks both invited Mrs Wilson to address them more familiarly, they were met with a polite but firm refusal. Jane was convinced that, coming as she did from a different part of the country, Mrs Wilson must have been accustomed to different social conventions. Elizabeth suspected there was something more to it, and that her friend wished to conceal her name for reasons of her own. As Mrs Wilson evidently enjoyed their company, however, and was willing to talk on most subjects that did not touch on her own history, Elizabeth was in all well pleased with the acquaintance.

The making of a new friend did not in any way diminish Elizabeth's affection for the others around her. Her heart could easily expand to accommodate all, and she was just as often in company with her friend Charlotte Lucas as she had been previously. It was her long solo walks which suffered from her additional sociability, and this she found she could very easily bear when the walk to Purvis Lodge still held such interest.

Charlotte was much less curious about their new acquaintance. "She seems a very respectable young woman, Lizzy, and although so young, she evidently has sufficient means to establish a home of her own." Charlotte's voice held a note of envy in this, and they returned to an old theme between the two. Charlotte, at thirty, was widely thought to have passed any opportunity to marry. Although her circle would never discuss this within her earshot, Miss Lucas was considered a confirmed spinster. Charlotte was more than aware of her status, particularly since the marriage of her younger sister Maria to a gentleman of a small estate ten miles away, but was grateful for the solicitude of her friends in not drawing it always to her attention.

"Do not regret, Charlotte! You may simply not have met your love yet. I hold out hope he will be the one to take Netherfield Park, and he will realise he needs a mistress of sense as well as beauty."

Charlotte laughed aloud at this. "Flatter my sense all you will, Lizzy, but we both know beauty is not my portion."

Elizabeth indicated her disagreement, but Charlotte laughed again before continuing pragmatically, "No, I am reconciled to my appearance, for it is the only one I shall ever have. I do not think I am destined for romance." She paused, then more wistfully said, "I do not regret that. But I fear dependence on others. I shall always be a burden to other people, and I would much rather have found a husband who could give me a home of my own. At least then I might be useful in keeping the house and any children."

Elizabeth's brow furrowed. Although three years past twenty, she still had a great deal of romance in her and had turned down two proposals from respectable men. They had admired her, but one had spoken little sense, and the other had shown her little respect. She was only grateful neither had chosen to transfer their offers to her younger sisters, for she could not help but feel none of them were yet ready to become a wife. Thankfully, although her mother had berated the men in private for pursuing and then slighting her daughter, she knew nothing of the proposals, or she would have berated Elizabeth still more. Jane was yet to receive any offers of marriage, although a good number of men had worshipped at the altar of her beauty before drifting away into nothing. Jane disliked speaking of her marriage prospects and had grown wary of any discussions on the topic, but Elizabeth held to the belief that the difficulty was only that her sister, like Charlotte, had yet to meet the man who would suit her best. Jane was not yet an old maid, she was sure.

"I do not understand you at all, Charlotte," she replied with mock seriousness, for they had long known how different their views were on marriage. "But enough of such topics. Who could trouble themselves over gentlemen when the world looks as glorious as this?" She flung her arms wide to encompass the new green of the trees in Lucas Lodge Park as the spring turned into summer.

"We can agree on that, at least. It reminds me of when you used to insist on coming here to build a bower."

"Oh yes! Perhaps we might build one now," replied Elizabeth with delight. "We would look quite the proper ladies, sitting surrounded by logs strewn with dying flowers. I could build a shelter between the birches as I used to do."

Charlotte nodded. "Yes, and tear your dress clambering up to reach, and cover your gown with leaf litter and mud. It would be just like old times."

"Except I would have to clamber higher to build the shelter big enough for us to sit under now. We are a little taller than we were then."

"I am, perhaps," Charlotte replied with solemnity. "I do not believe you have grown much taller."

Elizabeth laughed aloud and, assuring herself that there was no one in sight, ran ahead of her friend and skipped under the trees.

CHAPTER THREE

Although the elder Bennet sisters' friendship with Mrs Wilson continued to blossom, to most of Meryton society the lady had quickly been discarded as a person of interest. She was always polite, always ladylike, but she did nothing whatsoever to create gossip. Thus, she was relegated to an occasional mention in conversation, on the rare occasions when she was seen in the town purchasing ink or any other small necessities.

Meryton was just settling into a long summer of little news or entertainment when everything was thrown into disarray. Mrs Bennet, bustling into the drawing room after Sunday services, was evidently bursting with some news she had heard, and turned in a flurry to her husband, who had foolishly entered the room in pursuit of his reading glasses.

"Mr Bennet! Have you heard the news?" Enthusiasm made her shrill.

Elizabeth watched as her father winced and very deliberately crossed to the door before turning back. "I am sure you will tell me regardless, my dear Mrs Bennet, and more than once, so you had better get the first telling over and done with."

Mrs Bennet waved a hand at him in vexation but could not be long irritated when she was all a quiver with anticipation of unlooked-for delights.

"Netherfield is let!"

"Is it?" Her husband's disinterested tones did nothing to settle her as she reached the pinnacle of her joy.

"To a gentleman! A single gentleman, by all accounts, for he brings a sister to keep house for him. And he must be a man of considerable means to have taken such a property. Oh, Mr Bennet, when you visit him, you must invite him to dinner one evening. He will dine with us, and fall in love with Jane, and keep coming to dinner, and then he will marry her and we all shall be saved!"

Mr Bennet looked at his eldest daughter, who was focusing steadily on her embroidery with only the slightest flush to show she had heard. He smirked a little, but then his eyes met Elizabeth's, and he seemed to consider his words, saying only, "I am sure your table will be quite enough inducement for any gentleman to join us for dinner, Mrs Bennet."

"Oh, but he must fall in love with Jane and save us from the entail!" Mrs Bennet did not notice her daughter's hand hovering unmoving over her sewing. Elizabeth reached out and took it with a light squeeze.

Mr Bennet patted the door frame lightly as he replied, "Yes, well, Jane is a mostly sensible girl." With this mysterious comment, he departed for his study. Mrs Bennet was left bemoaning his lack of interest, and she bustled out of the room in search of a more sympathetic—or less overtly uninterested—listener in Mrs Hill, the housekeeper.

Elizabeth squeezed Jane's hand again. "Jane?"

Her sister carefully released herself from Elizabeth's grasp and, with a grateful glance, returned to her sewing, seeming to take comfort in the repetitive movement and the resistance of the fabric under her needle. "Mama is animated at the newness of it all, Lizzy. She will be calmer soon." Her voice was mild, although Elizabeth readily detected an undercurrent of disquiet. She resolved to do what she could to counter any schemes of her mother's when the gentleman came to dinner. She had no doubt it would come to pass. Her father delighted in teasing his wife, and was never in a hurry to complete any task he saw as onerous, but he knew what was required of him as the owner of Longbourn and the father of five unmarried daughters. Elizabeth could only hope his natural indolence and delight in needling his wife would not delay the first meeting for too long.

A week passed, in which Mrs Bennet only became more frantic as she learnt more details about the occupant of the great house.

"Lady Lucas tells me the new tenant of Netherfield is called Mr Bingley. A distinguished sounding name, do you not think? I am sure Sir William will be calling on him very soon, if he has not already done so! But you delight in vexing me, Mr Bennet, and you will not visit him!"

On it went until the following Sunday, and there was a great deal of interest from six of the seven people in the Longbourn pew to see the inhabitants of the long-empty Netherfield seats across the aisle from them. Mrs Bennet fluttered with her prayer book, turning to a page and pretending to be absorbed in it before closing it and shifting in her seat, watching the door eagerly. Lydia had ensured she was seated at the end of the pew, where she would be the first of their party to be seen, although Kitty would insist on speaking to her and demanding an answer, forcing her to turn her head towards her sister and away from the door.

Elizabeth was almost as eager as Mrs Bennet to see Mr Bingley, for whilst she did not share her mother's ambitions to have him marry one of them at almost any cost, she enjoyed new company and hoped he would be of a sociable turn of mind. Jane, although embarrassed and uncomfortable with her mother's schemes, harboured a secret interest that she would never admit to. She longed to be married and have a family of her own almost as much as her mother longed for it for her. She was entirely predisposed to like Mr Bingley and, although she kept her eyes modestly down for the most part, could not help but sneak a glance every time someone entered the church.

Of the two remaining, only Mary had no interest in the gentleman's arrival, being engaged in private prayer before the service began. Mr Bennet, although he looked at his wife and daughters with a sardonic and superior eye, waited eagerly enough for the gentleman to appear. He had called on Mr Bingley the day after hearing of his arrival at Netherfield, had been introduced to the other gentlemen in his party, and was looking forward to the moment when he would be able to greet them as acquaintances and see how his wife handled the shock. That the moment would take place whilst she was constrained by the behaviour expected in church only caused him greater amusement.

Mr Bennet was not disappointed. When Mr Bingley entered the church, a lady at his side and leading a party of another lady and two gentlemen, such murmurs arose that no one could be ignorant of their arrival. Even Mary glanced up from her hymnal, although for barely a moment. Lydia and Kitty leant out of their pew to see better, giggling freely. Mrs Bennet drew herself up with haughty reserve, prepared to face the smirks of her neighbours. She watched with narrowed eyes as Mr Bingley made his way to the pew, affably greeting everyone of his acquaintance. As he approached, she prepared an indifferent yet welcoming smile, hoping it might prompt the gentleman to request an introduction from the Lucases.

As it was, Mr Bingley's eye was drawn to their pew, although not to Mrs Bennet. His eyes flickered across the assembled daughters, lingering but a moment on Jane before he greeted Mr Bennet with a broad smile and a short bow. "Mr Bennet," was all he said before being hustled into his seat by the lady he escorted. For the rest of the service, however, his attention was drawn repeatedly back to Jane, much to Elizabeth's pleasure. She could not but notice that her sister, after one sweet and winning smile at the gentleman, gazed at her prayer book through the whole service without once turning a page. She could see why, for he was handsome and appeared amiable, as far as might be told from the few paces it took him from church door to pew.

Mr Bingley paid no mind at all to Mrs Bennet, who—her cheeks a bright shade of crimson and her usual volubility stifled by their location—continued to gape at him throughout the opening address and at intervals during the service.

Elizabeth noted that Mr Bingley was not the only one of his party to show interest in the Bennet family. After his friend greeted Mr Bennet, the tall man who entered the church last also acknowledged him, without smiling, before his eyes swept rapidly across the assembled women. He might have been handsome were it not that his face was utterly grave and a little pinched. He could not be older than thirty and was immaculately dressed. From the way Mr Bingley's companion attempted to draw the gentleman's attention her way and encourage him into the pew to sit by her, as she had her brother, it was clear he was unmarried and that the lady wished him to be otherwise. He paid no attention to her, however, and she was disappointed in her attempts, for his observation continued until the rest of the party was seated.

Elizabeth, noticing his scrutiny, wondered what he must be looking for. He had an abstracted air, as if his mind were occupied elsewhere, but he seemed to be counting them almost, looking at each of the women in turn before nodding to himself as though confirming some thought he harboured. She met his eye and was surprised when he held her gaze for a moment before again nodding abstractedly. She did not know what to make of it.

In contrast, Elizabeth's opinions of the other members of the Netherfield party were quickly formed. The lady at Mr Bingley's side, who she surmised to be the sister who kept his house, made little acknowledgement of anyone in the church beyond her party, except in a supercilious smile that did not reach her eyes. She was dressed in what Elizabeth assumed was London fashion, and her silks seemed excessively fine for their country church. She radiated disdain, and Elizabeth had to control her inclination to laugh at the lady's mien.

The other two members of the party struck Elizabeth as remarkably bland. They had nothing to either recommend them or to dislike. Perhaps they were dressed a little too fashionably, but they had less overblown finery than the other lady. They nodded politely to other members of the congregation but smiled at none. The lady seemed well pleased with herself, and the gentleman had a sleepy look that suggested he had risen earlier than was his custom for the sake of attending the service, but all in all, Elizabeth felt they were no more or less ridiculous than many others of their acquaintance.

All of this observation passed in the time it took for the party to be seated, after which the service began and passed without unusual incident. As soon as it was over, Mrs Bennet insisted on hurrying her daughters out of their seats as quickly as could be done with propriety, harrying them all out into the churchyard, where her urgency suddenly disappeared as she fretted around Jane and found a place for her to appear to best advantage. This achieved, she abruptly remembered it was imperative she speak to Lady Lucas, and that they would therefore need to wait for that lady's emergence.

Her manoeuvres were largely unnecessary, for Mr Bingley would have been drawn to the Longbourn party as he left the church even had they been standing in the darkest corner of the churchyard. Mrs Bennet's satisfaction at seeing him pause with admiration was great, and all intention to speak to anyone else was forgotten. Elizabeth, observing her mother's machinations, stood close to Jane to shield her as best she could, should it be required.

Mr Bingley approached as soon as he had performed the necessary niceties with the parson. His eyes left Jane for but a moment as he bowed to Mr Bennet, straying back to her as he requested an introduction to the ladies. Mr Bennet, with a sardonic smile, obliged, before Mr Bingley introduced the ladies that accompanied him. The lady he had escorted was, as Elizabeth had surmised, his sister, Miss Bingley. She greeted them all with polite condescension before stepping to one side and surveying them with barely concealed distaste. She again attempted to draw the attention of the solemn gentleman, but he remained at his friend's side as the other lady of the party, Mrs Hurst, was introduced, along with her husband. She proved to be another sister of Mr Bingley. The final gentleman was introduced as Mr Darcy. He deigned not to smile at the ladies but bowed gravely.

Bows being made, Mr Bingley immediately introduced the topic of the coming assembly and how pleased he would be to have an opportunity to become better acquainted with the people of Meryton. He addressed all of this to Jane, who smiled her serene agreement, and before many moments had passed, he had secured her hand for a dance. He then turned to Elizabeth for another and seemed about to continue through the ladies when Lydia put herself forward in front of Mary with a smirk. Mr Bingley was for a moment discomposed by her action, but then continued as though he had intended all along to secure Lydia's dance next. He would no doubt have asked Mary and Kitty for dances too, but at that moment his attention was called by Miss Bingley.

"Come, Charles! I am sure Louisa is keen to return to Lucy."

Mrs Hurst, who had been standing by, idly admiring her fan, looked up and agreed in languid tones. "Indeed, I do wonder how my poor child fares. Croup can be so terribly unpleasant for children, do you not you think, Mrs Bennet?" She did not wait for an answer but looped her arm through her husband's and pulled him away. Miss Bingley seemed to be about to do the same to Mr Darcy, but seeing her brother had made no move away from where he was standing, she instead seized him and with a pointedly polite farewell, followed her sister, looking back only to ensure Mr Darcy followed.

To her quickly concealed dismay, Mr Darcy did not do so immediately. Instead, he looked for a moment at the Bennet family, then addressed the eldest Miss Bennet.

"Has your first dance yet been taken, Miss Bennet?" She

indicated that it had not, and he continued, "May I request the honour?" Securing Jane's agreement, he then turned to Elizabeth and, in a similar form of words, requested her second dance.

Having settled this matter, Mr Darcy turned abruptly and followed the remainder of his party, cutting off Mrs Bennet, who only managed to exclaim, "Oh! Mr Darcy!" to his retreating back.

CHAPTER FOUR

Longbourn was soon in uproar. Mrs Bennet, having been denied the opportunity to encourage the gentlemen in person, fretted over the state of Jane's dresses, constantly changing her mind about the best way to do them over whilst complaining loudly that her sister Gardiner ought to have written to her with the latest London fashions.

"Do you not want to look your best for Mr Darcy, Jane? Mrs Long told me he has ten thousand a year, and he has asked you for your first dance! Although Mr Bingley was also particularly taken with you. They must see you in something new and fresh!"

"Yes, Mama," her daughter replied meekly, continuing to sew. Mrs Bennet huffed, and was about to depart to examine Jane's closet for the fourth time that day, when her eye alighted on Elizabeth, who was reading nearby.

"And what are you about, Lizzy?" Mrs Bennet wailed at her. "A book in your hand! You may not have your sister's beauty, but with a little effort you might look very well. Mr Bingley may very well offer for you, if Mr Darcy prefers Jane. Oh Jane, my beautiful daughter! If I could only get a little extra pin money, I might have bought you that lovely cherry silk! Oh, but you will look handsome, and if Mr Darcy does not wish to marry you, then Mr Bingley will. I must visit my sister Philips!"

With this, Mrs Bennet left, and her two eldest daughters heaved in unison a sigh of relief. After a moment, Jane spoke. "I do not mean to complain, but I sometimes wish Mama would allow me to prepare in peace. After all, any dress I wear will be new when we have only just met." She sighed again as she spoke.

"I think you do mean to complain," replied Elizabeth with a smile. "I do believe you are becoming churlish in your old age. You would not have spoken so a few years past."

"Oh, do not call me old! Mama means well, I know, but to be so constantly reminded that I have failed her. It can some-times be hard to bear." Her voice was unsteady, more so than Elizabeth was used to hearing. She pondered this fact for a moment before a suspicion dawned that her sister was, in her own manner, as keen to impress the gentlemen as their mother was.

"Do not allow yourself to think so. Why, no one could doubt that Mr Bingley at least is as conscious as anyone that you are the most beautiful woman in Hertfordshire. His interest was plain, it was only a wonder that he requested but one dance."

Elizabeth's sharp eyes did not miss Jane's fleeting look of consciousness. She was a little surprised; Mr Bingley was undoubtedly handsome, but they had spoken so little. It seemed precipitous for Jane to be so interested in him already.

"He asked to dance with you too, Lizzy. And Lydia," Jane added as an afterthought.

"Indeed. So he has proved he has good taste! For you are beautiful and dance like a sylph, and Lydia dances with such enthusiasm that he will be able to retire from exhaustion and devote himself to your comfort for the remainder of the evening. And," continued Elizabeth, smiling, "he has evidently realised that if he is to please you, he must also make himself agreeable to me by including me in his general goodwill."

"Lizzy," Jane smiled with indulgent affection. "I am sure you do not believe that any more than I do. Besides, it was not only Mr Bingley who engaged us to dance. Mr Darcy asked us too."

"Indeed! And he is to open the dancing with you. Perhaps Mr Bingley will be green with envy, and we shall see swords drawn at dawn in Netherfield Park, and you may weep over the slain as the victor claims you as his own."

Jane laughed, despite herself. "I think Mr Darcy only intends to be courteous."

"I think," Elizabeth echoed, "Mr Darcy intends to impress us with his superiority. Certainly the grandeur of his bow and the way he inspected us all in the church indicated that he meant us to understand he was a person of some importance."

"I thought he behaved like a perfect gentleman." Jane would have said the same of any man of their acquaintance, and Elizabeth discounted this observation accordingly.

"And what did you think of Mr Bingley?" she asked with teasing innocence.

Jane suppressed a smile. "I thought Mr Bingley behaved like a perfect gentleman."

The same sentence sounded very different with her

sister's subtle change of emphasis. Perhaps Jane truly was ready to admire and be admired.

The sisters' tête-à-tête was interrupted at this point by their two youngest sisters, who entered the room arguing loudly. Lydia was crowing over Kitty that she was to dance with Mr Bingley, and the older girl was loudly complaining that she was always overlooked, and as the older she ought to have been next invited to dance. Lydia pointed out that Mary was older than either of them, and delighted still further in the fact he had passed over two of her older sisters in her favour. Mary, following them into the room, said nothing, but opened her instrument and began to play. All peace was lost for the time being.

The days before the assembly proved trying all round. Amidst all the preparations, Elizabeth would escape as often as she could to visit either Charlotte or Mrs Wilson, sometimes with Jane but often alone. At Lucas Lodge, she found the solace of long familiar company, where she could complain about her mother with impunity. She rarely needed to, however, for Charlotte was so familiar with all of the Bennets that a mere sigh would produce sympathetic agreement. Charlotte provided an excellent supply of distraction, light teasing, good sense, and support.

At Purvis Lodge, Elizabeth found a different respite, for she was received with increasing enthusiasm. That she was welcome, she had never doubted, but she also felt she was being somehow useful. Mrs Wilson, still timid and reserved in some ways, was beginning to blossom with their companionship. Sometimes, her sons would be present, and Mrs Wilson would show an unexpectedly playful side as she interacted with them. At other times, the children would be occupied elsewhere, and the ladies would sit talking idly as they worked.

"How did you find the poems?" Elizabeth asked during one such visit. She had taken to bringing her embroidery with her and staying for a few hours when she was able. They had long abandoned formal calls to Purvis Lodge, although Mrs Wilson still kept strictly to form in her rare calls at Longbourn. Her friend smiled at her.

"They were beautiful. I have read Shakespeare's sonnets before, of course, but hearing you read aloud last time brought them alive in a way my governess was never able to. I had forgotten that poetry lived and breathed, and was not merely a construction of rhyme and metre."

"I am glad you enjoyed it. I do love to read aloud. Perhaps I might try one of the plays next."

"Oh, do! I used to love to be read to when I was a child. My mother had a beautiful voice."

"Did she read to you often?"

"Yes, when I was small, for she loved stories and sharing them with me. In her last illness, she would have me by her side daily. At first, she read to me, then, when she became too weak, I read to her, although I stumbled over every word."

"You were not confident at reading aloud then?"

"No. I-I was very young." Her eyes filled with tears, and Elizabeth reached out instinctively to comfort her friend.

"I am sure she loved you dearly. It is a great thing to have memories of shared moments, even though they may be tinged with later sorrow."

Mrs Wilson could not reply for some time, but as the quiet tears subsided, she smiled at Elizabeth gratefully. "It is a long while since I have spoken of my mother to anyone."

"Then I thank you for confiding in me."

They sat in companionable silence for a while, before Mrs

Wilson resumed their previous conversation. "You will read to me on a future visit?"

"Gladly, if you wish. Perhaps Jane might be persuaded too, as she makes an excellent nurse to my Juliet."

Mrs Wilson laughed. It was a melodic sound, rare, but becoming less so with time. "I would have expected it to be the other way round."

"Yes, you would have thought so, would you not? However, I am prepared to take you into my confidence if you will not reveal what I am about to say to anyone." Elizabeth looked at her friend in mock solemnity.

"I promise," Mrs Wilson replied faithfully, taking her cue.

"Jane is the better mimic, and the nurse sounds remarkably similar to my mother."

Mrs Wilson laughed again. Mrs Bennet was a creature of some awe for her, for she knew of few people who could speak so long, so loudly, or with such indecorous freedom. Mrs Bennet belonged to an entirely different breed of women to the one she recalled as Mama. "I long to hear it."

"And you will! Only, perhaps not until the assembly is over." Elizabeth held her work out and sighed at the amount still to be done. "It is a shame you are not in a position to attend the event. Do you like to dance?"

Mrs Wilson sighed, and hesitated, before tentatively admitting, "I have never danced at a public event. I used to dance at school of course, and at home before my marriage, at private family events. But never at a real ball." She sounded wistful. "I had hoped, when I was married...but it was not to be."

"In time, when your mourning has passed and you feel ready for greater society, I shall make sure a ball is held in your honour, even if I have to throw it myself! Although

Longbourn is better suited to a private dance. Netherfield is by far the largest property in our vicinity, and the best suited to a ball. Perhaps Mr Bingley might hold one," she added musingly. She was intent on a knot in her thread that needed untangling, and neither saw the expression on her friend's face nor heard the slight intake of breath at her words. When she did look up, Mrs Wilson was focused equally seriously on her own work.

"Did I tell you yet of Mr Bingley and his party?" Elizabeth asked idly.

"No, I do not believe you did."

"They are a thoroughly picturesque group. I am not sure our society has seen such beautiful or well-dressed people for some time. Excepting of course Jane. And you," she added, smiling. "You are exceedingly handsome, you know."

Mrs Wilson blushed. "As are you. But I do not think I am."

"That is a quarrel for another day, but I thank you for the compliment." Elizabeth paused and returned to her needle, and her friend breathed more easily until she spoke again. "I was speaking of Mr Bingley. He seems a very amiable man, prepared to dance with every maiden in Hertfordshire I suspect, although he had the good taste to appear the most enthusiastic to dance with Jane. He is handsome too, and they would make a fine pair. But I get ahead of myself! I have been spending too long listening to my mother. Mr Bingley seems all things affable, from what little I have seen, and therefore I have nothing to say about him.

"His sisters, however! Now they were delightful. Everything I might have hoped for from women of fashion. Miss Bingley's smile is a sight to behold. I have never seen one that expresses so much of her feelings regarding the people around her with such minute variations. I am not sure she would not have preferred to remain in town. She was handsomely dressed, although I doubt her shoes were the most suitable for walking on our country paths. Perhaps she wore her best for church, and next time I see her she will be in a walking dress with a sturdy pair of boots. Although, as that will likely be at the assembly, it would be odd attire for dancing."

Mrs Wilson giggled at this, although her eyes were firmly focused on her busy hands.

"I feel I ought to be able to say something of Mrs Hurst, Mr Bingley's other sister, and her husband, but whereas two minutes before a service and five minutes after felt quite sufficient to become acquainted with the primary points of Mr and Miss Bingley's characters, I find these two remain a mystery. I did, however, discover they have a child, who has recently had croup." Elizabeth's voice mellowed for a moment. "I feel for the child, for it is truly unpleasant. But I cannot help but wonder whether the child's croup was convenient to their need to return to Netherfield. However, tell no one I said so."

Mrs Wilson had taken her work across to the window, the better to see a particularly tricky part of the embroidery, which she held up to the light, her face turned away from her friend.

"That is nearly all of the party," Elizabeth continued, "other than one more gentleman. A Mr Darcy, who I think bodes well to be a very enjoyable study. He looked down on us all from his very great height with a most quizzical eye. I only hope we did not disappoint him in whatever he was looking for. He did not *appear* disappointed, but he had an inscrutable face. When he approached me and Jane for our hands at the assembly, I could not determine whether he genuinely wished to dance or whether he was following some form of unfamiliar courtesy. He has not asked anyone else for the favour, as far as I have heard."

"How odd." A note of something unusual in her friend's voice made Elizabeth look up, but Mrs Wilson still held her embroidery to the light, her face obscured, and she decided she had imagined it.

"Yes," she laughed. "He is to open the assembly with Jane and has asked me for the second. I hope he is a good dancer, for he seemed a terribly grave man, and I do prefer a partner who dances well if he will not smile occasionally."

"And what of the other man, Mr-Mr Hurst, was it? Will you be dancing with him, too?" This time there was no mistaking the catch in her voice, and Elizabeth looked curiously at her friend.

"No, Mr Hurst is married and showed no inclination to dance with unmarried women. It is Mr Bingley you are thinking of, and yes, he is to dance with Jane, me, and Lydia. Perhaps he might dance with Kitty too, but he was called away before he could mention it. Mary is more inclined to play than to dance."

Mrs Wilson was again examining her embroidery, but she turned back to Elizabeth with her usual calm but sad expression. She met her eyes with a small smile. "I find I am envious. I have never been asked to dance by a stranger."

"Then it is all the more important that Meryton hosts a ball when you are ready." Elizabeth spoke lightly, and by unspoken agreement they turned the conversation towards the recent exploits of Joey and Tommy, who had discovered they could, with the use of a kitchen stool, open the door to the larder by themselves, and had proved it by destroying a plum cake they found there. They were still suffering from the resulting stomach ache.

Only on her slow walk home did Elizabeth allow herself to spend a few minutes speculating on whether Mrs Wilson may have a prior acquaintance with Mr Bingley, and whether, if the early indication of his interest in Jane proved true, the pretty widow might prove a rival for his affections.

CHAPTER FIVE

T he Netherfield party arrived at the assembly hall ten minutes before the first dance was due to start. Pausing in the doorway, they were approached by Sir William Lucas, who escorted them into the room with enthusiastic conversation that none of them heard. Miss Bingley's eyes passed across the people of Meryton without interest; she disregarded her brother's good-humoured smiles to everyone and his sharp exhale when his eyes came to rest on Jane Bennet, who was deep in conversation with Miss Elizabeth and had not seen them enter.

He took a step towards their corner, but a chance comment from Sir William appeared to remind him of his duty to the eldest Miss Lucas. Miss Bingley and the rest of the Netherfield party declined to join the Lucases, instead standing away to one side.

"It is very gracious of you to consent to dance with some of the ladies here this evening, Mr Darcy. I did not know you were so fond of the activity." Miss Bingley's lip curled slightly as her eyes roved across the laughing and smiling faces, but she turned towards the gentleman as he replied, adopting her most teasing smile.

"I am not."

"Then whatever made you ask those Bennet girls to dance?"

Mr Darcy gazed across the room to where the aforementioned ladies were laughing at some private joke. "I am sure you cannot fail to have noticed, as I did, your brother's admiration for the eldest Miss Bennet. Nor are you ignorant of his susceptibility to flattery and to those whose motives may not be entirely pure. I am sure neither of us would wish someone we care about to be ensnared by false friends."

Miss Bingley's smile broadened. "Indeed not," she replied, looking back at the Bennet sisters with sharp eyes. She still could not comprehend what had possessed Darcy to offer the first dance to Miss Bennet and to follow it immediately with a set with the sister, to whom Charles had merely shown his usual embarrassing affability, but she would not complain at Mr Darcy showing such prodigious care for any of the Bingley family.

Mr Darcy took this as his cue to approach the ladies under discussion and to lead Miss Bennet to the dance floor, Miss Bingley looking on. She watched as three other Bennet girls each took their place in the line, silently comparing their partners, dresses, and deportment to that of Louisa, who had coaxed her husband into their customary single dance before the lure of the punch bowl grew too strong. Miss Bingley loathed that she was seated to one side whilst all her party danced, but glancing round the room she could not see a disengaged man she would not find it a punishment to stand up with. Her gaze took in the calculating eyes of the matrons as they watched her brother and his friend. To think she had left London for this!

. . .

NOT FAR FROM MISS BINGLEY, Mrs Bennet's lips pinched as she watched Mr Bingley take Charlotte Lucas to the head of the dance. Offering his first dance to Miss Lucas, indeed! She was glad the other gentleman had more sense. He at least stood up with Jane, and they made a fine, handsome pair. Well, Jane made them handsome. Mr Darcy might look better if he did not frown so often! But he was a gentleman of some means, so if not handsome then certainly distinguished. Yes, Jane looked a picture on his arm!

She watched them move through the set and caught a glance that passed between Jane and Mr Bingley with a satisfied smile. He was undoubtedly the surer bet. Perhaps not the richer man, but in line to be smitten, and with a little work, surely he might be the one? If Jane were not engaged this year, she would never be able to hold up her head in Meryton again! Oh, what would Mrs Long say?

As if conjured by this thought, Mrs Long broke into Mrs Bennet's uncharacteristic reverie. "Your Jane dances well this evening."

"Indeed, she does," Mrs Bennet replied with simpering enthusiasm. "Although she always shines on a dance floor."

"Indeed," Mrs Long replied with a smirk. "I recall her dancing beautifully at the gathering we held for Henrietta's engagement."

Mrs Bennet winced at the memory and was unusually silent. Mr Milton had appeared to be interested in Jane before his sudden discovery of Henrietta Long's one thousand pounds.

"Lizzy is also looking particularly handsome tonight. Has she a new beau you have not told us of?"

Mrs Bennet's eyes flicked to Mr Darcy. A private, motherly part of her wondered whether such an austere and sorrowful looking man would be best suited to her incomprehensible second daughter, but she gave it no mind. He had asked Lizzy to dance as well as Jane, and it would be a fine thing to get both of her eldest daughters settled. She would forward a match if she could.

"Oh, Mrs Long, you tease so! Why, you know very well that Lizzy will insist on going her own way. Whatever became of Mr Roberts who seemed so promising, I would dearly like to know! But perhaps she is destined for something better."

MR BINGLEY ENJOYED his dance with Miss Lucas, for she willingly made friendly conversation, but he could not but find his eyes wandering more often than they ought to where his next partner danced with his friend. Darcy seemed to be talking to her, which struck him as unusual. Miss Bennet answered him so sweetly! She was an angel to engage so with his taciturn friend. He watched them closely for a moment, but just then Miss Bennet happened to catch his eye, before rapidly dropping hers. Bingley looked away, abashed at being caught, and exerted himself to be more agreeable to his promised partner until he might be free to bask in the glow of an angel's smile.

His thoughts soon returned to his friend. Darcy was not one for conversation whilst dancing, but he appeared to have made an effort to ingratiate himself in local society by dancing with the most beautiful woman in Hertfordshire—nay, in England! And, of course, with her sister, who was also uncommonly pretty.

Darcy's unusual demeanour pleased Bingley. After so long spent aloof and isolated, burying himself at Pemberley, it would do him good to engage with new society. He was mightily glad his friend had finally agreed to assist him with finding a property. Why, it had been three or four years ago since he had first mentioned it, before—

Bingley stopped himself there. It would not do to dwell on such matters at a dance; he had undoubtedly been neglecting his partner in his abstraction. He turned to her again with a smile, and she raised an eyebrow with a quick glance at Miss Bennet—oh, Miss Bennet!—and a laughing smile.

As they finished, he bowed his thanks and escorted her from the floor with perhaps more haste than was his usual wont. Miss Lucas remained silent after a final exchange of pleasantries, but Lady Lucas appeared inclined to hold him in conversation for as long as he could be kept. Mr Bingley shifted from foot to foot anxiously, eager to be gone, but he was not a man to offend by cutting off a conversation mid-flow. He was beginning to despair of being able to reach Miss Bennet before they would be required to line up and step straight into the dance, when Miss Lucas, the wonderful creature, interrupted her mother.

"Mama! The next dance is soon to begin. We must not keep Mr Bingley from his partner." He beamed at her, acknowledged her curtsey, and did not look back as he headed swiftly across the room.

CHARLOTTE WATCHED Mr Bingley approach Jane, his hand already outstretched to take hers. Jane, with a blush, accepted his arm, and they turned towards the dance floor, apparently already deep in conversation. Charlotte smiled to herself. This would be something to tell Lizzy when her friend was no longer dancing.

Some while ago, when Mr Milton had seemed so smitten with Jane, they had nearly quarrelled over Charlotte's opinion that Jane was too serene, too difficult to read in her interest. After Mr Milton's attention had turned elsewhere, Elizbeth had not conceded the point, but Charlotte suspected she may have spoken to Jane on the matter. At least here there was evidence she was capable of showing interest—and all for a handsome face, for she could hardly know his character so soon! Charlotte hoped it boded well for the future.

Following the young couple across the floor—for such they appeared, for all that they had only just met—Charlotte's eyes lighted on an altogether different pairing. Somewhere in the middle of the line, Elizabeth stood with Mr Darcy. He was gazing seriously at her as he finished speaking, and she was looking back at him just as seriously, brow furrowed in an expression Charlotte recognised as showing that Lizzy found herself facing a conundrum. She wondered what it was they spoke of.

HAVING BEGUN their conversation with some standard pleasantries, Mr Darcy had, in fact, just asked Elizabeth how well acquainted she was with the local area, and she was wondering what answer he expected to such a question. She settled on stating the obvious as the dance began.

"I am somewhat acquainted with the area, sir, having never spent more than a month or two at a time away from it. Were you seeking a tour?"

Mr Darcy showed no sign of either amusement or offence at this sally, and Elizabeth was puzzled once again when he replied, "Thank you, but no. I was merely wondering where the nearest neighbours of Netherfield might be sited. We have spent the past fortnight establishing the household, and my friend is yet to call on many members of the local society."

Elizabeth thought this a roundabout way to ask a simple question, but she considered her answer until the dance brought them back within speaking distance. "My father's house is the nearest to Netherfield, for the parks adjoin. The two houses are some three miles apart. Lucas Lodge, Sir William's residence, is a mile or so farther. Haye Park also adjoins Netherfield land, but the house is situated some five miles from Netherfield House. Haye Park is occupied by the Gouldings. Have you been introduced?"

Mr Darcy indicated he had not, and they lapsed into silence. Eventually, he spoke again. "Only three such houses?"

"There is Ashworth, but that is seven miles from Netherfield and currently stands empty. Then there are other households beyond Meryton who form part of our circle, but they could not be called the nearest neighbours. Oh," she added as an afterthought, "and I suppose Purvis Lodge ought to be mentioned, for it is only a little farther away than Lucas Lodge is from Netherfield, although not in precisely the same direction. But the lady who lives there does not go out into society and attends church in another parish, so your paths are unlikely to cross."

As she spoke, she recalled her suspicion that Mrs Wilson had a prior acquaintance with Mr Bingley, and she watched Mr Darcy closely to see whether he had any reaction to the lady. Perhaps he might know of any connexion between her and his friend. She could not be sure whether she imagined the fleeting look of interest as the widow's name was mentioned. It was insufficient to determine whether Mr Darcy had any knowledge or suspicions tending in the same direction as her own.

The dance took them apart, and when he returned, Mr Darcy again resumed the conversation. "That must be an isolated life, to not go into society at all."

"Indeed, sir, it must." Elizabeth's voice softened. "But Mrs Wilson prefers it, for she is in mourning, and we do what we can to ensure she has company, when she wishes for it."

Mr Darcy nodded and said nothing. Elizabeth, finding the conversation had taken an entirely unexpected direction, decided it was time to turn it back to the people present in the ballroom. "Your friend Mr Bingley seems to be enjoying his dance with Jane."

Mr Darcy's eyes turned on the other pair, who were at that moment more engrossed in one another than ever. Jane had just spoken, and her eyes were lifted to Mr Bingley's with a gentle smile, whilst he had an air of light-hearted disbelief as he gazed back. Mr Darcy looked back at his own partner. "Bingley has an open heart. He delights in beauty, and no one could deny your sister is beautiful."

Elizabeth smiled broadly at this compliment to Jane. "I am much obliged to you, sir. One can never hear too much praise about a beloved sister. I think Mr Bingley's opinion is going to be the one she most prizes, however. I have never seen her so at ease with a new acquaintance."

Mr Darcy nodded absently. When he next spoke, it was to ask an entirely unrelated question.

"Are many ladies of your circle musical?"

"Most of us play," Elizabeth replied, "myself included. My sister Mary is perhaps the most enthusiastic musician in the area."

"But music is not your preferred pastime?"

"We have a range of interests and pursuits, Mr Darcy, as all accomplished young ladies ought!" She said the last with mock seriousness, and was pleased to see a small crack in his austerity in the form of a minute twitch at the corner of his mouth.

"Indeed," he replied gravely. "I have offended you. I beg your pardon."

"Freely granted," Elizabeth replied airily, but her mind turned over what Mr Darcy's conversation could possibly be about. He spoke not in pleasantries but with serious intent, yet his questions seemed oddly disconnected. She decided to ask some questions of her own.

"I understand you and Mr Bingley are both from more northern counties, Mr Darcy. What brings you to Hertfordshire?"

Had Elizabeth not made a point of studying him as she spoke, she might have missed the subtle change of his face as a look of something—discomfort?—passed across it. She was certain this time that she had not imagined it, although Mr Darcy schooled his features so well, it was gone in an instant. She waited for a response.

"Bingley wished to be close to London," came the eventual, bland reply, "and Netherfield was in want of a tenant."

Elizabeth had to be satisfied with this. "And how do you find our Hertfordshire society so far, Mr Darcy? Not too confining after London, I hope?"

"I spend little time in London."

"Ah, then I hope you will not find us overwhelming in our sociability. We are always keen to welcome new neighbours, and I imagine Mr Bingley will be inundated with invitations after this evening."

"I am sure he will do them all full justice."

"I am glad. I delight in dancing and good conversation, and would not want to be deprived of either by an unsociable neighbour. When you take a house in a neighbourhood, it is good to be of a mind to join their society." She thought for a moment before adding, "Although of course exceptions can be made. I mentioned Mrs Wilson before—she makes few calls and accepts few invitations, but she is in mourning. Truly, I like her, and am glad to call her my friend. I can forgive her for being a little shy of our neighbours in general."

Mr Darcy's face was turned away from her as she said this, once again observing his friend. Elizabeth glanced that way too. If Mrs Wilson was a rival to Jane for Mr Bingley's affections, it seemed to Elizabeth a certainty the battle was already lost, and her friend must concede to her sister.

Their conversation continued for the rest of the dance, but nothing of great consequence was said by either party. When Mr Darcy escorted her from the floor, Elizabeth found she had a great deal to think about, and was glad there was a short pause before the next dance began. She had found her partner puzzling—more handsome, now she had seen him at closer quarters, a good dancer, and more talkative than she anticipated, but to what purpose she could not fathom. Was he measuring the quality of their company for his friend? Perhaps Mr Bingley was particularly fond of music, and Mr Darcy sought to establish whether they would be capable of entertaining him. It was all most peculiar, and she wished to know more.

She was, however, convinced Mr Bingley had some prior knowledge of Mrs Wilson, and moreover, that his friend also knew something of it. Having settled with herself that she would not be curious about her friend's past, she found the subject occupied her thoughts more than ever. She resolved to set it aside, at least for the duration of the next dance. Perhaps a few words with Mr Bingley could shed light on the matter, but she would allow the conversation to go where it would and not seek to importune him with questions which might betray her suspicions.

She looked around for her dance partner, expecting him to be still attending Jane. He was not, however; her sister was in calm conversation with Mary, and Mr Bingley was not for a moment to be seen. She cast around the room until her eyes lit on Mr Darcy, easily spotted due to his height, and Mr Bingley with him. They were close to the door, not near enough to anyone to be overheard, and appeared to be having a minor disagreement. Mr Bingley evidently carried the day, for Mr Darcy, looking graver than ever, stalked across to Miss Bingley and invited her to dance. Elizabeth smiled to herself at the false humility the lady displayed on being so ungraciously engaged, but paid no more mind to the couple as Mr Bingley also crossed the room to approach her.

If Elizabeth had hoped she might be able to find out from Mr Bingley himself whether he had ever known her friend, she was disappointed. His conversation was pleasant, but after her perplexity at his friend's words, she found it easy to predict what Mr Bingley would ask and say. When he was not speaking politely of the weather or the dancing, his conversation would veer always and inevitably back to Jane.

It would have been irritating had Elizabeth not been content to hear his every compliment, to store up and return to her sister later. For all their admiration was evidently mutual, Jane was not one to think so highly of herself that she would expect such praise, and Elizabeth was determined she would be in no doubt of Mr Bingley's admiration. She could not with any decorum assure him of her sister's interest being equal to his own, but she did what she could to assure him his attentions were not unwelcome.

Elizabeth attempted, once or twice, to turn the conversation towards the neighbourhood and its inhabitants, but other than expressing in the broadest terms how much he looked forward to improving his knowledge of them all, Mr Bingley was not to be drawn. Short of simply announcing her friend's name and seeing what reaction she received, Elizabeth was unable to see a way to find out more. It was most vexing.

At the close of the dance, Elizabeth found herself without a partner but was not feeling starved of enjoyment and did not resent her state. Spying Charlotte on the other side of the room, she began to make the circuit to her friend.

As she passed the refreshments, she was momentarily caught in the crush and unable to make her way through. Waiting patiently for the chance to advance, she could not help but overhear a low conversation behind her. She did not need to turn to ascertain which two gentlemen spoke.

"You are fully aware I did not dance for my own pleasure. I have done my duty to your sister, but I shall stay no longer."

"You have spared us a day of Caroline's complaints by dancing with her, and I thank you. You ought to stay though, Darcy. The company is uncommonly good."

"I think the particular company you are referring to prefers your presence over mine, Bingley, and would not notice my absence."

"You ought to stay," Mr Bingley repeated. "You are too severe by half. It will do you good to spend more time dancing. Miss Elizabeth Bennet is an accomplished dancer and makes pleasant conversation, as well as being uncommonly handsome."

"She would have to be both a great deal handsomer and much more delightful to draw me from my current concerns." This last was said in a still lower voice, and Elizabeth pushed again at the crush in an attempt to move away from overhearing a conversation evidently not meant for her ears.

As a gap opened and she moved away, she heard Mr Bingley sigh, "Go, then. I cannot stop you."

Elizabeth's wonder at this conversation was immense, and she reached Charlotte with a look of perplexity that had her friend smiling teasingly. "Are you well, Lizzy? You look as though you have been entirely overthrown—or received another unexpected proposal."

"Oh, nothing of the kind!" Elizabeth managed to laugh, not yet ready to share what she had overheard, for she had yet to puzzle it out. "I am merely a little tired from so much dancing and so little refreshment. I was quite unable to pass the crush around the table and decided it would be better not to attempt to procure myself a drink."

This last being overheard by one of the young gentlemen of their acquaintance, he stepped in to offer to fetch refreshments for both ladies, which they gratefully accepted. Since he also took the opportunity to request Elizabeth's hand for the coming dance, she found that any hope she had of more than a moment's quiet reflection was denied her. As she sipped her drink, she watched Mr Bingley lead Lydia back to her mother and turn to Mary, offering a dance which her sister accepted with a great deal of surprise. With a smile, Elizabeth allowed her own partner to draw her back into all of the delight of an evening of dancing.

CHAPTER SIX

"Well, Lizzy. Perhaps I ought to hear your account of last night before your mother sees fit to give me hers."

Elizabeth smiled at her father's ill-concealed curiosity. In recent years, she had come to expect such an application from him following any event he did not attend. After an evening ball or assembly, it was usual for all of the women of the family except Elizabeth to sleep late. She had found she could never sleep long beyond her usual waking time, preferring instead to retire early the following evening. She would rise and find her father had held back his breakfast and would be waiting for her, pretending to read a news sheet or a letter. He would then proceed to question her on the details of the preceding evening.

This domestic ritual had begun a few years prior, shortly after a militia regiment had been stationed in Meryton. For much of their stay, nothing of note had occurred, except that the officers brought welcome variety to local society. Lydia and Kitty, then but fifteen and seventeen years of age, had

50

behaved like the children they had so recently been, but with Jane and Elizabeth present and able to curb their worst excesses, no harm had been done.

Towards the end of the regiment's stay, however, both of the eldest daughters had been invited to visit their aunt and uncle Gardiner in London. Left to the chaperonage of her indulgent mother, and with Kitty goading her on at every turn, something had occurred between Lydia and one of the militia officers. Elizabeth had never been apprised of the full details, but she knew that it had thankfully been caught before a scandal could develop, that it was not general knowledge, and that Lydia and her reputation were both fortunately unscathed. The regiment had departed Meryton not long after.

The incident awoke, for a time, a sense of responsibility in Mr Bennet. To begin with, he accompanied his family to assemblies and kept a watchful eye on his daughters. Sooner than he ought, however, he slipped back into old habits and stopped attending. With Elizabeth's return, he did at least continue to exert himself to find out what had occurred at such events. The intention was to catch any of Lydia or Kitty's wilder excesses early, but this purpose too had lapsed with time. Mr Bennet found he greatly enjoyed his daughter's accounts, which she gave with her customary wit, and he came to look forward to them for their own sake, and for the opportunity they created to make sport of his neighbours.

Lydia, for her part, had not been permanently affected by her experience with the officers. Although some of her privileges had been revoked for a time, her father was too indolent and her mother too indulgent for this to last. She felt more acutely the punishment that an invitation from the colonel's wife to join them in Brighton had been retracted, and had for a long time railed against what she saw as the fickleness of her former friend. This had not been made easier by Kitty's immense satisfaction that the honour accorded to her sister over herself had been rescinded. Kitty had gloried in her triumph over Lydia for many months after.

The effect of all this had been that Lydia and Kitty had become somewhat more restrained in their behaviour, at least in public, but years of being outshone by their unmarried older sisters had not improved them in essentials. Lydia remained bold and Kitty remained petulant, and they regularly caused their sisters to blush.

Elizabeth had thus far always been willing to indulge her father. If he would not be more active in bringing Lydia and Kitty up, then she could at least warn him of any serious concerns she might have. Thankfully, with the departure of the militia, their society was too unvarying for new opportunities for serious embarrassment to often arise. She would therefore enjoy a quiet half an hour observing some of the more idiosyncratic moments of whatever event she described, and laughing with her father at the follies and foibles of their neighbours.

On this occasion, however, Elizabeth could not but admit to herself that she was a little uncomfortable. Her younger sisters' behaviour, whilst loud and not irreproachable, had not been such as to cause unusual censure, unless one counted the astonished gazes they received from Mrs Hurst and Miss Bingley. But given the general disdain with which those ladies appeared to view the company, Elizabeth did not feel unduly troubled by their disapproval.

Inevitably, therefore, any account she gave would be focused on the one variation in society—the Netherfield party. Never before had her observations on events touched so closely on subjects so close to her own concerns, or Jane's.

For the first time, she considered that her father's approach to Meryton society was no less a form of gossip than her mother's, and no more admirable.

Irrespective of these musings, her father was expecting an answer. He steepled his hands and watched her with amused eyes.

Elizabeth smiled weakly at him. "You might admit, Papa, that you are curious about our new neighbours."

"I confess an interest in knowing what sport might be made of them."

"I am not sure Jane will thank you if you continue to make sport of Mr Bingley," Elizabeth replied. She wished to impress on her father that there was a real prospect of Mr Bingley's interest being fully in earnest. She therefore related the gentleman's obvious attention to Jane, including that he had asked her to stand up a second time, much to Kitty's chagrin, since he had not asked her at all. Elizabeth also gave her own impressions that he was a very gentlemanlike man and provided little of the sources of amusement her father favoured.

"Mr Bingley not to be laughed at? I hope for better from his companions."

Elizabeth assuaged his curiosity as best she could without touching on any of the details that were uppermost in her mind. It was something of an ordeal, and she inwardly sighed with relief when he finally settled back to his paper with the words, "I do believe we shall see a great deal more of the Bingleys and Mr Darcy, and I look forward to finding plenty to enjoy in their company. Perhaps they might have an opinion on the news from the continent."

Once she left the breakfast table, Elizabeth escaped outdoors for a solitary morning walk. For once, her feet took her to neither of her friends' houses. She wished to think over the previous evening alone.

Of Jane and Mr Bingley, she thought largely with satisfaction. It was surprising Jane had shown such a rapid and marked preference for the gentleman, but he seemed mannerly and good-humoured, and she had nothing ill to say of him. If Jane was going to give her heart away so easily, it seemed to be to a good man who would treat her well. Her sister might have to bear a little teasing for the rapidity of her inclination towards Mr Bingley, but Elizabeth could not but approve of the match, if on further acquaintance he continued as promising as he first appeared.

She was no closer, however, to understanding whether she had imagined Mrs Wilson's possible prior connexion to Mr Bingley. She had not succeeded at mentioning her friend's name to him when they were dancing, and neither had a later opportunity arisen. Either Mr Bingley had anticipated her questions and deliberately avoided them, which seemed altogether unlikely, or she had been unlucky. It was frustrating, but there was nothing to be done.

His attentions to Jane were too marked to imagine he had any intention of courting another, and if Mrs Wilson was not in society, they would be unlikely to meet. No, she must be satisfied that if any previous knowledge—any previous attachment—existed, it was firmly in the past. However much it pained her to think it might be an additional sorrow for her friend, she wished to see her sister happy, and Mr Bingley appeared likely to be the foundation of her happiness.

Elizabeth contemplated this conclusion for a moment before turning her thoughts to Mr Bingley's friend. Her mother, she knew, would seek to position her as a match for him, but the comment she had overheard had convinced her it was a lost cause. Combined with the fact that Mr Darcy had left the assembly after only three dances, causing much frowning and stifled offence amongst the people of Meryton, Elizabeth had to assume he was in attendance at the assembly—nay, even in Hertfordshire—only under duress.

Whatever business took him from the assembly, it had not been known to Miss Bingley. That lady had looked as surprised as anyone when her brother mentioned Mr Darcy had made his apologies and left, although she covered it rapidly. Soon after, she had turned to Lady Lucas and observed with a simpering smile, "Dear Mr Darcy is always so busy with the affairs of his great estate. I recall when I was last at Pemberley, the hours he spent out on business matters were prodigious. Why, what with that and the gentlemen's shooting parties, we ladies hardly saw him from morning until night!" Lady Lucas nodded, smiled, and made no comment.

Elizabeth smiled too at the recollection, but then her thoughts turned back to the gentleman himself. His conversation whilst dancing had been unexpected and not without some interest, for it had been different to the usual polite conversation of the newly acquainted. Mr Darcy seemed to have a genuine curiosity in the surrounding neighbours. Was he perhaps examining them all for their suitability for his friend? She had assumed he had asked her to dance because his friend had, but he did not seem to have attempted to make out her character.

He had shown some interest in Mrs Wilson, but not enough for her to discern whether he knew her history and how Mr Bingley figured in it. He had paid Jane a compliment but had shown little interest in discussing her. If his aim in dancing with them had been to test Jane's suitability for his friend, Elizabeth could not see how his questions suited his purpose. Why had he abruptly enquired after their musical accomplishments? Was musicianship particularly important to Mr Bingley?

Puzzling over her dance with Mr Darcy did nothing to enlighten Elizabeth on his character or purpose. Her thoughts turned inevitably to the conversation she had overheard. Mr Darcy had said he did not dance for his own pleasure. This she could easily believe, but why, if that was the case, did he dance at all, and ask such odd, disconnected questions whilst about it? It could not be for politeness' sake, for he had only asked the two Bennet sisters, in addition to Miss Bingley.

Inevitably, for they had been dancing at the fringes of all her thoughts since she first heard them, his final comments in the overheard conversation came back to her. She could not make out whether or not she felt insulted by his words. He had not disagreed outright that she was handsome and pleasant company, but apparently she was not sufficiently so for him to remain at the assembly. Evidently, nothing would have made him stay once he had reluctantly done his duty by Miss Bingley, so she was hardly surprised a new acquaintance would not. Yet she could not help but feel hurt. *Who else might have overheard his words?* Such a ready dismissal was surely not the sign of an agreeable man. Yet *she* had not found him disagreeable, merely puzzling.

Yes, Mr Darcy was a conundrum. Elizabeth suspected he thought himself above his company, attending a social event and then abandoning it after only three dances for other business. *Why could it not have waited one evening, whatever the matter was?* No, she was thinking in circles. The only conclusion she could draw with absolute confidence regarding Mr Darcy was that Miss Bingley was sure, at some point, to be disappointed.

Elizabeth had little opportunity in the following days to consider her impressions of the newcomers, for the usual business of life had to be continued. As the usual business of life consisted of social calls where everyone was discussing the newcomers, however, she found she had ample opportunity to consider everyone else's impressions of them.

SOON AFTER THE ASSEMBLY, the Bennet and Lucas ladies spent the afternoon together.

"Was Mr Bingley not charming, Lady Lucas? Dancing with Jane twice! His attentions were ever so marked, do you not think? Oh, to see Jane so well married, and mistress of Netherfield!"

"Indeed, it would be a fine thing," her friend concurred with genuine warmth and a kindly glance at Jane.

"You do not know he intends to make me an offer, Mama," Jane chided, but she could not meet Elizabeth's amused eyes.

"I do not think Mr Bingley is so very charming! He—" Kitty began, but she was cut off by Lydia.

"You only say so because he did not dance with you. I thought him a bore. Jane, when you marry him, I shall go to London with you and find someone more interesting."

Mary could not resist adding her own observations. "I found Mr Bingley to be a very proper gentleman," she stated. "He was kind enough to express a wish that there was an instrument at the assembly hall so that he might hear us all perform."

"Surely the sign of a man besotted," Charlotte murmured in Elizabeth's ear.

"Or a fool," countered Elizabeth quietly. "He knows not

what he says. But perhaps these visiting gentlemen set great store by our music. Mr Darcy also asked about it."

Mrs Bennet caught the name and required no further encouragement. "Mr Darcy! Oh, what a peculiar man! Why come at all if you are to dance three dances and then leave? Not a word spoken to anyone beyond his party, other than to Jane and Lizzy when he danced with them. It is a great compliment that he chose my girls. Did Mr Darcy say anything of note to either of you when he danced? You are the only ones who might be able to shed light on his character you know, for he danced with no others besides Miss Bingley. Such a fine man!" she cried happily before reverting to her concerns. "But then to have left, and no one the wiser about his character or his purpose! I am not sure that I ought not to warn you girls from him! But then, perhaps he had received an express from his estate and needed to deal with it at once. Such an estate he must have! A fine man, and he danced with you, Lizzy! Perhaps he will have a chance to dance with you again, and we may all get to know him better!"

Mrs Bennet would allow no interruptions whilst she made this speech, and Elizabeth decided she must have been quite bursting to express her conflicted views on the gentleman. When she finally sat back, slightly breathless, it was Lady Lucas who spoke.

"Mr Darcy's departure from the assembly was most peculiar. Did he say anything of consequence during his dances?"

"He was very proper when speaking to me," Jane replied. "He asked about some of our neighbours at the dance and whether any were absent. He seemed interested in knowing who the principal families were in the area, and how we are each connected."

"Oh, did he?" Mrs Bennet cut in sharply. "And pray, did he find our society met his exacting standards?"

"I do not think he sought to assess us, Mama. Perhaps he suspected he would have to leave early, and merely wished to prepare himself for future invitations."

"If he knew he was to leave early, he paid you and Lizzy quite the compliment," Charlotte commented.

"Oh, yes! He did show them a particular regard, did he not?"

It was clear to Elizabeth that even though her mother could not settle on her opinion of Mr Darcy, she grasped at her certainty that her daughters, as the only ones he had danced with beyond his party, were clearly the worthiest. Elizabeth could agree that singling them out so rapidly and so decisively might betray an uncommon interest, but as the only interest Mrs Bennet was capable of imagining was the romantic kind, and she had already in her mind settled that Mr Bingley was for Jane, Elizabeth sensed her mother had arrived at certain conclusions about where Mr Darcy's interest might be directed.

Just then, Mrs Bennet turned to her second daughter. "You did well to capture him for a dance."

"I did not capture him, Mama, and you must not say so," replied Elizabeth, thoughts about her inability to keep him from his pressing business lingering in the back of her mind. "I am sure Mr Darcy would have danced with more young ladies had he been able to stay."

As she spoke these words, her thoughts turned again to the question of why he had danced at all, if it gave him no pleasure? Was he merely being polite? Dancing with two ladies from the same family had created a belief, at least in her mother, that he intended to single out the Bennets. It remained a puzzle.

As they departed, Elizabeth told Charlotte that she and Jane would be visiting Mrs Wilson the next day. "Would you care to join us? I have spoken of you before, and she has expressed a wish to know you better."

With Charlotte's agreement, they made plans for a visit the following day.

When they arrived at Purvis Lodge, Mrs Wilson welcomed all three of them with a warmer smile than was usual when anyone other than Elizabeth and Jane was present. The children immediately rushed to commandeer Jane, who, with a brief smile at their mother, allowed herself to be seated on the sofa with a small boy either side and a book in her hands.

"I am not certain you have come to see me at all, Miss Bennet," Mrs Wilson said with a shy smile.

"Perhaps I ought to spend more time with you," came the smiling reply, "for Lizzy seems to have taught you how to tease."

This raised a small laugh from the young mother. "You do me a great service in providing my boys with some variety. We all look forward to your visits quite as much as your sister's." She turned to her other guests. "I am pleased you have come today, Miss Lucas. Miss Elizabeth has spoken of you a great deal. I hope we can be friends."

"I would be delighted," Charlotte replied. "Although I cannot promise my conversation will be half as lively as Lizzy's."

"Altogether wiser, however," came her friend's rejoinder, prompting another laugh. Elizabeth was pleased to see Mrs Wilson in such good spirits, and still more so that her two friends were comfortable in one another's company.

"How have you been, Mrs Wilson? It feels like an age since I saw you last."

"You have had a great deal to do to prepare for your assembly."

"Yes, and I come ready to tell you all about it." Elizabeth thought she saw a momentary shadow cross her friend's face, and hastened to add, "Although only if you wish it."

Mrs Wilson averted her eyes for a moment before looking up with resolve. "I would be pleased to hear about your evening," she said in a low voice.

"You do not know what you ask for, Mrs Wilson," Charlotte cut in, seeing the expression on her friend's face. "Lizzy's stories can be rather whimsical."

"Charlotte, you wound me!" Elizabeth feigned pain, causing her oldest friend and sister to laugh. Joey and Tommy looked confusedly on, before Joey tugged on Jane's arm and pointed at the book.

Elizabeth proceeded to give an account of the assembly entirely unlike that which she had provided to her father. Whereas he was only interested in the behaviour and speeches of his neighbours, for Mrs Wilson she gave free rein to her descriptive wit. Nothing escaped her retelling, from the difficulties she had encountered when having her hair arranged, until Jane swooped in to rescue her, to the footman who had almost been knocked into a trough by a startled horse but managed to escape by turning his lack of balance into some impromptu dance steps. She recalled a conversation she had whilst dancing with one of her friends, a young man recently engaged to a farmer's daughter. He was so disbelieving that his lady had accepted his hand that he had asked Elizabeth to reassure him on the point repeatedly, until she had given in and at every turn reminded him that Miss Barnes was soon to be his wife.

Everything was told with a deftness that left each of the women laughing, and the two small boys gazing in wonder at their mother, their book forgotten. Her laughter was shy, and checked regularly, but to her sons it appeared to be a rare and special treasure.

Elizabeth did not forget her thoughts on the Netherfield party, but she had no wish to create any discomfort for her friend. In truth, she knew them so little she could not describe their interactions with all the animation she had given to the rest of her story, so she passed over their names quickly. She saw no traces of consciousness in the young widow's eyes as she did so, and took this to mean her friend had steeled herself to hear them. She was surprised when, having exhausted her tale, Mrs Wilson broached the subject herself.

"You have said little of the newcomers you mentioned. Did you enjoy your dances with the gentlemen?"

"Oh, indeed yes!" Elizabeth replied, then hesitated before carefully continuing. "They were both excellent dancers. It is difficult to know them from such little conversation, but Mr Bingley seemed keen to please, and Mr Darcy...I confess I am not sure what his opinions were."

"What do you mean?" Mrs Wilson looked confused. Charlotte supplied the answer.

"Mr Darcy only danced three dances before leaving the assembly on some urgent business matter. He seemed content enough with his dance partners, but it is too little acquaintance to form an opinion of him, do you not think, Lizzy?"

Elizabeth's brow furrowed. She certainly did not know what to think of the gentleman, and it vexed her. "He is a puzzle."

"Perhaps there will be other opportunities to get to know him better," Mrs Wilson said in a distracted tone, gazing at the window.

"Undoubtedly there will." Charlotte smiled, "If his friend's interest in Jane is any indication, I think you will be seeing a great deal more of Mr Darcy, Lizzy. Someone, after all, will need to keep him occupied whilst his friend's attention is elsewhere."

Elizabeth turned in some alarm to see whether Mrs Wilson was discomposed by the revelation of Mr Bingley's apparent partiality for her sister, but she saw no signs of distress. In fact, Mrs Wilson had apparently not heard at all, for she called to her son.

"Tommy! Stop pulling at Miss Bennet's dress, dear. Come and sit by Mama for a time, and I shall ring for some refreshments for us all." Her son complying, she bustled to do as she stated, and the conversation was forgotten in a flurry of activity.

CHAPTER SEVEN

It was not many days after the assembly that the occupants of Netherfield called at Longbourn. The Bennet ladies were all about their occupations, Lydia and Kitty trimming bonnets and Mary copying music whilst their older sisters sewed, although the latter set aside their work when the guests arrived. Elizabeth concealed her smile as Miss Bingley and Mrs Hurst gingerly took their seats. They sat in state, immediately monopolising Jane's conversation. The gentlemen—Mr Hurst excluded, for he had chosen not to join them—stationed themselves close to the fireplace. Mr Bingley spoke readily to Mrs Bennet, but his eyes turned frequently upon Jane. Mr Darcy's eyes roved nowhere in particular, staying a little longer here or there, but never singling out any particular person over the others until, in a lull, Mrs Bennet turned to him.

"And did you enjoy the assembly, Mr Darcy? You left remarkably early."

"I had business to attend to," the man replied evenly.

"But you enjoyed your dances? You looked so well,

dancing with our Jane, but especially with our Lizzy. You have such a refined air whilst dancing."

Elizabeth winced, and as Mr Darcy's eyes turned to her, she averted her own, hoping he did not think her complicit in her mother's ill-disguised attempts to flatter.

"Thank you, madam," he replied stiffly.

Mrs Bennet was about to say more but was interrupted by a shriek from Lydia. "Mama, Mary has spilt ink on my skirts!"

Mary immediately replied, "I would not have done so had you not seized my arm like that!"

Mrs Bennet scolded, Kitty joined in the clamour, and for a few minutes Elizabeth felt as though she were back in the nursery with her sisters fighting over a doll. She eyed the guests. Miss Bingley and Mrs Hurst were sharing an expressive look that made her almost blush with shame. Mr Bingley, however, had seized the opportunity to cross the room and sit down next to Jane, and was speaking to her without paying any attention to her younger sisters.

When she turned her eyes on Mr Darcy, she was surprised to discover that his own still rested on her, his face impassive. Once again, she quickly averted hers. *Whatever can he be thinking?*

The next time she dared to glance his way, Mr Darcy was back to staring nowhere in particular, and Elizabeth breathed easier. The rest of the visit passed without incident.

They were to see their new acquaintances with tolerable frequency over the following weeks. Mr Bennet was persuaded to leave his study for long enough to accompany his wife and daughters when they called at Netherfield. The events with the militia had taught his youngest daughters to be better behaved when he was present, especially when not in their own home, and Elizabeth for once did not have cause to feel anxious for Jane's sake.

Even her mother did not seem to feel her usual broad hints were required, for Mr Bingley's marked attentions were such that no one could doubt his intentions towards Jane, nor her pleasure at receiving them. Whilst it was still early for an engagement, there was some amusement to be found in attempting to predict when his proposal would be forthcoming.

Elizabeth surprised herself by regretting that Mr Darcy was out riding when they called, and so was not present to see that there were occasions when her family were able to behave as they ought. She scolded herself internally for this thought, for whatever her mother might wish to forward between them, she had heard enough of Mr Darcy's opinions of herself to feel no desire to hear his thoughts on her family.

The following morning, Charlotte Lucas called with an invitation to a gathering at Lucas Lodge. It was to be a private affair, with only a few local families invited, but the inevitable inclusion of the Netherfield party was enough to throw Mrs Bennet into a flutter which left her daughters so harangued and harried that it almost removed the pleasure of anticipation. Mr Bennet withdrew to his study, but there was scant relief, for even there, Mrs Bennet's enthusiastic predictions for Jane's and occasionally Elizabeth's futures easily penetrated the walls.

Elizabeth sighed with relief as she stepped out of the carriage to think she had an evening of quiet conversation with Charlotte ahead. She was grateful for the variety produced by newcomers in society, but she could not but wish for a little more peace amidst her mother's enthusiasm.

Quiet conversation was indeed to be had, and Elizabeth found herself perfectly content until after dinner, when the ladies were called upon to play. Miss Bingley, as the newest addition to their number, performed first, displaying great technical skill and very little genuine feeling. Mary, who was so eager to perform that Sir William could not but invite her next, chose an equally difficult piece but performed with laborious precision that left no room for any feeling at all. It was a great relief to all when Mrs Hurst's turn came, and she chose something simpler, although her self-satisfied air marred the performance somewhat.

When after another few performances it came to Elizabeth's turn, she demurred from playing, instead persuading Charlotte to accompany her as she sang. It was an arrangement they had adopted around a year before, which suited them both; Charlotte found it drew unwelcome attention from herself and her adequate but unmemorable performances, and Elizabeth that it meant her woeful lack of practice was not put on show.

When their performance was concluded, the two ladies withdrew to their seats. They talked for a few moments before Charlotte observed that Mr Darcy's eyes had rested on Elizabeth more than once that evening.

"On me? You must be mistaken, Charlotte. I am neither handsome nor delightful enough to keep him from his business. Whatever his important concerns might be," she added with a laugh.

"Be that as it may, he is headed towards us, and I do not think it is me he seeks," Charlotte replied. Elizabeth turned to see that he was indeed crossing the room with long strides. He stopped before them.

"Miss Lucas. Miss Elizabeth."

Greetings performed, Mr Darcy stood silent for a moment, and Elizabeth and Charlotte exchanged a look.

"Are you well, Mr Darcy?" Charlotte eventually asked.

"Indeed yes, I am perfectly well, thank you." He lapsed into silence again, and Charlotte silently signalled to Elizabeth that it was her turn to attempt a conversation, but she was saved from having to find a topic by their companion regaining his voice.

"May I compliment you both on your performance earlier."

Charlotte nodded. "Thank you."

"Do you often perform together?"

"Yes, sir. Always, for preference, although it is not always possible. I am no great singer."

"And I sing far better than I play," laughed Elizabeth. "For until a truly portable pianoforte is invented, it is much easier to practise singing whilst I am walking."

She spoke this last to Charlotte, who was well acquainted with Elizabeth's aversion to regular application at the instrument, but she did not fail to miss a fleeting expression of amusement from the gentleman. Her good humour rose. He may not have been much delighted by her at the assembly, but she was certain he had some humour of his own beneath his solemn air.

"Are you much given to walking, Mr Darcy?" Charlotte asked.

Mr Darcy's answer was interrupted by Lydia's voice, carrying across all conversation.

"Mary, stop arguing with me, you must play a dance tune! There may be only half a dozen gentlemen present who are willing to dance, but I shall stand up with Kitty if I have to! I want to dance!"

Sir William immediately chimed in. "Dancing! Yes, capital idea, Miss Lydia. Miss Mary, would you be willing to oblige?"

As the couples formed on the floor, Lydia having immediately accosted one of the other gentlemen present, Mr Darcy turned to Charlotte. "Miss Lucas, might I have this dance?"

Charlotte was so astonished by this unexpected application that she threw a perplexed glance at Elizabeth, who was looking triumphant at this evidence that Mr Darcy was not showing any undue interest in her. As Charlotte accepted his hand, however, he turned to Elizabeth. "If you are inclined to dance, perhaps I might request the next?"

It was Charlotte's turn to look triumphant, and she followed Mr Darcy to the floor with a glance back towards her friend that was full of meaning.

When his dance with Charlotte finished, Mr Darcy lingered close to them for the few minutes it took Lydia to harangue Mary into another piece and find herself another partner, and as soon as the couples began to line up, he took Elizabeth's hand and led her to their place.

Sir William, looking on complacently, had beamed as Mr Darcy danced with Charlotte and now congratulated him on his choice of partners. "A man of discernment I see, Mr Darcy. Capital!" Untroubled at the lack of response, Sir William continued down the line offering praise to the other dancers.

Elizabeth did not wait to see whether her partner intended any particular conversation. "I had heard you were not fond of dancing, Mr Darcy. I did not expect the honour of being invited to stand up with you again." The challenge in her tone was unmistakable, she knew, but she would not have him thinking she meant to flirt.

"I assure you the honour is all mine," the gentleman replied, although with so little feeling that Elizabeth presumed he meant quite the opposite. She could not fathom why a man who had stated that he did not dance for his own pleasure was dancing at a private gathering, where he could certainly pass the whole evening without it if he so chose.

"Perhaps I misunderstood," continued Elizabeth, "and dancing is a favourite pastime?"

"I dance on occasion. Are you fond of it?"

"Very," Elizabeth rejoined.

"And what other pastimes do you prefer, other than walking and dancing?"

This question Elizabeth knew how to answer, and she did so at length. She told him that she enjoyed reading, although she did less of it than she ought, and delighted in good conversation with an intelligent partner. Mr Darcy asked pertinent questions and neatly avoided any attempts to direct them back upon himself, steering Elizabeth effortlessly through the conversation until the end of the dance.

"Did I pass?" she asked him sweetly as he led her back to a seat.

His colour changed slightly as he looked at her in astonishment. "Forgive me, I am not sure I understand your meaning."

"With such a detailed discussion of my interests, Mr Darcy, and none of yours, it felt as though I was being examined. I was merely wondering whether I passed the inspection." She smiled as she spoke, amused at his perplexity.

"I assure you I am ill-qualified to judge the pastimes of any lady." He bowed as he spoke, but the words came uneasily, and Elizabeth could not help but feel she had hit upon some nerve that he wished to conceal. Quite what it could be was beyond her comprehension. She eyed him as he crossed the room and invited Mrs Hurst to dance, paying no regard to the simpering smile of that lady's sister.

With so few younger gentlemen present, the third dance was the last, and Elizabeth spent the rest of the evening in conversation with her friend and sisters. If she paid any attention to Mr Darcy, it was only to notice that he appeared to have spent all his energy for social intercourse on herself and Charlotte, for he spoke only when addressed for the remainder of the evening.

In the days following their visit to Lucas Lodge, nothing was heard from Netherfield, and it became known that the gentlemen were engaged with shooting and fishing parties. With no particular events to plan for, Mrs Bennet began plotting when she might invite them to dinner and deliberating what courses she might serve. Her daughters settled back into their natural routine, and for a time all was peaceful at Longbourn.

After almost a week of quiet, a note came one morning, inviting Jane to dine with Miss Bingley and Mrs Hurst whilst the gentlemen were out. Mrs Bennet, sensing an opportunity, gave her consent immediately but insisted the carriage could not be had and that Jane must ride to Netherfield. Much to her daughter's horror, she made no secret of her hope it would rain, and that Jane would be forced by the lack of any equipage to stay overnight. It came as no surprise to any of them when, not two hours after her departure, a note was received indicating that Jane would not be home that evening.

CHAPTER EIGHT

Elizabeth stepped into the breakfast room at Netherfield to find the family party reaching the end of their meal. Only Mr Darcy was, once again, absent, and she fleetingly wondered whether he spent any time at Netherfield at all. Miss Bingley and Mrs Hurst eyed her with ill-concealed astonishment, whilst Mr Hurst, after a short glance in her direction, returned to his food. Only Mr Bingley stood to greet her.

"Miss Elizabeth!" She smiled at his salutation, for although her arrival was wholly uninvited and unexpected, he spoke as if it were the one thing he had most been hoping for. She returned his greeting, acknowledging the others in turn, then addressed him again.

"Please forgive my sudden intrusion at such an hour. I only came to enquire after Jane following the note we received early this morning."

"On foot?" Miss Bingley asked, eyeing the state of her skirts.

"As you see," replied Elizabeth shortly. "Would it be possible to be taken to her, please?"

"Of course, of course!" Mr Bingley jumped up again to escort her himself, sending his best regards and solicitations for Jane's health as he led Elizabeth to a room on the first floor.

Jane was in bed, and the pallor of her face had Elizabeth instantly at her side. She took her sister's hand and was rewarded with grateful eyes and the lightest of squeezes to her fingers.

Two hours later, Elizabeth made her way downstairs, where Mr Bingley, who had been in the library with the door open, the stairs visible from his seat, instantly accosted her. "How is your sister?"

"Thank you, sir, she is tolerably well, but the apothecary believes she is far too ill to be moved. I am afraid we may need to request your forbearance for a time whilst she recovers."

Mr Bingley immediately insisted Jane must stay until she was well and invited Elizabeth to remain to nurse her if she so wished. This being the one thing she had hoped for, knowing Jane would recover the sooner for her presence, she accepted gratefully and dispatched the necessary letter to Longbourn.

As Elizabeth had not eaten for some hours, Mr Bingley insisted on ordering her some refreshment. Elizabeth would have preferred to eat in Jane's room, but felt it would be churlish to say so in the light of Mr Bingley's clear desire to accommodate her. She accepted without protest, only grateful to be left to herself to eat so she could return to Jane as quickly as might be managed. She had only a few minutes alone, however, before she was interrupted.

A sound at the door made her look up, to be greeted by

the sight of Mr Darcy—but it was a Mr Darcy she had not previously encountered. He was dressed for riding, and from the state of his unbrushed clothes, he had only that moment returned. This, however, was not what gave Elizabeth pause.

Mr Darcy's face, usually pinched and drawn, was almost unrecognisable. It was considerably brightened by heightened colour, presumably from the exertion of his ride. His eyes as they met Elizabeth's were clearer and softer than she had believed them capable of. He looked younger, less stiff, undeniably handsome, and altogether astonished at her presence.

He collected himself and greeted her. "Forgive me. I was informed Bingley would be found here."

"Mr Bingley was here a few moments ago. I do not know where he is now."

"Ah. Thank you." He was silent for a moment. "You are well, Miss Elizabeth?" The interrogation in his voice encompassed a number of other questions, not least of which, Elizabeth assumed, was why she was currently eating in Netherfield's library.

She decided to answer the question he avoided and explained her presence, concluding, "I fear you will have to bear my company until Jane is well enough to be moved."

He made a polite reply to this, then each lapsed into silence, Mr Darcy looking thoughtful. Before either could speak again, however, Miss Bingley's tones were heard in the hall. "Oh, Mr Darcy! You have returned, we had quite despaired of you. Wherever have you been, out riding for so long?"

The change in him was instantaneous. The colour in his face from the ride remained, but he visibly stiffened, returning to his usual demeanour. Elizabeth was torn between pity for the man and a desire to laugh at the extraordinary transformation.

Miss Bingley bustled into the room, insisting Mr Darcy must eat and that she would arrange for some refreshment, but stopped short at the sight of Elizabeth so engaged.

"Miss Eliza Bennet! I was not aware you were still here." Her surprise was not greater than her disdain.

"Miss Bingley. I have been with Jane, and your brother has been kind enough to invite me to stay until she is further recovered. He also provided me with some refreshment. I am indebted to your cook, for it is a great deal for one person to eat. Mr Darcy would be welcome to share it if a plate is brought, to save the kitchen the inconvenience of preparing anything further."

Miss Bingley hesitated, but then eyed the room, as though choosing where she might sit displayed to best advantage whilst Mr Darcy ate. As if divining her thoughts, however, Mr Darcy hastily spoke.

"I regret that I ought to change from my riding clothes before eating. Miss Bingley, perhaps when Miss Elizabeth is finished, a plate might be sent to my room for me to take there?"

Miss Bingley nodded with obvious reluctance, and Mr Darcy retired. Elizabeth returned to her food, and after a few moments, the other lady departed. Only after she had gone did Elizabeth realise she had made no enquiry after Jane's health.

Elizabeth remained with Jane for the rest of the day until dinner, when, with her sister sleeping, she felt herself obliged to attend her hosts. Miss Bingley made up for her lack of solicitude earlier in the day by asking repeatedly after 'dear Jane', expressing suitable joy that she was improving, sympathy that she was still very unwell, and sorrow that it was yet too early to say when she would be recovered. Mr Bingley made similar expressions with rather more sincerity.

Enquiries concluded, conversation turned to other matters, and Elizabeth found herself quickly drawn into a discussion on the pleasures and benefits of reading with Mr Darcy. Whilst he was undoubtedly the better read of the two, with all of the benefits of a superior education, she was pleased to find she could often match and contend his arguments where their reading overlapped.

Miss Bingley, not wishing to be excluded from their conversation, contributed some lines from Shakespeare that bore little relevance to the topic at hand before sweetly smiling at Elizabeth.

"Which pieces did you study with your governess? Recitation was one of my particular pleasures at our seminary. Were you given a great deal to learn at yours?"

"No, for I neither had a governess nor attended such a school."

Miss Bingley smiled. "No governess, for five daughters! Why, surely no young lady could call themselves truly accomplished without the benefits of a proper education, do you not think, Mr Darcy? I am sure you would never have allowed your sister to be brought up so, for I recall you were always the best of brothers to dear Georgiana."

For the second time that day, Elizabeth saw Mr Darcy rapidly transformed by Miss Bingley's words. Through their conversation, he had been, if not open, certainly engaged with their discussion. He had paid attention to her words and responded to them thoughtfully and even with the occasional smile, although he had not lost his customary gravity. Now, however, all traces of feeling and humour seemed to withdraw from his face. The pinching became more acute, and Elizabeth fancied she saw shadows under his eyes that had not been there a moment before.

This reference to his sister clearly pained him. She could only assume from Miss Bingley's words and his reaction that Georgiana Darcy no longer lived, and that the lady's words had stirred some painful recollections. Having not been told as much, she was unable to go so far as to express sorrow for his loss, but she attempted to convey sympathy as their eyes met across the table. He held her gaze for the briefest of moments before looking away, finishing his meal in utter silence.

Mr Bingley had muttered something under his breath at his sister's words before loudly blurting out that it looked as though all rain had passed and the weather would continue fine for a time. Mrs Hurst, with a sharp glance at her sister and Mr Darcy, joined in the conversation, and the two of them carried it for some time, Elizabeth doing her best to contribute, although she continued distracted by Mr Darcy's withdrawal. Miss Bingley appeared to realise her mistake, for she did not attempt to speak to the gentleman again and wasted no time at the end of the meal in suggesting the ladies withdraw.

Conversation between the three ladies remained stilted until Mrs Hurst rang for her daughter. The child, not yet two, clung to her nurse until Elizabeth employed one of Jane's tricks and, paying no attention to the eyes peeping at her, opened a book of bright pictures to pore over. She soon found she had a companion and glanced at Mrs Hurst. The lady's eyes softened as she gazed at her daughter, and Elizabeth, who had largely dismissed her as a necessary chaperon for Caroline and of little independent interest, felt a corresponding soft-ening of her opinion. Their eyes met, and Elizabeth decided

Mrs Hurst loved her daughter dearly, yet did not have the first idea how to speak to her. It was evident she did not resent that Elizabeth captured Lucy's attention, being content to watch and listen to the child's incomprehensible prattle.

The ladies were entirely unaware what an attractive picture they made when the gentlemen arrived. Elizabeth had young Lucy at her side, laughingly describing an imaginary scene whilst the child listened wide-eyed. Mrs Hurst looked on in silence, affection and perplexity alternately playing across her features. Even Miss Bingley was focused on the child, although a sardonic smile played about her lips —most likely, thought Elizabeth, at the oddities of her descriptions to Lucy.

The gentlemen stopped at the door for a moment, two in silent appreciation, the other wondering loudly what they were waiting for. Upon seeing his daughter, however, Mr Hurst was across the room in a moment and had lifted her up high in the air with a smile, breaking the pretty tableau. The child giggled, he nodded, and his paternal duty done, he retreated to a chair.

Lucy held her arms out to Mr Bingley, and he in turn spun her around, causing Mrs Hurst to remonstrate, and the child to squeal with glee. Elizabeth could readily imagine a future not too distant where Mr Bingley would be similarly occupied with his own children.

Once set down, Lucy toddled across to her mother, who played with her curls and cooed over her. Elizabeth risked a glance at Mr Darcy to see how he responded to the child. As she did so, his eyes moved, and she doubted for a moment whether he had not in fact been looking, once again, at her. She shook off the thought, and watched as he took a chair and Lucy made her way across to him.

Unlike the other gentlemen, he did not lift her into the

air, but when she reached her arms out, picked her up only enough to place her on the seat beside him. She took hold of one of his arms, and he wriggled his fingers. With a laugh, she happily occupied herself trying to grasp them as he alternately pulled them away and allowed her to triumph in her game. Elizabeth was surprised at his gentleness, which both contrasted with and complemented his friend's exuberant play.

The presence of a child considerably softened the mood of the room, but after Lucy was taken to bed by the nursemaid, her influence evaporated. An attempt was made at cards, but Elizabeth and Mr Darcy both declined, and Miss Bingley was too distracted to play with any success. The game was abandoned, and Mr Bingley asked Elizabeth to play some music instead. Taking refuge in the request, she immediately concurred and chose one of the few pieces she could confidently deliver, a soothing air that seemed appropriate to her mood. She was not sorry when she was able to excuse herself and return to Jane.

CHAPTER NINE

The next day dawned fresh and clear, and as Jane was feeling brighter, Elizabeth slipped out into the grounds of Netherfield for some air before breakfast and a return to her sister's bedside. She was grateful to at first see no one, but as she moved farther from the house, she was brought to an abrupt halt by the sight of Mr Darcy, standing alone at the edge of a line of trees. He greeted her evenly as she drew closer.

"How is your sister this morning?"

"She has greatly improved, thank you, sir. I hope she will soon be well enough to leave her room."

"I am glad to hear she is recovering."

"Thank you." Elizabeth thought their conversation thus exhausted, but after a moment, he asked her what she thought of the grounds at Netherfield.

"I have always taken great pleasure in them, sir, although they are a little formal for my tastes."

"You prefer a more natural garden?"

She nodded. "Is my taste in gardening now to be examined?"

His mouth twitched in what she was coming to think of as his equivalent to laughter. "Bingley and I have been discussing some improvements to be made to this part of the grounds. We are limited, of course, by the terms of his tenancy, but perhaps you may approve of our plans."

"The grounds have been sadly neglected whilst the house stood empty," she agreed, her eyes trailing over the overgrown tangle of shrubs that formed this part of the garden.

He turned and gestured at an unusually dense section. "I believe some pleasant walks could be made through here with some judicious care."

Elizabeth, able to recall childhood frolics along some exceedingly pleasant paths that had once passed through this part of the garden, could do nothing but agree. When he began to walk elsewhere, pointing out features and how they might be improved under the plans he and Mr Bingley had devised, she readily walked alongside him. She was soon engaged in a discussion of the plans, and from there to asking Mr Darcy about his own estate. Speaking of Pemberley brought back some of the softened expression she had seen the previous day, and she could not doubt his deep affection for his home.

"You speak of Derbyshire with such love, Mr Darcy, you must long to be back there."

"I have rarely left it in recent years, but I am pleased to be in Hertfordshire at present." The statement was accompanied by no significant glance or sentimental tones, but Elizabeth felt an unexpected thrill course through her at his words. They could not possibly be meant for her—she had no reason to expect any such thing, despite her mother's hopes

—but a treacherous part of her that she refused to examine closely nevertheless hoped they were.

They headed together back towards the house to the breakfast room. Miss Bingley's expression at their simultaneous arrival caused Elizabeth another flutter of anxiety. She would have found it amusing, for she was certain she had not unduly courted Mr Darcy's notice, but her recent thoughts were still fresh in her mind, and she could not yet laugh at them.

Breakfast passed more easily than the previous evening's dinner. Mr Bingley, hearing that Jane was not yet ready to rise, insisted she stay at least another night, and Elizabeth with her. Miss Bingley seconded the invitation with polite indifference, bordering on coldness. Elizabeth disregarded the tone and thanked them as sincerely as if her hostess had shown her all the warmth of her host.

"Thank you both, your kindness is greatly appreciated. May I trouble your servants to carry two notes for me? My mother will be wishing to know we shall be staying longer, and it might save her the trouble of attending to Jane herself if she knows she is recovering."

"Of course, you will find writing materials in the library. They will be dispatched to Longbourn immediately."

"Only one is for Longbourn. The other is to my friend Mrs Wilson. She was expecting a visit from me today, and I must explain my absence."

"I have not yet ridden out today, Miss Elizabeth. I shall carry your letters for you." As Mr Darcy spoke, Mr Bingley shot a glance at his friend that Elizabeth could not interpret. It spoke of doubt, perhaps, or disapproval. Why he would disapprove of his friend carrying a gentlewoman's letters she could not imagine. He would not even need to call at either house; he was merely imparting a favour whilst undertaking his usual ride.

"Thank you, Mr Darcy, you are very kind. I shall write my notes immediately." With that, she rose and departed for the library.

Her letters entrusted to Mr Darcy's safekeeping, Elizabeth retired to Jane's room and remained there for most of the rest of the day. Her sister was much improved and, to Mr Bingley's clear delight, was able to join them for a short while after dinner. He was everything solicitous, rearranging furniture to ensure Jane's comfort, fretting about draughts and her proximity to the fire. Elizabeth was highly amused at his antics, although he stopped just short of being ridiculous, and she was not tripped into outright mirth. Jane, however, she treated to one of her most indulgent, teasing smiles. Her sister accepted both Mr Bingley's exertions and Elizabeth's notice with obvious, if subdued, pleasure. The gentleman appeared to feel himself thoroughly rewarded by the becoming smile she bestowed on him as he finally settled into a chair close by.

"It is a delight to have you with us, Miss Bennet. What entertainment would suit you best?"

"Oh, I am content to sit by and enjoy others' conversation this evening."

"Then conversation we must have! Miss Elizabeth, I understand you saw the grounds with Darcy this morning. What did you think of our plans for improvements? I hope you approve of the changes we intend to make?"

"Indeed yes," said Elizabeth with a laugh, "although as your friend spoke of his estate quite as much as he did Netherfield, I think he is trying to tempt you to create another Pemberley here in Hertfordshire."

Mr Bingley laughed. "And what if he is? It is a fine estate indeed, and the grounds are some of the finest I have seen."

"I entirely agree, Charles," cut in Miss Bingley. "Pemberley is one of the treasures of Derbyshire—might I even say, of England?" She addressed this last to Mr Darcy, who was unruffled. "I think the owner of Pemberley has great cause to be proud."

This remark did prompt a reaction. "I may once have thought as you do, Miss Bingley, but I have come to see there is little to be proud of in the chance of having inherited a grand estate. I love my home, but I did not earn it, although I seek to do so by caring for it as best I might. I would prefer to be respected for being a good landlord and managing my household well. Any dignity conferred by birth can easily be lost in a moment in the eyes of the world."

The last words were spoken in a rougher voice that betrayed some strong emotion. Miss Bingley coloured, having once again inadvertently displeased the one person whose favour she sought so assiduously. For the moment, Elizabeth pitied her, and so she turned to Mr Bingley with a different topic in hand.

"Are you fond of poetry, Mr Bingley?"

The gentleman blustered for a moment before replying honestly. "I am not a great reader. I do not know how people can sit for an hour together with a book. I find the words will dance over the page. Letters are even worse, but since I must read those, I confine my reading primarily to essential correspondence. Are you fond of reading, Miss Bennet?" He turned his eyes on Jane.

"I do not read as much as my sister," Jane replied gently, "but I have read a great deal of Shakespeare in my time. Elizabeth will insist on reading aloud, and although she is quite willing to read all of the parts, it can get a little confusing if she is left to do so."

"And you read aloud so beautifully," Elizabeth said with a smile. Jane shook her head slightly but made no reply.

"Would you read aloud for us now?" asked Mr Bingley with sudden enthusiasm. He sagged as Jane shook her head again.

"I am not sure I have the energy for that, but I would enjoy listening to Elizabeth read, if she would."

Elizabeth was more than willing. Despite her lack of governess and formal schooling, she knew many poems and sonnets by heart and was particularly fond of Shakespeare. She had no wish to appear to be putting herself forward unduly after the previous evening's conversation, however, so she preferred to read than to recite.

"Do you have any Shakespeare in the library here, Mr Bingley?"

"I shall find out at once!" He suited the action to the words, seeming glad to be doing something to escape difficult conversations and please Jane, and was back in a moment with a copy of the sonnets. "This was all I could discover for the moment. I must buy some more books. I shall order some the next time I am in Meryton."

Elizabeth took the book and turned to her favourite.

"Let me not to the marriage of true minds admit impediments," she began, reading the familiar words although she knew them by rote. As she read, she smiled to herself, for this was the love she held as the standard of marital perfection: a marriage of true minds above all else.

As she finished, she looked about the room. Miss Bingley was looking oddly at Mr Darcy, who Elizabeth was surprised to find had closed his eyes and appeared distracted. Mr Bingley and Jane were smiling softly at one another again.

Mrs Hurst was idly playing with her bracelets, whilst her husband poured himself another glass beside her. It was a curious assembly.

She turned to another famous sonnet, Jane's favourite, and again read aloud. "Shall I compare thee to a summer's day?" She playfully exaggerated the words, addressing Jane and feigning being overcome by her beauty. Jane smiled affectionately at the familiar teasing, and Elizabeth cast a subtle glance at Mr Bingley, who looked for all the world as though he were living the sentiments himself.

"What beautiful poetry!" Miss Bingley's languid tones cut through the room as Elizabeth finished. "I suppose a less formal education does lead one to the obvious choices. Do you recall, Louisa, how we were positively discouraged from reciting nonsense about something like the marriage of true minds?" Her sister murmured something in assent, looking thoroughly bored, and Miss Bingley continued. "What was it Madame used to say? Oh yes, I recall: 'a lady will always be able to offer something new and original at any exhibition.'"

"Forgive me, Miss Bingley, I was not aware I was being particularly called upon to exhibit this evening. I had thought I was reading for my sister's comfort and enjoyment in an evening amongst friends." Her wry emphasis on the last word appeared lost on her interlocutor.

Miss Bingley was on the verge of responding when Mr Darcy spoke. "Perhaps, Miss Bingley, the popularity of these verses suggests they are of a particular quality, and need not be mistaken for mediocrity. A great reader can bring something fresh even to the most familiar words."

The lady's attention was captured. "An excellent point, Mr Darcy! Of course, to be a great reader, one must have a certain tone and air when speaking, clear diction, and excellent expression."

"And to this, I would add a natural affinity with the words one is speaking, an ability to capture their meaning and convey it to the listener without pretension or conceit."

Miss Bingley was less satisfied with his answer than she had hoped. With a brittle smile, she suggested it might be time for music, and requested that her sister play.

Mrs Hurst took her place at the pianoforte and played until Jane, tired from the exertion of being amongst company, retired to her room, accompanied by Elizabeth.

As they departed in Mr Bingley's carriage the following morning, Elizabeth reflected on her stay at Netherfield. Direct them as she might, her thoughts kept returning to Mr Darcy and the puzzle he continued to present. She had seen glimpses of another man, with more feeling and less rigidity than she had believed possible. She had enjoyed his conversation, finding his understanding at least equal to her own and his knowledge far greater. He had shown such emotion at the recollection of his departed sister that her heart had truly warmed to him in that moment. She had seen him immovable, but she had also seen a softer side to his character, and she had been drawn to it. She still could not understand him.

A soft sigh turned her attention towards her sister.

"Jane?" She let the name hang in the air, a question she would not ask. Her sister turned to her and smiled.

"Mr and Miss Bingley were very kind to let us stay."

"I shall grant that Mr Bingley has been kind throughout. I am less certain of Miss Bingley."

"It must have been difficult for her to have two unexpected guests, one of them in need of nursing. She was kind, Lizzy."

"Oh, you will always be the sweetest of women. You do find the best in people, however much they may strive against it. And what do you think of Mr Bingley?"

"I like him very much. You know that."

Elizabeth smiled teasingly. "I do know that. I have never seen you so taken with a man after so little acquaintance."

Jane sighed happily. "It is altogether fast, I know. But there is something so pleasing about Mr Bingley. When he looks at me, I do not feel I am being considered like a horse taken to market. When he seeks me out to speak, he listens to what I say. I believe he may be the best of men, I truly do."

"If you who thinks well of everyone consider him to be the best, then I believe you are a hopeless case. I give you leave to like him. We know so little of his background, but I cannot believe he is not in love with you. I wish you joy."

"We are not engaged."

"A mere detail. He will ask you, for certain, and soon at that."

Jane smiled to herself and was silent.

CHAPTER TEN

The following day, all were up and about without any particular fuss. Jane, not giving any reason for the change, moved from her accustomed chair to one which gave her a view of anyone arriving. As such, she was the first to become aware of the appearance of a visitor. Hearing hoofs approaching, she sat a little straighter and glanced self-consciously at Elizabeth, but on turning to look out of the window, was greeted not by the sight of Mr Bingley on his horse, but by a stranger in a hired curricle.

"Mama, there is a gentleman arrived," she stated mildly. The others rushed with varying degrees of haste and curiosity to see who their visitor could be. They watched as a tall man in his late twenties dismounted without elegance and cast an appraising glance at the house. Mrs Bennet was loudly wondering who he might be, when her husband's voice answered her question.

"Ah, our visitor is here. I thought I heard some commotion. Had I not mentioned it to you, my dear? We are expecting a visit—indeed, are on the verge of receiving a visit —from a Mr Collins, of Hunsford in Kent."

"And who might Mr Collins of Hunsford in Kent be, pray?" Mrs Bennet's voice pierced the room, and Elizabeth turned involuntarily to see whether the gentleman had heard, one of the windows being ajar. He had not; he was currently brushing himself down and, by the way he nodded and spoke to the empty air, practising his greeting or, given the number of words involved, perhaps a speech or sermon.

"According to the terms of the entail on Longbourn, Mr Collins is my heir," Mr Bennet replied blandly.

His wife gaped at him. "Your heir? The man who will come to tear us all from our beds as soon as look at us? Oh, Mr Bennet! How could you invite him here?"

She burst into loud sobs, and was only partially quieted by Elizabeth, who with a reproachful look at her father, murmured, "Mama, he comes into the house. We must greet him as our guest."

Mrs Bennet was not one to recover herself quickly when overcome by her nerves, but she considered Mr Collins a gentleman to be placated and pleased so that he might treat them kindly when the time came. Therefore, with uncharacteristic fortitude, she swallowed her sobs and snapped at her daughters. "What are you huddling around me for, girls? Be seated and take up your work. He will not find us idle when he enters."

"What a remarkable recovery," Mr Bennet said sardonically, quietly enough that only Elizabeth might hear. She threw him another reproachful glance, for though less inclined to histrionics than her mother, she was acutely conscious that their future, as unmarried women of little dowry, might depend on this man about to enter their midst. Even Lydia and Kitty were conscious of it; they had withdrawn to a sofa where they whispered together in unusually hushed tones.

Mr Collins entered the drawing room and eyed the inhabitants with all the self-importance of a man inspecting his future property. His eyes roved across the daughters, lingering a long moment on Jane before Mr Bennet coughed, and the younger man stepped forward and addressed his host.

"Mr Bennet, I presume?" On receiving confirmation of this, he did not wait for any words of welcome, but pressed on immediately.

"My name is William Collins. I am delighted to make your acquaintance after so many years of correspondence. As you know, I come with the warmest of intentions, as suggested by none other than my noble patroness, Lady Catherine de Bourgh, to deepen the connexion that subsists between our families and strengthen the ties that bind me to your beautiful home."

Mrs Bennet drew a sharp breath in at the last words. They would be repeated and re-examined at length when she was not required to present her best manners. Elizabeth, however, was more curious about his reference to a connexion between their families, since until this meeting, Mr Collins's name had barely been spoken within the family, although the entail was the scourge of Mrs Bennet's existence.

When his eyes had wandered once again to Jane as he spoke of deepening the connexion, however, she had little doubt where his thoughts tended. She shuddered involuntarily.

Mr Bennet inclined his head slightly. "May I present my wife and daughters to you, sir? And then perhaps you would come through to my study."

Introductions made, Mr Collins bowed obsequiously to the assembled ladies and commenced a speech so dense with words and lacking in any discernible meaning that it was all Elizabeth could do not to sigh with relief when her father cut in with the welcome words, "Mr Collins. My study?"

As soon as the man could be persuaded to cease speaking and follow the older gentleman, Mrs Bennet cried out with an unquenchable torrent of words of her own that were not a great deal pleasanter to hear than those of their guest. Jane rushed to attend to her mother, seeking to placate her as best she could and calling Kitty to assist her. Lydia took the opportunity to poach a ribbon she had been coveting from Kitty's bonnet.

Once Mrs Bennet was calmer, Jane summoned Mrs Hill and gave instructions to prepare a room for their guest. This almost sent her mother into further paroxysms of anguish, but Jane, long used to her behaviour, remained unperturbed and continued to reassure her. In time, Mrs Bennet revived sufficiently that, when Mr Collins emerged from the study, she was able to perform the duties of a hostess and direct him to the prepared room. Elizabeth, seeing an opportunity, slipped out shortly after them and made her way to her father's study.

"Come, Lizzy," her father said as she knocked at the door. He had been expecting her visit.

"It was cruel, Papa," his daughter began with no preamble, "to spring Mr Collins on us so abruptly." She had long learnt that she alone of all the family could speak to him so freely, although he was not above teasing her for her freedoms.

Mr Bennet looked not a whit abashed. "Come now, I must have my sport. Your mother's reaction would have been much the same had she known for a twelve-month of his visit. Mr Collins has proved himself a wonder, and he aims to please. I have no doubt he will soon placate your mother and will be the apple of her eye."

"I hope you do not refer to his intentions towards Jane."

"You saw that, did you? Although it is no great surprise, for he was no better at hiding his interest than Mr Bingley. It will do him good to have a little competition for Jane's affections."

"You surely do not believe Jane could give her heart and hand to such a man?"

"I believe young ladies are capable of far sillier things than that. But I suspect your mother will not allow it, for she will by now have informed him of the hopes she has for the marriage of more than one daughter, and redirected his attention accordingly."

Elizabeth coloured at the sly smile her father gave with his words but did not look away from him. She had earned the right to meet her father on equal terms in conversation, and would not lose it now.

"If you are referring to me, I am not, to my knowledge, being courted."

"Indeed? I am pleased to hear it. It is so much more enjoyable to think it will be sprung upon you unexpectedly."

"Papa!" Elizabeth rose to go, but he put out a hand to placate her, and she slowly resumed her seat.

"Do not be missish. I am well aware your mother's ideas may run ahead of reality as regards potential marriage prospects for her daughters, and two dances from such a gentleman do not make for a proposal. But you may not wish to dispel any illusions she holds just yet. They will, after all, give her cause to direct Mr Collins's attentions away from you. I believe you will greatly enjoy his gift for giving compliments, as long as you are not their intended recipient."

Elizabeth feigned a laugh, and her father dismissed her with a wave and a final comment. "I look forward to more from Mr Collins. I believe he will be a fine addition to the family, one way or another."

Mr Bennet proved remarkably prescient in his assessment of Mr Collins. By the time Elizabeth returned to the ladies, he had made his way into Mrs Bennet's favour, for she smiled and simpered at him as they made conversation. As she questioned him, his history emerged, although bound up in so many flowery descriptions, panegyrics to Lady Catherine de Bourgh and her daughter, Anne de Bourgh, and abandoned trains of thought, that it took a great deal to decipher the essentials of his meaning. Elizabeth felt exhausted from listening, although she merely sat by, she and her sisters not being required by either party to join the conversation.

Mr Collins was a clergyman who had, through some unaccountable process, been lucky enough to be given a living by Lady Catherine, who appeared from his praise of her to be the centre and cause of all he did or said. Although he hedged the statement with false delicacy, it was quite clear his intention had been to take one of his cousins for a wife.

Regrettably—in Mr Collins's estimation—he had not been able to visit Longbourn when he originally intended. Lady Catherine had suffered some great disappointment—the details of which remained hazy but seemed to involve the collapse of her daughter Anne's marriage hopes—and had been unable to spare her clergyman, requiring his ministrations to assist her through a time of great distress. Mr Collins had therefore seen fit to take a wife from Hunsford village, who had borne him a son but had unfortunately not lived to see the child's first birthday. He spoke of his dear Margaret with affected sentimentality, but for the first time

Elizabeth felt she saw an undercurrent of genuine feeling, of sorrow if not grief, that made her feel more charitable to the man than she had yet been.

Now that his time of mourning had passed, and Lady Catherine's great trouble was sufficiently in the past that she could spare him, it appeared Mr Collins was resolved to revert to his original plan and seek one of his cousins as a wife, and indeed a mother to his young son, who had remained in Kent with his nurse for this visit.

Mrs Bennet seemed torn about which of her daughters to put forward to the gentleman. Undoubtedly, the prospect of Lydia being the next mistress of Longbourn was a fine one, even though the next heir would be the son of Mr Collins's first wife. Mr Collins, however, although initially looking at Lydia with admiration, was horrified at some unguarded comments she made within his earshot. Kitty, with no particular desire to be Mrs Collins but keen to be noticed, reprimanded Lydia with uncharacteristic primness, which turned to rancorous complaints when her mother's eyes passed straight across her and lit upon Mary. As she happened to be poring over a book of sermons, Mrs Bennet decided she ought to be introduced to his notice, and called her middle daughter from the table where she was seated to speak to their visitor.

Mr Collins's conversation was incessant, and lasted all through dinner and beyond into the evening, for Mr Bennet did not seem inclined to sit long alone with him after the meal. Elizabeth was greatly relieved when the time came to retire for the evening. She wondered how they would all survive the visit from their cousin.

CHAPTER ELEVEN

Mr Collins's visit proceeded much as it had begun. Mrs Bennet, having settled upon Mary as the daughter to be proffered to Mr Collins's notice, lost no opportunity to throw them together, thinking of all manner of errands for Mary to run, and insisting Mr Collins escort her as often as he could be persuaded. For his part, Mr Collins looked uncomfortable at being so thrown together with the plainest of his cousins, and for a time Elizabeth thought he might rebel against her mother's injunctions and attempt to pay his addresses to Jane or herself, regardless of any hints about other matrimonial prospects.

On the second day after their return from Netherfield, Miss Bingley arrived in state along with her sister to visit Jane and enquire after her health. The lady's unexpectedly friendly overtures were no doubt due to the fact she missed the company of her brother, who, she informed them, had gone to London on business but would return the following day. From the manner in which she spoke the word 'London',

Elizabeth wondered that she had not followed or insisted on accompanying him, but it appeared Mr Darcy was a fixture at Netherfield for the present, and where Mr Darcy was, Miss Bingley would remain, irrespective of the distinct lack of interest from the gentleman.

Miss Bingley and Mrs Hurst's visit allowed Jane to excuse herself from taking the walk that Mrs Bennet assiduously promoted for Mr Collins, Mary, and a very reluctant Kitty. Elizabeth found herself less fortunate, for she had business in Meryton, and Mr Collins declared himself eager to see the town in his cousins' company.

It soon emerged that Mr Collins felt it his duty to escort his cousin Elizabeth as much as his cousin Mary. Lydia had disappeared at the first hint of a walk, but Kitty had not been so successful and lagged reluctantly behind them. Elizabeth was relieved to discern from Mr Collins' stream of conversation that he had interpreted Miss Bingley's visit as confirmation of Mrs Bennet's suggestion that Jane would soon be engaged to Mr Bingley. Evidently, he was less convinced that Elizabeth was equally blessed in her prospects, for it was to her he turned as he extolled the virtues of his patroness and all the benefits of his position. It was more than she could readily endure, and when Kitty emitted a loud sigh, she rapidly fell back to walk with her. Kitty had no interest in conversation, however, being more inclined to meditate on her sense of injustice that even her own mother overlooked her, and walked sullenly at Elizabeth's side.

On reaching Meryton, Elizabeth was pleased to see amongst the usual mix of people that Mrs Wilson was emerging from one of the shops. As Mary and Kitty visited the draper's, she made her way rapidly to speak to her and apologise for her recent absence. Although she had occasionally ventured into the town when she first arrived, Mrs Wilson's visits had grown very rare, as she preferred to keep to the solitude of Purvis Lodge rather than brave even the friendlier stares and greetings of the townspeople. Elizabeth was at first a little displeased at her friend's reserve, for she spoke little and seemed in a hurry to depart. After a moment, however, Mrs Wilson met her eyes with a timid smile.

"Forgive me. I am not at ease when there are so many people. I would be pleased to see you soon. Perhaps you might call upon me the day after tomorrow?" Elizabeth gladly agreed, setting her friend's unwillingness to speak down to her natural reserve, and they parted with their usual degree of fondness.

If Elizabeth had hoped that by speaking to her friend she might escape her cousin for a moment, she was disappointed, for as she turned away, she found he approached her at as brisk a trot as behoved a clergyman.

"Cousin Elizabeth!" he called as he approached, although his eyes strayed to the retreating figure of the widow. "I am sorry to have missed the opportunity for an introduction to your friend. Perhaps on another occasion?"

Elizabeth could not be in the least sorry, for the thought of Mr Collins's particular form of civility being directed at Mrs Wilson was laughable and distressing in equal measure.

"Mrs Wilson is in mourning for her husband, sir, and goes little into company. I do not expect you will see her during your visit." Mr Collins expressed his disappointment at this information as sensibly as Elizabeth expected, and at greater length than she could endure.

It seemed to be a day of chance encounters, for not long after Mrs Wilson had left in one direction, Mr Darcy was seen approaching on horseback from the other. He dismounted as he approached the Longbourn party.

"Miss Bennet," he greeted her with a bow, although his eyes took in the proximity of her cousin standing at her side.

"Mr Darcy!" Elizabeth replied, her genuine pleasure tinged with heartfelt relief. The possibility of some sensible conversation was such a delightful prospect after half an hour of Mr Collins's ceaseless chatter that she beamed at the new arrival with a joy of which he could not be insensible. He met her gaze speechlessly for a moment, his cheeks reddening, before recovering himself enough to ask to be introduced to her companion.

Elizabeth looked round to find Mr Collins had drawn altogether too close to her side. She deliberately stepped away from him before providing the necessary information. The clergyman accepted the introduction with such a mixture of self-importance and servility that it was all she could do not to laugh aloud, and her eyes danced merrily as she turned back to Mr Darcy to find him eyeing the other gentleman with barely concealed disdain and not some little alarm.

"Hunsford? The village in Kent?" repeated Mr Darcy, a subtle note of curiosity in his voice that did not escape Elizabeth.

"Yes! I am lucky to be favoured with the gift of a living by Lady Catherine de Bourgh of Rosings Park. She is a most benevolent lady, and I have long benefited not merely from her gracious patronage but also from her extensive wisdom and knowledge. She was kind enough to acknowledge my late wife," here he offered a sentimental sigh, before continuing in a bright voice, "and to encourage me to heal the breach with the family of my dear, dear cousins since I have sadly been deprived of my dear Margaret's company." Any sorrow this time was concealed by a smirk at Elizabeth, who had trouble disguising her horror at his unsubtle insinuation. Mr Collins paid this no mind and turned back to Mr

Darcy with a sycophantic bow. "Do you know the village, sir?"

Mr Darcy's tone was aloof. "A little." He did not deign to say anything further, but at this moment, Kitty and Mary returned with their purchases.

"Lizzy, may we go back now?" Kitty asked, without waiting to acknowledge Mr Darcy's presence.

"I have one errand to run," Elizabeth replied. "I shall not be long, but my books have been at the bookseller's for a week now, and I must collect them. Of course," she added, seeing an opportunity, "I am sure Mr Collins would gladly escort you and Mary home if you would prefer not to wait, and I can follow on. I walk faster than any of you and shall soon catch up."

Mr Collins would hear of no such thing. He must wait for his cousin and would not hear of her walking alone. He smirked and simpered so frightfully that Elizabeth felt her ire rising. She could say nothing to change his mind, however, so she resigned herself to a walk home with Mr Collins once again doing his best to command her attention. She dropped a curtsey to Mr Darcy, who had business in another shop, and departed to collect her books.

On emerging from the bookseller's, Elizabeth was surprised to see Mr Darcy had also completed his business and was once again standing with her sisters and cousin. As she approached, she heard him asking Mary about the availability of new music for the pianoforte in Meryton. She was impressed; Mr Darcy was apparently not only conversing with her sister but had succeeded in finding a topic on which she could speak with some degree of sense. Elizabeth recalled that it was not his first enquiry into musical matters, but she could not imagine he wished to acquire it for his own use. Perhaps he hoped to persuade

Bingley to stock Netherfield with some different pieces to increase the variety of Miss Bingley and Mrs Hurst's performances.

As she approached, Mr Darcy greeted her again. "I had been intending to take the route past Longbourn on my return to Netherfield. That being so, I thought I might join you and your sisters and cousin on your walk, if it would not be unwelcome."

Elizabeth's smile made it abundantly clear his company would be exceedingly welcome, and she could not but laugh internally at her cousin's expression as he looked from one to the other.

They quickly settled into a walking party. Mr Collins appeared to reluctantly accept there may have been some basis for Mrs Bennet's hopes regarding Elizabeth's prospects, and made no comment as she walked ahead with Mr Darcy, but walked instead with Mary. Kitty, left to herself, lagged behind discontentedly.

Mr Darcy parted from them at the drive to Longbourn, mounted his horse and rode away without a backward glance, although Elizabeth lingered for a few moments to watch him go. They returned to the house, where Mrs Bennet, having observed them on the road from an upstairs window, came down to complain that no one had thought to invite Mr Darcy in, and to exclaim about her eldest daughters' marriage prospects. After Mr Collins retired to his room to write to Lady Catherine, her enthusiasm also extended to Mary's prospects, already seeing her as the future mistress of Longbourn, and it was some time before she could be persuaded to abandon the theme. Elizabeth was only grateful none of the gentlemen had been present to hear her effusions.

Lydia, having escaped the walk, had been thoroughly

bored, and now found her entertainment in goading Kitty for not yet having found a beau.

"And neither have you!" Kitty shot back. "So you hold your tongue!"

"Shan't," Lydia replied childishly. "I shall marry a colonel when Jane takes me to London. Or an admiral perhaps, or an earl! There's no one in Meryton the least bit interesting. No one is going to want to marry you, though, for you look so sour!"

Kitty's self-pity, already at a peak, overcame her, and she burst into tears and fled from the room, not to be seen again for some time. Jane chided Lydia gently, but the younger girl was unrepentant.

"Well, she never will find a husband if she is so sour all the time. Someone needed to tell her so."

When Kitty returned, Mrs Bennet was again discussing their marriage prospects, although with less exuberance than earlier in the day.

"And so, you see…oh, there you are, Kitty. Do you think Jane will be married before Lizzy? Or perhaps Mary will be first of all! My dear Lydia will have gentlemen falling at her feet I am sure, once she is in London and in the society of Mr Bingley and Mr Darcy's friends!"

Kitty took her seat with exaggerated primness, still looking peevish. Mrs Bennet, not needing anyone else to contribute to the conversation, continued with her speech, but after a moment Kitty spoke over her.

"I doubt it will be Jane married first," she said, glancing from under her eyelashes to see how her words were received. "If at all."

"Whatever can you mean, child?" Mrs Bennet exclaimed. "Of course Jane will be married! Mr Bingley is so in love with her, I am sure he will be at her side as soon as he returns from London. Oh! Perhaps he has gone to London to see about the settlement!" She was nearly lost in her reverie, but Kitty's next words commanded the complete attention of everyone present.

"Mr Bingley has been secretly calling on the widow at Purvis Lodge."

CHAPTER TWELVE

For a moment, the room was still and silent. Kitty sat with quiet smugness, clearly revelling in the sensation she had created. Even Lydia was uncharacteristically speechless, although she raised her hand to her mouth. Whether this was to disguise a gasp or a smile, Elizabeth could not tell. Mrs Bennet was the first to speak.

"Mr Bingley? What nonsense! Impossible," she scoffed, but her eyes, like Elizabeth's, darted to Jane, who sat unmoving, eyes lowered. "How could you suggest such a thing, Catherine?"

Kitty's eyes darkened at the use of her full name, and she frowned before she answered. "There is no need to blame me, Mama, he is not visiting me!"

"But you cannot throw such an accusation out without cause," Elizabeth interjected, attempting to conciliate before the conversation descended into acrimonious bickering. "What brings you to make it, Kitty?"

"I heard it from Nelly. Her brother works on the farm

closest to Purvis Lodge and saw him visiting. All of the servants were discussing it."

"Oh, Mr Bingley! We all praised him to the skies—and he was calling on another all along!" Mrs Bennet wailed. "To treat my Jane so! What can he be about, calling on that-that woman, who pretends to see no one? And to think we invited her under our roof!" She threw herself back on the sofa with inarticulate wails, and for once, Jane was not the first at her side.

Instead, it was Mary who rose. "A woman's virtue is a prized possession," she said inconsequentially, before continuing with a more practical offer to order some wine to aid their mother's recovery.

Mrs Bennet's groans became louder, her words still less distinct, but none in the room paid her any attention. Lydia, with a short laugh, continued adorning one of her bonnets with a new trim. Kitty's face changed, as her delight at the sensation she had caused turned to sulkiness once she realised that her moment was brief and she no longer held the room's attention. She picked up some embroidery, only to throw it down again a moment later.

Elizabeth was not insensible of the various reactions, but her sole focus as she crossed the room was Jane, who sat as if stunned. "Jane?"

Her sister turned unseeing eyes on her. "It cannot be true," she whispered. "It cannot. Or else there is some explanation, some other reason for calling on her than that."

"I am sure it is all a misunderstanding. You know how gossip can be."

Jane nodded absently, but immediately rose, and saying only, "Forgive me, Lizzy," she rapidly exited the room. Her feet slowed to a listless pace, however, as Elizabeth heard her climb the stairs. She stayed only to ensure Mary was attending to her mother, before following her eldest sister upstairs.

Jane was seated on the end of the bed, gazing out of the window. She smiled wanly as Elizabeth sat down beside her and drew her head to her shoulder.

"Surely you do not believe it?" she asked gently.

"I know him so little. Everything has happened so fast, but there is such goodness in his countenance and words. Could I have been deceived in his character? Have I been too quick to trust? He has made me no offer." Jane's voice was dull.

"Neither has he sought to take advantage of you, although he might have attempted it whilst you were at Netherfield if his intentions were not honest."

"No." Jane's voice came out as a breath. She drew away from Elizabeth and moved to unpin her hair. "But even if the report proves untrue, I have allowed my heart to be left too unguarded. Please excuse me to Mama and Papa. Perhaps I am still unwell."

"Perhaps." Elizabeth did not believe for a moment that Jane was ill, but after seeing she was not inclined to talk, reluctantly left her. She could understand that, whether she believed the accusations or not, Jane would not benefit from their mother's company for the time being.

Elizabeth returned slowly downstairs, her thoughts disturbed. Her mother, still in a state of agitation but less vocal in her exclamations, was still being attended by Mary. Lydia and Kitty had apparently made their peace for a time and were seated together whispering fiercely.

"Mama," Elizabeth said, "we do not know whether we ought to give credence to this report. There may have been a misunderstanding, and Mr Bingley has not done aught to injure Jane that we know for certain. We do not know why he was visiting Mrs Wilson, if indeed he has called on her at all."

Mrs Bennet sniffed. "Mr Bingley is a philanderer! Oh, my poor Jane, married to such a man!"

"Mama!" Elizabeth could not prevent the shock from sounding in her voice. "Mama, they are not married and have no understanding. We do not know what has truly happened. We must remain calm, for Jane's sake."

"And who are you to tell me what I must do? Speaking to your mother so!" Mrs Bennet's indignation was an improvement on her histrionics, although Elizabeth could not yet be calm.

"Mama, Mr Collins is our guest. It would not do for him to hear of rumours and gossip, not when our acquaintance with him is still so new. Not when he seeks to deepen the connexion between our families," she said with a glance at Mary, who met her gaze with an unreadable expression.

This argument seemed to break into Mrs Bennet's consciousness when being exhorted for calm did not, for she sat up straighter and her eyes widened. "Indeed! Mr Collins must not know, for he must marry one of you girls!" She looked around the room at her four assembled daughters. "None of you must breathe a word of this to anyone," she scolded, as if they had been caught doing that very thing. "Catherine! Lydia! Do you understand me?"

IT FELL to Elizabeth to inform her father of why his eldest daughter was suddenly indisposed. He was not inclined to believe there was anything at all in the report, and began to jest with Elizabeth about a good love story needing some turmoil before it could be brought to its inevitable conclusion. When Elizabeth uncharacteristically hung her head at his words, however, he was a little repentant.

"There, there. This will pass. I am sure Mr Bingley will prove to be a good man and this all to be a misunderstanding, as you say." Elizabeth managed to smile, but she did not meet his eyes as he reached out and tapped her gently on the shoulder.

Elizabeth left her father's study with her heart and mind still full of Jane's distress and Kitty's accusation. Hearing Mr Collins's heavy tread on the stairs, she changed her course away from her older sister and found herself taking the passage that led to the kitchen.

"Miss Elizabeth," Mrs Hill said as she spied the lady. "Does your mother require something?" Elizabeth winced inwardly at this reminder that her mother's indisposition had been evident to other members of the household, although she trusted Hill's discretion in dealing with her mistress.

"No, thank you," she replied; then with sudden inspiration, "I would like to speak to Nelly for a moment."

Nelly was called into the kitchen and bobbed a nervous curtsey at her summons.

Elizabeth glanced at Mrs Hill, who waited for further instructions, and indicated she was to remain before turning back to the anxious looking maid. "Nelly, I understand there has been some discussion about Mr Bingley visiting Mrs Wilson, the widow at Purvis Lodge."

Nelly nodded. "Yes, miss. My brother said he saw him calling one morning."

"Do you recall his exact words?"

"No, miss."

"Do you recall anything about what your brother saw? Which day it was, perhaps?"

"It was the day you returned from Netherfield."

"Your brother saw Mr Bingley call on Purvis Lodge the day Jane and I returned here?"

"Yes, miss. Oh! No, if you please, I saw Matty then. He must have seen the gentleman a day or two before that, I don't know when."

Elizabeth cast her mind back to her stay at Netherfield and whether Mr Bingley had been out for long enough to have called upon Mrs Wilson. Hope shot through her. "Are you quite certain it was Mr Bingley your brother mentioned?"

"Yes, miss. He said the gentleman from Netherfield called at Purvis Lodge, and Mr Bingley is the gentleman from Netherfield."

"There are three gentlemen currently residing at Netherfield. Is there the slightest possibility he referred to a different gentleman?"

Nelly had thus far borne the questioning with fortitude, but now the tears sprung to her eyes. "I...it is possible, I am not...he only said he saw a gentleman!"

Elizabeth breathed a sigh, doing her best not to distress the girl any further. "Thank you, Nelly." She did not dismiss her, but turned to Mrs Hill, who had busied herself preparing a tray of refreshments whilst they were talking. "I believe there has been a misunderstanding. Mr Darcy kindly carried a message for me to Purvis Lodge during his morning ride whilst I was at Netherfield, and I believe it is this which has prompted this rumour. I am sure neither Mr Darcy nor Mr Bingley would appreciate their business being discussed in the manner that it has reached me. Please ensure any information that has been put about by any of the servants is corrected, and that there is no further gossip."

Mrs Hill, who had heard much from Mrs Bennet's effusions about Jane's prospective hopes, understood Elizabeth's meaning and nodded. "It will be done. Shall I carry the tray through to your mama?"

"Thank you. I shall take it." And so saying, Elizabeth took up the tray and departed, her tread a little lighter.

She could hear Mr Collins's voice even from the kitchen, but it only required a moment to ascertain that it emanated from her father's study. She heaved a further sigh of relief.

Mrs Bennet did not wait for Elizabeth to set down the tray before she began complaining.

"Did Hill prepare this tray? She has sent the buns with currants in. They are sure to be too sweet. Currant buns always disagree with me, but no one ever considers my needs."

"Mama," Elizabeth said firmly, ignoring the complaint, "I have spoken to Nelly."

Mrs Bennet looked at her daughter with indignation. "Did I not tell you to speak to no one about the matter, Miss Lizzy? What makes it that you should be the one speaking to the servants?"

"Mama!" Elizabeth had been attempting to regain her mother's attention, and now raised her voice slightly. She went on hurriedly before Mrs Bennet could begin another speech. "I have spoken to Nelly, and I know what has caused this misunderstanding." She cast a glance at Kitty, who was focused on her embroidery, her face mutinous.

"Oh! I was certain it was all a mistake!" Mrs Bennet all but clapped her hands with glee. "Mr Bingley is so in love with Jane, not for a minute did I believe he could mistreat her! It must have been that boy's imagination entirely."

"No, he mistook Mr Darcy for Mr Bingley."

Mrs Bennet looked aghast. "Mr Darcy visiting the widow! Such a dour man! She is pretty, I grant you, but I would not have thought her such a temptress as to draw in such a man, for all his money. And you have called her your friend! You had better see her no more, Lizzy, she is no fit company for a lady. I always distrusted her with her mysterious ways. Snubbing our society, indeed! We are the ones who ought to snub one such as her!"

"Mama!" Elizabeth spoke sharply again, pained at hearing her friend so spoken of. "There is more. Nelly's brother saw Mr Darcy when he kindly delivered a note for me to Mrs Wilson when I was with Jane at Netherfield and unable to visit her. He was not calling on her."

Mrs Bennet looked at her daughter in perplexity. "What was Mr Darcy doing, delivering notes like an errand boy? You should not trouble him with such requests if you are to catch him!"

"He offered to carry the letter whilst taking his morning ride, and I accepted. It was really not a matter of any significance. But I think we can safely absolve the Netherfield gentlemen of any untoward behaviour regarding Mrs Wilson."

Mrs Bennet, determined as she was to marry the gentlemen in question to her daughters, needed no further persuasion, although her mutterings against Mrs Wilson's wiles took longer to subdue.

As soon as she felt her mother sufficiently placated, Elizabeth made her way to Jane's room. Her sister lay on the bed, awake and solemn. As quickly as she was able, Elizabeth informed her of what she had discovered from her conversation with Nelly. Her sister remained prone on the bed in silence as she spoke.

"All is well, Jane," she concluded. "Mr Bingley is innocent."

Jane smiled wanly. "I am glad."

"But you are not happy," Elizabeth stated, prompting Jane to sit up and look at her.

"I am relieved," she said slowly. "I hold Mr Bingley in high esteem and would not wish anyone to believe him capable of such things as Mama was suggesting." Elizabeth waited for Jane to continue. Eventually, with a sigh, she did so. "Yet I cannot help but wonder whether I have been wrong to encourage him so openly. Perhaps he does merely amuse himself, and I shall be exposed to ridicule as much as if he had proved to be calling on Mrs Wilson. Am I wrong," she whispered, a few tears falling gently, "to love him so, after so little acquaintance?"

Elizabeth's relief was great at the last words. Her sister's heart was won, and her natural sensitivity had asserted itself. On this she might reassure Jane.

"This will not do!" she said with a light laugh, pulling Jane to stand, then guiding her to sit in front of the glass. She busied herself with Jane's hair, which was in some disarray.

"You love him! That is a great thing, to love a man. If you do not know him well yet, then the answer to that is to know him better. When on his return from London he wishes to see you, and you wish to see him, then tell him the truth. If he is as good a man as I suspect, he will be willing to advance his suit more slowly and prove to you that your instincts are not wrong. If you like, I shall play the teasing younger sister and ask him all manner of difficult questions until you have all the answers you wish and, in comparison to me, he will see you for the paragon you are!"

Jane had brightened considerably during this speech and laughed at its conclusion. "We have enough teasing younger sisters not to require you to do anything unusual." She sobered again, before turning to face Elizabeth, who had just finished her hair. "How must poor Kitty be feeling?"

"Kitty?" Elizabeth responded in confusion.

"She spoke with such certainty. She must be mortified to have misunderstood matters so badly. She sought to warn me when she believed in Mr Bingley's perfidy, and I have said barely a word to her!"

"You are much too good." Elizabeth smiled at her sister, uncomfortably aware that she had not thought about Kitty for a moment. She was certain her purpose had not been to warn Jane so much as to create a sensation.

"We must re-join the others," Jane said with more firmness, and immediately rose to descend.

Mr Collins had also returned, and Jane and Elizabeth entered the room at the same time as their mother put forward the idea of a walk in the gardens. Jane's motive for immediately seconding the motion became clear when, as they set out, she drew Kitty to her side. The younger lady looked both sullen and alarmed but did not resist.

Mr Collins began speaking as soon as they were out of doors, comparing the grounds to those of Rosings Park and his parsonage in Hunsford. Mary walked dutifully at his side making no comment, for he seemed to require nothing else from his companion than the appearance of attending his every word.

The conversation during the walk must have proved satisfying to some of the party, for when they returned to the house, Mr Collins was still talking, and Kitty, although unwilling to meet anyone's eyes, had lost some of her sullenness. Jane slipped ahead of the rest of the party and disappeared into her father's study. The others separated naturally to attend to their chosen pursuits.

As they retired that evening, Jane informed Elizabeth that

she had suggested to their father that Kitty might benefit from some time away—from home, from Lydia, and from their mother's nerves. He had agreed to write to their uncle Gardiner to explore whether she might spend some time with his family in town.

Only once Jane was asleep, and she could examine her own feelings in peace, did Elizabeth allow the thought that had been at the back of her mind to come to the fore. She had suspected some prior knowledge—had even wondered about a prior attachment—between her friend and Mr Bingley. She was fully convinced that Kitty's accusations arose from a misunderstanding, but it had reawakened a question about Mrs Wilson's past that Elizabeth could not suppress.

Elizabeth awoke much earlier than usual, her mind still full of her friend and what her history might be. Unable to lie in bed for long once awake, she rose and dressed, making her way out earlier than usual to walk. Although she had no intention of calling on her friend at such an hour, Elizabeth's feet led her instinctively towards Purvis Lodge. Few were up and about yet, and she gloried in the peace and isolation of her walk, meeting no one on the familiar paths.

As she approached the house, Elizabeth's pace slowed involuntarily, and without realising it, she came to a stop, absentmindedly gazing at the frontage. As she stood, the door opened, and out stepped a figure she recognised instantly, although his head was turned away. A shout was followed by the form of young Tommy barrelling out to cling to the man's legs with the obvious intent of hindering his departure. Joey followed his brother out, and in the shadow of the door, Elizabeth could see Mrs Wilson calling her sons back.

They did as they were bid, but not before Elizabeth's gaze passed from the curly hair and sober visage of the man to that of the boy at his legs. Her eyes widened, and a gasp escaped her before she could contain it. At the noise, the gentleman's eyes flew in her direction, and they were both for a moment frozen in time, her eyes locked with those of Mr Darcy. With prodigious effort, Elizabeth dragged her gaze away, turned, and fled.

CHAPTER THIRTEEN

Elizabeth walked, entirely insensible of everything around her, for some time. She felt as though her mind had ceased functioning. All coherent thought had been removed, replaced with the one image of the tall man and the child who bore him such a resemblance.

Mr Darcy, visiting Mrs Wilson! This was unimaginable in itself, but the hour of the visit, when so few were abroad, surely indicated some clandestine purpose. The children appeared to know him—to be fond of him, even—and she could have no doubt this was not his first such visit. She could think of but one explanation for his appearance there, and could barely name it, even to herself.

Her friend, timid Mrs Wilson, living under the protection of a gentleman...of Mr Darcy! The thought horrified her. Such arrangements were not unknown, even in their quiet county, but she would not have believed either of them capable of it. Surely, she could not have been so deceived in her friend's character, or that of the gentleman? Yet it seemed she had. If she could be so soundly mistaken on this, what else could she have been deceived about?

Is Mrs Wilson truly a widow, or is she an unmarried lady seeking to conceal her shame so she can move with some freedom in society? Does she have a husband yet living whom she has left for Mr Darcy? Why has he not married her and set up house openly together? There was some disparity in their ages, for Mrs Wilson was still so young, but surely not more than ten or fifteen years, and she must be of legal age to wed. Mrs Wilson had spoken of schooling and was evidently a lady, unless she was still more deceitful than Elizabeth could rightly credit.

Surely she, who took great pride in her discernment and judgment of character, had not been so completely taken in by her friend? She had believed Mrs Wilson had some tragic secret she wished to conceal, but not this! Yet Elizabeth had seen the proof of it with her own eyes. What could it possibly mean? The thought of her friend, who had seemed all sweetness, having deceived her was troubling, and the more Elizabeth considered it, the more her ire grew. She had always prided herself on her discernment, yet she had been hoodwinked by a woman—*a girl!*—she considered her friend. It was not her situation that angered Elizabeth, but the deceit that had been played on her. *She feigned ignorance of Mr Darcy. I thought she responded to Mr Bingley's name, but all along it was Mr Darcy she knew.* Elizabeth's pace increased, her hands in her agitation unconsciously grasping the air in fistfuls as she marched, but her thoughts raced even faster.

I allowed myself to be deceived. She had seen a lonely young woman, and she had sought her out and made a friendship. It was unnecessary for Mrs Wilson to have feigned loneliness— living as she did, Elizabeth could not doubt she would feel her solitude. And it was no great wonder that she might not want her situation to be broadcast amongst her new neighbours and risk becoming an outcast before she was even accepted. *She was merely doing what was necessary to protect herself. It was wrong, but it was not maliciously done. It did me no harm to not know her circumstances.* No, Mrs Wilson had not behaved as Elizabeth would have wished, but it could be understood, if not excused. She stopped in her tracks and, not caring whether anyone might hear, screamed a little with frustration. *How could I have been so foolish? To have been so taken in, when I have thought myself so observant and wise?* She shook her head fiercely and marched on.

Her thoughts turned from the lady to the gentleman. She hardly knew what to think about *him*. She was not unaware of the ways of society, and she knew that some men who could afford it, and some who could not, kept mistresses. She knew too that Mr Darcy was sufficiently wealthy to be able to do as he pleased. Yet it seemed so unlike the man she thought she knew. She did not wish to think him dishonourable; he had seemed severe, solemn, even haughty, but he had never shown any sign of being dissolute.

She recalled his appearance at Netherfield when he returned from his ride, the uncharacteristic brightness in his face and air. Had he just come from Purvis Lodge? He had offered to deliver a letter for her there—the very letter that had prompted the events of the day before. Unless perhaps Nelly's brother had seen other visits by the gentleman. And *she* had unwittingly provided an excuse for him to visit his paramour! *Was that why Mr Bingley had cast that peculiar glance at his friend when he offered to carry the letters?* Again, Elizabeth berated herself for her failure to understand the meaning of what she had observed. She thought herself so clever, yet she had been so blind.

Mr Darcy had arrived in Hertfordshire after Mrs Wilson— he must have established her here, then followed after sufficient time to allay suspicion. But he had not taken Nether-field himself. *What brought Mr Bingley here? Is he aware of Mrs Wilson's situation? Is Mr Darcy as close friends with his host as he appears, or is he merely taking advantage of the good nature of Mr Bingley and the advances of Miss Bingley to suit his own purpose?*

During their very first dance, Mr Darcy had asked her about the houses in the neighbourhood; was he seeking information on where Mrs Wilson might be? *Or did he already know and wished to find out the nature of the society he had placed her in?*

Her heart stopped in her throat when she realised Mr Darcy had left the assembly early, and her suspicion rose regarding where he had been. What had he said of her? That she would have to be more handsome and far more delightful to keep him from his business. The thought was sickening; had she been handsome, would he have been tempted? Would he have sought to make her one such as Mrs Wilson?

Elizabeth was now far from Purvis Lodge, and passing a tree, she paused for a moment and leant her weight full against it. She examined her history with Mr Darcy, and with a heavy heart admitted to herself that she had found him stimulating in conversation, intelligent, and—she had thought—respectful in how he engaged with her.

I enjoy his company. I like him.

Perhaps her mother's enthusiasm for a match had turned her head, for whilst she was not in love, she knew she felt something which could easily grow into love. The thought of marriage to Mr Darcy had seemed unlikely, but neither impossible nor abhorrent. Now all such thoughts must be put aside. She had been blinded by her enjoyment of his company and her growing feelings. It was more evidence that her judgment was flawed, that she could be so taken in by a man who all along had—

She rubbed at her forehead. It was dizzying, attempting to understand what she had seen. *Did Mr Darcy ever show any sign that he desired my affection? Did he ever deceive me at all, other than in disguising his connexion to Mrs Wilson, or was it all my imagination that he had shown some preference for my company?*

It was too perplexing. She could not understand the truth, either of Mr Darcy's character or of Mrs Wilson's, but she was certain what she had seen today had made it impossible she could comfortably associate with either of them again; no friendship could survive such a betrayal. She deeply mourned the loss of her friend, and as she closed her eyes and leant her head back against the tree, she allowed herself for one moment to indulge what it might have meant to her to have Mr Darcy's respect and affection, if he had been the man she believed.

"Enough," she said out loud, although none but the crows in the adjoining field heard her. She deliberately stood herself upright, turned her feet towards Longbourn, and set herself the task of deciding what it was she must do with this information.

Could she expose the truth? Would Mr Darcy be scorned by polite society? He might be forgiven the indulgence, but the deception would be another matter if the people of Meryton felt they had been imposed upon. She thought of Mrs Wilson, subject to all the whispers of society and perhaps forced to leave her new home, and almost every feeling revolted. She might be barred from the society of her friend, but she needed time and space to examine whether she could be the means of her exposure. Jane and Charlotte would need to be warned, for any intimate association between Mrs Wilson and her friends must be at an end, but Elizabeth knew she could trust them with this secret, and they could decide together whether they ought to make the information generally known.

Having resolved to be silent, Elizabeth determined only that she would watch Mr Bingley carefully when he returned, to see whether she could ascertain the extent of his knowledge of the situation.

Thinking of Mr Bingley reminded her again it had been *his* name that she had believed Mrs Wilson reacted to. The thought made little sense to her now. Perhaps she knew Mr Bingley through Mr Darcy? Perhaps she had once thought to marry him before being persuaded to a different life? It was a mystery that Elizabeth would gladly see resolved, but she could not believe, now, that Mr Bingley had any culpability. His manners were so open, perhaps the opportunity would arise to mention Mrs Wilson's name to him, and all could be quickly made clear on that point.

Of Mr Darcy, Elizabeth could only hope that they would not often be in company together. If they were, she would have to avoid him as best she could, for she knew she would not be able to conceal her feelings. Surely, it would not be difficult not to see him, for although he had spoken to her more than he had to many people in Meryton, he would not now wish to risk his secret being revealed by seeking her out. She would be able to avoid him.

With these thoughts, Elizabeth reached Longbourn once again and braced herself to face her family. She had missed breakfast but did not feel the loss. Pausing to take a deep breath, she slipped inside the house and was grateful not to see anyone other than Mrs Hill, who readily accepted her request that she inform the family she had a headache, as she made her way upstairs to the peace of her own room.

CHAPTER FOURTEEN

Elizabeth was still in her room at noon, her feigned headache having rapidly become reality once she was no longer walking. She was grateful to discover that food had been sent up to her, for the long walk on little sustenance had finally had its effect, and she ate with more appetite than she would have thought possible an hour before.

By dinnertime, she concluded it was necessary to begin making the pretence that nothing out of the ordinary had occurred. Thankfully, her pale face and silence was attributed to her afternoon's indisposition, and no one required any particular exertion on her part through the meal or the remainder of the evening. She retired to bed feeling she had acquitted herself respectably, and that if she could only endure the next two or three days, she might develop sufficient perspective to be able to decide what action, if any, she ought to take.

Elizabeth was highly relieved when, the next morning, Mr Bingley called alone. She had all but forgotten Kitty's accusation against the gentleman in the shock of her recent discovery, but Jane's quiet reminded her that her sister had resolved to take time to better understand his character. She was glad of it; not knowing what he knew of Mrs Wilson, or what his opinion was on her situation, it was all the more important Jane took time to ensure she was certain of her own heart and Mr Bingley's intentions. It was quickly evident that his admiration for Jane had not diminished during his brief stay in town, but he seemed to be more reserved than his usual manner. Elizabeth put this down to the change in Jane's own demeanour; although she smiled and conversed, there was a new reserve in her responses that Mr Bingley could not fail to notice.

After a few minutes of desultory conversation, Mrs Bennet grew impatient with the new awkwardness between the couple and, demonstrating her firm belief in the efficacy of exercise for furthering attachments, suggested they take a walk in the garden. The gentleman accepted the suggestion eagerly, and Jane acquiesced quietly but not without a voiceless plea directed at Elizabeth that she would remain close by.

Once in the garden, Mr Bingley drew Jane gently but inexorably forward, only so far ahead that they might speak without being overheard. Elizabeth had no wish to eavesdrop but took care not to fall so far behind that her sister would be uncomfortable. She felt no reluctance at being left to walk alone, for her thoughts, although less frantic, continued on much the same theme as on the previous day.

Mr Bingley left for Netherfield without returning to the house, with the excuse that he had a prior engagement with Mr Darcy. Judging by his expression as he took his leave, Elizabeth thought the outcome of their conversation had been largely successful, although perhaps not quite everything he had hoped. He promised to call again the following day, which Jane accepted with a quiet nod. As they watched him depart, Elizabeth drew closer to her sister's side and took her arm. Jane smiled and, instead of making her way indoors, turned back towards the gardens.

They walked without speaking for a moment, until Jane broke the silence.

"Mr Bingley asked for my hand."

Elizabeth squeezed her sister's arm with an inquisitive look but waited for Jane to answer the obvious question.

"I told him I would like to know his character and background better first. He was surprised, but not offended, I think. He understands that it was not a refusal."

"I am not sure he has it in him to be offended."

"Perhaps that is one of the things I need to find out," Jane said calmly.

"Did you—" Elizabeth's voice was thick and choked, and she took a moment to clear her throat before attempting to speak again. "Did you tell him anything of what happened?"

"No," Jane replied. "Nor did I ask whether he knew Mrs Wilson, or anything akin to it. There will be time enough for that. I merely said his absence had given me time to reflect on how rapidly we had moved on such a short acquaintance. He wishes to speak to Papa tomorrow, to make his intentions clear, and I think we shall see more of him in the coming days and weeks."

Elizabeth felt a brief shiver pass over her as she realised that, unless Mr Darcy was as keen to avoid her as she was him, there was a high probability Mr Bingley's increased presence would make escaping a meeting with his friend and guest more difficult. Not wanting to yet disturb Jane's quiet happiness, however, she kept silent for the present on the subject uppermost in her own mind.

The following morning, Elizabeth's fears were confirmed when Mr Bingley arrived at Longbourn accompanied by Mr Darcy. She had steeled herself for this meeting but had not prepared for it to be made without the distraction of his friend's attention to Jane, for Mr Bingley had gone straight to Mr Bennet after only a passing acknowledgement of the ladies.

With Mr Bingley absent, all of her mother's enthusiasm was directed to her next two daughters, and she soon found a way to arrange them to her liking.

"Mary, what book are you reading?"

"A new volume of sermons, Mama."

"Sermons! Why, Mr Collins, would you recommend that particular volume? I am sure as a clergyman you know all the best writers."

Mr Collins's chest swelled. "I do pride myself on my extensive collection of literature suitable to the lot of a clergyman, although they would not disgrace the library of any gentleman. My noble patroness has been so good as to give me a number of suggestions on books that I ought—"

"How very interesting! Mary, do bring your book here and sit by me. You will be able to show Mr Collins and discover whether he holds a copy in his library. Perhaps he might help you with one or two of the more difficult passages."

Mary stood up obediently and crossed the room, where she proceeded to show Mr Collins the book.

"Ah! Yes, Mrs Bennet, this is by a very respected author. In fact, I recall—"

Only Mary heard what he recalled, for no one else wished to hear another of Mr Collins' speeches, and Mrs Bennet had already turned to Mr Darcy.

"Mr Darcy, that seat is placed a little close to the door. Can you not feel a draught? Perhaps you would prefer to move?" She indicated the chair Mary had recently vacated and which was closest in proximity to Elizabeth.

"Thank you, madam."

Elizabeth's horror and mortification was great as Mr Darcy crossed the room. She pondered whether it was better to disregard him entirely and risk her mother's wrath, or to attempt the impossible task of maintaining a neutral, indifferent conversation.

Thankfully, Mrs Bennet, having achieved her aim for the present, could not contain her natural volubility. She continued to carry on a largely one-sided conversation with the gentleman and required no contributions from her daughter for some time.

Elizabeth sneaked a surreptitious glance at Mr Darcy from under her eyelashes whilst he made some curt response to her mother. She regretted it straight away, for he noticed the movement and turned his eyes immediately on her. She was however satisfied on one point—in discovering whether he appeared at all affected by their last encounter. His appearance had once again undergone a radical change. Gone was the relaxed air she had observed at Purvis Lodge. Now, his bearing was rigid, his face drawn, and his expression closed.

Eventually, even Mrs Bennet's enthusiasm for talking waned, and she attempted to forward Elizabeth's match in her preferred manner, asking, "Would you care to take a walk, Mr Darcy?"

"Gladly," he replied shortly. Elizabeth felt him turn in her direction.

"Lizzy, perhaps you would accompany Mr Darcy. He might be pleased to see the rose garden. I am sure Kitty or Lydia might join you."

Elizabeth floundered for a moment, but then with cold

firmness replied to her mother. "Regrettably, I cannot walk today. My headache from my last long walk the day before yesterday lingers yet. It would be wiser to keep to the house."

"Nonsense! You have never declined a walk before. Why, you walked in the gardens yesterday with Jane and Mr Bingley."

"Indeed, and I found it did little to clear my head. Please excuse me from walking today."

Mrs Bennet was most disgruntled and might perhaps have exhorted Elizabeth further, but Mr Bingley returned to the drawing room at this point. He made for Jane without hesitation, although as he crossed the room, he exchanged a look with Mr Darcy. Despite all her recently-acquired knowledge, Elizabeth found she still could not interpret its meaning, and chafed at her ignorance of what he knew and what his opinions were. For a man of such open manners, it frustrated her that he had such unreadable communications with his friend.

Mr Bingley's return enabled conversation to flow more easily, for although he devoted most of his attention to Jane, he could not stop his general good humour, which required him to seek to make everyone present comfortable, even when he was a guest rather than the host. Mr Darcy spoke little but responded when addressed. Elizabeth did her best to behave similarly, but found that with Mr Darcy's ongoing silent proximity and, she suspected, scrutiny, her headache was back again in full force. Eventually, she lapsed entirely into silence.

After the gentlemen had departed, Elizabeth escaped as soon as she could to her room. Her solitude was quickly interrupted, however.

"Lizzy." The sympathy in Jane's voice was painful to hear

as she stroked her sister's forehead. "What has happened to affect you so?"

"I have a terrible headache." Elizabeth buried her face in her pillows as she spoke.

"A headache that started whilst you were out on the longest walk you have taken in some time, and which seemed to resurge during Mr Darcy's visit."

Elizabeth groaned. "I have the most unpleasant discovery to share, and I hardly know how to begin."

"Unpleasant? How so?" Jane had been standing by the bed, but came now to sit beside her sister as she gently took her hand. Elizabeth, with a sense of blessed relief, told her all.

Jane listened without comment until the end, although she gasped when Elizabeth told her what she had seen at Purvis Lodge.

"There must have been some misunderstanding, as there was with Mr Bingley," Jane said. "Mrs Wilson has been a genteel friend to us, I do not think she could be so much to blame. And Mr Darcy...I only know him a little, but you have spent more time with him and believed him to be a good sort of man. I am sure this must be a mistake."

"Believe that if you will, Jane. I do not know that I can doubt the evidence of my own eyes. The resemblance between Tommy and Mr Darcy is startling when you see them together."

"It is merely that they have similar hair, I am certain of it. Perhaps Mr Wilson had the same dark, curly hair. It is hardly an unusual style."

"Jane! I know it to be true. I have thought through every possible explanation, and this is the only one that makes sense of his presence at Purvis Lodge at such an hour. He was evidently not a stranger to any of the occupants."

Jane stroked her hand sympathetically. "How you must have suffered with this. Why did you not tell me?"

"Because I have been in such a quandary. I do not know what Mr Bingley knows of the matter, but I believe him to be a good man, and I did not want to hinder your happiness. But I intended to tell you soon, for we must be strangers to Mrs Wilson now, and I fear Mr Bingley may know something of the matter."

"Poor Mrs Wilson! How hard it will be for her to be isolated from us when she has so few friends nearby. She lives such a lonely life."

"I am sorry to lose her friendship," said Elizabeth, "for I like her very much and would never have believed this possible without the evidence I have seen. But I fear it must be so!"

Jane was silent. Elizabeth could see that her sister did not wish to agree, but neither could she present a convincing argument that it was unlikely.

"Poor Mr Darcy! He must have been uncomfortable when he called today." Jane brightened. "But the fact that he was here surely suggests he is innocent of the accusation. He must have known you would be present. Perhaps he was seeking an opportunity to explain what occurred."

Elizabeth could not help but smile at Jane's determination to see the best in everyone. "I cannot see it as you do. Perhaps he merely wished to maintain appearances and discover whether I would expose the truth to the people of Meryton."

Jane could not agree with this, and looked vexed that she could not see an explanation. After a while, Elizabeth ventured further. "I suspect Mr Bingley may know about Mr Darcy's relationship with Mrs Wilson," she said softly.

"What makes you say that?"

"Certain glances that have passed between them." She told Jane of the look she had seen earlier that evening and her recollection from Netherfield.

Jane looked thoughtful. "Lizzy, what would you think if I were to hint to Mr Bingley that you had shared this confidence? I do not need to reveal the details of it, of course, but his reaction might help us gain some insight into the matter."

Elizabeth pondered this for a moment. "Does this change your view of him?"

"On the contrary, it makes me more convinced, both that there is most likely to have been a misunderstanding, and that there is too much I do not know about Mr Bingley to marry him." She shook her head. "I do not see why he would give Mr Darcy a disapproving look about visiting Mrs Wilson if he supported their relationship. And his look earlier may have been out of concern for his friend. Mr Darcy did not look as well as usual this morning."

"You are too good. You always think the best of people."

"And I shall continue to do so until I am proved wrong. If you do not wish me to say anything, I shall not, but I think it may be of value, both in your understanding of Mr Darcy and mine of Mr Bingley."

Elizabeth would have preferred that the whole matter had never arisen in the first place, but as that was not possible, acquiesced. "Do you think we ought to inform Papa?"

Jane pondered this for a moment. "Not immediately. There may be much we do not know, and as Mrs Wilson is so little in company other than our own, I do not think there is any risk from not exposing her to the neighbourhood when so much is still uncertain. Perhaps in a week or two, if nothing further has emerged."

CHAPTER FIFTEEN

Mr Bingley called alone the following morning, but Mrs Bennet had sent an invitation to dinner to the whole Netherfield party for that evening. As this had been accepted, Elizabeth knew she would not long escape another meeting with Mr Darcy.

At Jane's insistence, Elizabeth had agreed to call on Charlotte rather than spend another day at home feigning disinterest in walking. She was yearning to be outside, and although she made a half-hearted attempt to insist Jane might wish her close by if her conversation with Mr Bingley proved difficult, Jane was adamant. Elizabeth forcing herself into stagnation at home would not serve either of them. After some resistance, the effect of the lure of exercise and air, the chance to see her friend, and Jane's unusual determination, had been too strong a combination.

Shortly after Mr Bingley's arrival, therefore, Elizabeth slipped out and made her way to Lucas Lodge. Charlotte was delighted to see her and was very ready to join her for her walk. They strolled the path and chatted idly for some moments before Elizabeth broached the subject of Mrs Wilson.

Charlotte listened in silence to all her friend had to say, and continued so for some time after she had finished, until Elizabeth uttered an anguished, "Well?"

"Why do you tell me this?"

Elizabeth was astonished. "Because you have called on Mrs Wilson with us and she numbered you, I think, among her friends. I thought it best to warn you, if she is now found to be unsuitable to be called such."

Charlotte considered this for a moment. "That is certainly a concern. If your perception of matters is correct, then we might be barred from her society."

"What other construction can be placed upon it?" Elizabeth was not often angry with Charlotte, but could not help her ire rising again, for it still smarted to feel that her judgment was not all she had thought it to be. "Mr Darcy was present at Mrs Wilson's house at such an hour, and clearly at ease in her company. Not to mention the striking similarity between him and Tommy."

Charlotte's response was immediate, but she reached out a hand to Elizabeth as she spoke. "Perhaps they are married."

"Married!" Elizabeth was aghast.

"Indeed. A man such as Mr Darcy might be expected to marry for connexions, but perhaps he has contracted a love match and, for reasons we cannot know, has found it necessary to conceal his marriage at present. He might have arranged for his wife to live apart from him under an assumed name."

"Impossible!"

"Unlikely, perhaps," Charlotte countered calmly, "but given what we know of Mr Darcy's character, no less likely than your interpretation."

Elizabeth stared at her friend, who continued, "Consider your perception of Mr Darcy so far. How did he seem at Netherfield?"

Elizabeth related the events of her stay. The entire account was tinged with sadness, and when Charlotte next spoke, it was with some compassion.

"I believe you were growing very fond of him. You have certainly become good friends with Mrs Wilson."

Elizabeth's brow furrowed at this. "I confess I am—*was*—very fond of Mrs Wilson. I cannot but believe she is forced into her situation by some dire circumstances unknown to me. But I barely know her, and still less Mr Darcy, as recent events have proved."

"You are determined he is to be the villain. Yet your description of his manner yesterday spoke more of distress than of anger or arrogance, and prior to that you have not been unwilling to become acquainted. If it was truly his intent to impose on the neighbourhood by installing his mistress here and concealing that she is such, surely he would either have avoided you so soon after your discovery or would have attempted to cow you into silence in some way."

Elizabeth was silent as she realised the truth of Charlotte's words. Mr Darcy's appearance and behaviour *were* marked more by anxiety than arrogance, and he had made an effort to remain in her company. She had asked herself why Mr Darcy could not have married Mrs Wilson, but it had never occurred to her that perhaps he had, and that Mrs Wilson was in truth Mrs Darcy.

Charlotte continued with gentle probity. "Were you beginning to care for Mr Darcy? Is it possible your reaction to this is not solely due to what you perceive Mrs Wilson's situation to be?"

Elizabeth's silence deepened, and she would not look at her friend. Charlotte pressed no further, but took Elizabeth's arm as they walked, and changed the subject.

"Tell me about your cousin. Has he proved to be everything you expected?"

A small laugh escaped Elizabeth, despite her abstraction. She was soon relating some of Mr Collins' speeches, although with less vigour than usual. She could not disguise how relieved she had felt at his attention being redirected from herself to Mary.

"I do not know what Mary thinks of the matter," Elizabeth concluded. "She accepts him without demur, but she does not seek his attention. She is such a quiet little thing when it comes to such matters." She thought this over for a moment, thinking of Jane and Kitty. "Perhaps the thing to do is ask her," she continued, almost to herself.

"I generally find it the best way to resolve doubt about what someone is thinking or feeling," Charlotte concurred.

Elizabeth returned to Longbourn deep in contemplation. Charlotte's influence had calmed her wildest flights of fancy but had given her thoughts a new direction. Her mind flew once again over her past interactions with Mr Darcy.

He had requested a dance from her and Jane on the very first occasion that they met. He surely had not merely been following his friend's lead. He had looked at each of her sisters as though he knew them by report, and it seemed obvious, now, that he had a prior acquaintance with someone who knew them. He had not asked the younger girls to dance; could he have been examining the suitability of Jane and Elizabeth, the two who had befriended Mrs Wilson, as friends of his wife?

Charlotte's explanation of his presence at Purvis Lodge undoubtedly fit better with his behaviour than her own tortured thoughts after her discovery. Yet it was a mystery why Mr Darcy, a man of considerable means and, presumably, influence, would need to conceal a marriage. Certainly, a marriage to a gentlewoman was nothing to be ashamed of, even if her status was below his own.

She wondered for a moment whether Mrs Wilson was of unknown parentage. She appeared everything ladylike; someone, too, must have paid for her schooling. It was not impossible she was the ward of someone wealthy. But as Mr Darcy's wife, surely she would be accepted into society whatever the circumstances of her birth? Yet Mr Darcy had said himself that he had rarely left Pemberley. Had his wife been at his side at his home, only to be set up in a separate household in Hertfordshire? *Why?*

Elizabeth's visit to Charlotte had both invigorated and further perplexed her. Her friend's practical sense had convinced her more effectively than Jane's hopeful optimism that there might be some other, more palatable, explanation for what she had seen than her first assumption. She could not, however, entirely reconcile herself to the idea that Mr Darcy could be married, to Mrs Wilson or any other. She had battled with the idea that he might not be worthy of the regard in which she knew she held him; she ought to be happier at the possibility he might yet be honourable, yet her feelings continued to revolt.

In such a state did Elizabeth return to Longbourn. Mr Bingley had departed, to join them with his household in the evening, and Elizabeth cast more than one quick glance at Jane. Seeing she appeared entirely calm and collected, however, Elizabeth was free to be thoroughly irritated by Mr Collins, who was once again attempting to solicit her notice in small but aggravating ways. She was reprieved by her father, who requested a moment of her time. Rising with alacrity, Elizabeth obediently followed him to his study.

She took a seat with caution, dreading that her father had noticed something of her recent distress and was about to make enquiries.

"Mmm?" her father asked, looking up from the book he had taken up.

"Why did you wish to speak to me?"

"Oh, I have nothing particular to say, child. Do choose a book."

Elizabeth looked as confused as she felt, and Mr Bennet sat back with a smile. "I merely thought you might appreciate some relief from our guest's attentions. Perhaps your mother will be able to redirect them back onto a more welcome course in your absence. I suggest half an hour will be enough." Having thus spoken, he returned to his reading.

Elizabeth felt a mixture of relief, gratitude, and irritation at her father's words. He had indeed rescued her, for the time being, for Mr Collins apparently did not intend to follow her into the study. She was pleased her father had not merely observed Mr Collins's continued notice of her but had also taken a step to relieve her, thereby removing the need for her to either make awkward excuses or to be inflicted with her cousin's company.

She could not refuse such an unexpected intervention. Indeed, she would usually have welcomed it, knowing it was, for her father, a sign of great consideration. Today, however, she was galled by his evident amusement at his solution to her problem, a feeling only made worse since it formed an obstacle to her main desire, which was to find a moment alone with Jane and discover whether she had spoken to Mr Bingley, and what the outcome had been if so.

Elizabeth took up a book as suggested and attempted to

read it, grateful her father was not more inclined to conversation this afternoon, for she did not think she could have sustained one. If he observed that she did not once turn a page he did not show it, appearing absorbed in his reading.

Eventually, Elizabeth found her mind had settled somewhat, and gratitude overcame any other feelings. Nevertheless, as she uttered a quiet thank you and slipped from the room, she hurried immediately to find Jane.

A quick tour of the house proved her elder sister was nowhere to be found. Mr Collins she could hear writing in his room, for he did not write in silence but provided commentary on his work as he wrote, rehearsing phrases and commending his own skill.

She imagined he wrote to Lady Catherine, and wondered whether he was an equally assiduous correspondent with the nursemaid left with his child. This made her wonder how long he intended to stay. If he meant to remain until he found a wife, and persisted in his attention to her, it would be a long visit indeed.

With this thought, she entered the drawing room. Jane remained absent, but Mary was leafing through some music and preparing to play. She stopped as Elizabeth entered.

"Were you looking for Jane? Mama has taken our sisters into Meryton."

Although it had indeed been Jane she sought, finding Mary alone seemed provident after Elizabeth's conversation with Charlotte. She therefore closed the door carefully and asked Mary for a few minutes of her time.

Mary was circumspect but acquiesced with a comment regarding the ties of sisterhood. She moved from her stool to the table, where she waited expectantly. Elizabeth hardly knew how to begin but settled on the simplest route. "I wanted to speak to you about Mr Collins."

Mary stiffened. Elizabeth took silence for agreement and continued. "Our cousin has, I think, proved a little confused regarding where his interest would be best directed. Forgive me if I speak out of turn, but do you wish for his attentions to be addressed to you?"

Her sister, unused to her opinion being so canvassed, had for once no proverb or sermon that immediately served her purpose. Surprised into matching Elizabeth's directness, she replied with a simple, "Yes."

Elizabeth in turn looked doubtful at this straightforward response. "You are sure?"

Mary's brow furrowed. "I know you do not view Mr Collins as he deserves, but he is a respectable man with a good situation. A fine situation when you consider the eventual inheritance of our home. He is a man of education, and there is a great deal I could learn from him. I believe I would be suited to the life of a parson's wife, and it would bring our mother comfort to know one of us will be the mistress of Longbourn after her."

This was quite as long a speech as Mary was given to making on matters other than morality, and Elizabeth listened to it with some surprise. "And what of the great Lady Catherine de Bourgh? How will you fare under her watchful eye?"

Mary thought for a moment. "I do not know. But I am prepared to find out."

Elizabeth was surprised at Mary's firmness. "I had no idea your views were so decided."

"I have had time to consider them. I had hoped Mr Collins was also more settled." Her voice was slightly morose as she spoke, and Elizabeth winced.

"You do not think I wish for his attention?"

"You do not encourage him. But I do not have your gift

for pleasing, and Mr Collins I think would prefer you over me. He only waits to see whether Mr Darcy has serious intentions and cannot be unaware of your recent quarrel." She stated this without recrimination.

Elizabeth blanched. "I have no understanding with Mr Darcy, nor do I have any particular reason to think we shall form one. I can assure you with great fervour, however, that I shall never accept any offer from Mr Collins. I shall continue to dissuade him as best I might if he continues to accost me, but if you truly wish him to pay you his addresses, you may wish to show him more encouragement."

"But I do not have your gift for pleasing," Mary repeated, a little plaintively.

"Nothing I do or say is intended to please Mr Collins! I cannot find his conversation enjoyable or his opinions satisfactory. But I think he will respond to someone who can, and who takes an active interest in what he has to say.

"Charlotte once told me a woman should show more interest than she feels in order to encourage a suitor. I cannot say whether she was correct, but I think Mr Collins might feel encouraged if he saw a little interest on your part."

Mary was thoughtful at this. They continued to sit together for some time in silence, and after a while, Mary returned to the instrument, where she began to learn her piece with an abstracted air. Elizabeth took up some sewing, and the two remained in silence but for the repeated strains of the music.

CHAPTER SIXTEEN

In time, the sound of the carriage indicated the return of their mother and sisters from Meryton. After much activity in the hall, they came in with such a clamour that Elizabeth could only manage one quick glance at Jane. Their eyes met, and Jane smiled with quiet reassurance. They were forced, however, to submit to their mother's account of the latest news she had received from her sister Philips regarding the town gossip. Since none of the names of Darcy, Wilson, or Bingley were mentioned, Elizabeth paid no more mind than was her custom.

Only when the time came to dress for dinner did Elizabeth finally succeed in obtaining a moment alone with Jane. She all but dragged her sister up the stairs, closing the door of her chamber behind them. "Well?"

Jane smiled at her fondly. "Has this been much on your mind? I am sorry we were not able to speak earlier."

"Not as sorry as I! But you must tell me how matters stand with Mr Bingley. You seem well, so he cannot have greatly distressed you, I think. Did he understand your hint?

Was he angry with you?" A sudden thought caused her to add in anguished impatience, "You did raise it, did you not?"

Jane smiled again. "I did. Sit down, and I shall tell you."

Elizabeth stopped where she had been pacing and did as she was bid, watching Jane warily as she took her own seat at the dressing table.

"Mr Bingley was not cross with me. In fact, quite the opposite. I had got only as far as mentioning you had walked past Purvis Lodge when he interrupted me. Apparently, it was a topic he particularly wished to speak to me about but had not known how to introduce it."

"He *wished* to discuss it?"

"Yes, he did. And I think it indicates there is indeed some misunderstanding."

Elizabeth frowned. "What did he say?" she asked with great urgency. Here, however, Jane sighed.

"Very little that will satisfy you, I am afraid. Although had you been there and seen his looks, you would be convinced he was genuine, I am sure. He said he was aware you had seen Mr Darcy at Purvis Lodge and that he feared there was some misunderstanding. But he would not tell me what the confusion was about. He was bound not to betray his friend's confidence but was determined to entreat you—in person, had you been present and the opportunity arisen, but failing that, through me—to allow an explanation. He said it matters not whether you speak to Mr Darcy or Mrs Wilson, but he sincerely desires you speak to them."

"What could cause Mr Bingley to be bound to secrecy?" Elizabeth returned, forgetting for the moment that Jane's purpose in speaking to Mr Bingley was to better understand his character and not to settle her own doubts. "There must be something they wish to conceal if he is not able to speak freely. The disguise and deceit cannot portend good things, can it?"

"I cannot tell what it might mean. I am as perplexed as you are." Jane reached for Elizabeth's hand and pressed it. "Mr Bingley's air was everything good, and kind, and I do not believe he would be encouraging you to speak to them if matters were as you feared. There must be some simple explanation which we have overlooked. I think it does Mr Bingley credit that he does not reveal his friend's secrets, if they are not his to reveal."

Elizabeth privately thought her first interpretation did look increasingly likely to be incorrect, but she could not yet rule out Charlotte's explanation. Either way, it seemed everyone was in agreement that the only way to uncover the mystery was to ask one of the principals about it, if a way could be found to do so, and with some reluctance, she was forced to concede the point. Speaking to Mrs Wilson was the more inviting path, but Mr Darcy would be present at dinner, and if the opportunity arose, perhaps she could get the worst out of the way more quickly. She resolved to allow the evening to pass as it would, and if the truth still eluded her, to make her way to Purvis Lodge in the morning.

They descended just as Mrs Bennet began to call that the carriage approached, and had barely taken their seats when the guests were shown in. Elizabeth could not this time stop her eyes meeting those of Mr Darcy. He was perhaps a little less haggard, although still pale and grave, and made no move to cross to where she sat.

Jane was soon in conversation with Mr Bingley and Mrs Hurst, paying no attention to the rest of the room. Mrs Hurst would occasionally seek her husband's agreement on some point she made, receiving an inarticulate grunt in response. Mr Collins was not in the drawing room when the guests arrived but offered a deep bow as he entered that encompassed everyone present. Elizabeth felt his eyes rest on the chair nearest to her and could not help a small sigh of relief from escaping when she heard Mary's voice address their cousin, mentioning a piece of scripture he had referenced the day before and asking him to enlighten her further.

It was difficult to read enthusiasm in Mary's sober tones, but as she was the only one present to betray any interest in him, after only a moment's hesitation Mr Collins crossed to his younger cousin. Elizabeth could hear Mary making an effort to ask him direct questions about what he said, and judging by the number of times he uttered the words 'my dear cousin' in patronising tones, he soon appeared to be enjoying himself greatly.

Three gentlemen in the room being thus occupied, two remained, only one of whom was at ease. Mr Bennet had joined his family on the arrival of their guests and was watching the room with amused eyes, occasionally offering a comment to Jane's conversation. Mr Darcy had taken a seat close to the fireplace; Miss Bingley sat across from him, attempting to engage him in conversation. He, however, spoke little, responding only when politeness proved it absolutely necessary.

Elizabeth was in agony. She wished above all things to solve the mystery that beset her, and Mr Darcy's presence in the room made her itch to know as soon as possible. She could see no way of introducing the topic or obtaining a moment of sufficient privacy to raise it, even obliquely, however, and despaired of having any opportunity to do so before dinner.

She had not reckoned with her mother. Mrs Bennet, attuned to any attention paid to her daughters by eligible gentlemen, was fully aware that something had occurred between her second eldest and Mr Darcy that had become an obstacle to her hopes. Not having had success with her previous suggestion of a walk, she eschewed the same plan immediately prior to dinner, but instead sought to distract Miss Bingley, who was commanding what attention she could from Mr Darcy.

"Miss Bingley, I was greatly admiring the lace on your dress. It is most becoming."

The lady raised an eyebrow at this statement and thanked her with perfect coolness, but Mrs Bennet was not to be gainsaid when she had a purpose, and she continued enthusiastically questioning Miss Bingley about her clothes. The lady was forced to respond or appear exceedingly impolite, and she chose the former, although her answers were as short as she could make them.

Eventually, Mr Darcy, whose seat lay approximately between the two and thus placed him directly in the middle of the conversation, rose and moved to the window. Mrs Bennet continued unperturbed, and Miss Bingley, although she cast an anxious glance at where Mr Darcy now stood, found herself unable to extricate herself from the conversation with politeness.

Elizabeth still could not see a way to speak to Mr Darcy, but he appeared as eager to speak to her as she was to him, for after a moment he addressed her.

"Miss Elizabeth, I wonder whether you could assist me. I appear to have lost my bearings. Judging by the position of the sun, this room faces east, yet I thought the stand of beech trees I can see across to my right was on the north side of the house."

Elizabeth's heart raced, but her courage rose as she stood and moved to where she might also see out of the window. He was drawn up to the full extent of his height, exuding tension, but standing so close, she could nevertheless feel his warmth and wondered whether his heart beat as fast as her own. She flushed at the thought, but as she looked up to reply, her blush was replaced by an anxious pallor at the pain she saw in his eyes. She replied as lightly as she dared. "You are mistaken, sir. The trees you are thinking of are all oaks. These are a mixture of oak and beech."

Mr Darcy stepped forward, closer to the window. "Ah yes, I see my mistake." He remained there for a moment, and Elizabeth wondered whether that was to be it after all. She could not believe he could have in truth mistaken beech and oak trees, however, and so she too remained where she was, looking out of the window in silence.

After a long pause, Mr Darcy stepped back again, and as he did so, passed closer to her. In a low voice, inaudible to any but Elizabeth with so many conversations in the room, he said, "I shall not stoop to plead for my own honour, but I will do whatever is necessary to protect that of my sister. Please call on her. Your sister too. Mine has been in great distress." His voice was almost level, but she detected a quaver in it that betrayed the emotion underlying the words.

The moment passed in an instant; Mr Darcy had returned to his chair and she soon followed to her own seat. There were no words adequate to express the turmoil of Elizabeth's thoughts. *His sister!* She savoured the word, rolling it around in her mind as though it were the taste of some fine delicacy. Could it be true? She realised with a start that she wished it to be so. Surely there could be no better explanation for what she had seen than for Mrs Wilson to be Mr Darcy's sister!

She recalled Miss Bingley's references to a sister when she was at Netherfield. She had believed the girl to be dead, but had anyone said so outright? She could not recall. Miss Bingley had undoubtedly referred to her in the past tense.

There was still a great mystery to be solved, but Elizabeth could not but feel great relief that it was not the one she had assumed. Whatever reasons Mr Darcy might have for concealing their relationship, they must surely be far more honourable than she had allowed for. And now he had proved that, whatever deception had been practised, she was to be trusted with the secret. She warmed slightly at this thought but dared not scrutinise the feeling too closely for what it might portend.

When dinner was called a short while later, Elizabeth's mood had improved such that she was able to meet Mr Darcy's eyes again, and with a rapid nod, indicated she would speak to Mrs Wilson. Some of the gravity lifted from him at this, and his eyes softened. She gave him a small smile, and each made their way to eat with greater appetite and easier conversation than she had thought possible only a short while before.

CHAPTER SEVENTEEN

Elizabeth found that the evening was to be endured rather than enjoyed, but this was less due to her previous turmoil than to a new anxiety to see her friend. She was burning with curiosity about Mr Darcy's words, and more than once found her attention drifting from the room, although with so many different conversations surrounding her she doubted many were aware of her abstraction. She pictured Mrs Wilson's suspense, knowing Elizabeth had fled her presence and not made her promised visit, and hoped Mr Darcy had exaggerated in his reference to her great distress. In the next moment she admitted to herself that this was highly unlikely, for Mr Darcy was not generally given to exaggeration, and her heart went out to her friend again.

That gentleman had appeared thoughtful throughout the evening, and weary as well, Elizabeth thought, as though he had been through some great exertion. More than once she saw him cast a glance her way, and set it down to his seeking to establish her reaction to his earlier statement. Although reserved, however, he was not entirely unable to converse, nor did he confine himself to the Netherfield party.

To Elizabeth's surprise, he voluntarily engaged Mr Bennet for some minutes in a conversation about the management of Longbourn, offering his own experience of managing Pemberley in comparison. Rather less to her surprise, although he spoke to both ladies, he evaded attempts by Mrs Bennet to enquire as to the extent and value of his estate and by Miss Bingley to eulogise the property as among the finest she had ever seen.

Mr Bingley naturally carried much of the remainder of the evening's conversation, but Mr Darcy responded with polite efficiency when required to do so. He spoke little to Elizabeth, except to ask after her health following her indisposition of his previous visit and whether she had recovered.

"Thank you, I am feeling much better. I ventured to Lucas Lodge this morning, and I hope to return soon to my usual pursuits and social activities."

"I am delighted to hear you are so far recovered. I hope you are soon able to do so." With that, he left her in peace, for which she was grateful.

The evening passed with fewer occasions to blush than Elizabeth expected. Her mother, having no one to boast to, had watched three of her daughters with smug satisfaction, storing up details of every attention paid to them to relate to her sister as soon as could be managed. Kitty had spoken of her forthcoming trip to town with great satisfaction, and Lydia, naturally, complained vociferously at the unfairness of Kitty's preference over herself. On the whole, however, conversation had been congenial, if not entirely natural between all parties.

In a quiet moment when the ladies left the table, Elizabeth was able to communicate a small hint to Mary. Thus, once the gentlemen had joined them, and Miss Bingley and Mrs Hurst had each displayed their prodigious musical talents, Mary approached Mr Collins to ask about his favourite piece of music. After his customary digression into Lady Catherine's opinions, he had eventually settled on a choice, and Mary had played it for them instead of one of her own choosing. Elizabeth was left to finish the evening's exhibitions with a simple air that she was more or less confident she could play without requiring too much concentration.

After the guests had departed and they had retired to prepare for bed, Jane had taken her arm with a questioning look, and Elizabeth had gloried in the relief of being able to smile at her and tell her Mr Darcy's words.

"His sister!" Jane's astonishment reflected Elizabeth's own, although she immediately betrayed the direction of her own thoughts. "Mr Bingley must be aware. That must be why he thought it so important you spoke to one of them."

"I hope to take his advice tomorrow," Elizabeth replied, "for I fully intend to call on Mrs Wilson. Will you join me? Mr Darcy particularly mentioned that I ought to take my sister with me, and I cannot think he meant Lydia."

"Why would he have meant Lydia?" Jane was confused, until a small sound from Elizabeth made her look up and smile. "I am glad you can tease again, Lizzy. You have been very distressed by this, have you not?"

"I confess I have thought of little else. I believe there is still some mystery to solve, for I cannot fathom why Mr Darcy could not openly acknowledge her if she is his sister as he says. I am hopeful, however, that there will be an answer when we see her."

"You do not doubt his word on this? I am sure Mr Darcy is honourable."

"I am sure he is," agreed Elizabeth. "And I do believe him.

Or, perhaps, I want to believe him. But I would like to speak to her as soon as I can, to fully comprehend how matters stand."

BOTH SISTERS AROSE EARLY the following morning, eager to solve the mystery once and for all, and they set off as promptly as they felt they could politely do so. Neither of them was inclined to doubt Mr Darcy's word, for they agreed he was a gentleman and that everything in his manner and words suggested he spoke the truth.

The great question, however, was why Mr Darcy would have concealed his relationship with Mrs Wilson to begin with. Although they approached the subject from every perspective, neither of them could explain it in the least. His manner when speaking to Elizabeth had made it abundantly clear he was not ashamed of the connexion; indeed, it had suggested he was devoted to his sister's good name. There must be something in their past which made this strange secrecy necessary; what it was, neither could fathom.

They reached Purvis Lodge and were greeted by the young maidservant, who showed them into a different room to that in which Mrs Wilson customarily received them. They found the lady sitting alone, playing her fingers along the keys of a beautiful pianoforte, although she applied no pressure, and no sound came from the fluid motion of her hands. She rose to greet them the instant they entered, a sudden surprised smile not disguising her pale and drawn face, or that tears had recently fallen from reddened eyes.

"Miss Bennet! Miss Elizabeth!" She greeted them with such joy and relief that it could not be feigned. Elizabeth reached out and offered her hands to her friend, who took them rapidly.

"Mrs Wilson. I am sorry not to have called upon you before." Her eyes traced her friend's face, looking for a resemblance to Mr Darcy. Much about them was different—she was fair, he was dark-haired, and although she was tall, her stature was nothing to his. Now that she looked for it, however, Elizabeth thought she could detect similarities around the jaw and eyes. She wished Mr Darcy were present, that she might compare them properly.

Despite her evident pleasure in their presence, Mrs Wilson showed a certain awkwardness at Elizabeth's apology. After murmuring some polite dismissal, she paused, then led them to seats close to the window, where two sofas faced one another. She sat on one, gesturing to the two of them to take the other.

"I have much to tell you," she began without further preamble. "I hope your presence here means my brother has been able to speak to you?"

Elizabeth smiled at the words. "Enough to have named you his sister. But he asked us to call on you, and it appears we do have much to learn."

Mrs Wilson nodded. "I am grateful that you came, both of you," she continued solemnly. "He followed directly after you that day, to explain, but he could not find you." She sighed softly. "I am sorry you have been deceived so much, and for so long. If you will hear it, I would like to tell you my tale, so you may understand why." Tears began to form in her eyes at these words, and it was Jane's turn to reach out and take her hand, leaning forward to bridge the space between them.

"Please do not distress yourself, Mrs Wilson. You do not need to tell us more than you are comfortable with."

"Then I will tell you all!" the girl replied, briefly fierce, although she returned immediately to her usual demeanour. "If you will hear it? It is a sorry tale."

"If it helps you to share your history, then of course we would be pleased to listen."

She prised herself gently free and sat back, gazing absently out of the window for a moment before turning back. "I suppose it must begin with telling you the name I once hesitated to reveal. My name is Georgiana...formerly Georgiana Darcy."

Jane and Elizabeth waited in silent contemplation whilst she paused again.

"My brother, Fitzwilliam, as you may have observed, is some years my senior. Following the death of my father some eight years ago, he became my guardian, along with a cousin of ours. He is the best of brothers and has been very kind to me—far, far kinder than I have deserved." She held up a hand to stay the interruption she saw on Elizabeth's lips.

"Please, do not say it. You will see the truth of it soon. Almost four years ago, whilst staying at the coast with a companion, I was persuaded to believe myself in love with a man I had known from childhood. With the aid of my companion at the time, he persuaded me to elope. He convinced me my brother was prejudiced against him, that he would not allow the match. He persuaded me that he could not bear to take the risk of being forcibly parted from me. I was fifteen years of age.

"Two days after we left for Scotland, Fitzwilliam arrived in Ramsgate to find me gone to be married to a man who, I later discovered, cared nothing for me. He had only two motives—the first to gain control of my fortune, and the second to wound my brother in the most painful way he knew how."

Elizabeth withheld her own shock but shared the horror she could hear in Jane's slight gasp. Mrs Wilson, however, continued with barely a pause, as though by allowing herself to tell her story, she must now continue to the close.

"Despite Fitzwilliam's pursuit of us, my husband had planned for such an eventuality and was able to evade him. My brother did not find us until I was irrevocably married. He caught up with us at an inn near York, where we had travelled after Scotland. At that time, I still believed myself in love with my husband, who had been everything kind to me at the start of our marriage, and I would not hear Fitzwilliam when he begged me to leave him. I believe he hoped I might be willing to live in seclusion at Pemberley—our home—and that my husband would content himself with his main object —my fortune. It was not to be so."

She paused for a moment, looking stricken. Elizabeth moved to sit beside the younger woman, again taking her unresisting hand. "You are distressed," she said. "Perhaps you wish to pause for a moment? Shall I order some wine?"

Mrs Wilson shook her head vehemently. "It is better to say it all at once. We moved around regularly, sometimes after only a week. Occasionally, we took lodgings but never stayed anywhere long. I was not taken into society, although my husband would disappear for hours at a time, expecting me to always be present on his return. I did not see my brother. At first, I was angry with him, for what I considered his betrayal in not supporting and recognising my marriage.

"Over time I began to see my husband was not the man I had thought," she continued, her voice growing hard. "I wrote to Fitzwilliam, giving our address at the time, but we had moved some distance before I ever received a reply. When I attempted to write again, my husband discovered it and forbade me from any correspondence except under his direction. He locked away the ink and paper, and made me account for every penny he gave me, little though it was.

Twice he allowed me to write. Each time he stood with me as I did so, preventing me from giving our address but providing details of an inn where letters would be collected. Each time I was told to ask Fitzwilliam for money.

"Occasionally, my husband would be absent for a few nights. I was not party to where he went and was never permitted to accompany him, but I understand now that some of these trips were to visit Fitzwilliam, taunting him and attempting to extract further funds from him. I do not know—*do not care to know*—what my husband did with the funds we had, but there never seemed to be enough of it, despite the thirty thousand pounds I had on our marriage. Whether the principal was tied up in some way, he truly had spent it all, or was simply avaricious I do not know. We had many creditors."

Neither of the listeners could disguise a gasp at the sum of money mentioned, but Mrs Wilson did not stop to wait for their exclamations.

"I do not think I need to tell you that my marriage was deeply unhappy. My husband was not cruel, to begin with, but he was often absent, leaving me with little money, no society, and no resources to support myself." As she spoke, her eyes flew to the instrument where she had been seated when they arrived.

"I could see no escape from the life I had tied myself to. Although he was absent for long periods, I lacked the courage and the resourcefulness to leave him." She paused and looked at the sympathetic, silent faces of her two listeners. "You are being so kind to me. If you wish, I need not continue."

"Please," Elizabeth said, "we want to understand."

"I would have carried on like this forever but for the solitary gift and solace to come from my marriage—my children.

I had long understood my own folly and had no choice but to endure it. For my sons, however—" Here she paused and shook her head, as though dispelling the rest of her words.

"As they grew, my husband began to take more notice of them. He would insist on dandling one or other on his knee and telling them of his exploits. I learnt more of his pastimes, his-his liaisons—"

As Mrs Wilson broke off with a sudden sob, Jane spoke quickly. "Please do not distress yourself. Allow me to ring for something for your relief." Mrs Wilson nodded through her tears as Elizabeth again sought to comfort her.

"I am sorry! I am so very sorry! I should not have said— You ought not—"

"Do not fear for us," Elizabeth replied as calmly as she could, although her voice shook. "If it relieves you, we would wish you to share your story."

The maid entered, her eyes wide and scared as she took in her mistress's state. Jane asked for wine, and the girl nodded sharply, all but running from the room. They remained in silence until the refreshments were brought by the housekeeper, who looked with some sternness at Jane and Elizabeth, then pointedly addressed Mrs Wilson. "Would you not prefer to take yours in your room, ma'am, if you are unwell?"

Mrs Wilson lifted her head and shook it sharply. "Thank you, Mrs Carmichael, I am well. Miss Bennet and Miss Elizabeth are my guests."

Mrs Carmichael continued to show her disapprobation but accepted the dismissal and silently withdrew. Once they were again alone, Jane handed Mrs Wilson the wine, and they each sat in contemplative silence whilst she took some tentative sips from the glass. After a time, Mrs Wilson once again spoke.

"You invited me once to address you by your forenames. Please call me Georgiana."

Elizabeth smiled gently. "Very well, if you will promise to return the compliment. Call me Lizzy, as my sisters do." Jane invited the same familiarity. A weak smile came to Mrs Wilson's face, and Elizabeth was emboldened. "Do you feel fortified, Georgiana? Would you prefer to speak of something else? We would not have you relive painful memories on our account."

"I relive painful memories daily. It is a great relief to share them. Fitzwilliam is kind, but I failed him when I married, and he feels it keenly."

"You did not fail him, dear Georgiana. But your brother is a good man," Elizabeth said with all the vigour of restored certainty.

Her friend smiled at her. "Yes, Lizzy, he is." She paused again before continuing. "What I am about to relate will, I hope, help make sense of my current situation. But before I relate it, I must beg one promise of you both."

"Of course, if we are able," Elizabeth replied. Jane murmured her assent.

"It is a burden I must place on you, but I beg you not to reveal my true name or circumstances, nor to speak of me as anything other than Mrs Wilson if anyone might hear. Very few know of my true identity, and it must remain that way."

CHAPTER EIGHTEEN

Their hostess watched her friends' faces anxiously. "You are uncomfortable with my request."

Elizabeth sighed with a quick glance at her sister. "I confess I do not like the disguise. But I can promise not to break your confidence. I have one request, however. Charlotte Lucas is aware of what occurred last time I was here and I think ought to be told of this. I can vouch for her discretion as for my own."

Mrs Wilson drew a hand across her eyes in a gesture that Elizabeth found reminiscent of her brother in moments of abstraction. "Fitzwilliam will be concerned with another knowing the truth, but I see it must be so. I like Miss Lucas."

Jane softly cut in. "May I ask, Georgiana, whether Mr Bingley knows of your situation?"

Elizabeth looked sharply at her friend, but was relieved to find she was smiling softly at Jane. "Charles knows who I am, Jane. You would not be betraying my confidence to speak to him."

"If you are quite certain?"

"Charles—Mr Bingley—is already aware of my situation, or as much of it as my brother has chosen to tell him. I have not seen him since he came to Hertfordshire, but he has been a friend to Fitzwilliam. He is an excellent man."

Jane blushed and hesitated. Mrs Wilson's eyes widened. "Please do not misunderstand," she added in great haste. "My brother has been friends with Mr Bingley since their university years, when I was a young girl. He was kind to me, and I have thought of him with great affection as an example of what a man ought to be. I know he courts you, and I am glad. *Glad*," she repeated forcefully, "that he has found a lady of equal sweetness."

Jane blushed again and gazed at her hands for a moment before looking up to reply. "He is the best of men."

Mrs Wilson smiled. "He is a good man. When Fitzwilliam told him of my predicament, he asked Mr Bingley whether he would be willing to resurrect a long-abandoned scheme of finding a house to take. His residence here is no coincidence but has given my brother a legitimate pretext for his presence." The two women were now smiling at one another in shared admiration of Mr Bingley's kindness.

"And what of his sisters?" enquired Elizabeth.

Mrs Wilson's eyes fell. "They are not aware."

"Does Miss Bingley know of your marriage? Would she not recognise your name?" Elizabeth thought back again to the one mention she had previously heard of Mr Darcy's sister. Did Miss Bingley truly believe Georgiana dead, or had she misunderstood the truth on that occasion too? Surely Mr Darcy would not willingly allow such a story to persist about a clearly most beloved sister? She wondered for a moment whether Miss Bingley would not recognise Mrs Wilson if she saw her, living in such close proximity, but since Georgiana attended a different church and neither lady was often in Meryton, she supposed it would be unlikely enough that they would meet.

"No announcements were made on my marriage that I am aware of, but I doubt it has remained a secret, and Miss Bingley takes such a—" She paused and blushed with a glance at Elizabeth before continuing. "A keen interest in my brother's affairs. Both Mrs Hurst and Miss Bingley were guests at Pemberley once or twice, but it is some years since I last saw them, and I do not know whether they would know me now. They do not know my present circumstances and are unlikely to connect my presence here with the child Georgiana Darcy they once knew. The truth is, Wilson is not truly my married name. It is Wickham. I shall explain, so that you may understand why this is of such importance."

She straightened her shoulders and began. "My husband was indifferent to me, but his only outright cruelty to begin with was in his separation of me from my brother. However, over time, our circumstances grew more straightened, and he made it clear to me that I was an obstacle to resolving his financial difficulties. Whether he felt he had the potential for another advantageous marriage or whether he had some other scheme in mind, I do not know. He would be more often out of temper and not in control of himself. I had previously felt unhappy in his company, and now I came to feel unsafe."

Mrs Wilson lifted a hand again to still the sympathy she could see on her friends' countenances. She was tearless and spoke without emotion. "The worst is nearly past. I was close to despair but had no wit or will to oppose him. As I was unresistant, he turned his attention to where he knew he could wound me most. I could bear anything for my own sake, but for my sons, I—" Her voice cracked again, but with a heaving sigh she forced herself onwards, gazing at the wall beyond Elizabeth's shoulder as though it held an image of her memory there.

"When I suspected I was again with child, I found the courage to approach our landlady. She had always spoken kindly to me, although we had little enough to do with one another, and one evening I asked her for paper and ink to write to my brother. She had none to offer me but she saw my condition and risked everything to help. She arranged for us to be carried away one evening in the cart of her cousin, concealed amongst his goods for the market in another town. She provided me with food and funds, enough to pay for us to reach Kympton, a village near my brother's estate. From there we walked.

"You may imagine the state we were in when we arrived, for I had carried my two brave boys for some distance and was close to collapse. Thankfully, we encountered one of the under-gardeners, who recognised me and helped me to bear them the final part. My brother was at home and gave us shelter immediately. It was a sorrowful reunion, but I felt more at peace than I had in a long time."

Mrs Wilson stopped and gazed out of the window, drawing a deep, shuddering breath. Not wishing to disturb her reverie and the brief respite it offered from the relation of her sad tale but anxious to do something to express her sympathy for her friend, Elizabeth busied herself with the refreshments, assisted by Jane, who was clearly equally pained by the story. Mrs Wilson declined the offer of another glass with a sorrowful smile before continuing.

"I was very ill on our arrival, and my brother feared greatly for my life. When my husband came to Pemberley, knowing I would have returned there if I could, my brother would not let him see any of us. They came to an arrangement, and I have not seen my husband since.

"I had thought I was safe at Pemberley, but after a few months of rest and quiet, this proved not to be the case. An attempt was made—Joey was in the care of one of the servants, and—" her voice broke, but she valiantly continued her tale. "My husband had reneged on his agreement with my brother and sought to reassert his rights over his children. He wished to hurt me, but I am certain his primary object was, as it ever was, to wound my brother and gain what he could from him."

Elizabeth had silently reached for Mrs Wilson's hand as she talked, and the lady paused and gazed at the hand wrapped around hers before sorrowfully acknowledging the horror on the faces of her friends. "The worst is past," she said with a pitiful attempt at a lighter tone. "He was not successful. I no longer felt safe, however, and pleaded with Fitzwilliam to conceal me and my sons from my husband. It pained him deeply to do so, for disguise of every kind is his abhorrence, but in the face of my husband's *rights*"—she said the last word with more bitterness than any of her previous speeches—"he agreed to help us. He sought a suitable home for us and pays all the expenses. The few servants here are all trusted Pemberley servants who agreed to join me. They know only as much of my situation as was necessary to assist them in protecting me."

"Oh, Georgiana," Elizabeth said sorrowfully, "how you have suffered. I am sorry I did not know this before."

Mrs Wilson laughed slightly, a shadowed, hollow laugh. "Young ladies such as yourselves should not be exposed to such things. I was innocent once but forfeited it on my marriage." The sudden bitterness in her voice did not cause Elizabeth to recoil, and she looked up to meet her eyes.

"When you came upon us that morning, we had been discussing whether or not to reveal my situation to you. Fitzwilliam was anxious on his arrival to know whether the ladies who had shown such friendship to his sister were to be trusted, and made an effort to become acquainted, particularly with you, Lizzy, for you have become the truest and dearest of friends. He has also come to think highly of you, and we were almost decided that it would be best to share the truth with you."

Elizabeth groaned. "Oh, that I had not run away! How you must have suffered."

It was Mrs Wilson's turn to place a comforting hand over her friend's. "I can hardly blame you. I can imagine how it must have appeared. You must have been greatly discomposed."

"I avoided speaking to Mr Darcy. To think, I might have understood matters so much earlier if I had only been willing to hear him!"

"But you know the truth now." Her voice turned anxious, and she suddenly seemed far younger. "You do believe it is the truth?"

Both Elizabeth and Jane confirmed their belief in her veracity, and their friend relaxed. None of them knew quite what else was to be said, until Jane asked after the children.

"I asked Mrs Carmichael to keep them away if you called. I think it is best. They know very little of all of this—they recall their father but do not know or comprehend what occurred."

"I understand," Jane replied. She glanced around the room, seeking an alternative source of conversation. "Your pianoforte is beautiful."

Tears filled Mrs Wilson's eyes. "It was a gift. A surprise from Fitzwilliam when I came here. Music has long been my joy, and I was deprived of it for so long. He wishes me to play again and believes it would help me, but I have not been able to do so. It belongs to the child I was before I married, not to the woman I am now."

"This will not do!" Elizabeth burst out with sudden vehemence. "Music does not judge you, and it certainly does not belong to any one part of your life. Come, let me play for you if you will not." She gently took her friend's hand and pulled lightly but determinedly until they were both seated where Mrs Wilson had been when they arrived, the bench being long enough to accommodate two.

With a questioning glance, seeking permission that her friend cautiously gave, Elizabeth began a traditional air. It was simple enough, and she played with determination and feeling that made up for her lack of skill. She did not look up to see her friend's eyes closed whilst tears silently fell.

As the piece came to a close, Elizabeth murmured, "Will you play?" Mrs Wilson shook her head mutely, but after a moment, she drew a deep breath and lifted one hand to the keys. Although it shook, she picked up the same air, playing it with one hand. Slowly, her other hand came dreamily to join it, picking out the lower notes. Elizabeth glanced at Jane, who was nodding in silence, and then at Mrs Wilson. Tears still fell silently from her eyes.

It was not more than a minute or two before she was overcome, but for those few moments she brought a richness, beauty, and sadness to the music that spoke directly to her companions. Elizabeth comforted her friend as best she could, until, through her sobs, Mrs Wilson was able to gasp a few words.

"No…thank you…to play again—"

They sat together for some time before Mrs Wilson recovered sufficiently to speak again.

"I am sorry, I had not expected—" She stopped again.

"You need not apologise. Please believe me."

Jane approached them at the instrument. "Perhaps you would be more comfortable if we were to distract you for a time. Might we read to you, perhaps?"

Mrs Wilson shook her head. "Thank you. But I fear I have overstretched myself today."

"Of course, you have exerted yourself a great deal to tell us so much. You must be wishing to be free of us and rest," Jane replied kindly.

"Oh, please do not doubt your welcome!" Mrs Wilson cried out with renewed emotion. "I wish to rest indeed, but to be able to share my story with you, to be able to call you my friends! You do not know what you have been to me, and I could not wish you away."

"It is best we go. But I think we can promise to call upon you again soon. Do you agree, Lizzy?"

Elizabeth did agree, vehemently, and Mrs Wilson smiled gratefully at them. She rang for someone to show them out, and Mrs Carmichael appeared with a rapidity that betrayed how anxiously she had been waiting for such a summons. Her gaze crossed from her young mistress at the pianoforte to the visitors with curiosity and some wonder. She led the way to escort the ladies out with a cautiously warm manner. Jane, anxious to give their friend the space she needed, rose promptly to depart. As Elizabeth followed, she was called back by a word.

"Lizzy?"

She paused in the doorway and smiled. "Yes, Georgiana?"

"I am not the only person glad of your friendship. Fitzwilliam holds you in high regard. I do not think his sorrow when you would not speak to him was entirely on my account."

Elizabeth could make no response to such an observation so contented herself with a soft, "Oh!" As this seemed to satisfy her friend, she departed, following Jane and leaving Mrs Wilson at the instrument, running her fingers over the keys.

CHAPTER NINETEEN

By unspoken agreement, Elizabeth and Jane returned to Longbourn by a much longer path than was their custom. Neither knew quite what to say, but both took comfort in their companionship. Occasionally, one would sigh or go so far as to say, "Poor Georgiana!" The other would wordlessly assent, and they would both walk on.

When they were only ten minutes from Longbourn, Elizabeth finally broke the silence. "I am glad we called on Mrs Wilson today, but it will be strange, returning to where everything is as it ever was. I feel as though I have lived a lifetime this morning."

"To have suffered so much, and so young! I can hardly comprehend it. At least she is safe here, however."

Elizabeth did not answer, for she wondered whether her friend's safety was entirely assured. Would her life be one of uncertainty and change, always living in the shadow of her marriage? The longer Mr Darcy remained in the area, the greater the risk, for surely Mrs Wilson's husband—*What was his name? Wick something. Wicken?*—surely he would eventually seek out Mr Darcy again when his current funds proved inadequate. And if that brought him to the area, the likelihood of discovering his wife would increase.

Mr Darcy, then, would have to leave. She wondered how soon this would come and whether he had already planned it. She could no longer deceive herself about the pain she felt at the thought.

"Lizzy?"

Elizabeth started abruptly from her thoughts. "I am sorry, I am still thinking over everything Mrs Wilson told us and how it might affect the future. What were you saying?"

Jane smiled sympathetically. "Only that we are nearly back and may need to gather our thoughts before we see the family."

"I fear I was proving your point. Let us try to talk of happier things. When does Kitty go to town?"

By exerting themselves, they were able to turn the conversation and the majority of their thoughts to lighter topics, and fortified themselves against the return to an unchanged Longbourn.

Upon their arrival at the house, however, they found all was far from usual. Mrs Bennet's voice could be heard from the open windows, exclaiming in joy, "Oh, Mary! Oh, my dear, dear child! Oh, 'Mrs Collins'! How well it sounds. 'Mistress of Longbourn'! We are saved from the hedgerows! Oh, where is my daughter? There is so much to discuss! Oh, Mary!"

Elizabeth and Jane exchanged a glance, one inclined to slow her pace and the other to quicken it. Jane won out.

With some reluctance, Elizabeth followed her sister into a house in mild uproar. Mrs Bennet was continuing to exclaim her joy at the prospect of a daughter married and all this particular marriage would mean. Lydia was almost as loudly exclaiming that she would not have accepted Mr Collins for the world, although nobody had suggested she ought. Kitty was observing that she might not be able to attend the wedding if it occurred when she was in London. Of Mr Bennet and the principals in the drama, there was no sign.

Mrs Bennet immediately accosted her eldest daughters and told them the happy news that Mr Collins had offered for Mary and that the dear, dear girl had accepted. The gentleman, having obtained Mr Bennet's consent, had gone to make preparations for his departure to Kent, to inform his patroness in person of his happiness and resume his duties until he returned for the wedding.

Mary was nowhere to be found, much to Mrs Bennet's chagrin. Having sent Lydia to examine her room for the third time, Kitty to the gardens and, in desperation, Jane to the kitchens, she threw her hands up in despair and called for Hill. Elizabeth quietly withdrew to her father and was only a little surprised to find he already had company.

"Ah, Lizzy," Mr Bennet waved her in. "I thought Mary here might need to escape."

Mary cast her sister an eloquent glance. Elizabeth hesitated only a moment before offering her warm congratulations. She could not begin to comprehend what Mary found so attractive about Mr Collins, but he was a fool, not a rake, and she could sincerely rejoice in Mary's future being secured.

"Thank you, Lizzy. I am happy." Mary spoke the words as a flat statement, but she exuded a quiet contentment that she had never had before. "Mr Collins is to return to Hunsford tomorrow. The wedding will be in one month."

Elizabeth said all that was appropriate before her father spoke again. "Perhaps it is time to go to your mother before her nerves get the better of her. She will no doubt have much to discuss with you."

Mary smiled dumbly at him and, with a last glance at her sister, left the room. Elizabeth and her father waited in silence until they heard a loud exclamation of, "Mary! There you are! Wherever have you been? No, do not try to explain, we have so much to do!" The voice receded, and a door could be heard closing.

Mr Bennet spoke first. "I am not sure Mary will receive a great deal of gratification from being the first married. I had expected it to be Jane. Although Lydia, I think, would have made the most out of being first."

Elizabeth smiled. "Mama will have quite enough enthusiasm to make up for any deficiencies on Mary's side. But she is not unenthusiastic so much as undemonstrative, I think."

"Indeed? That will serve her well if she is able to endure the strictures of Lady Catherine de Bourgh."

"If anyone is capable of it, it is Mary. And perhaps also Jane, although she is happier as she is."

"I expect every day to be consenting to an engagement, but it appears matters are taking longer than I anticipated."

"Jane is keen to know the man who wishes to marry her, Papa. She will be happier this way."

"With five daughters all grown up, what am I to know of modern methods of courting? I hardly know what to expect of any of you—Mary leaping into marriage with our delightful cousin, Jane shilly-shallying about marrying a man who clearly dotes on her, and you quarrelling with a man who by all common measures ought to outshine any you have met in your life. I hope that whatever he said to you yesterday evening has set you back on good terms again?"

Elizabeth blushed at this sudden evidence of her father's discernment and stuttered a reply. He laughed.

"Oh come, you girls will have your love affairs and secrets. I only hope, if you have your heart set on Mr Darcy, that he entirely deserves you. He is rich, to be sure, but your old father will be at sea without you as it is, let me not see you married to a man for the wrong reasons."

"I can assure you I would never marry a man merely because he is rich."

"But you will not confess whether you wish to marry Mr Darcy. Well, well, I shall let you young things go about your business. If you wish to have him, you might want to keep your wits about you. Your mother told me you went to see your widow friend. She was distressed the lady would soon be out of mourning and setting her cap at Mr Darcy. You have Mr Collins to thank for saving you from all her accumulated nerves on your return."

Elizabeth could not muster a laugh at these final pleasantries. Nevertheless, Mr Bennet was satisfied with his wit, and with a slight chuckle returned once again to his book.

THERE WAS no call from Netherfield that day, and although Elizabeth found she had plenty to occupy her mind with the morning's conversation and the news of Mary's engagement, she regretted not having the opportunity to speak to Mr Darcy. She was therefore as pleased as Jane when, the following morning, he was seen along with Mr Bingley riding towards the house.

Mrs Bennet seized upon them immediately, demanding congratulations for the impending wedding of her middle child. Mr Bingley was all delight and affability at the news, although even his patience appeared to be stretched when the newly engaged Mr Collins appeared and gave a long speech detailing not only his own joy, but the benefits of marriage as an institution. He closed with an exhortation to Mr Bingley and Mr Darcy to follow his example and to not hesitate in forming the expected engagements with his dear sisters.

Mr Bingley bore this as best he could, but when Mrs Bennet suggested all three couples should take a walk together, he seconded it with such rapidity that Elizabeth had to bite back a laugh, despite her general horror at Mr Collins' speech.

Prior to Mr Bingley's comical enthusiasm, Elizabeth's attention had been drawn to Mr Darcy's reaction to her cousin. After making the necessary congratulations, he had seemed to be entirely indifferent, until the reference to his own marital prospects appeared to take him by surprise. With admirable self-control, he did not turn his eyes once to meet Elizabeth's, and it was only because she observed him closely that she noted the knitting of his brow. She pondered what such an expression could mean and attempted to suppress the sinking feeling it produced in her.

Mr Collins and Mary declined to walk with the others, for he was soon to depart to return to Kent. "Lady Catherine cannot spare me any longer, and I am to return to her with all speed, although I shall be back within a month for marriage to my dear Mary." Kitty and Lydia also declined to walk. The two remaining couples, however, soon found themselves outside, and Jane and Mr Bingley fell rapidly into quiet conversation, heads bowed together. Elizabeth and Mr Darcy walked ahead, each busy with their thoughts, until they came to a path that stretched ahead of them across a meadow with no one but their companions in sight. Mr Darcy glanced around them and spoke in a low voice.

"You have called upon Mrs Wilson?"

"Yes," Elizabeth replied, a little breathless now that it

came to the conversation she had been so anticipating. "And many things have become much clearer."

"How was she?" His voice was choked with emotion, and Elizabeth fought her instinct to reach out and comfort him, uncertain whether he would welcome such a thing.

"Unhappy, but resolute. She found some relief in telling us her tale, I think."

He nodded soberly. "She has come to value your friendship very highly. I could not allow her to suffer any longer when I had the means to prevent it. She has endured enough."

"She has," Elizabeth agreed softly. "And I ached to hear her tell her story. She spoke of you with deep affection throughout it all, however. You have been the best of brothers to her."

Mr Darcy's eyes closed for a moment, and she thought she heard a small sigh. "I employed a companion who could not be trusted. I knew what her husband was before they married yet did not protect her from his advances. I was unable to save her from him when he had secured her fortune. All I have been able to do is descend to the depths of concealment to offer her what protection I can, in defiance of the law. I have failed her time and again."

"You were given the responsibility of guardianship at such a young age," Elizabeth protested. "You have done everything that can be done to support and protect her. Do not doubt, Mr Darcy, you have helped your sister. You have given her and her sons safety, security, and love when they had none! Why, when she played for us earlier—"

"She played?" Mr Darcy stopped and turned his eyes on her searchingly. "Georgiana played for you?" He looked around again abruptly; they were still far from anyone who might overhear, but he corrected himself nevertheless. "She played for you and did not merely touch the keys soundlessly?"

Elizabeth could not help a smile from entering her eyes at his eager questioning. "Indeed, she did. Not for long, but she played—and beautifully too."

He turned and carried on walking, more in possession of himself. "She has always played beautifully. I have long wanted her to resume her music. I have been attempting to gather what information I can about the availability of music and musicians hereabouts to see what might encourage her, but I have been unable to convince her. What brought it about?"

"She spoke of her music as her solace, and of how cut off she felt from it. I sat with her and played first. Perhaps," Elizabeth added, "it was desperation at the thought I might play again."

He did not smile but responded earnestly, "I am sure you mean no such thing. I have greatly enjoyed what I heard of your playing."

Elizabeth looked away across the fields. "Thank you."

After a moment, she spoke again. "I hope you did not think I was being flippant a moment ago. I am not insensible of the gravity of her situation—no one could be. I can only begin to conceive how painful it must have been to live as she did, and for you to see her suffer."

"You did not jest at her situation," he said softly. "Do not think I took it amiss. It has indeed been a difficult time."

They both were lost in their own thoughts for a while until Mr Darcy broke the silence. "It appears I owe you a great debt of gratitude. Telling you her story appears to have given her more than anything I have been able to do."

Elizabeth met his gaze, finding sincerity in his eyes and a new ease in his countenance. "You owe me nothing, Mr

Darcy. I am not sure I have rendered her such a very great service, but, if I have, I am glad to have been able to do so as her friend."

"Nevertheless, you do not know what relief you have given me. I am immensely grateful to you. And to Miss Bennet, of course."

This reminded Elizabeth that it would be best to inform him that she had Mrs Wilson's agreement to extend her confidence to Charlotte. Mr Darcy looked grave at this, but said with a sigh, "If it must be so, it can be no bad thing for her to have another friend. If you trust her, I have no objection to Miss Lucas being brought fully into our confidence."

Elizabeth was pleased at this additional sign of his approval of her judgment. She said all that was required, and they continued on their walk.

The route they followed was circular, so there was no need to turn back, but after a while they stopped and allowed the other couple to catch up with them. Noting the expressions on their faces, Elizabeth smiled and murmured, "I do believe Mr Bingley has taken Mr Collins's advice."

She was not intending to be heard, but Mr Darcy replied nevertheless. "I suspect you may be correct." She flushed, realising that her comment might be misconstrued, for Mr Collins had dispensed his advice freely to both Mr Bingley and Mr Darcy. She found she could not look up to see whether Mr Darcy was similarly conscious of it. When he next spoke, he made no reference to it.

"Your younger sister is to be congratulated on her engagement, but there is something I wish you to be aware of."

Elizabeth looked at him quizzically. "Regarding Mary?"

"Regarding Mr Collins." He paused, and Elizabeth wondered what he could possibly be about to reveal.

"I do not know whether you will recall this, but on my

first introduction to Mr Collins, he surprised me when mentioning the location of his living."

Elizabeth smiled at the recollection. "Yes, when we met in Meryton. I was very grateful to you that day for rescuing me from a surfeit of my cousin."

"It was no hardship," he said with mild amusement. "But there was a particular reason for my surprise. That living is in the gift of my mother's sister—one Lady Catherine de Bourgh."

Elizabeth's surprise was great. "Lady Catherine is your aunt!" she exclaimed in astonishment.

Mr Darcy's brow lowered. "As she disclaimed any connexion following Georgiana's marriage, I consider all association between us to have long been at an end."

Elizabeth pondered this new information. "Does this not pose a risk to Mrs Wilson? Mr Collins or Mary is sure to mention her. Or you."

"Mr Collins will no doubt already have mentioned me in his letters, but as he has shown no sign of recognition, I can only assume Lady Catherine refuses to speak or write about me at all. She would certainly never mention Mrs Wilson's marriage. She made it quite clear in the past she considers her utterly disgraced for marrying the son of a steward."

He spoke with evident bitterness, and Elizabeth wished again to be permitted to reach out in comfort, but it was an intimacy she dared not attempt. Instead, she tried to find a happier aspect to what he had told her.

"Then as long as your connexion remains unknown, we have nothing to fear in that quarter?"

"Lady Catherine, or her daughter Anne, could make Mr Collins and your sister aware of my sister's marriage, but they would have no reason to suspect that she and Mrs Wilson were one and the same. Nevertheless, may I request that you inform me if you or your sister hear anything relating to Mrs Wilson or myself that causes you concern?"

"Yes, yes, of course," Elizabeth replied. "What would you have us do if the news of your sister's marriage reaches Hertfordshire? Would it distress Mrs Wilson?"

"I hope it will not come to that, but it would be best to mention the connexion to her so it does not come upon her unexpectedly. And perhaps to also inform Miss Lucas, if there is a chance she could mention it unknowingly. But please do not speak of it to any others."

"Of course," Elizabeth said again, before adding with some wonder, "How unexpected to have such a connexion."

"It is one I would happily do without," he said solemnly, then added as an afterthought which caused Elizabeth once again to wonder precisely where she stood in his esteem, "although I would rather be connected to Mr Collins than lose your friendship."

"You can be assured of my continuing friendship, Mr Darcy," Elizabeth said quietly.

If he was about to reply, the moment was lost, because Mr Bingley and Jane having now approached close enough to be within hailing distance, Mr Bingley took off his hat and waved it in the air. "Darcy, I am the happiest man alive!" he announced with an expression that showed his sincerity in the belief.

Elizabeth's eyes were on Jane, who beamed and blushed in equal measure but remained silent until she was close enough to take her sister's hands and declare, "Oh, Lizzy!"

Elizabeth wished them great joy, and Mr Darcy followed with his own congratulations, and their solitary conversation was ended. As they continued their walk, the sisters fell behind the gentlemen.

"I am so happy. We had a good talk about everything, and

Mr Bingley—*Charles*—spoke so kindly of all that had happened. And when he asked me again, I could not refuse him. I love him so, and everything I know of him, everything we have spoken about, is confirmation that he truly is the kindest, the most affable, the most honourable of men. Oh, I do not deserve such happiness!"

"Indeed, you do," Elizabeth replied with a smile. "And Mama will surely be overcome."

Jane paused before replying. "It will bring her a great deal of happiness, and I am glad of it, but we have agreed not to announce our engagement immediately. Not that it will be entirely a secret," she rushed to add, "for Mr...Charles will go to Papa on our return, for his blessing. But with Mary so recently engaged, I do not wish to spoil the moment for her. Perhaps in a fortnight or so, or perhaps after the wedding. That is only four weeks. Not so very long to wait."

"I think your 'Mr Charles' will find that a very long time to wait indeed." The man in question was speaking to his friend and gesticulating enthusiastically as he walked ahead of them, occasionally glancing back their way with a broad smile.

"Perhaps," Jane agreed, "but I would not want to spoil Mary's moment! How strange, to have two proposals in two days."

"I do not believe anyone will find your engagement unexpected. Although I hope no one is anticipating the pattern will continue tomorrow."

Jane laughed. "That would be unlikely!"

After a few minutes of peaceful companionship, Elizabeth spoke again. "It is possible that Mary may not resent Mama's attention being diverted from her own marriage. A wise person once told me that talking to people is the best way to find out what they are thinking or feeling, you know."

"Why do I suspect you are presenting your own words to me as though they were a proverb?"

"Indeed not! Those were Charlotte's words."

"A wise person indeed."

"Jane, I am delighted for you. I believe Mr Bingley is a good man, but are you quite certain this is the right time to make this choice?"

Jane's eyes turned on her sister, clear and resolute. "Speaking to Mrs Wilson confirmed my opinion that Mr Bingley is the best of men. We talked about her situation. He has been pleased to be able to help her, in his way, and he is delighted we are now aware of her secret. He has been very concerned that Mr Darcy would unwittingly reveal something, despite all his precautions, and Mrs Wilson would be put in danger. But he is glad that she can be more open with us. Every word he spoke expressed compassion and consideration. I do not think I could be more convinced that this is the right decision."

Elizabeth smiled fondly at her sister. "Then I am content, and I wish you every joy."

Three of the party remained outside on their return to the house. Jane was unwilling to face her mother until Mr Bingley had spoken to her father, and Elizabeth was unwilling to leave her sister in such a state of anticipation and sweet anxiety. Whether Mr Darcy wished to remain with them or merely to avoid entering the drawing room alone need not be noted.

It would not have been thought Mr Bingley could appear more joyful than he had so far done, but on his return, they were confronted with the evidence that he was indeed capable of it. He took Jane's hands as soon as he was close enough and beamed at her in delight. Jane smiled softly up at him, and they were for a moment lost to the world.

As she retired that evening, Elizabeth contemplated all she had learnt. Her heart ached for her friend, and she longed above all things to be of use and to support her in any way she could. Mr Darcy's gratitude was evident, but he had given Elizabeth no particular encouragement nor shown her any unusual distinction beyond trusting her regarding his sister. Perhaps every attention she had ever received from him had arisen from fraternal affection. Mrs Wilson—she forced herself to use the name even in her thoughts rather than risk the accidental revelation of her secret—had suggested he valued her highly, but that might merely mean he trusted her.

She would not hope, she decided. She would smile on Mary's marriage, rejoice in Jane's, and continue to visit her friend. Any hope of anything else for herself would need to be set aside.

CHAPTER TWENTY

J ane, acting on Elizabeth's suggestion, talked to Mary the same day. She soon ascertained that, far from resenting Jane's engagement following so closely upon her own, her sister welcomed it. With the departure of Mr Collins so soon after their understanding was reached, Mary had felt the full force of her mother's undiluted enthusiasm and was very willing to share the honour with Jane; the thought rather bolstered her confidence than otherwise.

Thus it was that a note was soon dispatched to Netherfield to the effect that there was no requirement to keep Jane's engagement secret. A response arrived promptly, in the form of Mr Bingley himself. He brought with him a prettily worded message from his sisters, appealing for Jane's company the following afternoon and inviting all the Bennets to dinner with some other local families three days following, when a formal announcement would be made, in deference to Jane's wish to allow Mary a few days of primacy. Both invitations being accepted, he nevertheless found it was his business to linger, and the combination of his general affability,

Jane's radiant joy, Mary's reserved contentment, and Mrs Bennet's poorly repressed elation made for a pleasant afternoon for all at Longbourn.

Elizabeth had, at Jane's request, agreed not to speak of the engagement until the formal announcement had been made. Although it tried her patience to not be able to share her sister's happiness with her friends, the difficulty of keeping the secret was somewhat lessened by having the news both of Mary's engagement and her recent discoveries regarding Mrs Wilson to impart. She was conscious that, despite having permission to do so, she had not yet apprised Charlotte of all she had learnt regarding their friend, and the following day set out to walk to Lucas Lodge. Happily, Charlotte had evidently been thinking of Elizabeth too, for only a few minutes into her walk, they encountered one another near a bend in the road.

"Lizzy," Charlotte smiled. "I was on my way to visit you."

"And I you," replied Elizabeth, comfortably taking her friend's arm. "Although now we have found one another, perhaps you will walk with me instead?"

Charlotte was very willing, so Elizabeth turned back, and they walked together, chatting idly. Once they were clear of any risk of being overheard, Elizabeth quietly and hastily sketched the essential points of Mrs Wilson's story.

"So, you were almost correct, you see. There was another explanation, even if not the one you had supposed."

"It is quite the tale. How was Mrs Wilson?"

"She coped admirably well with the telling, although naturally found it difficult." She looked around thoughtfully. "We appear to be walking in the direction of Purvis Lodge at the moment. Would you be willing to call on her with me?"

"Of course, if you think she would welcome it."

"She allowed me to share her story with you, and I think

she is sorely in need of friends. I believe she will be glad to see you again."

They were shown into the house by Mrs Carmichael, who eyed Charlotte doubtfully but bestowed a more welcoming smile upon Elizabeth. She left them to wait a moment in the passage, and Elizabeth felt a sharp and painful joy to hear the soft sound of a melancholy melody.

Mrs Wilson turned from the pianoforte as they entered and smiled, but it was Joey who spoke first. "Miss 'lizbeth! See my horse!" He proudly held up a toy horse on wheels. Tommy looked up from where he sat playing with an identical one on the floor but ducked his head again at the sight of Charlotte. Elizabeth admired Joey's toy with suitable gravity and winked merrily at his brother when he glanced up again, being rewarded with a timid grin before he hid his face again.

"Lizzy! Miss Lucas. I am glad you have come." Mrs Wilson took Elizabeth's hands as she spoke. Her eyes crossed from one to the other, and she called the boys to her. With an affectionate embrace, she murmured, "Go with Mrs Carmichael, dears."

Obediently, the boys made to leave the room, but Tommy hesitated at the door. "Miss Benn't come soon, Mama?"

Mrs Wilson smiled. "I am sure she will, Tommy. But run along for now."

Once they were alone, she turned back to Elizabeth and Charlotte as though to speak, but words failed her. Charlotte, seeing her discomfort, stepped forward.

"Mrs Wilson, you must guess from my presence here that Lizzy has told me something of your story. You have suffered greatly." Tears rose in Mrs Wilson's eyes at the compassion in Charlotte's voice, and she attempted to speak, but Charlotte reached for her hand and spoke again. "Please, do not feel you need to say anything. You need not relive it again on my account, and your secret will go no further. I would like to be friends."

Mrs Wilson's manner calmed at this speech, and she replied softly, "And I, also."

Some ease having been restored to the conversation, Charlotte smiled. "I suspect you would rather talk about almost anything else." Mrs Wilson nodded, and she continued, "What say you to discussing the latest books we have read? Or would you prefer I tell you embarrassing stories from Lizzy's childhood?"

Elizabeth laughed, "That is a risky proposition! I am sure I could outdo you in the storytelling."

"Ah, but I never did anything in the least embarrassing."

"And what about the time you were caught sitting in the middle of the larder coated in preserves just before the new parson was to visit?"

"I was only there alone because I am some years older and could not have fitted through the window, even had I your gift for scrambling," said Charlotte. "As I recall, your dress was covered not merely in preserves but in grime from the windows and more than a few leaves from the bush you scrambled through."

Elizabeth laughed still more and addressed Mrs Wilson, who was looking from one to the other with shy astonishment, as though she did not know whether she ought to join in the laughter. "It is all true, I fear. I was very young, however. I was not always such a ragamuffin."

A small smile broke the face of their companion. "I-I once crept into my father's study to play and knocked his pot of ink over. It was the day my aunt Catherine was to visit, and although I was able to change my dress, there was nothing to be done about my fingers. She was exceedingly shocked about it. Fitzwilliam made a point of inking his own fingers the following day."

Elizabeth's laugh settled into one of gentler delight. This was a new level of friendship indeed, if Mrs Wilson was able to tell a tale of her childhood transgressions. She found the image of the grave Mr Darcy as a boy, deliberately applying ink to his fingers in a show of support for his sister, hugely charming. Her friend blushed, pleased to have amused her.

Having thus started, the three found that conversation came easily, Mrs Wilson and Charlotte comparing the antics of the youngest Lucas children with those of Tommy and Joey. When this conversation lapsed, Elizabeth shared the news of Mary's engagement before gently explaining the connexion to Lady Catherine.

Mrs Wilson paled slightly, and Elizabeth at once asked, "I hope you are not distressed? Your brother does not believe your aunt is likely to acknowledge the relationship."

Mrs Wilson shook her head. "I am not...that is not the word...it is only that...Aunt Catherine..."

Charlotte, with great compassion, cut in quietly. "You are a little afraid of her."

Mrs Wilson nodded, still pale. Charlotte smiled reassuringly at her. "There is no shame in feeling so. From all I have heard of her, she is a woman of strong opinions. Is she the aunt Catherine you mentioned earlier, whom your brother was so determined to stand up to on your behalf?"

Mrs Wilson nodded again, with a small smile at the memory. "Yes," she murmured. "I have not seen her since I was very young. We saw her rarely, for my cousin Anne was often too unwell to travel, but I always felt I greatly displeased her."

"You need not be afraid of her displeasure now. I tell you this only so you are prepared and are not taken by surprise should Mary's experiences in Hunsford be mentioned. But your brother does not think Lady Catherine will wish to speak of the connexion, and we need not speak of it any further now," Elizabeth said gently. "Now, what subject would you prefer?"

Mrs Wilson immediately replied, "I would be pleased to know how my brother fares. Have you seen him since you were last here?"

Elizabeth confirmed that she had.

"Did he seem well?" Mrs Wilson asked anxiously. "He cannot call every day without risking drawing attention to his visits. I have been worried about him."

"He seemed more at ease than when we last saw one another. He cares a great deal for your happiness, Georgiana."

"And I for his. When do you see him next?"

"I hardly know," Elizabeth admitted, "for I do not have such intimacy with the Netherfield ladies as to be able to call on them as readily as I do here. He occasionally calls with Mr Bingley, but if he does not, we have been invited to dinner at Netherfield in a few nights, and I imagine he will be there then." She checked herself. "It must be hard to be unable to be more in society. Would you prefer I spoke less of such engagements?"

"No!" Mrs Wilson spoke vehemently before gathering herself. "I-I mean I would not have you avoid such topics. It is hard, but it is not new to me. Your friendship allows me to hear about society, even though I am unable to fully participate in it."

"Will you promise to tell me if I am causing you pain?"

"I will," Mrs Wilson asserted earnestly. "Although I do not believe hearing about Fitzwilliam could ever cause me pain. I would be glad of anything you can tell me about him."

"Of course, if you wish it. Although I must warn you, if I am to particularly study him, I shall have to inform him I am conducting important research." Elizabeth laughed again. "I shall tell him I have been asked to present my findings to a learned society."

Mrs Wilson clapped her hands. "Oh, do! I shall be president of your learned society. Miss Lucas, perhaps you might be secretary, and Jane might be treasurer, if she wishes." She had all the girlish glee of a child, and Elizabeth was quite delighted. She continued the theme, rapidly spinning a picture of them as four earnest scholars, publishing papers for the sole edification of Mrs Wilson.

When the time came for Elizabeth and Charlotte to depart, there was reluctance on all sides, for their greater understanding had created a new intimacy, and each felt they had forged a still deeper attachment than had hitherto existed between them. Elizabeth left with a final promise that she would take great care to observe everything at the dinner party and furnish her friend with as many details as she could on her next visit. She wondered whether the particular news she would have to share, following the formal announcement of Jane and Mr Bingley's engagement, would give her friend any heartache, despite her previous assurances to Jane.

CHARLOTTE AND ELIZABETH parted at a fork in the road, each to return to their own home. Elizabeth rambled idly, contemplating how eventful life had become since the advent of the newcomers to Meryton, and how she had never spent so much time in a gentleman's company, other than that of her father and uncle Gardiner, as she had with Mr Darcy. This observation was strengthened as she approached Longbourn and saw Mr Darcy riding away from the house. As she approached, he reined in his horse and greeted her.

"I was informed you were out paying calls."

"Indeed, Charlotte and I have been visiting Purvis Lodge." She watched his face closely as she spoke and marvelled at his ability to school his features, although she did not miss the momentary eager gleam in his eye.

"And how were your friends?"

"Both very well, thank you. Mrs Wilson was, by the end of our visit, in as good spirits as I have ever seen her."

He nodded, but instead of riding away as Elizabeth expected, he dismounted his horse and joined her.

"If you have not yet had enough of walking, might I join you for a time? Perhaps in the gardens?" Elizabeth had no wish to deny him, or indeed herself, so acquiesced at once. Gesturing to a man to take his horse, he turned to walk beside her, and they began a slow circuit together of the paths through the gardens.

Elizabeth informed Mr Darcy in a low voice of all that had passed on the visit, emphasising that, bar the brief interlude regarding Lady Catherine, Mrs Wilson had been almost lively, that she and Charlotte were on excellent terms, and that Elizabeth herself was under strict instructions to observe him and report back.

"And what do you observe at present?" A smile glimmered around his eyes, although he spoke in measured tones.

"Oh, I hardly know. I have only just begun my study in earnest."

"In earnest?" he queried, his amusement growing.

She laughed, her joy rising. "Indeed, it is a whim of mine to study all of my acquaintance and try to make out their characters."

"And ought I to ask what assessment you have made of mine?"

She laughed again. "Certainly not."

"I am not afraid of you." His face bloomed into a full smile for a brief moment, startling Elizabeth with a feeling of warmth that lingered even when the expression was replaced with one more earnest. "Will you tell me?" he asked, and she looked at him quizzically before replying slowly.

"I have found you exceedingly puzzling, truth be told. Such a peculiar mixture of interest and aloofness, gravity and, occasionally, levity. Reserved yet full of questions. I have hardly known what to make of you, although I think I may have been recently provided with the key."

"We had been considering explaining matters to you. I am only sorry for the manner of your discovery."

"As was I. But it is past now, and we are friends again." She hardly knew whether she spoke of Mr Darcy or his sister.

"She will greatly benefit from your friendship when I leave Hertfordshire."

He was looking at her as he spoke, and she could not be certain whether she had successfully hidden the emotion she felt at this statement. He made no sign that he saw it, but turned away, and they continued in thoughtful silence.

"You said it pained you, hearing her story, but I was so intent on hearing how *she* was that I did not take the time to hear how *you* felt. I hope you were not unduly distressed?"

"No, not distressed, I do not think. I do not doubt her word, but it all hardly seems real. Stranger than anything you might read in a book. It pained me only as much as it hurt to think of my friend suffering such a life. The explanation brought clarity to many small anxieties."

"I am glad. I would not have you upset by it." Elizabeth

glanced at him again, but he still looked resolutely forward. "And your sister and Miss Lucas?"

"I believe their reaction was much the same as mine."

"I am glad," he repeated.

After a moment, he changed the subject. "Have you spent much time in town?"

"A little. My uncle and aunt Gardiner live there, and I have visited them during the Season sometimes."

"Where do they live?"

"On Gracechurch Street. My uncle is in trade." She wondered that he did not react to this, for many men of his wealth would disdain the connexion, but he merely continued with another question.

"And what do you make of London?"

"I have enjoyed my time there. The theatre is delightful. But I am glad I live here, amongst this," she gestured expansively at the greenery around them.

"Hertfordshire has many beauties. Have you travelled to many other places?"

"This is beginning to feel like another examination. You have already assessed my suitability as a friend to Mrs Wilson—where do your questions tend?" Her tone was arch and her eyes laughing, and Mr Darcy was unperturbed by the challenge.

"Perhaps you are not the only one who wishes to sketch characters."

"Ah, but I at least apply the same rigorous interest to everyone."

"I have no evidence of that. What is your assessment of Mr Bingley, for example?"

"Open as a book, anxious to please and easily does so, and smitten by Jane almost from the moment he saw her," she replied promptly. "What is yours of Charlotte?"

"A keen eye, a sharp mind, and a sensible conversational-ist," he replied, equally as quick.

Elizabeth laughed. "In answer to your question, I jour-neyed northwards with my aunt and uncle a few years ago, and we visited Chatsworth and the Peak, but I have travelled little beyond that."

"Then you have been to Derbyshire?" His eyes had turned to her again. "Where did you stay?"

"A place called Lambton. My aunt spent some of her youth there."

"That is but five miles from Pemberley!"

"Oh! I wish I had seen it. I have heard such praise of it."

"It is very dear to us."

"We visited one or two other such estates, but I do not recall visiting Pemberley. There was a house close to Lambton which we were told was closed to visitors at the time. I had no cause to particularly recollect the name, but it might have been Pemberley."

His face clouded for a minute. "That is very possible."

"Would you tell me more about it?" She turned to him with eagerness, and Mr Darcy had no difficulty in complying with her request as they returned to the house. Mrs Bennet, when they entered, very cordially invited him to eat with them. Although he declined, pleading that he had business matters to attend to and had already been gone too long, he remained with them for a short while before making his farewells and departing.

When Jane returned from Netherfield, she was bright and happy. Miss Bingley and Mrs Hurst had, in her estimation, paid her every civility in recognising her as their future sister. Much to Jane's delight, Mrs Hurst had sent for young Lucy, and the mother's manner had only warmed to Jane at the sight of her small daughter so happy and amused while playing with her future aunt.

Elizabeth listened to her sister's account of her visit with almost equal pleasure. She could not imagine either of the ladies being anything more than cordial at best, but Jane was satisfied, and as Jane was the one who would need to endure their company, that was all that concerned her.

As she told her sister of her own day, she blushed as a knowing smile crossed Jane's face. "So, Mr Darcy called upon you?"

"I hardly know what to make of it."

"Do you not?" Jane's air was so reminiscent of their aunt Gardiner that merriment quickly overcame Elizabeth, and Jane waited until she recovered before she persisted.

"Do you think he means to marry you? It is a marked attention to pay you if he does not."

"I do not know whether he was calling on me. He may have been visiting Papa."

"Would you like it, if he had been?"

Elizabeth made no reply as she reluctantly met her sister's eyes. Jane smiled sympathetically. "I do not think he is a man to deliberately mislead you as to his intentions."

Elizabeth again made no reply, and Jane reached out and gently prised apart her clasped hands, taking one in her own.

CHAPTER TWENTY-ONE

With two weddings to plan, Mrs Bennet was in a stew of emotions unlike any her daughters had seen before. They had given her, if not a calmer manner, at least a tangible event on which to focus her enthusiasm. Mr Bingley's dinner party, however, had somehow lodged in her mind as a particularly significant event. She therefore exhorted her daughters to dress as finely as it was within their power to do, and perhaps slightly finer.

Mary was soon exempted from this instruction on the understanding she was to adorn herself appropriately to her future married state. The clothes Mary considered suitable for a clergyman's wife, however, differed somewhat from her mother's idea of the same. It took Jane, acting as intermediary between the two, to quietly persuade Mary to add some light trim to one of her dresses.

The effect was to immediately soften the severity of Mary's costume, and Mrs Bennet pronounced she would do very well. Having thus achieved maternal approval without moving too far beyond the bounds of her own taste, Mary resolved to trim one or two of her other dresses in a similar manner, in the hope it would be acceptable to her future husband to see her so adorned.

Lydia and Kitty required no encouragement to dress up in a level of finery rather excessive for a dinner party, attiring themselves in all the lace and fripperies they owned. It took all of Jane's most careful persuasion to convince them to simplify their costume.

Jane herself favoured a simpler style, but on the eve of the dinner received a visit from Mr Bingley and an elegant necklace, which she accepted with a deep blush. Some small amendments to the rest of her outfit were necessary to complement the jewellery, and Mrs Bennet beamed at her with delight.

Elizabeth, as was not unusual, had the most difficult time of it from her mother. Mrs Bennet was determined Mr Darcy's most recent visit was a sure proof of his interest, and that Elizabeth ought to be dressed with all of the elegance of London society. Her daughter was equally convinced she would be much more comfortable, and therefore much better company, if she dressed as she always did. Elizabeth's will eventually won out over her mother's, but she had to pay the price of a great deal of protestation.

"Well, I only hope Mr Darcy does not have his head turned another way! For you will be sorry then and wish you had listened to your mother! Oh, my nerves cannot stand it. I shall have such a headache! I shall be able to think of nothing but your waywardness all day!"

Having got her way, Elizabeth nevertheless dressed with particular care. She was not immune to the knowledge that the engagements of two Bennet daughters would throw their family into the centre of all the local gossip, and wished to acquit herself well at the first social occasion where both engagements would be common knowledge. If she had any other motive, she chose not to admit it to herself, but her restored confidence in her friendships gave her mood such a lift that she was at her most bright and winning as she stepped into the carriage, rivalling even Jane in her radiance.

Mr Bingley received their party with all the honour that could be bestowed at such an event. His sisters, Elizabeth noted, looked less enthusiastic, but they made a point of receiving Jane with many expressions of joy. Miss Bingley appeared to take some pleasure in being able to murmur to Jane that she was convinced they were born to be sisters. It was unclear who exactly might have doubted this statement that she needed to affirm her belief, but Jane, glowing in the double happiness of Mr Bingley's love and her mother's joy, accepted it with perfect serenity.

Elizabeth was greeted by a small nod from Mr Darcy as she arrived, but he was deep in conversation with Sir William Lucas—or, rather, Sir William was deep in conversation with him—and he made no effort to break away. At dinner, she found they were seated some three seats apart on opposite sides of the table. Whilst she had not intended or expected to monopolise his attention, the inability to share even the most basic of pleasantries after their last conversation gave her no little frustration. Mr Darcy, however, appeared unmoved, although he looked her way occasionally. He spoke little, but responded readily, if briefly, when necessary to Lady Lucas and Mrs Hurst, who sat closest to him.

Elizabeth's natural inclination to be sociable bore her out, and she threw herself into conversation with her own neighbours with enthusiasm.

When Jane's engagement was formally announced, Elizabeth was carried away for a moment by her sister's radiance, Mr Bingley's warmth, and by the genuine congratulations of all those at the table. The announcement was surprising to no one, but it was nevertheless gratifying to the feelings of many that the affable tenant of Netherfield had chosen a bride from their number and had had the good sense to give Jane the recognition she was generally credited as richly deserving.

Aside from Elizabeth's pleasure in her sister's happiness, however, she found she did not enjoy the meal as much as she had anticipated. When the ladies retired from the table, Elizabeth had lost a little of her glow, and her irritation was only increased by Miss Bingley attaching herself to her side.

"Miss Eliza! Do come and sit with me."

"Thank you, Miss Bingley."

"Oh, of course you must call me Caroline. We are to be friends, you know! My brother will have you often in our company I am sure after he marries our dear Jane, and I for one am delighted we shall see so much more of you."

Elizabeth thought she could detect a sardonic humour in Miss Bingley's words, and could not quite bring herself to provide similar assurance so remained silent. Miss Bingley chattered on for some time, a series of platitudes and observations without expectation or need of reply that Elizabeth endured as best she could. She observed Charlotte and Jane, laughing together across the room, and even Kitty and Lydia, gossiping nearby with Charlotte's younger sister, Mrs Maria Ellsworth. She began to despair of having any enjoyment at all from this evening.

Miss Bingley was in the middle of relating the delights of London entertainments when Kitty, overhearing their conversation, turned to them both.

"Oh, do you speak of London? I long to be there, but Papa says I am not to go until after Jane's wedding. I do not see why I could not travel to London now. My aunt and uncle will be happy to have me, I am certain."

Lydia sighed noisily and turned to speak loudly and pointedly to Mrs Ellsworth. Kitty disregarded her and continued.

"I mean to go to balls and the theatre and all the entertainment you describe, Miss Bingley. You must tell me which particular theatres you recommend."

Caroline smiled a thin smile at Kitty. "I think you will find little to entertain you in London at this time of year. Society is very limited, unless one is willing to associate with those whose business keeps them in London all year round." She paused, then, "I think Jane mentioned your uncle was in trade?"

Kitty smiled airily. "Oh yes, but he travels in the summer sometimes. I am sure he could give up the business and buy an estate if he chose. Lydia and I have often talked about how he might. But he would keep the house in town, of course."

"Is that so?" Elizabeth did not like the look in Caroline's eye, but a sudden straightening of her posture and a change in her demeanour showed the lady had abruptly lost interest in their conversation. Elizabeth turned and saw the gentlemen entering the room.

"Mr Darcy! We were just discussing London's entertainments. I am unspeakably fond of the theatre. I was just on the verge of asking Miss Eliza whether she cares for it at all." She turned to Elizabeth expectantly, as though stating her intention to ask a question were the same as actually asking it.

"Thank you. I greatly enjoy it when I have the opportunity."

Miss Bingley did not seem to need to wait for any more answer than this. She turned to Mr Darcy, who had taken a seat nearby, and proceeded to catechise him on his preferences when theatregoing, dwelling more heavily on his box and who might accompany him, and on her extensive knowledge of the same places and people, than on anything that might happen on the stage.

It was a great relief to Elizabeth when Mr Bingley suggested Mary commence some music, and Miss Bingley was forced into silence. She had never heard that lady so voluble and could hardly imagine what might be the cause of it. She had little doubt why Miss Bingley had sought Mr Darcy's near presence, however, for when after a time the younger girls requested dancing, she turned in an expectant manner to him. He, however, had already turned towards Elizabeth and asked her whether she would favour him with a dance.

Elizabeth replied in the affirmative with no small pleasure, and with a satisfied nod he turned to Miss Bingley with a more solemn air, formally requesting a dance with his hostess. She replied with careful coolness.

"Thank you, Mr Darcy. I regret I shall not be dancing this evening. Please excuse me, I have been neglecting my other guests." With this, she swiftly stood and made her way across the room to where some other ladies were assembled.

As Mr Darcy led Elizabeth to the floor, they passed Sir William Lucas, who smiled at them genially. "Dancing with Miss Eliza again, sir! None can say otherwise than that you have excellent taste. Not for nothing is it said one wedding brings on another. Capital!"

Elizabeth attempted to hide her embarrassment at this speech and did not feel sufficiently mistress of herself to meet Mr Darcy's eyes until they had taken their places. To her surprise, his expression was gentle and warm. She flushed and looked away, and they began the figures without speaking. Mr Darcy made no attempt to break the silence and she, against her usual inclination whilst dancing, could not bring herself to address him. Eventually, she dared to meet his eye again, to find him looking at her with some concern.

"Miss Elizabeth, it appears—" he stopped, and she watched him gather his thoughts before looking at her expressively. "Would you permit me to call upon you tomorrow?"

Startled by the formality of the question into giving an equally formal response, Elizabeth after a moment of breathlessness gave him to understand she would be happy to receive him. His eyes softened, and she smiled weakly back. She did not in general think herself given to shyness, but found herself blushing and again unable to meet his eyes. She had thought of little else but this man and his affairs since he had arrived in Hertfordshire, and had been consumed by Mrs Wilson's story. She had thought her courage equal to anything, yet now, presented with his asking such a question with such gravity, she quailed, and hoped he would not observe it.

Mr Darcy did observe it, however, for he soon spoke again.

"Would you prefer we stood out of the set?"

She gathered her courage and shook her head. "No, sir, I would much prefer to finish our dance."

"Perhaps then some conversation might be in order. Will you comment on the number of couples, or should I?"

Elizabeth stifled a laugh and felt more herself. "I would prefer to speak about the weather. Or perhaps the state of the roads at present."

"What do you say to books?"

"I like them very well, sir. I find them exceedingly useful when I wish to read," she replied pertly. He smiled at this response and named some particular volumes, which kept them both thoroughly occupied for the remainder of the dance.

At the close of the set, Mr Darcy attended Elizabeth to Charlotte, who smiled warmly at her friend, and proceeded to engage them both in conversation. Elizabeth was soon laughing heartily, quite recovered to her usual good humour. She faltered only slightly when her eyes occasionally met his.

After a short while, Mr Bingley requested a dance, and Elizabeth was able to accept him with all her usual liveliness. She was pleased to see Mr Darcy remain where he was, continuing a conversation with Charlotte as she departed.

CHAPTER TWENTY-TWO

M r Bingley arrived the next morning still flushed with good humour from the evening before. In comparison, Mr Darcy seemed as solemn as he had ever been, and Elizabeth began to doubt her assumptions about his intentions.

She was greatly agitated and suffering from having had no opportunity to unburden herself to Charlotte the night before, or even to Jane in all the flurry of her delight. Elizabeth had garnered a quizzical look from her father when she had passed him the wrong plate at breakfast twice in succession, but otherwise her abstraction had escaped notice.

The ladies were settled at their usual occupations when the gentlemen arrived, interrupting an extract from a sermon on achieving felicity in marriage that Mary had insisted on sharing. Mr Bingley made at once for Jane and engaged her in quiet conversation. Mr Darcy paused only a moment at the door before similarly approaching Elizabeth and taking a seat. After exchanging greetings, Elizabeth attempting to appear entirely collected, her composure was thrown into complete disarray.

"Would it be possible to speak to you privately, Miss Elizabeth? Perhaps we might walk?"

Elizabeth, unable to trust her voice, was freed from the requirement to do so by Mrs Bennet, who at once loudly agreed it was a perfect day for walking. With hardly a moment's pause, therefore, Elizabeth found herself shortly afterwards once again at Mr Darcy's side, walking the garden. Jane and Mr Bingley strolled blissfully some way behind, entirely engrossed in one another.

Now that the moment had come, Elizabeth fought to regain her courage.

"Do you mean to frighten me by coming in all this state to call?" She cursed her voice for quavering.

"Not at all. My intentions are the reverse." He spoke calmly, but she thought she could detect some emotion in his words. "I am here to ask for your hand in marriage."

Elizabeth had, in one or two of her weaker moments, imagined Mr Darcy proposing. He had, in her mind, shown more obvious ardour. Nevertheless, she knew that, whatever the cause of his gravity in this moment, she had seen enough of his true character to know her own heart. It was therefore with a tremulous smile that she reached a hand out and began, "Mr Darcy—"

"I do not ask for an answer just yet," he cut in, before she could give one. Elizabeth drew her hand back. He saw her expression, and his manner softened. "I mean that there are some things you ought to understand, before you make your decision." She waited wordlessly for him to continue.

"My sister— Her current situation is so very precarious, and I will do what is necessary to protect her. My presence, so close to her residence for such a protracted period of time, daily increases the risk of bringing her husband to the area. I must therefore leave, and soon."

Elizabeth had expected as much, but nevertheless felt a pang at the confirmation of it. She remained silent, however, and he continued.

"I have estate matters and other business to attend to which will occupy my time for a month at least, but may take longer, and I am unable as yet to give a date for my return. I would like to be able to correspond with you. It will be valuable to hear how my sister fares from a source we have both come to trust. She does not always wish to tell me all, for fear of paining me, but not knowing the truth pains me far more. Bingley, of course, will be too much engaged with his wedding preparations to be of any real assistance."

Elizabeth could barely contain her astonishment at this speech.

"I would need to protect you from harm. In engaging myself to you, I am aware I place you in a position of risk. Wickham," he spoke the name as though the very act of doing so disgusted him, "sought out his wife not merely for her fortune but for her connexion to me. He might not see you as the same prize, but he is more than capable of seeking to hurt me, through you. I would therefore make no society announcement of our engagement, at least until I am able to be back with you to protect you if necessary."

He paused, but Elizabeth made no move to interject, and he continued without any sign he expected her to. "I am not stipulating a secret engagement. Your cousin and Sir William Lucas have both made it plain our match is considered a certainty, and I would not have you exposed to the risk of your neighbours thinking I had left you dishonourably. But they would be given to understand we had agreed to a long engagement, which I hope would prevent the news spreading too widely—"

"Mr Darcy!" Elizabeth did, at last, manage to speak. Stopping in her tracks, she waited until he also stopped a few paces ahead and turned to face her. "You seem to have forgotten that I have not agreed to any kind of engagement, long or otherwise."

His brow furrowed, and he looked at her for a long moment before saying slowly, "You are refusing my proposal?"

"I have not said so. I have not yet said *anything*, Mr Darcy!"

His brow cleared at her words, and he began to look shamefaced.

"I have gone about this all wrong." His words carried enough of a question that Elizabeth was able to muster a short laugh and reply.

"I had suspected you came today to make a proposal, but I did not expect it to be a business proposition. You wish to become engaged so I may write news of your sister to you? What does that portend for a lifetime together? I hold her in high regard, as I believe you know, but are you proposing marriage in order to have a local agent for a few months?"

She stepped closer. "You wish to protect me, but tell me in the same breath that you only need to do so because of our engagement, yet have not waited to hear whether I accept your offer?"

She moved still closer, until he was within arm's reach, but made no move to touch him. "You plan who we shall tell of our engagement, but Mr Darcy, we are not engaged. You are not solving a troubling estate matter. You are asking me to join myself with you for a lifetime and offering your life to me. Surely, that ought to be based on some form of affection or attachment, respect at least—something more than my value as a correspondent?"

He had been staring at her as she spoke, but at these words his eyes widened and he turned away from her, lifting his hand to his face. Elizabeth said nothing further, waiting to see how he would respond. When he began to speak, he was still looking away.

"I have gone about this all wrong," he repeated, with more conviction. "You are perfectly correct. What must you think of me?"

He turned back to look at her then with worried eyes. She met them unflinchingly but made no reply.

"Miss Elizabeth Bennet," he reached out for her unresisting hand, taking it gently in his. "Please allow me to tell you how ardently I admire and love you."

Elizabeth could not prevent a thrill passing through her at these words, but she only raised a sceptical eyebrow. He blushed slightly but continued.

"You do not believe me. Of course you do not, after such a speech. Yet it is true, nevertheless." He drew her hand through his arm and, turning, gestured to ask whether she would walk. Glad of the motion, she did so, and they fell into step.

"I believe I was half in love with you before we even met. My sister wrote with such warmth about the friendship you had offered and spoke so highly of you even after such a short acquaintance. I had been meaning to come regardless, Bingley's arrangements were well in hand, but when I read about you, I was particularly curious...drawn, somehow, to your description.

"When I first saw you, I knew you already and was disposed to like you. I had read my sister's words so often, I felt already acquainted with your family, although she mentioned your younger sisters only briefly. *Your* kindness, your recognition of my sister after she had suffered so much stood out from the page as though it were illuminated. I wished to ensure you were the friends you appeared to be, but I do not think I ever truly doubted it.

"I sought you out—Miss Bennet also, but it was you I sought most often and with the most determination. I did not examine my reasons for doing so, but if I had, it is likely I would have believed I wished only to ensure my sister's happiness by establishing her friend was all she appeared. Yet I think that, long before I knew it to be the case, I was seeking you out for myself. I do not often find I converse as easily as I have with you, especially on so short an acquaintance."

He took a breath and covered her hand where it rested on his arm with his own. Elizabeth, who had not been insensible of the quiet passion in his words, delighted in the touch.

"You have shown yourself kind and caring in your response to my sister, even more so since you have learnt what her recent life has been. You befriended her because she was alone, and although you understandably doubted what you saw that day at Purvis Lodge, you respected my word sufficiently to go to her and let her speak for herself. I have never known a woman so lively whose wit did not serve primarily to denigrate others, yet you retain a sweetness through it all that I cannot fail to admire."

Elizabeth felt the heat in her cheeks from such a declaration. She could not recall that she had ever received such a heartfelt compliment.

"I have long been given up by most of society as a lost cause and a confirmed bachelor, although some appear to think my not being at Pemberley indicates a new willingness to be drawn into marriage. I did not come to Hertfordshire in search of a wife, yet, if you are willing—if you have come to believe, as I hope you have, that you could entrust me with your heart—I have found one. And I would be honoured if you would accept my hand."

Elizabeth was no less astonished than she had been, but now her astonishment was suffused with a feeling of previously unfelt delight. She looked up at him with smiling eyes, the hand resting on his arm tightening so that he looked down to meet them. Warmth spread across her cheeks at what she saw, and she hurriedly looked away.

"When did you realise all this?"

He stepped closer, dropping her hand from his arm but in the same motion reaching to encase it in his own. His other hand reached to her chin, his touch gently requesting she lift it until she was once again looking at him. "That I loved you?" Elizabeth could not this time disguise her reaction to his words, and his eyes warmed as he continued. "I think, had I admitted it to myself, from the moment I saw you flee from Purvis Lodge. But I only examined my feelings after your cousin encouraged me to pursue my suit. Until that point, I had not stopped to realise I had one, but Mr Collins's comments caused me to reconsider my thoughts and actions. I quickly realised that even were my heart not engaged, my honour had been, and that making you an offer was the only path I could follow. I was not long in realising my duty and inclination were one and the same."

"So, Mr Collins brought you to this proposal?" Elizabeth laughed brightly, delighting in the amusement it brought to his expression.

"I would hope that now you are to be his sister you do not say as much to him," he replied with mock gravity.

"I think I can safely assure you I shall not," she replied with another laugh.

"In truth," he replied, mock gravity being replaced with his usual, natural kind, "Mr Collins made me examine my own feelings, which prompted me to better understand yours. I had decided only that, with my intention to depart, it would be better to speak on my return, perhaps making my future intentions clear before I went without entering into an engagement. I had intended to withdraw and to remain friends but not to excite any additional attention from the neighbourhood."

"Is that why you paid me little heed at dinner?"

"I wished to show I was not solely occupied with you, so finding myself among others, I exerted myself to remain there. I do not believe I could have lasted the entire evening, however. I would inevitably have been drawn to you somehow.

"It was Miss Bingley's influence that prompted me to ask you to dance as I did. I wished to demonstrate that she had no right, even though she is my hostess, to monopolise my attention as she attempted. And it was Sir William who taught me that further delay would only cause you harm. Your reaction to his words showed you were not unaffected, and your reaction to mine gave me cause to hope my affection would not go unrewarded."

"I was heartily embarrassed."

"But not at the thought we might be paired together?" The soft note of interrogation shot through her, and she shook her head lightly in response. "You are yet to give me an answer," he continued in the same soft tone.

"You know I can bring nothing to a marriage? I have no portion to speak of, no relations to boast of, and a family who often cause embarrassment."

He shook his head at this, capturing her other hand and pressing it lightly. "You would bring yourself. I can set no price on that, and ask for nothing more."

"In that case, I can only say I love you, and heartily consent to being your wife."

The smile that lit his face entranced her, and she was taken back to the glimpse of this man she had seen briefly at Netherfield. They remained as they stood for a moment, locked gazes and the gentle touch of his thumbs stroking across the backs of her hands communicating all that either needed to say. Eventually, it was Elizabeth who broke away, turning once again to walk.

"You voiced many concerns, at the start."

"I did," he agreed, his solemnity returning. "I ought not to have begun as I did, but those considerations had been uppermost in my thoughts, and once I had made up my mind to speak, they tumbled out first."

"Of course I shall write to you, although I shall tell your sister I intend to do so. I have no objection to avoiding the notice that such announcements must bring, although my mother may differ on that."

"Is there anything that will placate her, save public fanfare?"

"Presentation at court? A society ball attended by a duke or two? Introductions to any earls you might know for Kitty and Lydia?" She repented her words as she saw his face cloud. "I am sorry, I did not mean to vex you with poor jokes. You need do none of those things. Mama wants only the best for us, and she has long suffered at the thought of us all yet unmarried. I shall manage her enthusiasm and save you from it as best I can."

"I shall not live up to her expectations if she is expecting grandeur, or social connexions. I have not kept many of them up, although neither have I cut many outright."

"You do not need to live up to Mama's expectations, Fitzwilliam. You are more than sufficient for mine."

"Elizabeth." The reverent emphasis with which he spoke her name was enough to distract her from any other thought and as she gazed at him, he likewise seemed incapable of doing anything other than taking her hands again and drawing her wordlessly closer.

CHAPTER TWENTY-THREE

T he reception of the news of Elizabeth's quiet engagement to Mr Darcy was all that one might expect.

Mrs Bennet was thrown into such a heady mixture of joy that her nerves overtook her, and she was forced to retire to her room for much of the day, although not before insisting that Mr Darcy and Mr Bingley both stayed for dinner. Her recovery was rapid once she considered all of her dearest acquaintances in Meryton who would wish to hear of the match.

Mr Bennet, although he had wholly expected the engagement, frowned a little on the man who was to rob him of his favourite daughter. An hour's conversation in his study, however, apparently reconciled him to the idea that Mr Darcy was a man of sense, and by dinner he had recovered his equanimity sufficiently to request Elizabeth pass all manner of dishes, attempting to catch her in a state of distraction equal to that of the morning.

Jane was delighted; Mr Bingley was equally overjoyed, and only regretted that Mr Darcy's planned absence meant they could not combine their weddings into one grand celebration.

Mary, once reassured that there was no set date and that there would be no planning for Elizabeth's marriage until she was installed in her new life as Mrs Collins, wished her sister joy.

Kitty congratulated her sister with neither disdain nor enthusiasm, while Lydia greeted the news with an exclamation that it had been obvious for weeks and therefore was of very little interest. She did, however, congratulate Elizabeth, and asked whether she might have the choosing of the colour of her new dresses for the wedding.

Charlotte's congratulations, when Elizabeth made her way to Lucas Lodge a few days after the engagement, were warm and sincere. If she felt either inclined to point out her early perception of attachment or a pang of jealousy at her friend's good fortune, she concealed her feelings well.

Meryton society was soon full of the news, and for three days Elizabeth's grand match was the favourite topic of gossip in the town. The prospect of a long engagement and the generally reserved manner of Mr Darcy compared to that of his good-natured friend, however, soon meant that this match declined in interest compared to the more immediate prospects of her sisters.

The reaction that was of most importance to Mr Darcy, however, and which Elizabeth valued as highly as that of Jane and Charlotte, was that of the lady resident at Purvis Lodge. It was agreed that Elizabeth would be the one to call and inform her; much as Mr Darcy regretted missing the opportunity, he was particularly keen to ensure his visits were infrequent and irregular enough to pass unnoticed now that not only his sister's reputation but also Elizabeth's was at stake.

Elizabeth, therefore, called on Mrs Wilson the day after her engagement. Jane, preparations for her wedding requiring her attention, sent her regrets, and Elizabeth hoped her promise to visit within a few days would be sufficient to placate the children.

Tommy and Joey were out in the gardens for their daily exercise when Elizabeth arrived so were spared the disappointment of the absence of their favourite. She was shown into the music room, which now betrayed evidence of frequent occupation. Mrs Wilson rose from the bench immediately and welcomed Elizabeth warmly, eager for company and news, and they both settled for a long visit.

Elizabeth's recent happiness had cast a rosy glow back across her memories of the dinner party, and her account of it paid no heed to her own disappointment in the earlier part of the evening. Instead, it was a lively retelling of half-observed conversation and flights of absurd fantasy regarding the meanings of various overheard snippets of everyday speech.

When her narrative approached the end of dinner, Elizabeth hesitated. Mrs Wilson noticed and looked troubled.

"You have bad news."

"No, no not at all," Elizabeth hastened to reply. "Only I am not sure it will be entirely without pain for you."

Her friend waited expectantly. Elizabeth had been wondering how to break the news of her sister's engagement, but in the moment could do nothing but state it as simply as she could.

"Mr Bingley—"

"—is engaged to Jane," Mrs Wilson finished for her. "You

need not fear I shall break down at the news. I have been expecting it."

Elizabeth reached out for her hand. "And you are not troubled?" She paused, considering her words before once again deciding on the direct approach. "I confess I was concerned you cared for him yourself."

"No," her friend replied, although a slight quaver in her voice betrayed more emotion than she pretended to feel. "At least..." She paused.

Elizabeth waited for Mrs Wilson to continue, and when she did not, softly interposed, "I apologise for raising it. Let us talk of something else."

A vehement shake of the head was all the reply for a moment, but then the lady managed to speak, the words coming more easily once she had begun.

"No. I have told you the worst of my story, it would relieve me to speak of this. Even Fitzwilliam knows nothing of it. I am not in love with Mr Bingley, I am certain. I told your sister the truth—he was kind to me as a child, and I came to see him as the best sort of man, for he is the opposite of all that my husband embodies.

"In some of my darker times, I have held him up as the image of what a man ought to be, and have made from that image what I believe would be required for me to truly love someone. But it is not him. I know that. It is his shadow or reflection, embellished in my thoughts. Although my brother has many acquaintances, he has few close friends. Mr Bingley was one of the few good men I knew beyond my family.

"I am delighted for Jane. I believe she will make Mr Bingley an excellent wife, and he will make her the best of husbands. I can see she loves him dearly, and I wish them well."

Elizabeth still held Georgiana's hand, and she pressed it

comfortingly. A grateful smile was followed by a small shake of Mrs Wilson's head and a soft laugh. "I would not choose to sound maudlin. Tell me more about the evening."

"Before I do, may I enquire as to your feelings regarding Miss Bingley?"

"Oh! I barely know her. She visited occasionally as part of a larger party but noticed me little when I was small. As I grew older, she made as if to befriend me, but I could make nothing of her conversation. It was all chatter, I did not know even half of the people, places, or fashions she wished to speak about, and she did not wait to hear my own contributions."

"Had you said so before today, I would not have thought you were describing Miss Bingley at all," replied Elizabeth, "for until this dinner party I had never heard her speak more than a few sentences all at once. But I have discovered for myself that she can be talkative, when she chooses."

"How odd." Had Mrs Wilson been bolder, Elizabeth might have described the air of her next comment as teasing. As it was, her manner betrayed an eager interest in Elizabeth's reaction. "I usually found she was at her most talkative when we were in company. Particularly when Fitzwilliam was present, as I recall."

Elizabeth's eyes sparkled. "Now that you mention it, she did invite your brother to join us when the gentlemen entered." She had not yet decided how she would reveal her own engagement, but could not deny the eagerness in her friend's eyes. "If Miss Bingley wished to attract your brother's attention, however, I fear she was disappointed, and I cannot bring myself to laugh at her. He rapidly made it clear his intentions lay in another direction." A smile crept across her face, and Mrs Wilson responded instantly by jumping to her feet and clapping her hands with childlike glee.

"Oh! Did he—? Are you engaged to my brother? Oh, do, do tell me you are to be my sister!" She reached out her hands, and Elizabeth took them again, standing with her friend, who was trembling with anticipation at the sight of her beaming eyes.

"I had thought to make more of the evening before I confessed, for he did not propose, but he asked rather formally whether he might call on me."

"And did he call?"

"He did, and yes," she said, unable to hold off a moment longer from her friend's joy. "I am to be your sister."

"Oh! Oh, Lizzy!" she cried, sounding remarkably like Jane. "Oh, you make me so happy! What a wonderful thing. A sister, and that it should be you. I knew he felt more for you than he admitted, I knew he cared for you, but to think you are to be his wife!" Her exclamations continued, saying nothing new of note but celebrating their new connexion. After a time, she calmed sufficiently to resume her seat, insisting that Elizabeth tell her all.

In deference more to Mr Darcy's good intentions than to absolute truth, Elizabeth did not tell quite all to his sister, but enough of the latter half of his proposal that Mrs Wilson was, by the end, breathless and tearful. "Oh, it is beautiful! Fitzwilliam is the best of men, and you are the best of women, and I could not be happier at this news!" She immediately threw her face in her hands and began to sob, and Elizabeth, with some concern, drew closer to her and placed a comforting hand on her back.

"It is too much!" she whispered brokenly through her sobs. "Too much. Such happiness—a sister! Such beautiful words, and I-I shall never— Oh, Lizzy!"

Elizabeth had no words suitable for her friend's extremity of feeling, and sat helplessly by, offering what comfort she could in gentle contact and soothing words. After a time, Mrs Wilson recovered sufficiently to speak more clearly, if tonelessly.

"I am sorry. I have been hoping for this, and I am so delighted for you both, I truly am. It is only—"

"I believe you," Elizabeth replied gently. "It must be hard for you to feel yourself shut away here."

Mrs Wilson nodded speechlessly before drawing a breath and meeting her eyes. "I do not wish to dwell on such things. Tell me what your plans are. Is Fitzwilliam still intending to leave Hertfordshire?"

"Yes. He says he will be gone for at least a month, and we cannot set a date for our wedding until he knows when he can return."

"I wish I could be there!"

"Perhaps you can. There will be time enough to consider how it might be managed. There is no prohibition on anyone attending church for a wedding, you know."

Mrs Wilson assented to this, although still with evident reservations. Elizabeth, desirous of seeing her friend's countenance brighten before she departed, gradually coaxed her to speak of other things.

They were interrupted in their tête-à-tête by the arrival of two small boys in the company of the young maid, grimy from their exertions but full of chatter about their play. Their arrival naturally became the focus of both ladies, and the four formed a happy party, with only a little grass and dirt being scattered from the sleeves of the two young gentlemen over the dresses of their mother and future aunt.

Elizabeth's visit to Purvis Lodge was not without pain, but on the whole had been satisfactory. Her greatest regret was that it had not been possible for Mr Darcy to be present.

She wondered how he would have borne Georgiana's sorrowful assessment of her prospects, and settled, in the end, on gratitude that she, and not he, had been the one to bring the news of their engagement.

CHAPTER TWENTY-FOUR

Mr Darcy had arranged to leave Netherfield in a week's time but made the most of the interim to call upon Elizabeth as often as Mr Bingley called upon Jane. Invariably, his visits would lead to a walk, and Elizabeth was grateful the weather held dry, for she could not have endured much more of the flattery her mother showed him, rivalling even Mr Collins in her obsequious courtesy.

The walks were delightful to them both, and their conversation flowed freely. Mrs Wilson was a recurring topic, once they were beyond earshot of anyone else. Elizabeth was highly amused by the rhythm they created, where she would discuss the sister when she was with the brother, and vice versa. She had no doubt that, on the one fleeting visit he made to Mrs Wilson, she was the primary topic of conversation, and teased them both mercilessly to discover what they might have said. Mrs Wilson only giggled and told her it was all in her favour. Mr Darcy looked solemn and refused to tell her, although a play around his lips gave Elizabeth all the encouragement she required to press him until he finally owned to some decidedly complimentary sentiments. The three shared a peculiar kind of intimacy, having never once all been in company together, but they were all equal partners in their three-way conversation, and found a great deal of pleasure in it.

Jane was as occupied with Mr Bingley as Elizabeth was with Mr Darcy, but joined her sister one afternoon in calling on Mrs Wilson. She was received with an enthusiasm which betrayed no lingering sorrow on the latter's part. She received a still warmer welcome from the two young gentlemen, who had been out in the gardens on their arrival but now insisted on making their way indoors, commanding all of Jane's attention so rowdily that it was eventually decided the entire call would be better held in the garden. Even Tommy danced and played to see Jane again, matching his brother in liveliness although not in volume, and she found herself admiring all manner of leaves and twigs, and even a worm her young friends brought for her to see.

Elizabeth's account of the visit when she saw Mr Darcy the following morning caused him for the first time to laugh aloud in her presence, much to her delight. Although he had heard much of her lively wit, her gift for storytelling was less familiar, and he greatly enjoyed her rendering of Jane's enthusiasm at each new presentation from his young nephews. Once the retelling was done, he pressed her for more stories, and Elizabeth was incapable of refusing the eagerness with which he sought to learn all he could about her. He favoured accounts of her own antics and experiences over tales of society, teasing her for details and rewarding her with smiles that came more readily the more time they spent in one another's company.

Elizabeth, for her part, was discovering that Mr Darcy, aside from being abominably teasing when he chose to be, was a man of sober thought and strong opinions, characteristics which she admired the more as she discovered that he listened to and valued her own contributions. He was never patronising, but focused intently on her when she spoke and gave responses that were sometimes measured and thoughtful, accompanied by the caress of her hand where it habitually rested on his arm, and at other times playful, the familiar twist at the corner of his mouth on these occasions becoming a source of increasing fascination to Elizabeth.

For a time, all thought of their coming separation or the worst of Mrs Wilson's plight was set to the back of their minds, as they revelled in the happiness of their engagement and their mutual delight in one another.

Towards the middle of the week, an invitation was received for both Jane and Elizabeth to join the ladies at Netherfield for the afternoon, and afterwards to remain to dine. The gentlemen were engaged during the day but would be returning for the meal.

The promise of the evening with Mr Darcy was reason enough for Elizabeth to accept the invitation with enthusiasm, but she could not but admit to herself that she felt some curiosity regarding how Miss Bingley had reacted to the news of her engagement. She had seen nothing of the lady since the news had broken, and Mr Darcy had only stated that she had offered her congratulations without further comment. She could not imagine Miss Bingley wished to celebrate the news, and wondered whether her wit would be more pointed or her manners more sullen at events having taken a turn so different from her hopes.

As it happened, Miss Bingley greeted her with studied calm. She showed far greater civility to Jane than to Elizabeth, but her manner was polite, if entirely lacking in interest. She congratulated her on her engagement with neither a smile nor a sneer, before moving rapidly on to other topics. As they took tea, Elizabeth allowed Jane to carry the conversation, which she did without hesitation. Mr Bingley's sisters, whilst not warm, responded politely to every overture Jane made, and occasionally one of them would make a show of recognising the close relationship they would soon have. Elizabeth joined the conversation only when Jane invited her to do so, for she found she could offer little to Miss Bingley and Mrs Hurst's observations.

After tea, Jane asked Mrs Hurst about some drawings they had spoken of on her previous visit, asking whether it would be possible to see them. "Of course," Mrs Hurst replied, rising at once as if keen to leave the table. "They are in the library. Shall we view them in there?"

Jane followed her out, leaving Elizabeth wondering what form of conversation she would manage to make with Miss Bingley. To her surprise, the lady smiled at her with, if not warmth, at least some recognition of the awkwardness of the moment.

"I understand Mr Darcy is to leave Netherfield in a few days. Do you know when we should expect his return?"

"Indeed not," replied Elizabeth. "He says his business will take him away for at least a month."

"Then he will miss my brother's wedding?"

"I can only assume so."

"What a pity. I suppose, however, there is much to do to ready Pemberley for a mistress. It is such a large estate, and little has been done for its improvement in recent years."

"Indeed." Elizabeth wondered whether Miss Bingley sought to impress on her that she was unready for the management of Pemberley, but the lady's next words left her speechless.

"Yes, since poor Georgiana was married, he has hardly

had any guests, although we were fortunate enough to be invited to stop there on our way to and from the North. He was exceedingly affected by his sister choosing to marry the son of his steward, of all people. We all hated to see it, when she could have made a much better match. Mr Darcy all but withdrew from society and refused to have the marriage spoken of in his company. It was as though she had died, for he never speaks of her now. I suppose he took a house for them somewhere and tried to forget her and the connexion she made."

Elizabeth was convinced her feelings showed full upon her face, and she took a moment to control her features before replying levelly, "I am aware of his sister's marriage."

"Oh! Why of course, he need have no secrets from you, I am sure." Miss Bingley had the decency to look abashed, and paused for a moment before saying pointedly, "You need not fear my interference."

Elizabeth coughed at the unexpected words and could not find a suitable reply before Miss Bingley continued.

"Forgive my plain speaking. I shall not make Mr Darcy's life uncomfortable whilst he remains under my roof, nor do I seek to make yours so. I am not sure we shall ever be close friends, you and I, but we are likely to be in company together again, and I would not be openly at odds. He has made his choice, and I know when to withdraw from the field."

She turned her eyes on Elizabeth now and eyed her critically. "Do not think me a fool. I see no use in dissembling with you. I had hoped that having Mr Darcy to myself out in a place like this"—Elizabeth winced to hear her home so easily dismissed—"would serve me well, but I know when I am bested and when to withdraw with what is left of my dignity. It is not as though it is the first time." She muttered the last to herself, and Elizabeth felt a pang of pity. Unlike Elizabeth and her sisters, Miss Bingley had been in society and had been brought up to expect that her fortune would secure her a good match. Yet here she was, close in age to Elizabeth and with the advantage of numerous London Seasons, but still unmarried.

She consciously drove the pity from her voice as she replied, suspecting Miss Bingley would not welcome it. "Thank you for being so candid, and for your consideration." She could not trust herself to respond further.

Miss Bingley nodded, and Elizabeth marvelled that, even whilst humbling herself as she had just chosen to do, she managed to maintain such an air of condescension.

"When Charles marries, I shall depart to London with the Hursts, so if you wish to gloat, it would be better to have it all done now."

"I have no intention of gloating, and I hope you do not think I am doing so. I have never sought to compete with or slight you, and I hope we can be on good terms with one another."

Miss Bingley looked askance at this statement, as though she could not comprehend that Elizabeth would not want to make the most of her triumph in winning Mr Darcy, but she made no comment other than to smile thinly and ask whether Elizabeth cared to follow the others through to the library. Glad to put an end to an uncomfortable conversation, Elizabeth agreed, and they rose in unison.

Other than a pleasant visit by Lucy Hurst, little of note occurred in the remainder of the afternoon, and by the time Mr Bingley and Mr Darcy returned to the house, Elizabeth was feeling a little stifled by the empty politeness. She had amused herself by storing up odd moments that might serve to entertain Mrs Wilson, but found there was remarkably little for her wit to alight on.

The genuine pleasure she betrayed on Mr Darcy's joining them was rewarded with slightly embarrassed delight on his side, for although he had grown used to displaying his affection when alone, he remained reserved in company. He made his way with alacrity to sit by her side as his friend did the same to her sister. Elizabeth resisted the temptation to glance at Miss Bingley and see how she took this sign of his preference. Their conversation, whilst entirely unexpected, had made her view the lady's situation with more sympathy than she would have otherwise done, and she wished to prove, to herself as much as to Miss Bingley, that she did not view her happiness as a triumph.

With Mr Darcy's presence, Elizabeth's wit was largely restored, and she would have engaged any in the room in sparkling conversation. He, however, was determined to have her all to himself, and spoke to her quietly, leaving his hosts to fend as they would. Elizabeth indulged him freely in this until he began to ask for details of her day, when she merely smiled and raised a finger in teasing admonishment.

"None of your inquisitions today, sir! We are in company and must behave as such." So saying, she turned to Mrs Hurst and asked her about her plans regarding returning to London on her brother's marriage. Mr Darcy, after one quiet groan only audible to her ears, succumbed, and although he reverted to much of his usual gravity, engaged in the wider conversation when there was a requirement to do so.

Only after dinner, when cards were brought out for the Hursts, who persuaded Jane and Mr Bingley to join them, did Elizabeth allow Mr Darcy to again command her full attention. Miss Bingley, on the suggestion of cards, had declined, and had instead crossed the room to idly leaf through a book of illustrations left on one of the tables after the visit by Lucy Hurst. Elizabeth and Mr Darcy were left alone at the fireside, and he at once moved to sit on the sofa at her side.

"I would much rather have had you all to myself," he began, unexpectedly petulant. "We have precious little time as it is before I have to depart."

"We do," agreed Elizabeth lightly. "And you have done very well to endure it," she added, as though he were a small child. He looked at her sharply to find her eyes laughing at him, and his mouth twitched, fighting against the smile that she knew sought to break through.

"We shall have to have company sometimes, after we are married, you know," she continued. "You will not always be shutting yourself away at Pemberley."

"I thought we might consider taking a house in Hertford-shire," he replied in guarded tones.

She looked up sharply at him. "I would certainly be glad to be close to my sisters," she replied with quiet emphasis. "Although I hope we shall not always be away from Pember-ley. I long to see it for myself."

"And you will, when we are married. It will be difficult, returning alone, but I must go there for a time. I cannot always keep away from home, however much my heart might currently be in Hertfordshire."

Elizabeth did not begrudge the knowledge that even were she to be in Derbyshire at his side, a part of his heart would be in Hertfordshire yet. Her response, silent as it was, left him in no doubt hers would not be resting in Longbourn all the time he was forced to be away.

After a time, their tête-à-tête was interrupted by the sound of voices, as Mr Hurst called out, "And another game to me. You ought to count your cards better, Bingley."

"I have no great mind for cards," replied Mr Bingley,

"when we have such pleasant company for conversation. Here, Darcy, you cannot always be billing and cooing over there. There are not so many of us that we cannot all engage in conversation for a time."

Elizabeth's eyes played a merry dance at Mr Bingley, of all people, chastising his friend for acting the lover, and with a laughing smile at Mr Darcy, whose head dropped in resignation before he acquiesced with a sigh, she turned to the others to do as they were bid.

CHAPTER TWENTY-FIVE

Mr Darcy's last week in Hertfordshire passed all too quickly. He began the week with quiet good humour, but by the end of it, he was as grave as he had ever been. Elizabeth, whilst she did her best to lift his mood, could not disguise her own feelings regarding his coming departure.

"It will be so strange after you have gone. I have grown used to your company and conversation on my walks. I shall miss you so."

"I am deeply sorry to be leaving you here. If it were not —" he left the words hanging, and Elizabeth squeezed his arm compassionately.

"I understand. The longer you stay, the greater the risk. And it is important to you that Pemberley enjoys your presence once in a while."

"I have never been so reluctant to return there. Even in recent years, Pemberley has been a steadfast companion. It will not have changed, but I have. I shall be leaving a part of myself behind in Hertfordshire."

"Perhaps then, you will be comforted if you know a small part of Hertfordshire travels with you." Seeing that this thought only seemed to make him inclined to be more maudlin, Elizabeth added, "Perhaps a small box of soil would serve the purpose?"

This brought the required acknowledgement, in the form of a short laugh, but they each felt the impending separation came too soon, was to last too long, and was far too uncertain. Silence fell between them, not uncomfortable, but the result of each being occupied with their own thoughts. Eventually, Mr Darcy spoke again, with a solemnity that seemed sepulchral to Elizabeth's ears.

"I shall leave the address of my cousin, Colonel Fitzwilliam, with you. If Wickham should enter the neighbourhood, you may tell your father all if you think it best. I have spoken to Georgiana on the subject, and she agrees that you may do so. Please also write to both me and my cousin by express. Fitzwilliam is in London at present and may be able to reach you more rapidly." He hastily sketched out a description of his cousin's appearance, dwelling particularly on an injury to his leg that would mark him out, then continued, "I shall give him this ring"—he indicated a signet ring he wore—"as a token, so you will know him. He can be trusted."

"I hope these are unnecessary precautions," she replied as lightly as she could manage, although her voice caught.

He stopped and drew her to him. "As do I. But I must make them. You understand that?"

Elizabeth nodded and, feeling tears rising, leant her head against his shoulder. He lifted a hand to her hair, and they stood together, neither speaking. Eventually, Elizabeth pulled away and smiled up at him, her eyes brighter but still glistening.

"This is not how I would part from you," she murmured.

"Nor I. Let us speak of other things." They turned and continued their walk, but despite their intentions, neither felt inclined to converse, and it was some time before they began again.

When the time of Mr Darcy's departure came, Elizabeth presented him with a handkerchief embroidered with his initials entwined with hers. "Do not look too closely at the handiwork," she told him, "for I cannot be accountable for the quality of my embroidery in such a week as this has been."

Mr Darcy traced it with his fingers. "I am sure I have seen none finer," he replied, deliberately covering with his thumb the corner, where the thread had caught. Elizabeth laughed, as gaily as she could, and thanked him with teasing sweetness for the undeserved praise.

He fished out his own handkerchief. "I had not thought of tokens. But perhaps you may like this in return for yours." She took it and admired the neat lettering of the embroidery in the corner. "It was sewn for me a few years ago," he commented, watching her, "by someone who is very dear to me."

Elizabeth looked up at him quickly. "You have others?" He nodded. She accepted the handkerchief gladly but could not prevent tears gathering in her eyes at the prospect of his absence. She stepped closer and embraced him, leaning her head against his shoulder and breathing in the scent of his clothes. She was comforted to feel his arms encircle her, holding her close.

After a moment, she heard his voice, low and close to her ear. "Elizabeth."

She lifted her chin to meet his eyes and found them close to her own, looking at her tenderly. "Elizabeth," he said again, his voice aching. His lips came down towards hers, hesitating briefly as he searched her eyes for permission to continue, until Elizabeth lifted her mouth to meet his. The warmth of the kiss spread through her, and she tightened her grasp, clinging to him and savouring the new sensations it brought. When they broke apart, she was momentarily stunned, and simply gazed at him, her eyes round. He smiled reassuringly, and after a moment followed it with a short laugh.

"I shall savour the memory of this moment," he said, running a thumb across her cheek, then leaning in closer to murmur in her ear again. "For the kiss—" he chuckled, a hand pressing warmly against her back when she shivered, "and because it may be the only time I shall ever render you speechless."

Such a remark ought not to be allowed to pass without retaliation, but with their parting looming, Elizabeth was content to only return the compliment in kind, rising on tiptoe and silencing him from further teasing with another kiss. She settled back on her heels with an eyebrow raised in challenge, but he merely lifted the back of his hand to her cheek again. "I love you," he said, his voice cracking slightly. "I love you," he repeated more firmly.

"And I love you," she returned, prompting that quirk of his lips which now spoke to her not only of repressed smiles, but of a promise of future kisses.

It was with some reluctance that they returned to the house.

AFTER MR DARCY'S DEPARTURE, Elizabeth found she was not left to indulge any tender feelings for long. Mrs Bennet had an extensive list of tasks to complete ahead of

Mary and Jane's weddings, and Elizabeth threw herself into the preparations with a will. Mr Collins arrived at Longbourn a week before his wedding, accompanied by a tired-looking woman who carried in her arms a small, wide-eyed child. He greeted Mrs Bennet and Mary with every flourish he could muster, and his remaining cousins with a combination of condescension and flattery of which Elizabeth had never seen the like.

Mrs Bennet and Mr Collins made all that could be made of his arrival, fretting over rooms and other arrangements, and it was some time before the family reconvened to sit with their guest. Once they were settled, however, Mr Collins turned with great dignity to the nurse, who had hitherto been left largely to her own devices but had complied with the instruction to bring his son to join the family.

"Give me the child," he commanded her. The nurse silently made to do as she was bid, but the boy wriggled and sobbed at being taken from the comfort of her arms, and Mr Collins could not get sufficient purchase to take him. He attempted to command the boy to come to him, then to cajole, although in tones little more conciliatory than the commands. As his frustration grew, his voice grew louder, and young William, startled by the increased noise, clung still tighter to his nurse.

Elizabeth felt desperately sorry for the child, and even a little for her cousin, for he evidently did not know how to begin endearing himself to his son. She could feel Jane trembling at her elbow, each of them desperate to intervene but neither of them feeling they had any right to do so.

Elizabeth had just resolved she must do something to help matters, when she was astonished to see Mary standing abruptly and crossing to take a seat by the nurse. Mary herself appeared no less surprised; having done so much, she sat rigidly still, her eyes on the child but making no move to take or speak to him.

"My dear!" Mr Collins exclaimed. His attention, like that of all in the room, had been arrested by Mary's action.

"I must learn to be a mother, sir. It might begin at once," Mary said quietly. The nurse, hearing these words, looked fearfully at Mr Collins, who seemed momentarily perplexed. He was not a man to be long silenced, however, and soon found his voice.

"My dear Mary! This is just the excellence I recognised in you almost as soon as I saw you, and which led me to choose you for my lifetime companion. Lady Catherine de Bourgh was so good before I left Kent to tell me I ought to prepare you for being a mother as soon as possible. 'For Mr Collins,' said she, 'none know better than I the travails of mother-hood, and your wife will need to be a motherly sort of person to bring up another woman's child.' She is always so atten-tive to such matters!"

Mary did not reply, although a look of slight alarm had crossed her face. She held a hand out tentatively to the child, who had fallen silent since the threat of being removed from the arms of his nurse had receded.

"William," she greeted him sincerely as she cautiously touched his cheek. The boy merely looked at her, making no movement to either respond or to resist. Mr Collins launched into a lengthier explanation of Lady Catherine's advice on raising a child, not observing his future wife's inattention. She was cautious, and glanced often at Jane or her mother for confirmation that her approaches to the child were accept-able, but she persisted in her attempts at attending to her future son.

Mary's attempts to build an attachment to her child continued over the days preceding her wedding. Although young William was far from happy when not with his nurse, a small advancement came when Mary requested he sit nearby as she played the pianoforte. She found in the boy an enthusiastic audience, who made no objection to either mistakes or to endless repetition and would crow loudly at the merest sound from the keys.

His only discernment, Elizabeth noted with a smile, appeared to be a preference for livelier tunes, an inclination which, whilst not exactly in line with her own, Mary appeared willing to indulge for the sake of the response she received from her juvenile audience. Mr Collins would sit by, nodding condescendingly at his son with his new mother and occasionally seeing fit to inform them of Lady Catherine's opinion on some trifling matter or other.

MARY'S WEDDING day dawned clear and bright, and happy were the feelings of mother and daughter at the prospect of a future secured. Mrs Bennet's thoughts on the minutiae of Mary's wedding day were interspersed with happy premonitions of standing on the steps of Longbourn, gracious hostess to her son and daughter Collins.

Mary's own feelings on the marriage were remarkably settled, and although she too looked at Longbourn with fond ideas of her return, she had confided to Elizabeth her great, if somewhat vague, hopes for the part she might play in Hunsford. She looked forward to quiet evenings devoted to learning from her husband and, as the benign lady of the Parsonage, days spent imparting her own largesse and wisdom to the people of the village. Elizabeth was grateful Mary was not entirely lost to pragmatism, however, for stowed in her luggage alongside her book of favourite sermons was a small collection of recipes, discreetly presented to her by Mrs Hill and the cook that morning. The book contained some that would be familiar to Mary, who, after seriously assessing all she might need to do following her marriage, had quietly sought some lessons on the management of a household with fewer servants than she was accustomed to.

Mr Collins's feelings on the marriage were the subject of a long and tiresome speech that he made no fewer than three times between rising and the hour of his departure with his new wife. They were to return directly to Hunsford, his leave of absence not extending to a further Sunday away from his duties. Altogether, although the departure of Mrs Collins caused some genuine tears to be shed amongst her family, even Mrs Bennet joined in the hearty collective sigh of relief as Mr Collins turned away from his final parting salutations.

The residents of Longbourn were not left for long to feel the loss of Mary. Jane had insisted she would not overshadow her sister still further by combining the two weddings, so the space of a fortnight had been allowed between one marriage and the next. Although many of the preparations had taken place side by side, final details had still to be settled, and the day after parting from Mrs Collins, her mother was alive with preparations for the future Mrs Bingley.

Elizabeth, although she did not entirely neglect her friends or her correspondence, was almost as occupied as Jane and Mrs Bennet by preparations on behalf of her most beloved sister. The fortnight passed with such rapidity that she wondered at the end of it how she had so little noticed the elapse of two whole weeks.

Miss Bennet became Mrs Bingley in due course. It was universally agreed that the bride outshone any other in living memory, both in her beauty and in the radiance of her happiness. Mrs Bennet looked on with satisfaction, and Jane with admiration, at how fine Mr Bingley looked in his new coat, standing at her side. Elizabeth was swept away in her delight for Jane, setting aside Mr Darcy's absence and immersing herself fully in all the joy of the day.

After two nights at Netherfield, Mr and Mrs Bingley departed Hertfordshire for a short visit to London, followed by a tour north to meet Mr Bingley's family. With them went Kitty, who they were to carry to the Gardiners' home in London. The Hursts and Miss Bingley had departed from the wedding breakfast, and Netherfield was left empty once again.

At Longbourn, the sudden change from five daughters to two affected all the remaining family, and for some days the house and its occupants were subdued. Even Lydia seemed to feel the loss of Kitty, although she bore a sulky air at her sister being taken to London when she was not. Elizabeth felt Jane's loss sorely and found herself heading more frequently than ever to visit her friends. Charlotte would often join her on her visits to Mrs Wilson, and Elizabeth found that promoting the developing friendship between her oldest friend and her newest assisted her in adjusting to her suddenly much reduced society.

CHAPTER TWENTY-SIX

Following so many departures in rapid succession, there was a marked increase in the quantity of correspondence entered into by the inhabitants of Longbourn.

Elizabeth and Mr Darcy settled into a regular routine, and she came to time her weeks by the days where she sat down to write and those where she would receive a letter addressed in his even hand. She regaled him with stories of daily life at Longbourn and the comings and goings of her family; he, in return, wrote long missives detailing some of his daily life and the preparations required for Pemberley to receive a mistress. As promised, she also wrote to him with news of his sister, although they were both careful not to name her, unwilling to risk her exposure more than was necessary, even in a private letter.

Their correspondence was not merely an account of the happenings of their own lives, however, but a continuation of the conversations of their week of courtship. Elizabeth found she liked having Mr Darcy as a correspondent. His letters, whilst primarily characterised by thoughtfulness and pragma-tism with only the briefest of forays into entertainment or romance, confirmed her belief that he was a man of good sense. He shared his thoughts freely on the topics they discussed and spent time exploring any opinions she expressed, explaining his views without condescension when they differed from hers. He also sought her views on various matters of household management that might be expected to require a contribution from the mistress of the estate.

Whether he had learnt the lesson of his proposal or whether he merely expressed himself more readily on paper, a portion of each letter was always devoted to tender words of his regard. He made no secret of his gratitude for his sister's sake, but also wrote with great affection of Eliza-beth's intelligence, the pleasure he found in conversing with her, and even, in a moment of particular effusiveness, decried that her letters left him dependent on his own memory to recall the captivating expression of her eyes.

All of Mr Darcy's affection, however, could not prevent the need to extend his absence for a further month. The letter in which he informed her of this necessity was full of regret and, though it gave her no particulars, left no doubt as to the reason for the extension.

Nothing would keep me away from you, Elizabeth, but the happiness of one other person I hold dear. I have been attempting to gather information to prevent any unpleasant surprises. The extension of my recent stay in Hertfordshire allowed some enquiries I had set in motion to become mired in confusion, but I believe I now have some credible information which I strongly hope will allow us to guard against any unexpected arrivals. I intend to oversee the investigation into the matter, and I could be required to travel at short notice.

I may become a less regular correspondent for a time. Do not think the worst if this is the case. I shall put arrangements in place to ensure your letters reach me, but I may have fewer opportunities for writing.

As though making a silent apology for this news, the paragraph was followed by some particularly warm sentiments on Mr Darcy's part that Elizabeth soon came to learn by heart.

It is lonely, on my travels, my loveliest Elizabeth, and I find myself thinking back to the days I spent walking at your side, and forward to the days I shall spend with you living by my side, for the rest of our days. I did not know, when I entered Hertfordshire, that I would be finding a light I would happily follow, a life I am eager to cleave to, a heart I consider it my greatest privilege to call mine. Yet these are what I have found. I could not have believed, before meeting you, that such a perfect combination of kindness and compassion, intelligence and wit could exist, yet I have found it does, in you. More than that, all of these virtues I so admire are contained in a person as delightful as I could have ever hoped to know. Have I told you yet, my dearest, how beautiful you are? I know I have called your eyes captivating, but have I confessed why I find them so? Let me attempt to do so for a moment. Allow me to tell you, as I ought to have done when I failed so dreadfully to present my suit, of your manifold beauties.

I have never been insensible of the attractions of your person, although I confess I would not allow myself to properly perceive them at the start of our acquaintance. Absence and longing have made me bold, and so I shall start with the most scandalous: your figure, whether dancing, walking, or held close in our brief embraces, is entirely pleasing. Your simple and unstudied elegance has made

*dancing or walking with you a pleasure I could never forgo, even
were it not to be augmented with the delights of your conversation.
Taking your hand in mine, having it rest lightly on my arm, feels as
natural as breathing, and I miss it every day that I am apart from
you. None of this, however, compares to the beauty of your countenance. I shall endeavour to avoid any trite descriptions of your
cheeks, or your lips, or your eyes, but each of them is a study in itself
that I cannot tire of tracing in my mind. I long to again have the
pleasure of seeing you before me, that I might feel the soft line of
your cheek, taste the eager, tantalising press of your lips, and lose
myself in the light and expression of your incomparable eyes. I regret
that I had no time to have a miniature of you taken before I travelled, but in truth no pen or brush could do you justice.*

*Do not think that these sentiments replace my admiration for your
fine qualities of heart and mind; without these, you would not be
yourself, and I love you for them. But do not doubt that it is all of
you, body and mind, that I love. I will return to you, and soon, I
hope, and although there may still be many trials ahead, I shall be
better able to face them with you, my darling, at my side.*

Such a letter could only heighten the loss she felt at his
absence, but she would not blame him for his need to protect
his sister. She only wished, helpless as she was, that she
could do more to support them both, and take away the ever-
present shadow looming over them.

Mr Darcy's letters were eagerly awaited by Elizabeth, but
of interest to the whole family were the letters received from
the three daughters who had recently departed the house.
Each packet from Jane included separate letters to both her
mother and Elizabeth, and frequently also for Mr Bennet or
Lydia. Jane's letters to Elizabeth were full of her happiness
and warm praise of her dear Charles, alongside sweet expres-

sions of hope for Elizabeth's own future felicity. To Mrs Bennet, Jane wrote primarily of her social engagements and gowns, and her mother made much of every word. No social call between Mrs Bennet and her particular circle of friends was complete without all the ladies present speaking familiarly and fondly of Mrs Bingley of Netherfield Park.

Of Mrs Collins they spoke with perhaps less fondness but no less interest. Although Mrs Bennet was inclined to dwell on the happy thought that Mary had secured the future of Longbourn for the family, the more clear-sighted amongst her friends were conscious that she should expect to have many years ahead of her as mistress of a country parsonage. Mary's letters, addressed always to her mother but including without fail a particular message to each of the other occupants of Longbourn, contained detailed accounts of the house, of young William, and of Mary's new responsibilities. Lady Catherine de Bourgh appeared in sundry mentions, which collectively served to demonstrate that she was as attentive a patron as Mr Collins had intimated. Mary made no complaint, but Elizabeth wondered how her sister could bear the officious commands of the noble lady at every mention of Lady Catherine's advice, which ranged from insisting on changes to their regular orders from the grocer to the suggestion that Mary ought to learn to draw, and covering every point in between.

Lady Catherine's guidance apparently did not extend merely to the couple at the parsonage but to all their relations, whom, according to Mary's letters, their patroness had enquired closely about. Mrs Bennet sniffed and exclaimed through these parts of the letters, and Elizabeth hoped, rather than believed, that she restrained herself from pouring out her protestations into her replies to Mary. Elizabeth was also highly amused to discover that *she* appeared to be a subject of particular disdain for the lady. The cause of this was clear from a passage in one of Mary's earliest letters:

> Lady Catherine was most kind about Jane's marriage and suggested that were Mrs Bingley to have cause to visit us in Kent, she would be willing to receive her call as my guest. I fear, however, that Lizzy's match does not meet with her approbation. When I informed her that she was engaged to Mr Darcy, Lady Catherine sat for a moment wholly silent, in a manner such as I have never seen, before informing us that Lizzy might do as she pleased, but that she would have no part in it. I cannot think why this would be, but she would not say anything more on the matter, and we were not invited to dine with her the following week, but she now appears to welcome us again and enquires most particularly about Jane, Kitty, and Lydia whenever we see her.

Mr Bennet had some sport at the idea that Lady Catherine de Bourgh might have considered herself as having had any part in the engagement to begin with, until Elizabeth explained the connexion and that there had been a breach between the lady and Mr Darcy some years before. Her father was surprised and amused to learn of their relationship, and it was with some difficulty that Elizabeth was able to extract from him a promise not to write to Mary or Mr Collins on the subject. The promise was at last given, but was not without cost, for Elizabeth was forced to endure many jests by her father on the subject.

One happier outcome of Lady Catherine's excessive interest in the activities of the family at the parsonage was that she had insisted Mr Collins purchase a small pianoforte that happened to be on sale from the effects of a local spinster in the village.

Lady Catherine insisted on the purchase. There are a number of instruments at Rosings Park, although I have not heard that either Miss de Bourgh or Lady Catherine play, and she had graciously invited me to use the pianoforte in Miss de Bourgh's companion's room. She informed me I would trouble no one, but I fear she must have then changed her mind, for after only two visits to play as invited, Lady Catherine became insistent that it was my husband's duty to provide me with an instrument. It was fortunate that one could be found so cheaply. Young William sits by me, clapping his hands with the music, and I find it does not distract me after having so long played with the sounds of Longbourn all around me. I have offered to play for Miss de Bourgh, for music can be such sweet solace to an invalid, and Lady Catherine tells me she has a deep appreciation for it. However, I have not been encouraged to do so. I am yet to meet Miss de Bourgh, for she is suffering from a serious bout of illness that keeps her to her room. Lady Catherine is convinced she will recover soon, and I hope to be able to play for her then.

Kitty's letters were the shortest of the three, and the most irregular. Initially, they boasted of her delight in the whirl of social calls, plays, and dresses in a manner so pointedly designed to vex Lydia that she refused after the first week to hear a word of them read. Over time, however, there were indications that the separation from her sister, the influence of Mrs Gardiner, and perhaps a longing for home were beginning to affect Kitty. Whilst her letters were still full of the delights of her London experience, they lost some of their gloating tone and began to demonstrate an interest in the activities and concerns of the Longbourn residents.

The loss of three Bennet sisters and the Netherfield party was not without effect on the wider Meryton society. Miss Bingley and the Hursts were not regretted, and Mr Darcy's absence was mostly notable for the fact it left Elizabeth in that undesirable situation of a long engagement. As Mr Bingley's manners and amiability had made him popular in the community, however, and as Jane was universally liked, they were much missed. Even the absence of Mary and Kitty, although not as highly regarded as their eldest sister, was felt, for although Mrs Bennet would object to any suggestion that their society was small, the loss of two of their number meant a corresponding loss of two points of interest.

Meryton seemed to be settling into a period of some dullness, and it was therefore with great enthusiasm that Mrs Philips made an announcement to her sister over tea one afternoon. "Have you heard? There are two new gentlemen come to town!"

With two daughters still without marriage prospects, Mrs Bennet was all attention in a moment. "New gentlemen! Well, I am sure we are always ready to welcome newcomers."

Mrs Philips needed no more encouragement to tell what little she knew. "They are a Mr Jackson and a Mr Grey. They have taken lodgings for two months, although they are likely to stay longer."

Mrs Bennet's mouth twisted at the news they had not taken the great house at Stoke, or at least the smaller Ashworth. "And are they respectable gentlemen?"

"Sir William Lucas has called on them. I have encouraged Mr Philips to do so, but he delights in vexing me! Lady Lucas believes they are perfectly respectable, if not of extensive means."

Mrs Bennet's mind digested this information. She would have expected something greater for Lydia and Kitty, in the light of Jane's marriage and Elizabeth's engagement.

"Well, Sir William may do as he pleases. Perhaps one of them will take a fancy to Miss Lucas, although I cannot see she is likely to marry now. I, for one, shall not be throwing my daughters at these two gentlemen just because they are newly arrived. Why, we know nothing of them, nor why they chose to come to Meryton."

"Indeed, Sister," replied Mrs Philips. "They might be rakes or rogues!"

"Indeed!"

Mrs Bennet's eyes gleamed. By the time she and her daughters were seated in the carriage home, she was convinced the two newcomers were romantic heroes. Lydia was entirely ready to participate in her mother's vision, speculating that they were highwaymen or bandits and imagining herself caught up by some dashing rake before converting him from his wicked ways.

Elizabeth, not in the least inclined to participate in this particular flight of fancy, did what she could to bring her mother and sister to speak sensibly, but was eventually forced to give it up as a lost cause. Instead of enduring the conversation for the rest of the ride home, however, she asked to be let out where the road divided to pass Lucas Lodge, and with great relief made her way on foot the last distance to call on Charlotte and have some sensible conversation.

CHAPTER TWENTY-SEVEN

Mrs Bennet did not have to wait long to meet the new arrivals in Meryton, for an invitation was soon received from Mrs Philips to an evening gathering. A visit from the same lady followed, confirming that her husband had called on the gentlemen, who were also expected to attend.

"So, you will get to meet them after all, dear sister! I must admit, I am curious. It is so rare that anyone new arrives, yet this year we have been inundated with newcomers! Although Longbourn has had an unfair share of the attention. Perhaps I ought not to invite you at all, to allow the rest of society a turn!"

"I am sure I do not know what you mean! Of course Mr Bingley did take to Jane ever so quickly, and Mr Collins to Mary, and then of course Mr Darcy—"

"Indeed, Sister. Every new gentleman in town has proposed to one of your daughters!"

Mrs Bennet, very willing to be reminded of her good fortune, would have continued the conversation in this vein, but Mrs Philips was full of the newcomers and what their business might be in Meryton, and her sister was soon drawn into the conversation.

As she stepped into her aunt's drawing room, it felt to Elizabeth as though all of Meryton must have turned out for the event, for the room was crowded. She made her way around the edge as best she could to Charlotte, stopping every few steps to return the greeting of some neighbour or other. When she reached her friend, she was immensely grateful to see that she had somehow reserved her a seat, and dropped gratefully into it.

"I do not think I have ever seen Aunt Philips's drawing room so busy!" she exclaimed, her eyes scanning the people in the room.

"It is certainly a large turnout for an evening gathering, although I think I can guess the reason." Charlotte indicated the far corner of the room, where two gentlemen stood.

"Ah, the strangers!" Elizabeth replied. "I am afraid Lydia will be disappointed. They do not look like romantic heroes."

"What does a romantic hero look like?" asked Charlotte with a teasing smile.

"Oh, I could hardly say. Dark, perhaps, and brooding. With a flashing eye and a dashing smile."

Charlotte laughed. "You have read more novels than you admit. But I agree that these gentlemen do not meet that description."

Indeed, they did not. They were both well dressed, although the taller of the two, who Charlotte informed her was Mr Jackson, had clothes of a cut and fabric that suggested he was the wealthier. He had a fine countenance and figure, but with a slight redness around the face that made Elizabeth think of Mr Hurst. Unlike that gentleman, however, he spoke with his immediate neighbours with what appeared from a distance to be an air of engaging charm. Mr Grey was both less handsome and less florid than his companion but was also readily engaging in conversation.

It was well into the evening before Elizabeth was introduced to either of the men. Although always ready to make new acquaintances, life had become too eventful for her to have any unusual interest in them. When they did eventually meet, she found Mr Jackson had an undeniably pleasing appearance, but that the redness of his visage was more pronounced. Whether this was due to their greater proximity or was in tribute to her aunt and uncle's hospitality, she could not have said. She was also able to see that his clothes, whilst fine, bore signs of wear that suggested they were not of recent make. Mr Grey's clothes, in contrast, were less expensive but were in better condition. They were all things pleasant—Mr Jackson could even be considered charming—and they engaged Elizabeth and Charlotte in easy conversation. Elizabeth, accustomed to sketching the characters of the people she met, found them perfectly agreeable companions and entirely uninteresting.

Elizabeth was soon after this accosted by her aunt to join a card table and, after some confusion as the various players took their seats, found herself seated near Mr Jackson, who smiled winningly at her and remarked with good humour, "I shall do my best this evening, but you must forgive me if I play ill. When I am amongst new people, I am always keen to get to know them, to the detriment of my attention to the game."

"Do you find yourself amongst new people often, Mr Jackson?"

"More often than I would like. It has been my fate to roam the land in recent years, although I hope to settle in one place soon and come to Meryton in the hopes of making that possible. I had heard a house here might be to let, but I have discovered this evening it was taken earlier this year, so my visit might be in vain."

"I hope you find somewhere suitable," Elizabeth replied. She turned her attention back to the game, but Mr Jackson seemed intent on conversation.

"I think Netherfield would have suited me perfectly, but I hear the current tenant intends to stay in the area, having married a local lady."

"Indeed, sir, that is Mr Bingley's intention."

"Did I hear correctly that his bride was your sister?"

"Yes," Elizabeth said, "they are currently in the North, visiting Mr Bingley's family."

"Ah. I also heard," he offered a particularly charming smile, "that you are to be congratulated on your own engagement to a friend of Mr Bingley's, Miss Bennet. Please allow me, although a stranger, to offer my warmest felicitations."

"Thank you." Elizabeth's smile warmed as she thought of Mr Darcy.

"Is your betrothed not here this evening?"

"Regrettably not." It being Elizabeth's turn to play, she turned her eyes to her cards as she spoke. After a moment, he too turned back to focus on playing, chatting with another of his neighbours and demonstrating a skill which belied his early claim of being unable to both converse and play.

Lydia, who had declined cards and had instead been laughing loudly in the corner of the room with some of the younger gentlemen, appeared to grow bored of their conversation and came and sat by her sister, offering advice in a too-loud whisper on which cards she ought to play. She soon grew tired of this, too, and loudly exclaimed, "Laws, Lizzy, I hope there will be more to do when Mr Darcy returns and marries you. Then you can take me to London for some real entertainment!"

Elizabeth winced at Lydia's speech and hoped that those around her would be good enough not to acknowledge it. Mr Jackson, however, did speak.

"Darcy! I have heard that name before. Not the same Darcy, I suppose, of Pemberley in Derbyshire?" he asked.

"Yes," Elizabeth replied, "that is Mr Darcy's estate."

"And you are to be married to him! You are indeed to be congratulated. It is reported to be particularly grand. An estate to be proud of, by all accounts."

"I have yet to see it, sir."

"Ah. Of course. I hope you will not be deprived of his company for too long."

"His return date is not settled." Elizabeth was finding this interest in Mr Darcy a little peculiar, but as Mr Jackson appeared to accept this answer and returned to the game, thought little more of it.

Elizabeth wrote to Mr Darcy of the newcomers and of her impressions of them, but received no reply. It did not unduly concern her; he had, after all, told her to expect less regularity in his letters. He had hinted that he had tracked Mr Wickham's location, and the knowledge that he was working with such determination to protect his sister soothed any anxieties she may have had.

The two gentlemen appeared settled in Meryton, and their affable manners meant they were widely welcomed. It soon became known that, although Netherfield could not be had, Mr Jackson sought another house in Hertfordshire, or perhaps in one of the surrounding counties. The gentlemen would disappear on long excursions that lasted well into the evening, and it was widely discussed that they were visiting suitable properties.

The Bennet ladies found the gentlemen pleasant enough company. Mrs Bennet had no aversion to either of them marrying one of her daughters, but her recent successes had made her less inclined to pursue a match of no obvious grandeur, so she saw no reason to encourage Lydia into their notice. Elizabeth found them amiable and sufficiently charming, but neither sought their attention nor received it in any unusual amount. Lydia, however, felt otherwise, and was often to be found at one or other of their sides when they met, laughing at some joke or listening to their stories. Elizabeth saw no particular interest from the gentlemen to cause alarm, but neither did they appear to object to having a young lady so eager to place herself before their notice, and both dispensed their charm and conversation freely. She wished that Lydia would be more circumspect, but knew any attempt to influence her would be met with resistance so contented herself with quietly observing her sister's behaviour for the time being.

Watching Lydia did not stop Elizabeth from collecting impressions of the events she attended to share with Mrs Wilson. She told her tales with animation, always bringing a smile to her friend's face. She had been paler and more anxious since the departure of her brother from the area. He may have been concerned that his presence would draw Mr Wickham to the neighbourhood, but Elizabeth could see the security that his proximity had also given her friend, and her heart ached to see her need for such comfort.

She told Mrs Wilson of the newcomers and, nervous to broach the subject, asked whether there were any Jacksons or Greys amongst Mr Wickham's associates.

"Not that I am aware of," Mrs Wilson replied quietly. "Although I hardly met any of them, and I could not say either way with any conviction."

"Mr Jackson mentioned he had heard of Fitzwilliam, but I suppose that cannot be uncommon?"

"I hardly know. Before I was married, I think Fitzwilliam was considered one of the prizes of the marriage market," she added with a sly grin.

"Luckily for him, I am his equal in all things," Elizabeth replied solemnly. "Why, I was once gifted an apple by the most popular boy in Meryton. I was the envy of all my set, for he was six and quite the catch for a four-year-old such as I. Regrettably, I spoiled the moment by taking a bite, announcing that I hated apples, and throwing it onto the floor. I do hope Fitzwilliam is better behaved."

"No wonder he never married you if you spurned his gift!" Mrs Wilson laughed. "Whatever happened to him? Ought I to be jealous on Fitzwilliam's behalf?"

"I believe you can be easy on that point. He is now the blacksmith, and is married with four adorable children."

In the absence of her brother, Mrs Wilson took more comfort in such whimsical conversations than in tales of life beyond Purvis Lodge, and so Elizabeth delighted in indulging her with stories of childhood misadventures, and they spoke little more of the new arrivals. Elizabeth was glad of conversation with her friends, for at Longbourn, companionship was severely restricted since the marriage of her dearest sister. She was, inevitably, more often in Lydia's company, but their common interests were few, and conversation was cumbersome until they eventually settled on discussing the news from their sisters' letters. In this, they found a subject they could both take enjoyment from, and on days a letter was received, they found themselves actively seeking one another's company to share what news they contained.

One evening, they were to attend a small dinner at Lucas Lodge. Elizabeth had arranged to spend the day with Charlotte, so had missed letters from both Jane and Mary. Lydia was in high spirits in the early part of the evening and spent it laughing gaily with a number of the gentlemen present. After dinner, however, she made her way to Elizabeth's side.

"Lizzy, you missed two letters today. Only Kitty did not write. If it were not for Aunt Gardiner, we would know nothing of how she fares!"

"Oh, I am sorry to have missed them. What did they have to say? Did Jane mention whether they have travelled to visit Mr Bingley's uncle, or did they decide to extend their stay with his cousin?"

Lydia immediately began repeating all of Jane's news in great depth, her flow of words sufficiently entertaining that it drew the attention of one or two of those seated nearby. After a time, she exhausted her memory, and Elizabeth was able to speak for long enough to ask after Mary's news.

"Oh, she is well enough. Most of her letter was about an illness young William has had. It was frightfully dull."

"Oh! Poor child. Has he recovered?"

"Oh yes, he is quite well again. Beyond that, she mentioned Lady Catherine half a dozen times, and Mr Collins only twice! What a bore it must be to be married to him!"

"Lydia!"

"I know you think so too! Oh, but she did have one funny piece of news! She has finally met Lady Catherine's daughter...what was her name? Oh, it is not important—"

"Anne," interjected Elizabeth.

"Oh yes. Anne de Bourgh. Such a plain forename for a pretty surname. Mary was saying she spent the entire evening puzzling because she thought she reminded her of someone but could not place who. Then it came to her. Can you guess?"

"Not at all."

"Well, it was your friend! Mrs Wilson! She says Mrs Wilson is taller, but they are both so pale and have just the same features. She said that once she had realised it, she mentioned it to Mr Collins, and although he had only seen Mrs Wilson once, he quite agrees! Isn't that peculiar?"

Elizabeth had not realised the danger in time. Lady Catherine was Mr Darcy and Mrs Wilson's aunt, and Anne de Bourgh their cousin. Resemblance between such close relations was not unknown, but Elizabeth would have wished that Miss de Bourgh looked more like a de Bourgh cousin rather than like her friend.

"Most peculiar indeed," she said, as easily as she could manage. "I suppose it can happen that two people can look uncommonly alike, even if they are entirely unconnected." Although Elizabeth knew it was impossible to attempt to suppress talk about Mrs Wilson, and that any attempt to do so would only draw attention to her friend, she preferred not to engage with it any more than was absolutely required. This was all the more important when it could risk her friend's secret being discovered. She glanced around those seated nearby, but Lady Lucas and Mrs Long were deep in conversation and made no sign they had heard or took any interest in Lydia's speeches. Mr Jackson, although he also sat nearby, was engrossed in admiring some sketches in a book on the table.

As Elizabeth looked his way, he glanced up. "My apologies, I was taken by these drawings. Did you address me?"

"No," Elizabeth smiled, relieved that no one appeared to have heard the conversation. She was not sorry to change the topic, however, and readily took the opportunity offered. "I did not, but since we are speaking, the sketches are wonderful, I agree. I believe they were mostly drawn by Miss Lucas's sister Mrs Ellsworth, before she was married."

"She has an excellent eye. There are many views here that I am yet to encounter in the neighbourhood. Perhaps I ought to spend some more time locally and try to discover some of them."

"I do not believe they are all to be found in Hertfordshire, but there is much to admire in the view from Oakham Mount." She did not think there were any views that were close to Purvis Lodge and was immensely grateful that the best vistas lay in the entirely opposite direction.

"Thank you for the recommendation. I do believe I shall make some time to explore locally. It would be a shame to live here for any length of time and not know the immediate vicinity."

"Would you like me to describe where the views in the drawings are, Mr Jackson?" interrupted Lydia, not wanting to be left out of the conversation. "That might help you to find them." He thanked her gratefully, and Lydia, needing no further encouragement, promptly moved to a chair by the table where she could examine the pictures more closely.

CHAPTER TWENTY-EIGHT

Sir William Lucas took great pride in his position as a leader in his community. He was therefore highly pleased to be able to announce that another assembly was planned in Meryton, as well as immensely gratified by the general welcome that the news received.

The preparations for this assembly caused significantly less disturbance at Longbourn than the momentous one where Jane and Elizabeth first danced with Mr Bingley and Mr Darcy, but Mrs Bennet could not be entirely restrained from old habits. Mr Darcy not being likely to return in time to attend, Elizabeth found her mother was once again willing to overlook her appearance to a great extent. Lydia, however, was thrown into her usual frenzy of preparations, and she and Mrs Bennet between them made as much noise as though all the sisters were still at home. Lydia took to going to Meryton almost every afternoon to purchase trimmings, until Elizabeth dreaded what her father's reaction would be when the bills were sent in.

Elizabeth again found refuge in the quiet companionship

of her friends, and they settled into a regular routine, Charlotte usually accompanying her to call on Mrs Wilson. They would be greeted warmly by the household servants, who since her engagement had treated Elizabeth as though she were already Mrs Darcy. Mrs Carmichael went so far as to ask to speak to her on one visit, where she thanked her for making her 'young missus' so much happier. "Forgive me for speaking out of turn, ma'am, but I have known her since she was just a mite, and she is another creature. She was always such a solemn, lonely child, and I have never heard her laugh so much as when you are by. When the master returns, it will be a pleasure to see you as his wife." Elizabeth found much to be pleased with in this vote of confidence, and resolved anew to be everything she could to both her husband and his sister.

Often, the boys would be in attendance, and Elizabeth would bring Jane's letters so she could read out excerpts, which Jane never forgot to include, addressed to Mrs Wilson and her sons. She sent her kindest regards to the mother and particular tales and observations specifically for the children.

"I do not know how Jane does it, Lizzy. She never forgets us in her letters, and she must be so very busy."

"Oh, Jane is a wonder. No one has a larger heart, and it just seems to grow with everyone she meets. I can only hope I shall be so attentive to my friends when I am married!"

"You need not have any concerns about me. I shall write to you daily whether you write back or not. I am quite resigned to being an old maid and shall have nothing better to do," Charlotte put in lightly.

"Perhaps Fitzwilliam will find a friend who will fall madly in love with you and insist on marrying you and taking you to live in a villa in Italy. Then you will be the one who is far too busy to write for all the balls and entertainments you will attend." Elizabeth laughed, although she felt a pang of sorrow as she spoke. She had not before considered how left behind Charlotte must feel as she saw her younger family and friends married, whilst she was still dependent on her father.

The day before the assembly, Charlotte was unable to join Elizabeth in her visit to Purvis Lodge, being required by her mother. Elizabeth had promised to bring her ball gown to show Mrs Wilson, so ordered the carriage and made her way there alone. She was feeling particularly cheerful, having just received a long letter from Jane, full of enthusiasm for her husband, his family, and all the experiences offered by her tour. As Elizabeth alighted from the carriage, however, she was greeted by the sight of Mrs Carmichael already waiting at the door, her face pale and drawn. Elizabeth's mood changed at once.

"What has happened?" she asked as soon as she approached the house. "Is Mrs Wilson well?"

"Mrs-Mrs Wickham is well, miss." Elizabeth's eyes widened, and Mrs Carmichael nodded slowly. "I am instructed to take you in, miss, if you wish to go, but…"

Elizabeth hesitated only a moment. "I will go to her," she said, "but I have brought the carriage." She turned to signal to the coachman. When he approached, she introduced the two, then addressed Mrs Carmichael. "Please ensure Porter is stationed close to the room, in case there is any need for him. Has Mr Darcy been written to?"

"Mr Wickham gave us a letter to send from Mrs Wickham only this morning, miss." Elizabeth nodded and made her way into the house.

Instead of taking her into the music room, Elizabeth was shown into the drawing room. As the door opened, she heard a familiar voice address the housekeeper. "Excellent, our visitor has arrived. Leave the door ajar, Mrs Carmichael, and remain in the passage. I wish to ensure Miss Bennet is comfortable."

Elizabeth's colour rose, and she berated herself for not having discovered the truth before this moment. She would not allow him to think she was intimidated, however, and she unflinchingly met the eyes of the man she had believed to be Mr Jackson.

"Mr Wickham," she said coldly. He was standing behind a chair on which Mrs Wickham was seated, her face ashen and her eyes dull. "Georgiana!" she cried, her warmth returning, and rushed to her friend's side, kneeling and taking her hands.

Mrs Wickham lifted her eyes, but they were sorrowful and frightened. She was a shadow of the person she had been even when she first arrived in the neighbourhood. "Lizzy," she whispered, "I am well."

"Of course you are well, my dear. It has been a trying time since our misunderstanding and separation, but we are happily reunited. Miss Bennet, please do take a seat." He spoke with his usual affable charm, as though this were an ordinary social call. Elizabeth stayed for a moment by her friend, unwilling to leave her side, but Mrs Wickham nodded at her, and she slowly did as she was bid.

"I apologise for the little subterfuge in our early acquaintance. My wife is not the only one who has found concealment necessary. I am delighted to have found her, however, at last." He rested a hand lightly on her shoulder. Mrs Wickham closed her eyes briefly but showed no other sign of having felt the contact. "I understand you already know a version of our history, but please do not doubt, my wife means a great deal to me, despite our regrettable misunderstanding."

Elizabeth could not conceal a shudder at his words and the ease of his manner. Mr Wickham let it pass unnoticed, but he moved around to take a seat near his wife, taking her unresisting hand in his. "It has been a great hardship, being separated from Georgiana and my children for so long, and I do not intend to be parted again. We wrote this morning to Darcy to tell him of our reunion, so I believe you will soon have the happiness of seeing him again. I look forward to calling you sister."

Elizabeth ached for her friend, who seemed barely able to speak in her husband's presence. She was glad the children were not present; how Mrs Wickham must be suffering to see them together with their father again.

"What a surprise it was, to arrive in a small country town and to discover Darcy had been here! Had I known he had left Pemberley, I would have been glad to follow him here earlier, but sadly I was not privy to the news. I understand the attractions of the area, of course," his manner changed almost imperceptibly, his eye running for a moment over Elizabeth before the mask was replaced, "but I had not realised until recently that his prolonged visit was due to the presence of my own dear Georgiana. I merely found it a convenient place to spend a few months to allow time for some of my more eager associates to cool themselves a little. It was chosen because my friend Mr Denny, whom you know as Grey, considered joining the militia for a time. He heard from his friends that this town had been remarkably accommodating to the officers here."

Elizabeth felt ill. She knew enough of Lydia's experience of the militia to believe that some of the officers' ideas of entertainment would not at all fit with her own. She would have moved, but her friend's eyes pleaded with her to stay. Mr Wickham was clearly enjoying himself, and she thought that the more information she could provide to Mr Darcy and his cousin, the more they might be able to do to help Mrs Wickham. She heard Mrs Carmichael cough in the passage, and her courage rose. She did not believe Mr Wickham would hurt her physically, whatever he might be doing with his words. She would remain.

"I have your sister to thank," Mr Wickham continued, his eyes on Elizabeth. Her heart sank that his mind had moved from the 'entertainment' to be found locally to Lydia. What foolishness had she been involved in now?

"Two of your sisters, in fact," he continued, "although one I have not had the pleasure of meeting. I am particularly grateful to Miss Lydia for sharing the news from your other sister's letter that my wife bears a likeness to Miss de Bourgh. It has been many years since I saw that lady, but even as children it was remarked upon that my wife and her cousin bore an uncanny resemblance, although one was so sickly and one so strong." Elizabeth shuddered as she saw Mrs Wickham's eyes close briefly at these words, but Mr Wickham continued without commenting on it. "Miss Lydia taught me to hope I might once again be reconciled with my dear wife. I am hugely indebted to her. Denny was lucky enough to chance upon her in Meryton last week, and she has been most accommodating." Elizabeth recoiled, and he smiled wolfishly. "She told us of your friendship with my wife and her brother, and gave me everything I needed to ensure we were brought back together. I shall tender my thanks in person, of course, for she has promised to dance with us both at the assembly tomorrow."

Elizabeth's heart dropped. The thought of Lydia, younger even than Mrs Wickham, dancing with this man horrified and disgusted her. With his smooth and plausible manners, no one else would see the true horror of the moment. She wondered whether Mrs Wickham would be left at home, knowing that her husband was enjoying the society she had so long denied herself, and her eyes went involuntarily to her friend. She still sat motionless, but Elizabeth thought she detected a slight trembling. Mr Wickham lifted the hand he still held and clasped it with his other one.

"Georgiana will of course be attending and is looking forward to dancing too. I understand she has chosen not to join local society, and I look forward to introducing her to all my newfound friends. I also count on a dance from my fair sister, Miss Bennet. I am sure Darcy would want to know his bride is on good terms with his brother. Now," he stood up briskly, "it has been a pleasure speaking to you, but I have some business to attend to, and I must spend some time with my sons. I shall leave you to discuss dresses or whatever it is that ladies discuss. I look forward to seeing you tomorrow." He made a full, flourishing bow, accompanied by a smile that could only be called triumphant, and left the room, closing the door behind him.

Elizabeth flew at once to her friend's side and seized both her hands. "Dear Georgiana!" she said, gazing into her face, shrouded as it was in misery. "Tell me that he has not hurt you!"

"He has not laid a finger on me," Mrs Wickham replied dully. "Nor on the children," she added with a little more confidence, but she said nothing more.

"And Fitzwilliam has been sent for?"

"He has. But I do not expect to be parted from my husband again. He...he will not allow it. He tells me he rather likes this house, and Hertfordshire, and intends to settle here with me. The children... I am so tired, Lizzy. I cannot run again."

She was rather exhausted by the effort of this speech and

took long, tearless gasps of breath as Elizabeth drew her into an embrace. "Fitzwilliam and I will not abandon you. You do not have to bear it alone."

"It will hurt Fitzwilliam deeply. You must not let *him* bear it alone. He will need you more than ever now. Please do not abandon *him*," begged Mrs Wickham.

CHAPTER TWENTY-NINE

Elizabeth's heart could not take everything that the day had thrown at it. It swelled at this woman who, even in her evident and great distress, thought only of her children and her brother. It almost broke at the thought of the grave and good man who would himself be heartbroken by his sister's state. She thought of her own sisters, and for once thought least of Jane. She thought instead of Mary, gone to be the wife of a fool, a mother to another's child, and subject to the whim of an officious patroness; Kitty, so often neglected and left to follow the example of the only sister who noticed her, however cruel that attention could sometimes be; and Lydia, the youngest, boldest, and most foolish of all, so desperate for love and attention and unchecked by parental guidance that she might already have exposed herself and her family to terrible shame. She could not bear the weight of her heart in that moment, and found herself sobbing as her friend could not, crying tears enough for both of them. Her release of emotion seemed to affect Mrs Wickham, and the two women were soon crying softly together.

The door opened and Mrs Carmichael entered. Mrs Wickham looked up with reddened eyes and managed to gasp out, "We are not hurt." The good lady nodded compassionately and quietly withdrew.

Once they had recovered sufficiently to speak again, Elizabeth attempted something of her usual tone. "There is little to be done until your brother arrives. Did you still wish to see my dress for the assembly?" Mrs Wickham nodded mutely, and Elizabeth drew it from where it had been carefully folded in her basket, laying it out for her friend to admire. Rallying herself, she pointed out particular details, and the two attempted to converse easily. It was little use, however, and after a short while, Mrs Wickham spoke again softly.

"I am so sorry that our friendship has led you here."

"I would not change it if I could," Elizabeth said solemnly. "I am glad to be able to call you my friend. I hope one day you will find your happiness."

Georgiana sighed. "You once kindly wished to see me dancing. Tomorrow, it appears you will do so, but not in the circumstances I think you meant."

"No. But I hope there will be some small pleasure to be had in being out in and seeing society, my dear friend. You deserve better than being hidden away from the sight of the world."

"I am not sure I do."

"I am certain of it. And one day, we shall see you happy."

Elizabeth chafed against the ride home in the carriage, for at times of distress she found the motion of walking a soothing release. Having stayed so long with her friend, however, she knew she had to return to Longbourn to arrange an express to Colonel Fitzwilliam. She did not know whether there was anything that could be done for her friend, but she could not be easy until she had tried everything in her power.

On her return home, Elizabeth wrote two short notes and arranged for them to be dispatched immediately, before making her way to her father's study. She paused for several moments before knocking. When her father's voice invited her in, she entered with an air of such uncharacteristic sorrow that her father stood up to welcome her. "Take a seat, Lizzy, and tell me what has happened," he said with such unusual concern that it was all Elizabeth could do not to break down in tears once again. She resisted doing so, however, and started from the beginning of her tale. Mr Bennet listened in silence, watching her over the top of his glasses. He continued without speaking for several minutes after she had finished.

"Well?" Elizabeth asked eventually.

Mr Bennet sighed heavily. "I have long expected Lydia to become caught up in another minor scandal, I had even thought it was possible for Kitty to do so. Jane and Mary would never expose themselves but are both so willing to listen to the views of others that I could readily see them being taken in. I never expected it would be you who would become ensnared in such a matter as this."

Elizabeth had not seen him so affected since the time of the militia, and her heart sank. "I have not been taken in, sir. Mrs Wickham is my friend, and the situation she is in, whilst partly of her own making, is not to be envied. Mr Darcy is an honourable man, and from the time I discovered the truth has always been entirely open and honest."

"Yet you find yourself involved in this business with these excellent people. Are you in any danger from this husband of your friend? Will he seek to use you in some way to reach Mr Darcy's pocket as he has used his sister? Whatever possessed you to walk into that house today? Do you realise what hurt he could have caused you?"

"I—" Elizabeth could not form an answer to this question. She had thought only of her friend's likely distress and not of her own safety at all.

"It was foolhardy. Utterly foolhardy. I can only thank God that no harm came to you."

Elizabeth hung her head at the unexpected forcefulness of her father's manner, but lifted it sharply at his next words.

"I do not see what protection I can offer from such a man, except to bar you from leaving the house without a footman or myself to escort you until Mr Darcy returns."

"You would not imprison me because of this, Papa?"

"I cannot see that I have a great deal of choice." He rose from his seat and moved round the desk to join her and take her hand. "I could not bear the thought of you being hurt, and Mr Darcy would certainly not forgive me if you were not protected. I do not doubt he will soon be here, and then we can agree what steps are best to take. But until then you must not become a pawn in this Wickham's game."

Elizabeth was silent, although her eyes were pleading for mercy. Mr Bennet continued relentlessly, however. "I once almost failed to keep a daughter safe, and it seems we are at risk again. Please fetch Lydia. It is best we understand at once what she has exposed herself to."

Elizabeth did as she was asked and soon returned with her sister, who entered the room with a sullen air. Lydia rarely chose to spend time in her father's study, and had come to associate it with the rare occasions that he took it upon himself to reprimand her for some infraction or other. She silently took a seat and waited to hear what he had to say. Elizabeth made to leave, but remained at Mr Bennet's word and also took a seat.

"I understand, Lydia, that you have been regularly to Meryton this past week."

"Well, I needed some ribbons for my dress, but then I bought the wrong colour and had to return them, and when I looked at my gloves, I noticed that one was damaged from a burn from when Kitty borrowed them last, and—" she was quieted by her father raising a hand.

"That is enough. Despite my concern over what the bill for all of this will be, your shopping habits are not the reason I asked you to come here. Have you been meeting anyone on these excursions?"

Lydia tossed her head. "I may have. I can meet who I like, I am not a child!"

"You have not yet reached your majority and remain under my protection. Have you been meeting any gentlemen?" he asked. The last word was spoken in a manner that implied it was not his preferred epithet.

"It is hardly my fault if I encounter him when I am walking into Meryton!"

"Who? And how frequently?"

"Why does Lizzy have to be here? It is nothing to her!"

"Your sister is here at my invitation." He did not repeat his question, but Lydia for once proved not indomitable, for after eyeing her father in fright for a moment, she answered him.

"Twice. Or three times. But I did not arrange to meet Mr Grey, I only told him I was often in Meryton!" Lydia tossed her head again, her show of defiance creeping into her voice.

"And has he taken any liberties with you?"

Lydia did not reply. Mr Bennet waited, and the silence stretched out between them.

"He kissed me. In the woods by Milking Lane. He asked to meet me again." It was almost a whisper.

"I see. Do you recall the events of three years ago?"

Lydia's face blanched. "Yes, Papa," she replied meekly.

"And you recall what we discussed about meeting gentlemen without my express permission?"

"Yes, Papa." This was a side of her family Elizabeth had never seen. She was painfully aware that her father was an inattentive, negligent parent, particularly of the daughters who did not share his humour and interests. She had always thought Lydia bold in the face of anything, able to shrug off any complaint or reprimand and continue on her merry way. Yet here was her father, as severe as she had ever seen him, and her sister quiet and compliant. Had Mrs Bennet joined them and informed them that she was taking a vow of silence, she could not have been more surprised.

"You will not be going to tomorrow's assembly, or to any other public or private event where gentlemen will be present that I have not expressly approved of you associating with. Nor will you be receiving any allowance for three months to come."

Lydia frowned and appeared sulky, but she nodded her head and only said, "May I leave?"

"You may." She stood up immediately and made her way to the door, where she turned.

"Mama will not agree with you," she said in a pale imitation of her usual defiance. Her father merely stared at her, and she left the room.

Mr Bennet removed his glasses and rubbed his eyes with a sigh. Elizabeth was uncertain whether to depart, but after a moment her father spoke again. "It appears Lydia has both more sense and less than she did three years ago. She is a fool to have allowed such familiarity once again, knowing where it could lead, but she has shown some sense today in not protesting against the restrictions placed upon her."

"I have not seen Lydia in such a condition before."

"You do not know how close she came to ruining you all in the past. I had thought she had learnt to keep her flirtation to public meetings where they can do less harm. It appears I was wrong."

"She is right that Mama will be disappointed she cannot attend the assembly."

"I shall speak to Mrs Bennet. First, however, we should decide whether you ought to attend. If your friend will be present with her husband, it will cause a great deal of scandal, and we do not know what he may attempt. You would be better off removed from the entire situation. I would send you to London were it not that Kitty is already there, and I do not like to impose further on your uncle Gardiner."

"I would prefer to attend the assembly. If Georgiana must endure a public revelation of her story, presented in any way her husband chooses to present it, I would choose to be there to support her."

"Your presence would link you closely to the gossip."

"My engagement will do that whether I am present or not. My absence would imply I was ashamed of the connexion, and I am not ashamed of Mr Darcy, nor of his sister. It would only fuel the gossip."

"But Mr Darcy will not be there. Mr Wickham may seek to hurt you in some fashion."

"I would like to support Mrs Wickham," Elizabeth said quietly.

Mr Bennet sat back. "I shall think further on the matter. I have not been the father I should. Please ask your mother to come to me." Elizabeth accepted her dismissal and was soon in her own room, thinking over the events of the day and writing a long letter to Mr Darcy. She would not send it until she had a response to the express, but it was some consolation to write and to imagine that the addressee was present to help her see a way through the difficult tangle in which she found herself.

CHAPTER THIRTY

T he following day dawned with all the vigour and glory one could hope for, but the mood at Longbourn was far removed from the anticipation that usually preceded an assembly. Lydia was uncharacteristically quiet; at breakfast, she was alternately sullen and contrite, and the rest of the time kept largely to her own room. Mrs Bennet also vacillated in her opinions; one moment she protested vehemently against Lydia's exclusion from the evening's entertainment, the next she vigorously blamed her and bewailed that she would never find Lydia a husband if she would keep behaving so. The strength of her reactions kept her confined to her room for much of the day, bemoaning the state of her nerves.

Elizabeth did what she could to maintain the peace and to quiet Mrs Bennet, attending her mother through the morning, but she sorely felt Jane's absence. She fought the impulse to be resentful that she, too, might be denied the pleasure of dancing, even if it be as protection rather than punishment. She did not approach her father's study, where he had closeted himself soon after breakfast and remained all morning; her thoughts, however, often led to him and whether he would allow her to support her friend at the assembly.

During the afternoon, Elizabeth was summoned. Had her mind not been so full, she might have laughed at the trepidation she felt over the simple matter of whether she was to attend a social gathering or not. As it was, she entered the study prepared to receive the worst. Unexpectedly, however, she found her father was not alone but was accompanied by a gentleman she did not recognise.

"Come in, child," Mr Bennet said quietly, gesturing to a chair. Without preamble or an attempt at an introduction, he continued, "Do you know this gentleman?"

Elizabeth looked at him. She estimated he was perhaps ten years her elder. He sat upright in his chair with one leg raised on a small footstool. Against his chair rested a cane. He met all the particulars of Mr Darcy's description of his cousin Colonel Fitzwilliam, but without any confirmation, she replied with a cautious negative.

"If I were to tell you his name is Colonel Fitzwilliam, and he claims to be Mr Darcy's cousin, would you be inclined to believe him?"

"That would depend, Papa, on whether he could present any credentials." She looked at the stranger as her father spoke, and saw a nod of approval at her words. Reaching into a pocket, he produced a gold ring which he held out to her.

"Mr Darcy's token," she said, taking and examining it before returning it to him.

"In case you suspect me of having obtained it by underhand means, when I last saw Darcy, he informed me that, in the event we met, I was not to ask you too many questions lest you accuse me of attempting an inquisition."

At the last statement, Elizabeth's face broke into a smile. "I am sure you have far less reason to be curious than he," she said with a light laugh. "I am pleased to make your acquaintance, Colonel Fitzwilliam, although I might wish it were under happier circumstances."

"Sentiments I share. Although I assure you, I have every reason to be curious, and indeed grateful. It has been many years since I have seen my cousin laugh."

"It remains all too rare an occurrence," Elizabeth replied, now perfectly at her ease.

"To return to our conversation," interrupted Mr Bennet, addressing their guest, "please forgive my initial suspicion. There have been too many cases of false identity in Lizzy's recent experience as it is."

Colonel Fitzwilliam sat back in his seat and eyed Mr Bennet coolly. "Forgiveness is freely given, Mr Bennet. In fact, I found it rather reassuring than otherwise that you appear to be taking greater care with your daughters than I understand has previously been the case."

Mr Bennet looked affronted, but then sighed in resignation. "No, I have not been the father I ought to have been. I cannot fault your reprimand."

"It was not intended as a reprimand, sir, so much as a plain statement of fact. It is my turn to ask forgiveness, for speaking so plainly to my host without invitation. Too long in the military, with a particular responsibility for maintaining discipline, has made me accustomed to direct speaking. It is not a habit I have shaken off, despite—" he completed his sentence with a gesture at his raised leg.

Mr Bennet nodded. "Very well, very well," he said, evidently wishing to move to a different topic. "Let us get on to the matter in hand. You are here because Lizzy sent for you, and Lizzy sent for you because Mr Darcy asked her to, in the event Mr Wickham appeared in Hertfordshire."

"Indeed."

"What are your intentions, now you are here?"

"To ensure Mr Wickham does not attempt to interfere with your daughter, or any of your family."

Mr Bennet looked up sharply. "What of your young cousin?"

"Much as I would like to call the man out, I have no power to help her. My guardianship ended upon her marriage, and I have no right in law to come between a man and his wife. Not that I could chase him off if I tried," he added with a short bark of a laugh. "I shall see her, if I am permitted, but I do not expect Wickham to allow me entry to the house, and an attempt at a clandestine meeting will only serve to increase the risk to her at home. I shall of course be ready to assist Georgiana, if there is any service I can render to her, but my primary purpose in being here is to ensure that her husband does not attempt to harm Miss Bennet in his bid to hurt Darcy."

Mr Bennet eyed his visitor thoughtfully. "And how do you intend to do this?"

"In any way you and I—and Miss Bennet—see fit."

Mr Bennet nodded. "You will stay here at Longbourn, of course."

Colonel Fitzwilliam accepted the invitation with thanks before turning to Elizabeth. "You wrote to Darcy?" She nodded. "He will arrive here soon, perhaps as soon as tomorrow evening. In the meantime, we must decide what protective measures are necessary. Would you relate the circumstances of Wickham's arrival in the neighbourhood and your meeting with him yesterday? It will help us understand his movements, and any actions we can take that might be of use to Georgiana."

Elizabeth set aside her joy that Darcy would soon arrive and, keen to help her friend, related all she knew, from the first arrival of Mr Wickham and his friend in Meryton through to her visit to Purvis Lodge the previous day. Her habit of observation had served her well, and she was able to recount most of the conversations she had had with him in detail. Her usual storytelling habits proved unhelpful, however, and more than once, Colonel Fitzwilliam interrupted her with a question or to direct her back to the most pertinent facts, all the time making notes in a small notebook.

At the end of her tale, he sat back and looked over his notes for some time before looking up at Mr Bennet. "May I speak freely in front of your daughter?"

The older gentleman looked at him with piercing eyes but nodded slowly. "There seems little advantage to concealing anything now. But please spare her any graphic account of his misdeeds."

Colonel Fitzwilliam turned to Elizabeth, who was hiding her relief that her father had not sent her away. She may not be able to act, but she wanted to understand. "Miss Bennet?" he asked.

"I would prefer to stay," she replied simply. Colonel Fitzwilliam nodded and began to speak.

"I suspect it is an unhappy coincidence that Wickham found his way here. He has no reason to conceal his name unless he is hiding from creditors. Darcy has always resisted attempting to use his debts to imprison him, concerned that Georgiana would be tainted by the association, but this may be something we can use to work on him. From what you reported of his conversation, however, I believe he intends to take advantage of Georgiana's presence here to set himself up in the neighbourhood as a gentleman of means.

"He has no fear of Darcy's arrival, for all the time that Georgiana is with her husband, Darcy will not act in a way that could hurt her or the children. It is not in Wickham's interest to attempt to rile Darcy at present any more than he already has, for he is in the stronger position with regards to his wife and will be well aware of it." The colonel's voice hardened. "He is too much of a coward to be a violent man, except when cornered, but he does not need to be. He is more than capable of wielding words as a weapon.

"I think it unlikely he intends any direct harm to you at present," he continued, in an attempt to reassure Elizabeth. "He will not hesitate to turn matters to his advantage, however, if an opportunity arises. His more unpleasant behaviour is usually confined to the shadows. If he wishes to appear a gentleman locally, as I suspect, he is not likely to risk that by harming the daughter of one of Meryton's principal families. However, if he could see a way to do so without risk to himself, he would undoubtedly take it. I therefore suspect you need not fear attending events such as this evening's assembly, but would benefit from appropriate protection from your father or other trusted gentlemen."

Colonel Fitzwilliam looked from Elizabeth to Mr Bennet before continuing. "Wickham will be eager to establish a strong link to Darcy, so is likely to make much of your engagement once he has established his own situation as Darcy's brother. It is for you to decide, Miss Bennet, whether you wish to acknowledge the connexion, but it would serve Georgiana ill to rile him too much. The arrival of Darcy is likely to be an opportunity to him, not a threat. He will be seeking to secure funds and will have more chances to do so if Darcy is present."

Mr Bennet and Elizabeth had listened in silence to this assessment of Mr Wickham's character, motives, and behaviour. There was nothing to be said. Colonel Fitzwilliam observed their expressions for a moment before he continued.

"Mr Bennet, I intend to attend the assembly this evening, if it is possible to do so, and I would appreciate your introduction. I am hopeful my presence will serve to dampen the worst of any malicious display of Wickham's power over Georgiana. My preference would be for Miss Bennet to attend also, if she wishes, for my cousin will be sorely in need of kindly faces. Even had her situation not been as it is, she would have been nervous under the scrutiny of so many people. I can offer your daughter my protection, if required."

Mr Bennet appeared entirely at a loss. He looked speechlessly at Elizabeth for a long moment before turning back to his guest.

"Thank you, Colonel Fitzwilliam," he said, his voice unusually hoarse, "for expressing so clearly the situation we find ourselves in. I admit I am reluctant for Lizzy to attend any event where this—" he paused, "'gentleman' will be present, if he could make her at all uncomfortable. And despite your assurances, I cannot help but feel he is a dangerous man." Elizabeth made as if to speak, and he held up a hand to silence her. "However, if she is determined to attend, I will not stop her. I will insist, however, on accompanying her, which is not my usual practice with such events, and if I believe for a moment she is at risk, will not hesitate to return with her to Longbourn immediately. Elizabeth, do you understand me?"

"Yes, Papa."

"I am grateful for your offer of protection, Colonel, but suspect that despite my advanced age, I shall be quicker on my feet should there be a need. You are of course welcome to join us. Lizzy, your mother will insist on attending, and we shall not hear the end of it if I bar her from an event to which you are permitted to go. Which leaves me with the problem of Lydia remaining here alone. Would that your sisters were still at home! But Mrs Hill will have to serve as companion for the evening, and I shall ensure a man is also about the house." With this, he sat back, the uncharacteristic execution of his duty as a parent having utterly exhausted him. "Go to your mother, child, and inform her that Colonel Fitzwilliam will be staying here as our guest."

Elizabeth was glad to escape the conversation, and before going to find Mrs Bennet, slipped quietly into the garden, where she breathed the air to steady herself. She would not be intimidated by Mr Wickham, or by this strange situation she found herself in. She felt her courage rise as she thought of her friend, and how everything she did now seemed to be in her name and for her benefit. The knowledge of what Georgiana must be enduring strengthened her resolve, and with renewed determination she went to inform her mother of their visitor.

Mrs Bennet made many complaints about the effect on her nerves of yet another gentleman visitor arriving without notice, although she at once set about ordering a room to be prepared. She was slightly consoled that, as far as Elizabeth knew, Colonel Fitzwilliam was a single man. Although a little old, perhaps, she nevertheless saw no harm in ensuring her youngest daughter looked her best when the gentleman came through to join them.

Despite his military bearing when speaking of Wickham, once amongst the ladies, Elizabeth was surprised to find Colonel Fitzwilliam was very capable of being the affable gentleman. He answered Mrs Bennet's questions with ease, conversing lightly and readily on any topic that occurred to her, and even engaged Lydia's attention with some light-hearted tales of life in camp. He was not so changed that either his manner in her father's study or when exchanging pleasantries with the ladies appeared false, but he seemed to be a man accustomed to adjusting his behaviour to fit the needs of his companions. Elizabeth could not help but be impressed by the way in which he skilfully eluded any attempts by her mother to pin him down regarding his marriage prospects without seeming to offend her in the least. By the end of the conversation, it was somehow known to all in the room that Colonel Fitzwilliam was not in need of a wife such as Lydia Bennet, without either Lydia or her mother feeling slighted by the fact.

Elizabeth thoroughly enjoyed Colonel Fitzwilliam's company. He was a man of sense and good humour, open to teasing and being teased, and a fine conversationalist. She wondered whether there were any of Mr Darcy's relations she would not be pleased to know, for the showing so far spoke very highly for him. Colonel Fitzwilliam, having apparently read her thoughts, chose this moment to mention Lady Catherine de Bourgh, and to state that he would be pleased to call on Mrs Collins when he next visited his aunt. Elizabeth was rather abruptly reminded by this that it was highly probable Mr Darcy, like any other person, did have some relatives at whose behaviour he might blush, as well as those Elizabeth was so pleased to be newly acquainted with.

Later, when she came downstairs ready to depart, she found her new friend waiting alone. As she entered, he remarked, "Darcy will not forgive me for being in a position to escort such a vision to the assembly when he is not here."

"I am sure Mr Darcy would happily forgo the assembly

portion of the task," she replied with a matching smile, which faded as she added, "Particularly this assembly."

His smile was understanding, but he had said all that he had to say of Wickham for the present, and he pursued his theme. "I suspect you are right. I am glad you have the measure of the man already. We have not had the opportunity to speak on private matters, but please allow me to say that I heartily approve of his choice of bride. He was happier, when I last saw him, than he has been these past three years, and I do not believe that is solely due to the relative contentment of Georgiana when he left Hertfordshire. You do my cousin a great deal of good, Miss Bennet. If I were inclined to be a jealous man, I might almost resent his good fortune. Alas, marriage is not for all of us poor younger sons."

"Thank you for the compliment," she laughingly returned. "I do intend to be happy in marriage if I can possibly manage it, and I believe Mr Darcy will suit me well as a husband."

CHAPTER THIRTY-ONE

I t was a peculiar feeling to step into the assembly hall. Everything was much as it always had been; familiar faces met and mingled, and her mother was soon in the midst of a chattering throng. Elizabeth, however, felt far from her usual self. She could not contain a small shudder as she heard her mother's piercing voice declaring, "Poor Lydia has had to be left at home, she was so upset to be excluded." Thinking it better not to wait to hear what her mother would tell people of the reason for Lydia's absence, she moved in the opposite direction, glad to see Charlotte turning to smile her way. Mr Bennet and Colonel Fitzwilliam both looked intently around the room before exchanging glances. It was the younger man who followed Elizabeth, Mr Bennet making his way to sit with some of the older gentlemen, who had positioned themselves with a clear view of the door so that they might gossip at their leisure about each arrival.

"Charlotte! May I introduce you to Mr Darcy's cousin, Colonel Fitzwilliam?" The introduction had been expected by the gentleman. Mr Darcy had mentioned Charlotte's friendship with his sister; Elizabeth had told him her friend was entirely in Mrs Wickham's confidence.

"I am pleased to make your acquaintance, Miss Lucas. Regrettably, I am here more on business than pleasure. We are expecting the arrival of my young cousin and her husband, and I wish to keep on my guard for it." He sat down. "As you will see, my dancing days are over, or I would be sure to secure you each for a set."

Charlotte returned his greeting readily, she and Elizabeth taking seats alongside the officer.

"He is in Meryton, then?"

"Yes," Elizabeth replied in a low voice, "and already known to you. Mr Jackson revealed his true identity to me only yesterday."

"Mr Jackson!" Charlotte was surprised, but after a moment's thought, she added, "Did he come here to search for her, following Mr Darcy?"

"No, it all appears to have been an unhappy coincidence. But here he is, nevertheless."

Charlotte nodded. "Poor Georgiana."

They had managed to communicate this much discreetly, but the assembly hall was no place to inform Charlotte of all that Elizabeth had learnt. She therefore merely responded with a squeeze of her friend's hand, and the three waited without speaking, observing the happy throng around them. After very little time, the ladies were approached to dance; Elizabeth was too agitated to consider it, although Charlotte departed for the first set.

The first two dances had already been completed and Charlotte was speaking to her mother in a separate part of the room when a disturbance at the entrance indicated the arrival of someone of note. Colonel Fitzwilliam rose to his feet, the advantage of his height allowing him to see past the throng. "They are here," he said quietly, before turning to meet Mr Bennet's eyes. Elizabeth looked towards the door, keen to see how her friend fared.

Mrs Wickham was not dressed in her widow's weeds, but the change made little difference to her demeanour. Her gown was light grey and her manner submissive, although she looked timidly about her. Mr Wickham stood tall and proud, smiling at the massed people of Meryton as though it were the most ordinary matter in the world to appear at the assembly with a reclusive widowed lady on his arm. Catching the eye of Sir William Lucas, he made his way directly to the gentleman, disregarding the murmurs and sidelong glances that followed them. Mrs Wickham stepped meekly at his side, looking at no one, her face pale. Mr Denny, who had followed them into the assembly hall, did not remain with them but made his way to the punch table, where he was soon surrounded by curious gentlemen.

Elizabeth watched as Sir William greeted Mr Wickham with some confusion, which only increased as an introduction was made to the lady on his arm. She was clearly making a great effort to appear at ease, although her eyes dropped frequently to the ground before being lifted up again with a start when her husband shifted at her side. At one point, Sir William looked around the room until his eyes lit upon Elizabeth, beaming at her with avuncular affection. Elizabeth could not discern, but had no difficulty imagining, the word 'sister' forming on Mr Wickham's lips.

What story Mr Wickham was choosing to tell, Elizabeth could not imagine, but he regularly placed a hand over his wife's on his arm, casting smiles her way that she attempted to return. It evidently sufficed for Sir William, for at the end of it he reached out to shake the other man's hand. He also spoke to Mrs Wickham, apparently kindly, for her eyes fixed on him with gratitude before the couple moved away.

Mr Wickham now turned to Elizabeth, smiling at her with a grace that would have been charming had she not known him for the man he was. She could not bring herself to smile in return as he crossed the room to greet her, Mrs Wickham still passive at his side. She did not see Mr Bennet, who crossed to speak to Sir William as soon as the couple had parted from him.

"My dear sister," Mr Wickham began, but stopped and paled as his eyes met those of Colonel Fitzwilliam, who had resumed his seat and was not visible until one was at close quarters. The colonel's face darkened, and he did not stand. Wickham recovered quickly. "Fitzwilliam! I had not known we were to be honoured with your company."

Colonel Fitzwilliam gave the slightest of nods in acknowledgement, but had turned his attention to Mrs Wickham, who bore the first genuine smile since she had entered the room. "Richard!" she exclaimed in quiet delight before glancing at her husband with some apprehension.

Mr Wickham, however, had apparently decided that causing a scene was not in his interest. He made no further acknowledgement of Colonel Fitzwilliam, instead turning back to Elizabeth and addressing her.

"What a pleasure it is to be able to bring my wife to an event such as this. I have just been explaining to Sir William the unhappy circumstances of our separation. Alas, I was too trusting of one on whom I thought I could depend. I thought him honest, but found a trail of debts and broken promises across the country in my name, in places I had never so much as visited. I thought him faithful, but he whispered poison in my ear, separated me from my dear wife, then had me believe she had died, breaking my heart. I have been forced to assume a false name whilst I roamed the country, desperate to find some comfort but unable to settle, unable to reveal my true name for fear of being driven away or pursued for another man's debts. Oh," he cried, "would that I had known she too had been deceived into believing it was necessary to conceal her name! But such is the insidious venom of a silver-tongued serpent. If only we had not grown estranged from my dear brother Darcy, then I might have applied to him and brought on a happier reunion. I have learnt my lesson, however, never to put my trust in the appearance of goodness and fine words of another! Yes, I have learnt my lesson and am a humbled man, once again reunited with my dear, dear Georgiana."

He had delivered this entire speech boldly, not taking his eyes from Elizabeth, and she did not mistake the relish in his eyes as he related it. Only at the end, as he spoke his wife's name, did he cover her hand with his and turn his gaze to meet that of Colonel Fitzwilliam.

Elizabeth was stricken with horror and disgust. Such a flimsy explanation; she could not comprehend how it could pass for plain truth to anyone. Yet she could not deny that his prevarication had every appearance of genuine feeling, and that his manner gave the tale a plausibility that only one who knew the truth could deny.

Mr Wickham observed her disquiet with a small smile and, unperturbed, continued. "I look forward to welcoming all our friends and associates to Purvis Lodge. All we need to be happy is my dear brother's return, that we may heal our past breach and reunite as one family."

Elizabeth was feeling altogether unwell, but with a glance at Mrs Wickham, managed to respond. "I am sure Mr Darcy will not delay a moment once he knows of your presence in the area, Mr Wickham."

He bowed in acknowledgement. "In the meantime, I hope that after I dance with my wife, you will favour me with a turn, Miss Bennet, in celebration of our future connexion."

"Thank you, sir. I regret I am not inclined to dance this evening." She looked him full in the face as she spoke and did not miss the fleeting sneer that crossed it.

"Regrettable," he replied, "especially since your sister appears to not be present this evening. I had been looking forward to dancing with you both."

Their conversation was interrupted by the approach of Mr Bennet, who had left his conversation with Sir William and arrived in time to hear the last exchange. He immediately came and stood behind Elizabeth, a hand upon her shoulder, not acknowledging any of her companions. "Are you in need of anything, Lizzy?"

"No, Papa," she replied levelly. "I have just been informing Mr Wickham I shall not be dancing this evening."

"Very good," her father replied.

His eyes met those of Mr Wickham, who smirked before turning coolly to his wife. "A new dance is beginning. Shall we, my dear?"

She took a deep breath, then said with nervous emphasis, "I would like one word with Lizzy first, if I may."

Mr Wickham's eyebrows raised, but with a smirk, he replied, "Of course, dear Georgiana. I could deny you nothing," and stepped away in a show of giving them privacy. Elizabeth turned to her father, who with a sharp look reluctantly nodded and retreated to sit alongside Colonel Fitzwilliam.

Elizabeth doubted that any of the men were out of earshot, but turned to her friend nevertheless, attempting to read what she hid behind her closed expression. "Georgiana?"

"I am well. I am pleased to see you, and it comforts me that my cousin is here. But please do not...do not attempt— Oh, it is better this way. George's version of our story. There is nothing to be gained from refuting it."

Elizabeth took her friend's hand. "You are sure?"

Georgiana met her eyes, and Elizabeth's heart wrenched to see the tears that pooled there. "Please," she said quietly. "It is better this way," she repeated.

"Until your brother arrives," Elizabeth replied, "I shall promise to do as you wish. I have no way of proving anything as it is, and he has broken no law that I know of. I cannot speak for Colonel Fitzwilliam." They both turned towards him. With a thunderous look in his eye, he slowly inclined his head, showing that he had both heard and acquiesced.

Mrs Wickham smiled weakly as her husband stepped back to her side.

"My dear, the dance is commencing," he said easily, and took her away to their places without a backward glance.

Elizabeth helplessly watched them. Mr Wickham danced well, with every appearance of grace and enjoyment. Mrs Wickham's movements were precise and controlled, evidently the result of the finest tutors. The couple barely spoke, however, and although he smiled widely and freely, she did not smile at all. Elizabeth turned away. Mr Bennet and Colonel Fitzwilliam were still talking in quiet voices, although they acknowledged her as her eyes fell on them. She turned back and saw her mother making her way across the assembly hall. Not feeling equal to Mrs Bennet's obvious desire to gossip, she turned another way and made for Charlotte, who was standing alone.

As soon as she reached her friend, words burst from Elizabeth, although she kept her voice low. "There is nothing I can do. She is a shadow of herself."

Charlotte took her hand. "There is a great deal you can do. Mr Wickham proposes to stay in the area. You will still be her friend. And Mr Darcy will return soon."

"To be drained of every penny he has in his sister's name," Elizabeth replied bitterly.

"Perhaps matters will turn out otherwise. Perhaps things are not so bad as they appear at present."

A smile played around Elizabeth's lips for the first time that evening. "Where has Charlotte gone? Tell me only that you are sure there has been some misunderstanding, and that Mr Wickham can only have had good intentions, and I shall believe you are turning into Jane. Oh, how I miss her!" she finished plaintively.

Charlotte murmured something sympathetic just as they were joined by Mr Bennet.

"Mr Wickham caused you no harm, Lizzy?" her father asked at once, watching the man unconcernedly dancing.

"No. I cannot comprehend anyone believing his story, and I hate to see Mrs Wickham so distraught. But he has not hurt me."

Mr Bennet scrutinised her closely. "The story is improbable, but not entirely implausible. I think we shall have a hard job to refute it."

"You heard Mrs Wickham ask that we not attempt it," Elizabeth replied dully, turning away from the dancing. "I do not know what Mr Wickham has said to her, but I think she fears some form of retribution if we do."

Mr Bennet grimaced. "A sorry business all round."

As the evening continued, Elizabeth found herself the subject of many stares and whispers. Mrs Bennet succeeded in accosting her, declaring, "Well, what is this about your friend? Who would have thought she remained married all along, and entirely unaware of it! It must have come as a great surprise to you to discover she was no widow after all. And they each concealed their names! Why, they might never have found one another again but for the happy chance of Mr Wickham happening to visit the area! How delighted you must be for your friend. And to be able to come into society and dance! Although she seems a little timid. I am sure she will be glad to be amongst society again, once she has adjusted to her situation. Perhaps I ought to arrange a small dinner at Longbourn. I shall speak to my sister about when her next evening is planned." Having allowed no opportunity for Elizabeth to respond, she bustled off in search of Mrs Philips.

Elizabeth spent the rest of the evening with either Charlotte or Colonel Fitzwilliam, and often with both. Mr Bennet, apparently satisfied that Mr Wickham intended no active injury to his daughter, increasingly withdrew to the company of the gentlemen. Although Elizabeth's spirits were low, Colonel Fitzwilliam and Charlotte combined their efforts to maintain a steady stream of harmless anecdotes and conversation in an attempt to keep her distracted from Mrs Wickham's plight. Charlotte occasionally stood to dance, but Elizabeth steadfastly refused all requests, pleading a slight indisposition.

Mr Wickham kept his wife close by his side for a full hour after their dance, sometimes parading her about the room, at others stopping to speak to one or other of the people at the assembly. Eventually, however, he signalled to his friend, and Elizabeth watched as Mrs Wickham was led to the floor by Mr Denny, where she went through the motions of a further dance. As it concluded, Mr Denny glanced at Mr Wickham, who had removed to a group of some of the younger men, known only by sight to Elizabeth. At a nod from the taller man, Mr Denny led Mrs Wickham to Elizabeth.

"I understand you are close to Mrs Wickham," he said without preamble. "Perhaps she might sit with you?" Elizabeth was very glad to welcome her. Mr Denny seemed about to make some further remarks, until he glanced up and saw Colonel Fitzwilliam in his seat close by. His colour changed instantly, and he turned abruptly on his heel. Colonel Fitzwilliam did not acknowledge the man's behaviour, but his eye followed him across the room with a furrowed brow.

Mrs Wickham smiled with timid warmth at Elizabeth, and still more so at her cousin, but her smiles were marked with the weight of the evening. "Richard," she said softly, barely audible above the noise of the assembly, "it is a pleasure to see you."

Colonel Fitzwilliam shifted forward in his seat. "It is always a pleasure to see you, Georgiana." His eyes roved across her face, and he asked with some urgency how she fared.

"I am well," she said, although her passive manner contradicted her words. "I think this day could not have been put off forever. I am glad to have had time to form friendships"—she acknowledged Elizabeth as the latter took her hand—"and to build a life for myself here. Better to be settled somewhere than to live as we have lived. I hope Joey —I mean, young George—and Tommy will be able to meet other children if we are to stay here."

Colonel Fitzwilliam's brow darkened. "George?"

"We are to call Joey by his christened name. He is learning to answer to George." She continued in a low voice, unable to meet the eyes of her companions. "He has been generous to them. They are very pleased with their father."

Charlotte, who had been detained by a dance partner, joined them in the silence that followed. Seeing Colonel Fitzwilliam settle back in his seat and Mrs Wickham recede into herself, Charlotte once again exerted herself to make conversation, and for the sake of the younger woman, Elizabeth joined her. Nothing of any importance was said, but Mrs Wickham appeared content to listen. Her eyes, however, were frequently directed towards her husband, who did not deign to look her way. That he was enjoying the company of the gentlemen was evident by the flash of a flask being quietly passed between them, and occasional outbreaks of raucous laughter from that corner of the room.

Only after supper did Mr Wickham approach. "Come," he said, his speech less clear than usual. He made no acknowledgement of Colonel Fitzwilliam, although he turned a smile on Elizabeth.

Mrs Wickham stood up at once. "I hope I shall see you all very soon," she said.

Her husband leered. "Yes, do join us, my dear Miss Bennet. My sister! My dear soon-to-be sister. Darcy's a damned fool but he's picked a fine one—" he stopped speaking and squinted slightly as Mr Bennet, who had made his way over as soon as he had seen Wickham approach, inserted himself deliberately in front of Elizabeth.

"Damned fathers! Worse than brothers," Mr Wickham mumbled as he turned away. "Come, Georgiana," he added in more commanding tones, offering her his arm.

"Thank you, Papa," Elizabeth said, but her eyes trailed the two people leaving the assembly hall.

"I believe it would be best if we allow them some time to depart, but we shall not stay long ourselves."

"I am ready to leave at any time."

He patted her hand, already searching the room for Mrs Bennet. "I shall go and ensure your mother is also prepared."

Elizabeth turned to Colonel Fitzwilliam, about to speak, but was distracted by the sound of a commotion from outside. "Georgiana!" The colonel attempted to get to his feet as he shouted but was unable to do so quickly, and by the time he had risen and found his cane, there were already crowds of onlookers at the windows and doors. Elizabeth caught snatches of the conversation.

"Did you see?"

"It was Long's horse again I think…"

"…Wickham, um, Jackson, you know the man…"

"There is something the matter with that horse!"

"The man was drunk! He probably…"

Elizabeth turned wide-eyed to her companion, but he, with a remarkable turn of speed on his damaged leg, was already close to the door, pushing his way firmly through the crowd. She made to follow but was stopped by her father. "No. I do not know what has happened, but you will not put yourself in his way again. Colonel Fitzwilliam will see to Mrs Wickham's safety, if needed. I do not think he will let his injury stand in the way of that. There is nothing you can do to help tonight."

Elizabeth chafed against her father's words, but meeting his eyes, realised he would not be gainsaid. Reluctantly, therefore, she crossed the room to wait impatiently at the edge of the crowd, hoping to hear something of her friend's state. There was no more enlightening information to be gleaned, however, and as the people dispersed, no one could tell her what had occurred beyond the assembly hall after her friend departed.

CHAPTER THIRTY-TWO

Colonel Fitzwilliam did not return, and when the press of the throng had receded, Mr Bennet decided they would depart without him. Mrs Bennet maintained a constant stream of chatter throughout the entire journey, not noticing the tension in her companions. Much of it related to the Wickhams, and Elizabeth was hard pressed not to correct her mother's many misapprehensions. Knowing that any attempt when she was in the full flow of speech would be disregarded or dismissed, however, she remained silent. Her mind was occupied with what might have happened.

They were met at the door to Longbourn by an uncharacteristically flustered Hill. "Oh, Mr Bennet!" she announced as soon as the carriage door opened. "Miss Lydia—" she got no further, as Mr Bennet cut across her.

"What has she done? Is she safe?"

"Safe, sir, yes. She is with the maids in the kitchen. But, sir, there was a man creeping about, and Miss Lydia seemed to know him."

This was enough to have Mr Bennet striding into the house, calling, "Show her to my room," over his shoulder. Mrs Bennet, who had not mentioned Lydia since the Wickhams had arrived at the assembly, at once started to follow, protesting in piercing tones that Lydia should be treated so cruelly. A single quelling glance stopped her in her tracks.

For the next hour, Elizabeth was once again much occupied attending to her mother, who maintained a continuous stream of complaints about her nerves. Lydia had not entirely usurped her interest in the gossip surrounding the Wickhams, and the two subjects jostled for a place in Mrs Bennet's thoughts and words. Elizabeth soothed and placated her as best she could. Her mind, however, was all the time occupied by the whirl of her own thoughts, no less centred on her sister than her friend. The two became increasingly tangled in her mind, until in her weariness she was barely able to distinguish between them. When she eventually retired, she had expected to be wakeful, but her exertion with her mother had left her exhausted. As soon as she had prepared herself for bed, she found herself overcome by drowsiness and fell asleep.

Despite the lateness of the hour that she retired, Elizabeth's habits prevailed, and she found herself awake at close to her usual time, unrefreshed but unable to remain where she was in her wakefulness. Rising, she dressed and made her way quietly downstairs. Her father, in keeping with his own habits, was waiting for her at the breakfast table. He seemed to have aged overnight, and Elizabeth went to his side and placed her hand on his shoulder. He reached up and patted it with a reluctant smile. "Well, well, Lizzy," was all he said.

She hesitated as she sat down, before asking quietly, "Lydia?"

"Will keep to her room today. You may see her."

"Is she well? What happened?"

Mr Bennet shook his head. "She was very foolish, but no permanent harm has come of it."

Elizabeth wished to ask more, but something in her father's countenance told her she would not obtain more information on the events involving her sister. It was a source of frustration, to still be shut out of his confidence when there appeared to be so much at stake, but she knew it was fruitless to ask once he had made up his mind.

Instead, she enquired, "And Colonel Fitzwilliam?"

"Has not yet returned. I expect we shall see him in due course."

Conversation lapsed, and they finished their meal without speaking again. Elizabeth kissed her father's head as she left, and was rewarded with another pat on her hand. She made her way outside to walk in the garden, deep in thought. She had ached for Mrs Wickham yesterday and longed now to hear she was unharmed. Colonel Fitzwilliam's continued absence suggested that something serious had occurred, but it was also reassuring. He would not tarry at other business; if he was absent, it would be because he was with, or working to support, his cousin. Her mind roved over everything that had brought them to this point. So much sorrow on her friend's part, all stemming from the silver words and false heart of one man. She toyed with the thought for a moment of what life would have been had Mrs Wickham not been persuaded to her marriage, but discarded the thought almost at once. Without it, she would not have met her friend, or Mr Darcy. She could not be grateful for her friend's situation, but neither was she so romantic that she imagined destiny causing them to meet in other circumstances. There was no joy to be found in exploring what might have been.

Her thoughts turned to Mr Wickham, and she shuddered. How easily everyone had been taken in! How readily he twisted the truth to become a tale of lost love reunited. How might such words have worked on her, had she not known better? How might they have worked on Lydia?

Lydia! Her confused thoughts of the evening before once again presented themselves to her mind's eye but with sharper clarity. Despite being so different, her friend and her sister had each shown themselves susceptible to sweet talking and false promises. For Mrs Wickham, it had led to her current unhappy situation and the mysterious event that closed the assembly. Lydia was as yet safe, but something had occurred yesterday to put her at risk. Twice now she had come close to exposing herself, nay, her whole family, in some manner. What had happened to her sister the previous evening?

Lydia had already confessed to meeting Mr Denny. Elizabeth had not seen him after he had left Mrs Wickham at her side and exchanged that curious look with Colonel Fitzwilliam. Had he been the man at Longbourn last night? What might he have said to Lydia? What might she have almost been persuaded to do? Lydia had been keen to put herself in the way of both Mr Wickham and Mr Denny, laughing and flirting with the men. Elizabeth had been troubled by her behaviour, aghast at the thought Lydia might have exposed herself to ridicule and shame. Yet, for all this, Elizabeth had not taken the time to speak to her sister or to better understand her.

She had been so caught up in Mrs Wickham's story that she had failed entirely to consider that of her own sister. With an urgent tread she began to return to the house, berating herself at every step. She had admired the unselfish affection Mr Darcy and Mrs Wickham each felt for the other, but she had not emulated it. Except perhaps with Jane, who hardly required it, she had not acted for her sisters. Whatever might be happening to Mrs Wickham, there was nothing Elizabeth could do; for Lydia, however, she could attempt to rectify her failings.

When Elizabeth knocked at the door, Lydia invited her in with no good humour.

"Well?" Lydia asked. Elizabeth overlooked her tone and sat down.

"I came to see how you are," Elizabeth replied. "A great deal has happened recently, and although we have been so much more in company together, I have not taken the time to truly listen to you."

Lydia looked askance at this statement. "Laws, Lizzy, what can you mean? We have talked more these past weeks than in the past three years."

"Yet I find I barely know my youngest sister and have taken little interest in her concerns."

"My concerns? They are all ribbons and flirting."

Elizabeth flinched at Lydia's bitter retort but strove to express what she meant. "I cannot comment because it appears I have never taken the time to find out. How are you feeling?" She asked the last with great concern, thinking of all that had happened.

"You sound like Jane," Lydia said with a snort of laughter. "Do you think you have to take her place now that she is married?"

"No." Elizabeth strained to keep her temper even. "I was hoping we might understand one another better."

Lydia laughed again, the same snort of derisive amusement. "I am easy to understand! I wanted to dance and enjoy myself, and now I am stuck here."

Elizabeth stood to leave. "I am sorry to have disturbed you," she said, making her way to the door.

"Yes, go! Call on your perfect friend Mrs Wilson. You like her better than me anyhow."

Elizabeth froze in place. She turned slowly to Lydia and spoke with quiet emphasis. "Her name is Georgiana Wickham. Her husband, Mr Wickham, is known to you as Mr Jackson, but has now resumed his proper name. She is Mr Darcy's sister, and fled a terrible marriage, but now her husband has found her and will make her life miserable once again. Colonel Fitzwilliam, as well as being Mr Darcy's cousin, is also Georgiana's. She eloped, Lydia. Eloped with a man who pretended affection but had none. And she has been paying the price of her folly ever since."

Lydia's face had paled, but she replied defiantly, "Then she is a fool if she cannot look after herself. I am sure when I marry, I shall choose more wisely."

"Wisely? Lydia, when Mr Denny called last night, what did he say?"

"He did not...he said nothing...I did not listen to him!" Lydia's declaration was fierce, if not articulate.

"Did he try to convince you to join him in some folly?"

Lydia looked shamefaced but spoke defiantly. "No."

"Very well," Elizabeth replied, working to subdue the inclination to severity. She made no move to leave, but watched her sister, who seemed to be deep in thought. Lydia twisted her hands together in an unusually nervous movement.

"He said he would marry me," she said suddenly. "When he kissed me. He said he would come for me some day and take me away to Gretna Green."

"If he meant to marry you, surely he could have come to

the house honourably and openly called on you," Elizabeth said, cautiously returning to her seat.

"But it was so romantic! To think of him riding off with me to Gretna Green, clinging to him on the back of his horse!"

"All the way to Scotland?"

Lydia frowned. "You sound like Papa," she said sulkily. "It is all very well for you, with your rich and dull Mr Darcy. But I need adventure! I want to live!"

Elizabeth looked at her quizzically. "There is more than one way to live. And rash decisions can lead to a lifetime of misery."

Lydia responded with an inarticulate noise. She said nothing more, her gaze apparently tracing the patterns above her bed. Elizabeth at first thought to remain with her, but sensing that the conversation had ended, she stood up to leave. "I am sorry I have not spent more time listening to you. I am here if you wish to talk."

"Until Mr Darcy returns," Lydia said without turning to her.

"Even then. He will not keep me from my sister if you need me. He understands the importance of family all too well, but even if he did not, I would not allow it."

When she returned downstairs, Elizabeth found her mother had gone to call on her sister Philips. Her father was in his study but merely waved her away. Colonel Fitzwilliam, apparently, had still not returned. Elizabeth took up her sewing, but finding her attention wandering, instead took pen and paper and attempted to write to Jane. She was thus occupied when she heard the door open. Turning, she saw Colonel Fitzwilliam, dishevelled in the clothes he had worn the previous evening. She stood up at once.

"Colonel Fitzwilliam! What news?"

He shook his head. "Would you be so good as to call for some food? I have not eaten. I must refresh myself, but if your father is amenable, I shall explain all once I have changed my clothes." Elizabeth nodded and set about meeting his request before making her way to Mr Bennet's room.

When Colonel Fitzwilliam re-joined them, looking more presentable if not any less tired, Elizabeth longed to enquire after her friend but restrained herself whilst she ensured his leg was comfortable and that he had ample sustenance. She was grateful when he took only a few bites of some fruit, then began to speak.

"Georgiana is well." He took another few bites as Elizabeth felt relief wash over her. "Do you know what occurred after Mr and Mrs Wickham left last night?"

Seeing two heads shaking, he sat forward. "The details are hazy, but something happened to frighten one of the horses waiting outside. Whether Wickham startled it or whether it had some other cause, he was close by when it occurred and attempted to catch a hold of the bridle. The horse reared, Wickham fell, and he was under its hoofs in a moment. It did not kill him," he stated, responding to Elizabeth's small gasp, "although it might have been better if it had. Both his legs were trampled. The other horses were affected and almost bolted. It was only a quick-thinking footman who managed to successfully seize and calm them that stopped the whole equipage from causing a greater disaster. Had that happened, Georgiana would surely have been hurt.

"Wickham was vocal in his pain. It took six of us to lift and move him, intending to take him to the inn in town, but he insisted with a stream of invective—forgive me, I ought not to say so much in front of a lady, but it was so—insisted that he be moved to Purvis Lodge. He would not allow me near him, although I have seen wounds just as bad and worse. The other men, not knowing what else to do, took him home as requested, although it was a foolish thing to do. Wounds like that ought to be looked at and treated as quickly as possible. It fell to me to escort Georgiana home. It was lucky that you had made sure to introduce me as Darcy's relation, for no one questioned my right to do so. She was badly shaken by the whole affair.

"At the house, all was in uproar, for he could not be got up the stairs. The housekeeper arranged to have a bed made up on some boards in one of the downstairs rooms, and he was placed there. The wound was cleaned and a doctor called, but he will be confined to his bed for a long time to come.

"I slept in a chair in the room with him, supplying him with brandy and nursing him as far as he would allow. In the morning, a nurse was sent for, and she has taken over his care. After ensuring Georgiana was well, I sent an express to Darcy, although whether it will reach him if he is on his way here, I cannot tell."

"It seems Mr Wickham is intent on supplying the neighbourhood with sufficient gossip to last a year," Mr Bennet said drily. He waved off Elizabeth's protest at his words. "Will he live?"

"That depends on whether his wounds were treated quickly enough. They are severe. If he does recover, I doubt he will have full use of his legs. He will not be the same man. If infection sets in, his chances are slim."

Mr Bennet nodded. "Not to be wished upon anyone, even one such as Wickham. Is there anything to be done?"

"I do not think so. I was hoping to persuade Georgiana to

impose on your hospitality by leaving the house and bringing the children here, but she appears to believe it is her duty to remain with him. I convinced her to sleep a little whilst I took Joey and Tommy out to play, but recent events have taken their toll. She will stay and mark time at his bedside. She will have no respite. Even his friend appears to have deserted him. I thought the man would be happy to live off his hospitality, but he did not appear nor send any enquiry. I sent to his rooms to ask him to send Wickham's remaining possessions but was told he had not been seen."

Elizabeth and her father exchanged a glance. Colonel Fitzwilliam did not miss the wordless exchange. "You know more of the man?"

Mr Bennet looked stern. "Not in as many words."

Colonel Fitzwilliam looked quizzical. "Mr Bennet," he said abruptly, "your family have, for happy and desirable reasons," he tipped his head respectfully towards Elizabeth, "become closely involved in my family's affairs. I do not know whether this man means further harm to Georgiana. Please do me the goodness to speak plainly if you know anything which might help."

"Papa," Elizabeth interjected pleadingly, "please."

Mr Bennet scowled, but sighed and replied, "It concerns my own family's reputation."

"Miss Lydia," Colonel Fitzwilliam replied with a nod. At Mr Bennet's further scowl, he added, "It is no great leap of imagination, sir. Your youngest daughter was clearly unhappy at being excluded from the ball, her mother hardly less so."

Mr Bennet sighed and sketched out Lydia's recent history with Mr Denny. Colonel Fitzwilliam listened until the end, where he said musingly, "Denny. A more recognisable name than Grey."

"He had a peculiar reaction to seeing you yesterday," Elizabeth added.

"Indeed he did. I am a familiar enough figure, in certain circles. I shall write to London and see what can be discovered about Mr Denny. He appears to have forsaken Wickham, but I would like to ensure there are no more mysteries."

CHAPTER THIRTY-THREE

E lizabeth had decided that she would, one way or another, contrive to visit her friend. Mrs Bennet had talked of making up a basket of treats to send to the two boys, who, she had said, 'must find it hard to have their father found and lost in such a short space of time'. Elizabeth thought she might volunteer to take the basket. If Mrs Wickham was not accepting visitors, she would simply leave the gift, in the hope her friend knew she was thinking about her. She was still determining how her father might be persuaded to allow it when an interruption redirected her thoughts.

Mr Bennet being occupied in his study and Colonel Fitzwilliam having gone to enquire after his cousin, the Bennet ladies were sitting together in a moment of unusual peace. Mrs Bennet was at her sewing, Elizabeth was attempting to sort through the tangle of threads in her own sewing basket, and Lydia played with a kitten she had acquired from the most recent litter born to the Longbourn cats. The interruption came in the form of Mr Darcy, arriving at the house and being shown directly into Mr Bennet's study.

Mrs Bennet was all activity at once. "Mr Darcy has returned!" she declared. "Why did you not tell me he was expected, Lizzy? Why, I hardly have a good joint for dinner! He will need a room, of course. With Netherfield empty, we cannot leave him to stay at the inn. We shall have wedding preparations to think of now! Oh, there is so much to do!" She rang the bell with every sign of enjoyment.

Lydia spoke without looking up from the kitten, who was attempting to catch a piece of thread that Elizabeth had just painstakingly untangled. "You are a sly thing. Why did you not say? You are as bad as Papa!"

"I did not know he was coming," Elizabeth replied, unable to stop a small smile from playing about her lips. She grew quickly solemn, however, as she thought of what had brought him back to Hertfordshire. "I expected he would return soon, but he sent no word ahead."

"Well, he is here now, and look at you! In an old gown and nothing to tempt the man at all!" Mrs Bennet surveyed her daughter with a critical eye. "Why, he will forget why he ever proposed to you if you present to him like that! Go and change! No, stay, there is no time. We shall just have to do what we can." With that, she pinched Elizabeth's cheek to redden it.

Elizabeth pulled away with an exclamation. "Mama! I am sure that if I did well enough for Mr Darcy before, I shall do well enough for him now." Mrs Bennet was about to protest, but at that moment, Hill entered and informed Elizabeth she was requested to attend her father.

"You spend more time in that room with the men than is entirely proper for a lady!" Mrs Bennet grumbled, at the same time tugging on a wayward fold in Elizabeth's dress and pushing her towards the door.

Elizabeth's eyes were searching for Mr Darcy the moment she stepped into the room. She could not restrain a gasp at the sight of him. He was a shadow of himself; pale, noticeably thinner, and graver than ever. His eyes met hers with a small spark of warmth, but his smile was tired and wan.

"Miss Bennet," Mr Darcy said in greeting. "Elizabeth."

Elizabeth felt unexpectedly shy under Mr Darcy's steady gaze. Although she had waited and longed for it, she had not prepared herself for his return and was overwhelmed by relief, happiness, and, unaccountably, nerves. Even in her anxiety at all that had occurred, she was overcome by an instinctive wish to tease, to conceal her sudden timidity. She dropped her own curtsey, lowering her voice to copy his. "Mr Darcy," she said solemnly before raising her eyes with an echo of their usual expression. "Fitzwilliam."

She saw the twitch at his mouth, small and fleeting though it was, and was satisfied. She turned to her father, who was looking on. "Mr Darcy has just come from Purvis Lodge," he said. Elizabeth's eyes flew back to Mr Darcy's at the mention of his sister's home, but he stood unmoving.

"How is Georgiana?"

Mr Darcy's reply was in the anguish in every line of his face. He was not yet ready to speak of his sister's plight. She wished to comfort him, and cast about for how she might best offer some relief.

"Do you need to refresh yourself at all? Or would you perhaps prefer to walk?"

"Thank you. I ate before I left my sister. I would be pleased to walk with you."

The day was grey and slightly breezy, but with no immediate sign of rain. As they stepped into the garden, Lydia protesting at being expected to follow in their wake, Elizabeth asked again after Georgiana.

Mr Darcy sighed. "She is not happy, yet she is determined to do what she sees as her duty by him."

"Is there anything I can do?"

"Would you call on her? I believe she is more in need of a friend than ever."

"Gladly, but I believe Papa may object. He has been cautious ever since he learnt the truth."

"As he should be. I shall speak to him. Wickham can do you no harm at present. You are unlikely even to see him."

Elizabeth nodded before shivering.

"Is it too cold for walking? Would you prefer to be inside?" He spoke more solicitously than he had done before her father, and she returned him a soft smile.

"I would rarely prefer to be inside. Besides, we have always walked together, it is where we are most ourselves. Now, will you tell me how you are?" she continued, taking his arm.

"I am well, thank you," he replied formally.

Elizabeth stopped and contemplated him. "You are not," she replied. "You have not been taking care of yourself."

"I have had much to do. And much to think of."

"Except eating and sleeping?" She gave him an arch look that did not disguise her concern as they continued walking.

"I have been on the road a great deal of late."

Elizabeth nodded. "When did you leave Derbyshire?"

"Three weeks ago."

"So long!" Elizabeth was astonished. "Wherever have you been?"

"Out seeking traces of Wickham in Northamptonshire," Mr Darcy replied through gritted teeth. "He has left a trail of debt and worse in his wake. I have done what I can."

"Why did you not tell me?"

"I departed suddenly, based on some information I had received. The source was correct, except less recent than I had been led to believe. I could give you no direction, but I had a man stationed to bring any letters to Northampton. I did not wish to burden you with my adventures when you were already carrying so much for my sister. I would have been here sooner but for the delays my absence occasioned. If only I had known that the man I trailed had made his way here."

"You could not have known."

"You told me of the newcomers to the area. I ought to have been on my guard, even if you were not, but I was too confident of the value of the information I already held."

It was said without intent of wounding, but Elizabeth felt his remark as the severest reproof, and felt a wave of sorrow that she had not protected her friend; indeed, it was through her association with Elizabeth that Mrs Wickham's secret had been revealed. "I am sorry my letters were not sufficient to warn you, Fitzwilliam. You proposed so I might write to you of Georgiana, to aid in her support, yet I failed to give you adequate warning of Mr Wickham's arrival. Had I but been clearer, you might have discovered his presence sooner and been here to prevent..." she fell silent as a traitorous sob rose abruptly in her throat.

Mr Darcy's hand found its way to cover hers where it rested on his arm, but it was a moment before he spoke. "You could not have prevented this. You had no knowledge of the man, or of his appearance. Would that I had been able to send an image of him to help you, but I burnt the only one I know of following their wedding. I could not bear that it sat in a place of distinction in my father's effects. Georgiana's every letter to me whilst I was away spoke of how grateful she was to have a friend—to have you as her friend. I could not have asked for more from you. Ought not, perhaps, to have asked as much as I did. I was foolish to believe I could hide her in this way. It was only a matter of time until she was found. I am the one who has failed her. At every turn I have failed her as a guardian and as a brother. I did not protect her from being taken in by his false words. I can do nothing to ease the burden of her marriage. I could not keep her safe at Pemberley, and I left her here to once again fall into Wickham's hands."

Hearing the despair in his voice did more than any reassurance would have to restore Elizabeth to herself. "You have not failed her," she replied, desperate to reassure him. Lydia's presence preventing any closer embrace, she stroked his arm with her thumb, hoping it would convey the comfort she wished to impart. "You are not at fault for Mr Wickham's actions. Everything Georgiana has suffered has been due to him. *He* persuaded her to believe herself in love, *he* convinced her to elope. He could have chosen to enjoy his victory by living comfortably within Georgiana's income. His indifference need not have harmed her so much as it has, had she been allowed to go into society, to have friends and access to simple comforts, but he chose to live as he did and keep her cut off from the world.

"When he found her here, he could have taken her away to set himself up as a local gentleman in some other neighbourhood, rather than parading her in Meryton and trumpeting his connexion to you. He has at every stage been the only person responsible for his actions." Every word she spoke strengthened her own conviction of their truth; she could only hope he was similarly convinced.

A small sigh of relief escaped his lips. "Thank you, Elizabeth," he murmured. She sensed that he was not entirely able to accept her argument, but she did not push the matter further.

"What are your plans?" she asked.

"I understand Colonel Fitzwilliam is staying at present. I shall need to speak to him. But I intend to stay in Meryton."

"Will you stay at Longbourn? Mama is expecting it."

"I am uncertain as yet. Georgiana hopes I shall remain at Purvis Lodge."

"What will Mr Wickham think of that?"

"I spent a short amount of time with him when I visited. The pain of his wounds meant he was not often lucid, but if he recovers, he will contrive to present it as an irrefutable sign of our connexion and an indication that I shall support them both."

"Could you bear to be in the same house with him?"

"I would not have chosen it. But I can bear a great deal for Georgiana's sake. It might give her some respite."

"You have already borne so much."

"Yet it has not been enough."

Seeing that he was once again slipping into maudlin reflections, Elizabeth squeezed his arm, again wishing she could embrace him.

"You will stay to dinner today, at least? I am afraid Mama will wish to expedite our marriage now you have returned. I cannot promise a quiet meal."

"Would it placate her if we set a date for our wedding?"

Elizabeth could not hide her surprise. "Do you wish to?"

"Do you not?" Mr Darcy replied with almost equal consternation.

"I had not thought beyond your return," Elizabeth confessed. "I would of course be pleased to settle on a date. But I have no wish to force a commitment you are not ready to make. You must surely wish to assist Georgiana first."

"I do not wish to wait. I have engaged my hand and my honour to you. The right thing to do is to marry you. When I discovered that Wickham had made his way here, it was not merely for Georgiana that I feared. I did not know what he might do to harm you. That he would be seeking to hurt me through you made the thought no easier to bear. Elizabeth, you said earlier that I proposed so we might correspond. Recalling my lamentable first attempt at a declaration, I cannot deny it. Please do not think, however, that I wish to go back on my word.

"In truth, having corresponded with you, my affection has only grown. Your letters have given me more cause to be hopeful for the future than I have felt these past three years. I would like to set a date for our marriage, unless you have any objection to doing so other than your belief that you are following my wishes."

Elizabeth smiled at him. Her eyes relayed her response, but her words did not follow sufficiently rapidly for Lydia, who from her position behind them interjected, "Hurry up and agree so we can go back inside, Lizzy!"

Mr Darcy looked at Lydia in surprise, and Elizabeth blushed. "You ought not to have been listening, Lydia."

Her sister shrugged. "There is nothing else to do out here. Besides, I am only hurrying you on. If you want to kiss him, I promise not to tell."

"Thank you," Elizabeth replied with some emphasis, unable to meet Mr Darcy's eyes. She turned and walked on faster, the gentleman adjusting his pace to match hers until they had increased the distance between them and her sister.

With a hint of a smile, he commented, "I believe she is out of earshot now."

Elizabeth looked up at him then, still a little warm in the face. "I apologise for Lydia's behaviour."

"You need not. She meant well, I believe, even if her approach was unusual. Besides, my thoughts are not dissimilar to hers," he added. Elizabeth's eyes were drawn to where she knew that teasing twist would be at the corner of his mouth, and when he asked, in a lower voice, "May I kiss you?" she hesitated only a moment. Glancing round her to seek Lydia, she saw her sister was not only out of earshot, but had stopped, apparently taking a new and sudden interest in horticulture from the manner in which she inspected a tree. Her embarrassment at her sister's words was replaced by a pleasant tingling of anticipation, and she nodded once before lifting her lips to his.

When they parted, Elizabeth planted one or two further short kisses on his mouth before a giggle from Lydia brought her to herself. Looking round, she found her sister apparently still contemplating the same tree, and she blushed again. Seeing that Mr Darcy, despite having instigated the moment, was also discomposed by Lydia's obvious attention to their proceedings, she turned and began walking again at a brisk pace. "What must you think of my family? Mama will be just as embarrassing. Once we set a date, she will trumpet your wealth and status wherever she goes."

He caressed the hand that still sat lightly on his arm, "I have long learnt that my own family are not above reproach. You simply have the advantage of only having met the best of them."

"Are there many others?"

"No, my family is very small. I have no near Darcy relations, only some distant cousins. In addition to Lady Catherine, on my mother's side I have an uncle—Colonel Fitzwilliam's father. He is a good man. His other children, the viscount and the colonel's sisters, were of the same opinion as Lady Catherine regarding Georgiana's marriage, and I ceased any association with them long ago. But that is all I shall tell you for now. I shall gladly answer any further questions you may have, if you will first set a date for our wedding."

He accompanied his last words with a tone of mock severity, and Elizabeth laughed. "Very well. We shall marry six weeks from now. It will be clearer in a week or two what Georgiana's situation is, after which you will have more time to prepare. Also, Jane will have returned by then. And Kitty," she added after a moment's thought.

Mr Darcy gave her a small smile and lifted her free hand to his lips. "Very well. Now that is settled, I shall gladly keep my promise, but I fear Lydia is correct and we ought to first return to the house. You are shivering again."

As they turned back, Lydia looked curiously at them, and then in great surprise at Mr Darcy when he offered her his free arm. She took it, however, and Elizabeth tried not to be amused at the manner in which she paraded back to the house.

Mrs Bennet's joy at the news was unbounded. The delay since their engagement had dulled her most enthusiastic outbursts, but they emerged with full force at the prospect of all the preparations that would be needed. "Oh Lizzy! You fine, fine girl! To have secured such a wealthy man! The pin money! I shall have to see about everything. There is so much to be done!" she declared. Elizabeth sighed and was grateful Mr Darcy had chosen to spend some time with her father rather than face her mother's first outburst.

Colonel Fitzwilliam had returned to Longbourn whilst they were walking, and the three gentlemen were closeted together for some time. When the younger gentlemen did eventually join the ladies, it was the colonel who crossed to Elizabeth with rapid strides and sat by her, offering his heartiest congratulations. His cousin loomed sternly over him, saying, "I find you are in my seat," but he merely laughed.

"You will have all the time in the world to sit by your fair lady, Darcy. I shall be leaving Hertfordshire in a day or two. Spare her to me for half an hour." He turned his back on his cousin and commenced telling her an anecdote. Elizabeth smiled resignedly at Mr Darcy, who shook his head ruefully and took himself to another seat at no great distance from her, where he was promptly accosted by her mother.

The evening passed as pleasantly as could be hoped when the minds of three of the party were constantly drifting to another, less happy house. Elizabeth took quiet satisfaction in having set a date for their wedding but felt little inclined for celebration. Mr Darcy evidently felt similarly conflicted, for he responded to all the questions Mrs Bennet posed about their wedding with great solemnity. Towards the end of the evening, he drew Elizabeth away from the room, back towards the window where he had first told her of his sister.

"Your father has given permission for you to go to Purvis Lodge under my escort tomorrow."

"I would dearly like to see how Georgiana fares."

"Then it is settled. I shall return there tonight and stay at least until my cousin departs Longbourn. By then I shall know whether it is better to remain there or not."

CHAPTER THIRTY-FOUR

True to his word, Mr Darcy called promptly the following morning to escort Elizabeth, who was to travel in the carriage as he rode alongside. She wished she might be in a position that enabled them to talk more easily, but as they drew closer, was grateful she was able to reflect and prepare herself without being subject to scrutiny, even that of Mr Darcy.

Mrs Wickham met them at the door in person. She looked weary, and bore herself with a new solemnity that reminded Elizabeth strongly of her brother. Elizabeth ran forward without a second thought, seizing her friend's hands gently and then instinctively drawing her into an embrace. Mrs Wickham responded with a soft, "Oh!" of surprise, but after a moment of rigidity she accepted and returned the gesture.

After a few moments, Elizabeth drew away, embarrassed at her spontaneous display. She stepped back to allow Mr Darcy to greet his sister after his hour-long absence. As he did so, she remembered the moment she had last seen the two of them standing on this step. How different everything was now from how it had been then! They made a handsome picture, despite their shared gravity, and she found herself instinctively tracing their faces for similarities. The likeness was not uncanny, particularly with the light reflecting from Mrs Wickham's golden gloss and contrasting with her brother's dark curls, but both shared features that she also recognised as belonging to young Tommy. Joey, in contrast, evidently took more than his name from his father. As they spoke, the mannerisms of brother and sister were such as to heighten the resemblance, until Elizabeth wondered how she could ever have been mistaken about the nature of their relationship.

Mrs Wickham led them to the music room, where the pianoforte had been covered by a sheet. Elizabeth looked quizzically at her friend.

"It troubles George," Mrs Wickham said quietly, "to hear it play. It disturbs his rest." She placed a hand lightly on the covered instrument, as though apologising for neglecting it, before inviting them to sit. She turned to Elizabeth, and in an attempt at her usual manner, asked after her family.

"They are well, thank you," Elizabeth replied. "Jane is looking forward to returning to Netherfield, and Kitty is also expected back in a few weeks. I long to see them again. How are you?"

"I am also well, thank you." The words tripped off readily, politely, but without conviction.

"It must be a hard time for you at present," Elizabeth said with compassion. Mrs Wickham met her eyes slowly before looking rapidly away. Elizabeth was about to enquire further when the door opened and the two small boys entered. They too were changed; they walked gingerly, with exaggerated caution, closing the door quietly behind them.

"Miss 'lizbeth!" Joey forgot himself when he saw her and

shouted with joy, then stopped himself abruptly, looking nervously back towards the door as though expecting a reprimand. "Miss 'lizbeth!" he repeated, in softer tones. She held out her hands to both boys, and they came immediately to her to be greeted.

"Do you see this basket at my feet?" she asked solemnly. They nodded in unison. "Do you think you might carry it to the kitchen for me? You must be very careful."

"Treats?" Tommy asked with wide eyes.

Elizabeth smiled at him. "Perhaps there might be one or two special treats for two boys who can carry it safely between them. They have been sent by Mrs Bennet, my mother." They eagerly picked it up, jostling about so that Elizabeth was glad she had brought her smallest basket, and that it contained nothing but buns and crumpets that could withstand a certain amount of tumbling. After a moment, however, they got the basket between them and set off, comically staggering at the weight of their burden.

"Slowly, boys," Mr Darcy called behind them, and their uneven trot settled into an exaggerated walk, although no less stable. Their uncle stood and held the door, and they could be heard proceeding down the passageway with great care.

Mrs Wickham had watched the entire exchange, her expression warming as she did so. "That is very kind of your mother, Elizabeth," she said with more feeling than she had hitherto mustered.

"It is nothing out of the ordinary that they might not get at home, but she thought it might help them to have a distraction. How do they fare?"

Mrs Wickham looked pensive. "They are finding it very difficult. George is not often conscious, but when he is, loud noises can provoke him to anger. It is not directed at them, but they are too young to understand. It is not easy for them to be so quiet."

This was the longest speech she had managed since her visitors had arrived, and Elizabeth seized the opportunity it presented. "Perhaps you might bring them to Longbourn," she offered. "They could play more readily there, and Mama would be pleased to welcome you all. Although I am sorry not to be able to offer Jane as an incentive."

Mrs Wickham looked troubled. "I do not think I could leave George," she murmured abstractedly. She looked to Mr Darcy, who had been observing the exchange between the two women with a curious expression, part pleasure and part pain. "I ought to be nearby," she said with a note of question in her voice, as though seeking his confirmation of her words, "in case I am needed."

Mr Darcy shook his head. "You know my views, Georgiana. You do not need to always be ready to tend to him."

"But he may ask for me," his sister said with a hint of a plea in her voice.

"In his state, he might say anything. It is not good for you to be shut away here."

Mrs Wickham smiled sadly. "I have been shut away here for some time, Fitzwilliam. Now at least it is because it is my duty to be here."

Seeing they were not likely to agree, Elizabeth spoke again. "If you are not yet ready to leave, would you consider allowing me to take the children for a visit? It will do them good to be able to run and shout, and they will be safe at Longbourn."

Mrs Wickham looked doubtful, but at that moment the sound of a loud crash in the passage was followed by an inarticulate roar from the other room. Without knowing it, she winced, and her brother again stood and went to investigate.

He returned mere moments later, informing them that the maid had dropped an empty coal scuttle but that nothing was damaged and no one hurt, although she was greatly shaken. She had been dispatched to the kitchen for respite from the continued shouts of the injured man.

Mrs Wickham stood up with an air of decision. "I shall go to him," she said firmly. "You may take the boys, Elizabeth. Thank you. Perhaps Fitzwilliam could attend you and escort them back for dinner?"

Mr Darcy was reluctant to abandon his sister and could not be persuaded to leave, but he agreed to call later that afternoon and escort his nephews home. They, for their part, were delighted to hear they would be returning to Longbourn with Elizabeth, and as soon as they were in the carriage, Joey demanded to know whether they might make as much noise as they chose.

"Perhaps not as much as that," Elizabeth replied with a small smile, "but you may make a little noise, and you may run on the lawns, and if you are very good, I shall play hide and seek with you."

Elizabeth was as good as her word, and although her mind often drifted to her friend, did her best to conceal any unhappy feelings before the children. Mrs Bennet showed her own sympathy for them by providing a quantity of sweets far greater than Elizabeth recalled ever having been permitted. Lydia, not usually a favourite of small children but having no more desirable occupation, also appeared, and having found a ball to amuse herself, soon found she was expected to share her treasure. She would not admit that she found the pastime of idly rolling and tossing the ball to the two small boys entertaining, but found that a full half an hour seemed to pass without once pitying herself for her condition.

Mr Bennet, not finding the foolishness of children nearly

so entertaining as that of adults, kept to his study. Colonel Fitzwilliam was at first with him but soon abandoned his companion to entertain himself with his young cousins, delighting them in his willingness to engage in rough and tumble play and to dirty his coat in the process, before he took himself to visit their mother. All in all, it was considered a splendid afternoon by the two young gentlemen. When their uncle called to escort them home and sat for a time with the Bennet ladies, they both fell sound asleep on the sofa and had to be carried to the coach to be returned home.

The following day, Colonel Fitzwilliam departed Longbourn to return to London. He left on excellent terms with all the Bennets, but particularly with Elizabeth, who thanked him for his prompt appearance and all he had done to support her family, as well as his own.

"There is no need to thank me, Miss Bennet. We shall soon be family too. It is for me to thank you. The change you have wrought on Darcy is remarkable. He has borne his sister's present condition far better than I would have anticipated, and I think this can be largely credited to you." Elizabeth demurred, but they nevertheless parted with a mutual sense of satisfaction in a new friendship having been established.

Little changed for the next few days. Mr Darcy called daily. Sometimes he joined the Bennet family for a meal, but he was most at his ease when he and Elizabeth escaped to walk together. They spoke less of Mrs Wickham than had been their custom; he found the subject of his sister's strong sense of duty painful, so Elizabeth took it upon herself to talk of other matters. Sometimes, she coaxed and teased him in a light-hearted manner; at other times, they spoke of Pemberley and the many matters of estate and business that still occupied his correspondence. On alternate days, Mr Darcy would escort Elizabeth to Purvis Lodge, where she performed the same service, with slightly less success, for Mrs Wickham. She did succeed in coaxing her out into the garden, the children often playing nearby, where they would walk and talk of anything Elizabeth could think of. Mr Darcy, occupied at a desk at the window of his room, confessed after one such visit that he was less diligent at his correspondence when these walks took place, and that more often than not his eye was following the two ladies rather than the action of his pen.

Mrs Wickham's reserve continued, and Elizabeth found that, although she might be diverted from her thoughts at one moment, it took very little to remind her again of her husband's situation. In the middle of a conversation, she would sigh, and sometimes observe that she ought to relieve the nurse. She grew paler as the days drew on and there was no sign of any change. Mr Darcy's demeanour became increasingly as it had been when he first entered Hertfordshire. Elizabeth might once have found amusing the contrast between the stern gentleman and Mrs Bennet's enthusiastic wedding preparations, but she was too caught up in similar concern to notice it. Mr Bennet had no such reservations. The danger to his daughters having passed, he had recovered much of his usual indolent good humour, and although out of some residual feeling and respect for Mrs Wickham's plight he did not attempt to jest with Elizabeth, in the quiet of his own room he chuckled as he compared the effusions of his wife with the sternness of his future son.

A little over a week after the assembly, instead of the expected visit by Mr Darcy, Elizabeth received a note during breakfast, apologising for keeping away.

Wickham showed signs of improvement late last evening and even called for Joey and Tommy, who spent a short time in his company before he again grew too weary. Overnight, his condition deteriorated rapidly, and as I write this, he has descended into a stupor. Georgiana sits with him. I suspect today will see an end to his suffering.

The note finished with an exhortation not to attempt to visit, and a promise to send word when there was anything to be told. Word came that same afternoon that Mr Wickham had indeed succumbed to his injuries, and that Mrs Wickham, so recently restored to the status of wifehood, was once again a widow. Elizabeth, after conveying the important points to her parents, absented herself to her room, where she finally abandoned herself to the emotion she had held at bay since Mr Wickham's appearance.

CHAPTER THIRTY-FIVE

Mr Darcy called again the following morning with the intention of spending an hour at Longbourn before returning with Elizabeth to Purvis Lodge. The weather, however, prevented them from escaping to the garden. Instead, he was forced to endure Mrs Bennet's well-meaning condolences.

"Oh, Mr Darcy! What a loss it must be to you and your sister! To have been parted from her husband for so long, then to lose him all over again. She must feel it deeply. And back in her widow's weeds! Her grey dress was becoming, but she would do better with some colour, I think. Perhaps a deep blue. Yes, I could see her looking handsome in blue, once her mourning is past. Oh, what a sorry tale it is! And her boys! I must see about sending something over for them. Let me see, what might we have?"

She began reviewing a series of dishes and treats that might serve to brighten the mood of two small boys, and soon became entirely absorbed in the thought. Elizabeth turned her eyes in mute apology on Mr Darcy, who had sat stiff and blank-faced through the entire speech. Thinking a distraction might be in order, she instead asked after Colonel Fitzwilliam.

"I have not heard from him these past three days. I believe he has been much caught up in some business for his father, but I wrote express yesterday to inform him of Wickham's death. I do not doubt he will return to Hertfordshire soon to see Georgiana."

Mrs Bennet, hearing Colonel Fitzwilliam's name, once again pushed herself on their attention. "Colonel Fitzwilliam! Such a gentlemanlike man. Had he but a few thousand more a year he would be an excellent match for any young lady. What must he have looked like in his regimentals? Why, when I was a girl, I was very fond of the soldiers." She continued in this vein for some time. Elizabeth was not sorry to escape to the quiet of the carriage.

Georgiana was not waiting to greet them when they arrived at Purvis Lodge. Being shown in, they found her at the pianoforte. The lid was closed, but her hands were running over the smooth wood as she gazed through the window at the rain falling on the garden. She leapt to her feet as they entered, discomposed by being discovered in her reverie. Tommy and Joey were seated in one corner with a book between them. They jumped up too when their mother did and came to crowd protectively at her skirts.

"Fitzwilliam, Elizabeth. I did not expect you so soon." She had regained a little of her colour but had not lost her solemn demeanour.

"I could not have kept away, as long as my presence is welcome," Elizabeth replied before greeting the two boys who stood before their mother. After a moment's contemplation, Joey held out a small hand for Elizabeth to shake. With great gravity she did so, offering the same courtesy to Tommy, who accepted it with more reluctance.

"Come, children." Mr Darcy had moved to the door, and now stood waiting for the two to join him. "I have some business to attend to, and Mrs Bennet has once again sent a basket. Let us leave your mama and Miss Bennet."

Tommy tugged on Elizabeth's skirt. "Miss 'lizbeth," he whispered.

She smiled at him. "Yes, Tommy?"

"I don't want Mama sad. Make Mama laugh?"

"I shall do all I can to help her," she replied sincerely. Tommy nodded several times very rapidly, and at another word from his uncle, left the room.

"Welcome indeed," Georgiana said with greater feeling as Elizabeth led her to a seat.

"I am sorry, my dear, for all you have endured. This has been a difficult time for you."

She received in response a wan smile. Elizabeth longed to draw out her friend, to encourage her to talk of how she was truly feeling, and was wondering how to begin when Georgiana surprised her by voluntarily introducing the subject.

"Do not speak ill of him, please, please do not. It was painful, at the end, to see him suffer so. George was always so strong, so much a master of himself. Whatever he may have been since our marriage, I could not help but recall him as he was when I idolised him as a child." Her eyes misted with tears and memory, and Elizabeth, unable to think of anything soothing to say, merely took her hand.

"My brother cannot understand," Georgiana continued softly. "He has for so long seen me as a child who needs protecting and George as the villain to be kept at bay. He has done so much to help me, and I do not mean to complain, but I cannot speak to him of our marriage. I cannot speak my heart."

"Your heart!" Elizabeth could not contain her astonishment. "Did you love Mr Wickham?"

Her friend shook her head, tears still gathering in her eyes, although they did not fall. "I do not...I think...I hardly know." She paused, gazing once again at the rain. "I do not think so. But it is not easy to believe he is gone. He has figured so large in my life, even in these past months. I hardly know who I am, if I am not George Wickham's wife. Even at the end, when he did not ask for me, did not recognise me, I still knew who I was. I do not know what it means to be his widow."

"You are Georgiana. You are Fitzwilliam's sister, my friend, and Jane and Charlotte's friend. You are mother to two wonderful boys and the most accomplished at the pianoforte of anyone I have had the pleasure to hear. You are the bravest person I know."

Georgiana's reaction may have been a laugh or a sob but was suppressed so rapidly as to be unable to tell the difference. "I do not feel brave," she said quietly.

"When you do not feel it, but continue regardless, doing what you know must be done, that is when you are at your bravest."

"And what must I do now?"

"I wish I knew," Elizabeth admitted sadly. "Endure a little longer, for there will be visits of condolence to face, and I am sure there will be matters relating to his life and passing to resolve. Then perhaps we can see you smile again."

Georgiana attempted to overcome her sorrow at this, but Elizabeth, seeing the effort it cost her, laid a hand on hers. "Do not feel you need to pretend for me. You need not smile for my sake. I only wish it for yours." Seeing that her friend was still greatly discomposed, she began speaking of Joey and Tommy, and planning some activities that might serve to entertain and distract them. Georgiana listened in silence, but the topic was ideally suited to engage her interest, and after a time, she began to participate in the conversation.

When Mr Darcy returned to the room, he appeared pleased to discover Georgiana looking a little happier. He paused in the doorway a moment, watching them speak quietly together. Before he could make a move to announce his return, Elizabeth rose and said, "Now, you promised me you would attempt to play. It need not be long, and it certainly need not be lively, but I would be glad to see you make the attempt before I depart."

Georgiana followed obediently to the instrument. As they crossed the room, Elizabeth welcomed Mr Darcy. "Fitzwilliam!" She greeted him with a smile. "Georgiana and I were going to see whether we could find some music. You may stay, if you promise to be quiet."

Georgiana had looked up at his name, and her eyes had warmed, but she bent her head again as she took a seat alongside Elizabeth, who opened the instrument, asking, "Do you require music to follow?"

Georgiana shook her head and lifted her fingers to the keys, where she waited for a moment, her breathing audible. As soon as she began to play, however, tension dropped away from her frame, and she was rapidly lost in the music. She chose an old country air rather than an elegant presentation piece, and Elizabeth began to softly sing along with her friend. She again noticed Mr Darcy, drawn inexorably towards them, and raised her voice slightly that he might hear them both. His countenance betrayed his satisfaction at hearing the two women so in harmony, and when tears came to his eyes, she recognised them as betokening joy and gratitude as much as any residual sorrow. When the music ceased, he rose apparently on an impulse, taking her hand and planting a light kiss on her fingers before turning to Georgiana and reaching for her. Instead of taking the proffered hands, his sister leapt from her seat, clinging to him as her tears flowed.

When they eventually subsided, he took from his pocket a handkerchief to offer to her. Observing the stitching, he returned it and found another in its stead which he passed to Georgiana. Elizabeth, who had seen his action despite her own eyes threatening tears, felt a warm leap of affection that settled comfortably in her heart.

Elizabeth was thoughtful on her return to Longbourn. Georgiana had revealed a great deal more than Elizabeth had expected of her, and had left her with the conviction that something must be done to allow her to escape the long shadow cast by her marriage. What that might be, however, entirely escaped her.

Colonel Fitzwilliam returned to Meryton but chose to stay at Purvis Lodge, where he was much engaged with Mr Darcy. The day after his arrival, he called at Longbourn, was shown directly into the library, and remained closeted with Mr Bennet for some time. When he emerged, all three ladies were surprised to discover that Mr Bennet joined him, with an air of resignation and weariness.

"Well, my dears," he said, resting his hand on his youngest daughter's shoulder before taking a seat. "Colonel Fitzwilliam brings the answer to one of our mysteries." He gestured resignedly to the younger man, who had settled himself in a chair facing them all.

"I undertook some investigations into the man Denny, or Grey as he called himself," he clarified, cutting off the question he could see forming on Mrs Bennet's lips. "I shall not trouble you with all the details, but suffice to say, he has long been an associate of Mr Wickham's, and his fortunes have risen and fallen alongside those of his friend. During a recent downturn, when funds were particularly scarce, he joined the militia. No doubt he was seeking a source of income, and apparently he retained sufficient funds or friends to purchase a commission. Shortly after he joined, a spate of thefts occurred from the colonel of the regiment. Whilst the cause of these was being investigated, Mr Denny deserted his post and disappeared."

Mrs Bennet burst out in a wailing cry. "Oh! Oh! Such a man to have been allowed among us! And Lydia! Oh, my poor—"

Colonel Fitzwilliam cut her off before she could continue. "Madam, there is more to be told." Mrs Bennet, unused to being interrupted in such decided tones, ceased her complaint in surprise, although she continued to emit small cries and moans through the remainder of Colonel Fitzwilliam's tale.

"Having spoken to some of the officers from his regiment, it seems likely Mr Denny heard from them of the town of Meryton. When he wished to leave London for somewhere out of the way, he appears to have recalled the name of the town and made it his destination. Having no personal connexion with the place, he had good reason to assume it would not be the first town he would be sought in. At some point in his flight, he was joined by Mr Wickham, and so they came here.

"As far as I have been able to ascertain, Mr Denny was not told the specifics of Miss Lydia's history," he continued, nodding to Lydia, who was wide-eyed at the tale. "I am well known amongst the military and militia. He must have recognised me at the assembly and fled potential discovery.

His attempt to include Miss Lydia in his flight was, I suspect, opportunistic rather than deliberate design. Perhaps he held a mistaken belief that her openness made her agreeable to such an approach.

"Mr Denny has been apprehended in another town. He had fled only as far as Buckinghamshire. It is possible his trial will be reported. Therefore, Mr Bennet has judged it best that I present the situation to you now before it becomes general knowledge. Miss Lydia, I do not believe your name will be mentioned or reported, but it is important that you understand the gravity of the situation. Gossip can be cruel, and we cannot rule out the possibility."

Lydia bit her lip and hung her head. She had always imagined it would be thrilling to be caught in the middle of such events, but under the piercing stare of Colonel Fitzwilliam, Elizabeth could see her sister felt unusually cowed.

Mrs Bennet once again began to exclaim and to bewail her nerves, working herself into such a frenzy that there was nothing to be done but for Elizabeth to escort her mother upstairs. She attempted to explain the truth of Georgiana's situation, or at least to convey that Mr Wickham was not exactly as he had appeared to be. She was partially successful; Mrs Bennet came to understand the man to be a gamester, which sent her into new paroxysms of surprise. When she had calmed sufficiently for Elizabeth to be able to return, she resolved not to broach the subject further with her mother unless there were any new developments that made it necessary. Returning downstairs, she found her father and Colonel Fitzwilliam engaged in a game of chess, Lydia sitting nearby gazing out of the window. Elizabeth, recalling that she had seen Georgiana similarly alone and thoughtful, went and sat with her, placing a hand over her sister's. Lydia looked up in surprise.

"No great harm has come to you, Lydia, and we are all grateful for it. I think, though, you are not happy. Will you talk to me?"

Lydia shook her head emphatically, but then laid it on her sister's shoulder. "I miss Jane," she murmured.

Elizabeth felt a pang that she could not offer the comfort that their sister could, but merely said, "As do I. She will be back with us soon."

"But not here, and not the same," Lydia replied. "I miss Kitty too, but her letters are so different now. I shall not know her when she returns."

"Perhaps you will find that you are also changed," Elizabeth replied gently. Lydia merely sighed.

CHAPTER THIRTY-SIX

The days passed rapidly in a flurry of activity. Mr Wickham's funeral was attended by more than one curious gentleman of the town, and Georgiana found herself facing calls from all the women. Most were scrupulously polite, and some were entirely kind, but all were curious. Elizabeth was with her friend as she received some of these calls, and it soon became clear that rumours abounded regarding Mr Wickham's debts and the truth of their marriage. Although none would ask directly, she knew Mrs Long and her aunt Philips enough to recognise the knowing looks that they shared when they happened to visit at the same time. She attempted to raise the matter with Georgiana, but found her concerns were soundly rebuffed.

"It matters not, now. Let them believe what they will. I no longer have need for concealment. It is all in the past."

Try as she might, however, Elizabeth could not be unaware that the town not only freely discussed Georgiana's marriage, but also her own engagement.

"Your friend Mrs Wickham must be suffering a great

deal," her aunt commented, not unkindly, one day at tea after dining at Longbourn.

"It has been a difficult time for her," Elizabeth agreed, not without some caution. It was a relief to be able to speak more freely about her friend, but her habit of being restrained regarding Georgiana was not yet entirely overcome. She had no wish to prolong the inclination of the townsfolk to discuss her situation.

"Mr Wickham seemed such a charming man, but if the stories are to be believed, he had a great many debts, and of the worst kind, too!"

Mrs Philips eyed her niece as she spoke, gauging her reaction. Seeing Elizabeth had nothing to say on the subject of Mr Wickham's financial situation, she continued lightly, "What I cannot understand is why Mr Darcy felt it so necessary to conceal their relationship. There is nothing so very shocking about having a sister!"

Elizabeth's colour rose, and her aunt leant forward with sudden interest. "Did you know, my dear?"

Elizabeth hesitated only a moment before deciding there was no benefit in concealing this part of the truth. "Not at first, but he informed me before our engagement."

"How peculiar of him to conceal it at all! Did he explain why? He does not seem a man for secrets. I wonder what else he might be hiding."

"Mr Darcy is an honourable man," she replied, "and there are honourable reasons for all of his actions. Forgive me that they are not mine to discuss."

"Oh yes, an honourable man!" Mrs Bennet's voice startled them both with her interjection. "And a rich one too! Why, he informed me himself that the ceiling of the ballroom at Pemberley was painted by a member of the Royal Academy! Now, what was the name? Oh, it matters not! I am sure once

Lizzy is mistress there, we shall be given a tour by the master himself! No housekeeper for us!"

For once, Elizabeth was grateful for her mother's effusions, turning the conversation as they did away from Mr Darcy's actions. Georgiana might be prepared to accept and defy society's scrutiny, but she was sure her brother would not find it easy to bear that his behaviour contributed to the gossip surrounding her. In this, however, the gentleman surprised her. Georgiana was, if not welcomed in society, at least accepted, and was not suffering from the attention; Elizabeth continued to be a favourite amongst the local population. He, therefore, was content to let matters stand as they were, confident that soon enough, other subjects would rise to be of more interest to the people of Meryton.

In this, Mr Darcy proved entirely correct. Shortly after the funeral, Meryton's chief source of gossip began to shift from the story of the young widow to the reopening of Netherfield. Many were keen to see how Mrs Bingley had adjusted to married life, and hoped that the return of the couple would herald a new variety of social activity. They had spent the final part of their tour in London, and were to bring Kitty back with them on their return, although Mrs Bennet had argued vigorously that Kitty would be better staying in London where she might have a better chance of finding a husband.

The Bingleys returned to Netherfield one evening, keeping Kitty with them for the night, so it was not until the following day that Elizabeth would be reunited with her sisters. Mr Darcy, Colonel Fitzwilliam, and Georgiana had all been invited to Longbourn for dinner. Georgiana had declined, not yet feeling equal to being among so many people all at once, but her brother and cousin had accepted and were to join them in the afternoon. Elizabeth set out to take a solitary morning walk, but soon found her isolation interrupted by the sound of another pair of footsteps, approaching from the opposite direction. As she rounded a corner, she smiled in delight. "Charlotte!"

Charlotte Lucas greeted her with a wide smile, then exclaimed in mock severity, "I was on my way to complain of your neglect, Lizzy. I have not seen you once since the night of the assembly."

Elizabeth took her friend's arm and turned about on the path to walk alongside her. Matching her tone with exaggerated contrition, she replied, "I am acutely sorry for it. Can you ever forgive me?"

Charlotte dropped her teasing tone and squeezed her arm. "I believe our friendship is of sufficient good standing to survive," she said. "You have had much to occupy you, I am certain. How is Georgiana? When I called on her with my mother, I was unable to tell how she is coping."

Elizabeth sighed. "It is very difficult for her. I think she would welcome a visit from you without Lady Lucas. Perhaps you could come with me to visit her one day. Mr Darcy and Colonel Fitzwilliam do a great deal to lift her mood, but I believe she needs some friends around her too."

"I can certainly do so. I would have called before, but I did not wish to intrude. I imagine she has been kept very busy," Charlotte replied.

"She has had many callers, it is true, but would value the company of friends more than all the well-meant curiosity of her neighbours. I am concerned for her."

Charlotte promised to call on Georgiana soon, before turning her attention to the furrow of Elizabeth's brow and her slower step than usual. "And how do you fare?"

"Me?" Elizabeth's brow furrowed still further.

"You may not like to admit it, but you are troubled,"

Charlotte said kindly. "Have you encouraged Georgiana to discuss her feelings?"

"Yes, of course. It is part of healing."

"Indeed. And have you talked of your own?" She smiled knowingly at Elizabeth's silence. "Come, Lizzy. Talk to me."

Once she had begun, she found that the entire story poured from her unchecked. Charlotte listened in silence to her impressions of Georgiana, of her fears for how she would escape Mr Wickham's continuing hold over her life, of how she worried that Mr Darcy took too much upon himself. Elizabeth found intense relief in the telling, a relief she had not known she needed.

"Have you spoken of any of this to Mr Darcy?" Charlotte enquired when Elizabeth finally ran out of words.

"No, not at all. He is busy at present, tying up Mr Wickham's affairs. It would not do to burden him."

"Yet you are soon to be his wife."

"Do not think I do not care for him, Charlotte, or that he cannot be trusted with my happiness. Everything is happening so rapidly, but he is the best of men—I have seen it in his deeds, I have heard it in his words. I love him, with all my heart, and I know he cares equally for me. But he has so much to cope with at present, I could not burden him with this. I am lucky to have friends around me to confide in," she added with a grateful glance.

Charlotte smiled affectionately. "I hope matters settle soon so that you may begin your married life without this shadow looming so large over you."

"My married life! Oh, what a thought that is. Starting another life, with a new name and a new home."

Charlotte squeezed her arm. "It is an adventure to be sure, and one you are well fitted for," she replied. Elizabeth knew she did not imagine the catch in her friend's voice, and would have turned the conversation, but Charlotte began questioning her further, and Elizabeth was soon speaking with animation about her many hopes for the future and of her anticipation of what Pemberley would be like. As she recalled passages from Mr Darcy's letters, his deep attachment to his home was clear, and Charlotte commented that Elizabeth was fortunate in how much he trusted her and sought to make her a genuine part of his life and establishment.

"You will have to come to visit us at Pemberley once we are settled. I think you and Mr Darcy will be fast friends, and Georgiana will be as pleased to see you as I am."

"She will remove with you, then, on your marriage? I wondered whether she would see out her lease at Purvis Lodge."

Elizabeth paused to reflect on this comment. "I had not thought about it. I suppose I had assumed she would live with us. Her brother will certainly want her to, and Purvis Lodge cannot hold very many happy memories."

"I do not know. It is where she found true friendship, perhaps for the very first time in her life."

"That is a bittersweet thought, Charlotte."

"Perhaps. But it means there has been sweetness, and in time it will outweigh the bitter."

ELIZABETH'S OPPORTUNITY TO confide in her friend brought her new energy, and when the Bingleys arrived at Longbourn and she and Jane flew into one another's arms, she was less distracted than she might have been. She greeted Kitty with almost as much enthusiasm, genuinely pleased to be reunited. She had feared her sister might be petulant at her stay in London not having been extended, but she showed no sign of being anything other than pleased to be at home.

The reunion between Kitty and Lydia was slightly more circumspect. Elizabeth observed that they were each cautious, and they circled one another in conversation as the family and guests sat down together. Lydia was subdued compared to her usual self and kept darting nervous glances at Colonel Fitzwilliam. "Oh Lydia," Kitty said with animation, "I do not think I told you in my letters, but I brought a magazine with London fashions for you to look at. One of the pictures has a lady in such a shade of orange! I thought when I saw it what a good laugh you would find it. Shall I go and fetch it?"

Lydia accepted the offer, and the two were soon poring over the pictures and giggling together. Neither was quite as they had been before. Lydia still took the lead, and at one point pulled the magazine sharply from her sister's hands to look more closely, but when Kitty offered an opinion, she waited and listened almost every time. Kitty, in turn, looked about for recognition for her good deed in establishing a conversation with her sister, and pouted a little when she did not receive it, but when Lydia began to show enthusiasm over a particularly garish outfit, she took genuine delight in her pleasure. Elizabeth, although scarcely able to tear herself away from her own most beloved sister, was pleased by the picture they presented.

When Mr Darcy and Colonel Fitzwilliam arrived, the latter glanced once at his cousin and immediately put himself into Mrs Bennet's notice. The other gentleman, seeing that Elizabeth and Jane were deep in conversation, readily joined Mr Bingley and Mr Bennet's discussion.

The dinner party proved a pleasant evening. Mrs Bennet had excelled herself to present a good table, and the newcomers brought enough news and variety of conversation to entertain all.

"One piece of news we are yet to share," remarked Mr Bingley during the dessert course, "is that my sister Caroline is to be married."

"Married!" remarked Mrs Bennet. "Well, good luck to her. Is it a good match?"

"Oh, excellent," replied Mr Bingley with a smile. "Mr Hartford has offered for her before, but Caroline was always so certain that London was to be her home, she would not consider it. His father is a cousin of an earl, you know, and he is a distinguished member of York's society."

"She was busy preparing her wedding clothes when we saw her in London," added Jane. "She will be pleased to introduce York to the latest fashions."

Everyone agreed that it sounded an eminently eligible match. Only Mrs Bennet wondered aloud why she had not accepted such an excellent offer before; Mr Darcy's eyes met Elizabeth's, and she restrained the laugh that threatened at the expression she saw there.

With so many people present, there was little opportunity for private conversation, but it was soon agreed between Elizabeth and Jane that they would go together to call on Georgiana in the morning, before returning to Netherfield to spend the entire day together. Lydia and Kitty were to join them in the afternoon and stay to dinner, Lydia having been given dispensation to do so by her father. Mr Darcy and Colonel Fitzwilliam were soon talked into joining them. Georgiana they could not speak for, but Jane resolved to persuade her, if she could, during their call.

Towards the end of the evening, Elizabeth and Mr Darcy managed a few quiet words together. Mindful of her earlier conversation with Charlotte, Elizabeth broached a topic that had occupied her mind for much of the day.

"It is odd to think I shall soon be changing my name and embarking on a whole new life."

"Not unpleasant, I hope?"

"No," she smiled. "It is just there has been so much occupying us recently. I hardly feel that I have had time to prepare for all the changes that will come upon us."

"I do not think you need to prepare. You will make an excellent Darcy just as you are."

Elizabeth's face warmed at this, and she laughed to cover her embarrassment. "You see, I ought not to blush at such an absurd speech! Ours is not a marriage of convenience or alliance, yet Georgiana's plight has formed so much a part of our courtship that we have hardly had the opportunity to act as lovers do. I hope you do not think I am lacking in affection because I have had neither time nor inclination to tease and coax sweet sentiments from you?"

He looked at her in mild surprise. "I do not find you lacking in anything, Elizabeth. I am confident that I have your affection as surely as you have mine." He lifted the back of his fingers to her cheek for a breath, and smiled as it flushed again. Elizabeth was satisfied.

SHE HAD INTENDED to walk to Purvis Lodge the following morning, but Jane insisted on the carriage. As Elizabeth settled herself in a seat and set off, her sister seized her hand.

"I am sorry to deny you your exercise, dearest Lizzy, but I do not think I could walk so far at present."

"Oh! Are you ill? Did you injure yourself?"

"Not precisely," replied Jane with a radiant smile.

"Although it is important I follow the doctor's advice for the next few months."

Elizabeth caught her meaning immediately and wrapped her other hand around the two already joined. "Jane!" she breathed in inarticulate delight.

"Oh, Lizzy!" Jane replied, her smile unfading although tears sprung to her eyes. "I am so happy!"

Georgiana and Jane were both overjoyed to see one another, and Elizabeth retreated slightly, pleased at Georgiana's animation at having another friend returned. They were not long left alone, however, for Joey and Tommy soon burst into the room with cries of "Miss Benn't!"

"It is Mrs Bingley now," their mother told them.

The two boys stopped and peered cautiously at Jane. "She looks same," Joey said doubtfully.

"Do you remember that she got married?"

Joey nodded.

"When she married Mr Bingley, she changed her name."

"Like I'm George when Papa came?"

"A little like that."

"Will she be Miss Benn't 'gain? I'm Joey now."

"No, she will stay Mrs Bingley."

"I stay George?"

"Not if you do not choose it, until you are a man."

"I will be Joey, not a man." Having thus decided, the boy held out a hand to Jane to take and made an attempt at a bow. Jane returned the handshake and a curtsey, and soon found herself in a corner with the two boys, listening to a full account of their latest escapades.

"I do not think she came to see me," Georgiana said quietly. Elizabeth looked at her with concern, but to her relief found her friend smiling.

"I suspect Jane will soon find a way to devote all of her

attention to you whilst keeping them happy, but in the meantime, I am afraid I shall have to suffice."

"I think we shall manage very well," Georgiana replied. "I should like to keep you all to myself until Fitzwilliam appears. After that I shall have to share you."

"Or else we shall have to share him," Elizabeth laughed.

Georgiana merely smiled and made no reply.

CHAPTER THIRTY-SEVEN

Georgiana's habitual reluctance to go into society and her recent formal widowhood were no match for Jane's quiet persuasion, and she was brought to agree to join them for dinner at Netherfield. After all, Jane observed, everyone in attendance, bar Kitty and Lydia, were already counted amongst Georgiana's friends. All knew her story, and none would demand anything of her that would cause her discomfort. Jane vouched solemnly that her two youngest sisters would not be permitted to trouble Georgiana, if they proved too lively for her to bear. When she protested that such a late addition to their numbers would inconvenience her friend, Jane recalled that she had fully intended to invite Charlotte Lucas as well, and begged a sheet of paper to send a note to Lucas Lodge with the invitation. Georgiana bowed to the gentle pressure, and at last consented to come.

Jane and Elizabeth returned to Netherfield deep in conversation, which continued unabated until they were interrupted by the entrance of their other guests. Kitty and

Lydia arrived first, followed not long after by Mr Darcy, who came alone. After greeting the ladies and informing them that Colonel Fitzwilliam remained at home but would escort Georgiana later, he chose to withdraw with Mr Bingley and leave the ladies to one another's society. The four sisters had a pleasant time of it; all were pleased to be reunited, and there was much news and exclamation to be passed between them. They had only an hour together before the gentlemen, drawn by the sound of conversation and laughter, could no longer resist interrupting them. Mr Bingley devoted himself to Jane and Lydia, and it fell to Mr Darcy to entertain Elizabeth and Kitty.

The latter fell silent during the ensuing conversation. The engaged couple gradually receded into a discussion that she could not join, full of unspoken words and significant glances. At first, they spoke only of Georgiana, but conversation then ranged to Pemberley and to their planned stay in London immediately after their wedding. Kitty quietly withdrew, unnoticed by either, to sit with her other sisters and Mr Bingley.

"I am a little nervous at the thought of meeting your family."

"You need not fear," he assured her. "It is only my uncle and aunt whom you will meet, and they are good people. You have met Colonel Fitzwilliam, and my other relations will not be introduced to my wife. Especially not when Georgiana is in residence with us."

"Perhaps it will be possible for the breach to heal, with time."

His face darkened. "It is too late for that."

Elizabeth reached to take his hand. "Do not think so. You feel it deeply, but there is always hope for reconciliation." His eyes met hers, and she thought she saw the stirrings of belief in them, although he did not smile. "I am afraid you will not escape meeting my cousins when you meet my uncle and aunt Gardiner. They will insist on seeing me and will not spare you their interest either. They are good children, but likely to be more so if you happen to have a pocketful of sweets or curiosities."

"I shall endure it as best I can," he said solemnly, but the familiar twitch of his lips told her she had succeeded in lifting his thoughts.

It was with some surprise that they discovered from Kitty's re-approach that it was time to go and dress for dinner.

Kitty had promised Lydia that she would teach her a new coiffure she had learnt from Aunt Gardiner's maid in London. Jane having pleaded her duty as hostess to exempt her from modelling the new style, Elizabeth soon found herself seated before a glass in the guest bedroom, trying not to wince as her two younger sisters flitted together around her head. She was pleasantly surprised, however. Without a single cross word, and with Kitty taking the lead without a murmur from Lydia, they successfully arranged her hair into a style more becoming than Elizabeth had expected.

Charlotte had already arrived when they descended, although Georgiana and Colonel Fitzwilliam had not yet appeared. It was not long before a carriage was heard, however, and Mr Darcy excused himself, shortly after followed by Elizabeth. She found Georgiana and Colonel Fitzwilliam divesting themselves of their outer garments in the entrance hall, with Mr Darcy pacing nervously nearby.

"Oh, do give over, Darcy. You will wear out Bingley's floor." Colonel Fitzwilliam sounded more amused than irritated, but Mr Darcy came immediately to a halt. Elizabeth crossed to Georgiana. She looked around her nervously and clung to Elizabeth's hand when it was offered.

"What do you need?" Elizabeth asked softly, drawing her aside. Georgiana attempted to speak, but her throat was dry, and she was unable to say a word. Her eyes flickered nervously between the three of them. Elizabeth tried again, in a lower voice so that the gentlemen could not hear. "Who would be your preferred companion for braving an entrance? You need not speak if you can indicate it some other way."

Georgiana looked nervously at Elizabeth before nodding slightly in the direction of her cousin. Elizabeth too inclined her head, to show she understood, and stepped away to Mr Darcy. "Come, Fitzwilliam," she said gently, taking his arm. "We are all friends here. The colonel will ensure she is comfortable."

Mr Darcy looked at her in astonishment and seemed about to protest, but Elizabeth was brooking no opposition. She looked up at him, eyes beseeching. "Please," she added. His eyes moved briefly from hers, seeking his sister, who was standing quietly with his cousin. He did not speak, or smile, but met her eyes again before turning and escorting Elizabeth back to the drawing room.

As they approached the room, Elizabeth looked up at him again. "Thank you," she said with sincerity. He looked down on her with anxious eyes, and she smiled comfortingly. "All will be well, my love."

He looked startled at the endearment, but it brought a hint of colour to his cheeks and a softness to his eyes that almost translated to a smile. "Thank you, Elizabeth," he replied, his voice caressing her name. "I have not had the opportunity yet to tell you how beautiful you look. You always do, but your hair is particularly becoming this evening." He reached out to play with a loose curl, and Elizabeth's blush was accompanied by laughter in her relief that some of his tension had lifted. She smiled at him as he continued to thread the curl through his fingers, and replied in a tone torn between playfulness and solemnity.

"I do not think it would be fair for me to accept such compliments without confessing that I think you the most handsome man that I have ever known, as well as the best of them."

Delight spread across his face at this statement, and they lingered a little longer in the passageway, exchanging soft words of affection, before the sound of approaching footsteps had them returning to the others.

When Georgiana entered, she looked much younger than her true age. Gazing nervously at the assembled guests, she smiled at her brother, Elizabeth, Charlotte, and Jane. She looked a little frightened by Kitty and Lydia but, with a little effort, managed a smile for each of them too. As her eyes rested on Mr Bingley, she looked timid and self-conscious, and Elizabeth remembered her confession that she had idolised his memory in contrast to the reality of her married life.

Mr Bingley, entirely unconscious of the nerves he was creating in his guest, stepped forward with a broad smile. "Mrs Wickham," he said warmly, "and Colonel Fitzwilliam. It is a pleasure to see you both again, and to welcome you to my home. I believe no introductions are needed."

Georgiana bit her lip, then, "None, thank you Mr Bingley, I am acquainted with everyone here. I would prefer—" She paused. "If it is not too much to ask, that is, if it would not be too forward of me, I would prefer to be called Georgiana by everyone present."

Mr Bingley smiled broadly. "And you must call me Charles, as you used to when you were a child," he replied.

He seemed about to continue, but Jane, seeing their guest was not yet composed, stepped to his side.

"Welcome, Georgiana," she said gently. "Will you come and sit with me? I was so caught up with your dear boys this morning that I feel we have hardly had the opportunity to speak so far."

Georgiana looked gratefully at Jane as she steered her to a farther part of the room and began to engage her in quiet conversation. After a few minutes, Charlotte moved across to join them. Elizabeth was pleased to see her friend visibly relaxing under their welcome, and to see Mr Darcy also lose some of his rigidity as he saw that he need not have feared too much for his sister.

Dinner passed rapidly and very pleasantly. As they finished, Colonel Fitzwilliam sat back with a satisfied sigh and commented, "Mrs Bingley, I can only offer you the compliment that you set as good a table as your mother."

Jane accepted the praise with a light blush and unaffected pleasure. As they stood up to withdraw, Elizabeth murmured, "As fine a table as Mama and no one was in the least embarrassed. You do yourself credit."

"Hush," her sister replied with an admonishing smile.

Kitty and Lydia dominated conversation in the drawing room, but they were not long alone, for all of the gentlemen were keen to return to them. On doing so, Mr Bingley immediately suggested some of the ladies perform. As Charlotte demurred and none of the others counted music amongst their accomplishments, Elizabeth rose and invited Georgiana to join her.

"It is not a public display," she whispered with mock severity, "and I shall scold you if you think of it as one. You are performing them a service, for if you do not play, they will be forced to listen to me."

Georgiana giggled slightly and obediently took her seat.

"Shall I turn pages, or sing, or hold my tongue?" Elizabeth asked her.

Georgiana inspected the music on the pianoforte. "Turn for me, please," she replied. "Then you must play, whether it will be a punishment or not."

As soon as her fingers touched the keys, the young widow was once again lost to the music. Elizabeth smiled as she followed the notes, for she noticed that Georgiana either had some previously undiscovered skill to read music with her eyes closed or else had only accepted her assistance to bolster her confidence. She had some leisure to turn and inspect their audience.

Lydia was fidgeting slightly in her seat, restless as she always was when asked to sit and simply listen. For Lydia, music meant dancing, and she hated to sit through it, but she was making a good show of attending, at least, and not attempting to chatter.

Kitty was listening with an air of studied politeness that was new to Elizabeth. She had grown more mature in her absence. Jane and Mr Bingley were seated together, hands joined, smiling in contentment and occasionally exchanging quiet comments. Colonel Fitzwilliam sat with his foot up on a stool, enjoying the picture his cousin and Elizabeth made. He noticed her gaze and tipped an imaginary hat to her. Charlotte sat slightly back from the others, watching the scene with an unusually placid smile on her face. Elizabeth wondered what she might be thinking.

Mr Darcy's thoughts were no mystery. He had taken a seat with a clear view of the ladies at the pianoforte, and he watched them with frank awe, taking in both Georgiana's contentment to be playing to a room full of friends and Elizabeth sitting reassuringly at her side. As her eyes met his, she saw the hint of tenderness that she had seen in the passage develop into a full-blown smile, which she willingly returned.

As the piece finished, Georgiana was overcome by shyness and would not play again. Mr Darcy jumped up and approached the instrument. "Georgie," he said softly. She looked up at the childish nickname, long abandoned. "Come," he said simply. She looked gratefully at him as he escorted her to a seat and placed himself between her and the room, where she could take some time to recover out of general sight.

Elizabeth played and sang, and although she made many more mistakes than the younger woman, she sang with such feeling and expression that even Lydia, at the end, commented on it. Elizabeth intended to retire from the instrument, but Lydia had not finished, for she announced to the entire room, "I wish I could dance."

"Dancing! We ought to have some dancing," agreed Mr Bingley. He looked at Jane, "You will not?" She shook her head, and he turned and surveyed the room. "Miss Lydia, I shall dance with you, if you will. Darcy, your cousin cannot dance, so you must stand up with someone. Miss Kitty or Miss Lucas, either will do."

"I shall stand up with you, Kitty, if Mr Darcy will not," Charlotte interjected, seeing that the gentleman was still much occupied with his sister's comfort. Kitty smiled broadly, and the two took their places.

Mr Bingley turned back to Elizabeth. "You will play?" he asked.

She nodded, before laughingly adding, "Very ill, but well enough for friends, I hope."

The dance began. Elizabeth's eyes could not help but wander to Georgiana, who watched the proceedings with a longing look, and she felt a little sorrowful.

As the dance ended, she was minded to cease rather than pain Georgiana any further, but to her surprise, Lydia had crossed the room to sit by the young widow's side. Charlotte, also noticing, caught Elizabeth's eye before abruptly moving across to speak to Kitty and Colonel Fitzwilliam. Elizabeth hesitated, then moved to sit near Mr Darcy, lest she should be needed to pull Lydia away. He was looking severely at the youngest Bennet, also ready to intervene if she caused his sister any discomfort.

To both of their surprise, Lydia's voice was full of compassion when she spoke. "You would like to dance, but you do not feel you ought," she said, looking carefully at Georgiana. "If you wish it, we are all friends here, and none of us will think you any less proper for it."

Georgiana's eyes widened at this. "I could not dance!" she whispered, but there was longing in her tone.

Lydia nodded thoughtfully. "I understand. You think it would be wrong. I only know some of your story, but I know you were married before you had even come out. You should not be denied dancing after the life you have led. No one need know beyond the people in this room."

Georgiana visibly wavered. "I know what it is like, to have sweet words poured in your ear until you are ready to be overcome," Lydia continued. "It is so easy to be swept away. I could have been like you, but for the chance that I was discovered before it was too late. And then I showed everyone I did not deserve my fortune, because I was almost as foolish again. If it would be wrong for anyone to dance, it is me. I do not deserve to be able to, and it is only good fortune which separates us. If it will make you happy, please dance. I swear we can all be trusted. Kitty will swear it too, and I know you trust all the others, even if you do not know the two of us."

Mr Darcy looked severely at Lydia. "You do not need to dance, Georgie. If you prefer to be quiet here, or with your friends, or to return home, you may do so."

Georgiana looked at him contemplatively for a moment, then said with unexpected firmness, "I would like to dance, Fitzwilliam. I would like to dance with you."

Mr Darcy's brow furrowed. "Are you sure?"

"Yes," she said simply. "That is, if no one here objects to it."

Elizabeth, who had heard the whole exchange with great astonishment, gathered her wits to respond. "No one here will think the worse of you for it, Georgiana."

Jane, Charlotte, and Kitty made no objections to the proposal, and Mr Bingley looked delighted. Colonel Fitzwilliam declined to comment either way, but it was clear from his smile that he was pleased at the prospect. Only Mr Darcy still seemed uncertain. Taking advantage of Charlotte speaking quietly to Georgiana, Elizabeth drew him aside and looked at him expectantly. He sighed. "I am only concerned to know she is at ease," he answered her unspoken question.

"She has chosen this," Elizabeth replied. "If she is able to make her own choices, that is the surest sign we have that her confidence is growing."

Mr Darcy conceded the point and, with a happier air, returned to his sister with a bow. "May I have this dance, madam?" he asked with all the formality of the grandest ballroom.

"With pleasure, sir," she replied, her smile warm although still timid.

They took their places. Mr Bingley approached the two youngest Bennet sisters and looked between them. "I would dance with both of you if I could!" he said jovially, "but it is Kitty's turn, I think."

Lydia accepted this with good grace. "I would much rather watch Georgiana dance," she said, "for I have already said she deserves it more than I do." So saying, she took a seat alongside Jane.

Elizabeth was hard pressed to get through the music. She found her eyes moved constantly to the brother and sister on the floor, so that she fudged the notes and caused both Kitty and Mr Bingley to miss their steps. Mr Darcy and Georgiana, however, moved through the dance in perfect synchronicity, until Elizabeth found she was playing the music to match them, rather than to lead. Unlike when she had danced at the assembly, Georgiana's face bore a contented smile, new colour in her cheeks, and to the precision of her movements was added a gracefulness that became her well. Brother and sister made a delightful picture as they moved through the figures, and when it finished, he drew her into an embrace that spoke less of his need to protect her and more of the love that was the source of his solicitude.

Mr Darcy escorted his sister to take a seat with Charlotte, where he knew she would find some quiet conversation, before making his way to where Elizabeth tidied the music at the pianoforte. Without announcing himself, he spoke low in her ear. "The next time there is dancing, Miss Bennet, you will not be able to hide behind the pianoforte. I expect to be dancing with you."

She turned to face him with a merry smile. "The next time there is dancing, sir, I expect I shall no longer be Miss Bennet."

His face broke into a smile again. "No, I think you will have another name by then, Elizabeth."

CHAPTER THIRTY-EIGHT

Elizabeth's supposition was incorrect, for having had one evening gathering prove so successful, Mr Bingley insisted on arranging another before the wedding could take place. Georgiana did not choose to dance again, but willingly played to allow her brother and Elizabeth to do so. As they took their places, Elizabeth laughingly asked Mr Darcy what subject he would question her on today.

"I prepared for this evening by dressing my hair and reviewing all you have told me of Pemberley, in case you wish to test my understanding or my powers of recollection."

Mr Darcy's smile came more readily than had once been the case. "I believe I have all the information I need at present. I would not want to exhaust all conversation before we are even married."

"You clearly still have much to learn about me if you believe I shall ever run out of things to say, sir."

"Indeed? In that case, I defer to your superior conversation skills, and shall say nothing but 'yes', 'no', and 'is that so?' for the remainder of the dance." Elizabeth laughed aloud, and Mr Darcy looked smug.

"Oh, you are insufferable when you want to be!" she exclaimed with delight.

"Is that so?"

Such moments gave both Elizabeth and Darcy great pleasure as they prepared for their wedding. Although they were busy with preparations, they met daily, sometimes at Longbourn and sometimes at Purvis Lodge. Others, too, soon started gravitating to Georgiana's home, until not a day went by without a call from Charlotte or Jane. Lydia and Kitty visited together, and although it could not be said that there was a close relationship between the three younger women, they found enough common ground to occupy them all for their visit.

Joey and Tommy delighted in all the new company and soon discovered which of them could be relied upon to bring them sweets. They still preferred Jane's company above any other, but discovered that Kitty usually brought with her a treat of some kind. Charlotte did not often bring them gifts, but on the occasions she did so, she somehow contrived to provide them with something particularly special, so that they came to eagerly anticipate her visits. Lydia did not think to bring gifts at all, but when they demanded something of her, found bits of ribbon in her pocket, which they took greedily and hid away for later use.

Thus, the days passed happily and busily. Shortly before the wedding, Colonel Fitzwilliam departed for London on business for his father, promising to return ahead of the day. Mr Darcy, eager to make the most of the opportunity to have Elizabeth and Georgiana to himself, contrived to keep all guests other than Elizabeth away from Purvis Lodge. Joey and Tommy had been taken on a visit to

Netherfield, and he intended to have a quiet day with the two ladies.

The day began peacefully enough, and they were soon each about their own occupation, Elizabeth and Georgiana sewing whilst Mr Darcy wrote letters at a desk in the corner. Their tranquil productivity was interrupted, however, by the sound of hoofbeats and carriage wheels. Mr Darcy groaned and put down his pen, but before any of them had got so far as to reach the window to discover who had arrived, the answer reached them in the form of a loud voice in the passage demanding, "Where are my niece and nephew?"

Elizabeth looked up at Mr Darcy to find he had frozen on the spot, his face stony and pale. She glanced at Georgiana, who had also paled, shrinking back into herself. It was no great struggle to piece together the identity of the visitor before the lady entered the room, followed by the anxious maid, who announced with a nervous curtsey, "Lady Catherine de Bourgh, ma'am."

Lady Catherine stood regally in the centre of the room, eyeing first Mr Darcy and then Georgiana with a haughty expression. The gentleman looked back coldly. Georgiana looked stricken, and Elizabeth moved discreetly to her side. She was not discreet enough, however, for Lady Catherine at once turned her gaze hawk-like upon her and sharply asked, "Who is that?"

"Lady Catherine, may I present Miss Elizabeth Bennet, my future wife," Darcy replied, his voice hard. "Elizabeth, this is Lady Catherine de Bourgh."

"Mr Darcy's aunt, and sister of his most beloved mother," the lady continued sharply.

He did not acknowledge the words, but enquired with no attempt at civility, "Why are you here?"

"I have come to call upon my dear sister's children." Lady

Catherine stiffly took a seat, gesturing irritably to Darcy. He did not match her action, but crossed to the window, closer to the younger ladies.

Lady Catherine looked around her. "Such a small room," she stated.

Her eyes fixed on her niece. "Now that the unfortunate business of Georgiana's marriage is dealt with," she sniffed as she spoke, "we need to remove the stain of that man's name from her, so it can be completely forgotten. I have with me a list of suitable candidates who would be willing enough to take her for her connexions after the proper time. I doubt that man left her with anything to live on."

Mr Darcy's face had already been pale, but it grew only paler. He was for a moment speechless, and Lady Catherine continued without waiting for a response.

"Of course, I could have written, but having heard of your intended marriage," she cast a glance over Elizabeth, who set her jaw and lifted her head defiantly, "I thought it better to come in person. As though Georgiana's misalliance were not bad enough, you seek to ally yourself to this person! The sister of my own parson's wife! Have you no regard for your connexions? Your family? Now that the steward's son is dispensed with, your engagement to Anne will be renewed. I am sure this girl will be more than happy to be suitably compensated for the loss."

Elizabeth bristled, and would have spoken out had she not felt Georgiana trembling at her side. Comforting her friend was of more immediate importance than confronting her accuser, and she gently took Georgiana's hand and squeezed it.

Mr Darcy had taken his eyes from Lady Catherine only briefly during this speech, to see how it affected the ladies. Seeing the flash in Elizabeth's eye and the movement of her hand to Georgiana's, he seemed satisfied. He turned his attention back to his aunt.

"You have insulted me, my sister, and my future wife in every possible way. You made it abundantly clear three years past that you would have nothing to do with us, and I intend to honour the wishes you stated then, for they accord entirely with mine. You know perfectly well that I was never engaged to Anne. I hope you think better of my mother than that you would believe any son of hers would go back on his word in the manner you suggest. Georgiana requires no husband. She has a home for life at Pemberley. She certainly needs none of your choosing. You will leave the premises and will never importune any of us again."

Lady Catherine fumed. "How dare you speak to me so!" she snapped. "I have travelled here from Kent to protect my dear sister's legacy, and you refuse my assistance! Have you lost all pride in your name that you will shame Pemberley so, by bringing to it this woman as mistress and your disgraced sister to live with you? You do not deserve to bear the name Fitzwilliam."

"Your choice to journey here was not of my making, and you can have nothing further to say to me. I am my own man, and, having been so fortunate as to win her, I will marry the woman I love irrespective of you or any other person." With that, he stalked across the room and rang the bell, staring in frosty silence at his aunt. When the maid came, he said coldly, "Lady Catherine is leaving now."

Lady Catherine drew herself up to her full height. "You will persist in this folly! You will never be welcome at Rosings again!"

"A loss I have lived with for the past three years and see no hardship in continuing," he replied.

She turned on her heel and stalked from the room. Mr

Darcy followed her, standing at the doorway of the house to ensure she climbed into her coach and departed.

Georgiana still trembled, but as soon as her aunt left the room, she crossed to the window and stood, wringing her hands with agitation. Elizabeth summoned a maid and ordered a glass of wine, hoping it might help to relieve her friend's distress. When it arrived, she pressed it into her hand. "Will you drink this?" she asked. Georgiana did so, sitting in a nearby chair and sipping at the glass. She showed no inclination to talk.

Mr Darcy found them thus on his return. "I am sorry you were both exposed to Lady Catherine's behaviour. I have given instructions that she be denied entry to the house if she returns. She will not trouble us again." He looked from one to the other before drawing a chair over to sit with them. "Georgie?" he asked gently. She lifted her eyes to meet his but did not speak.

Elizabeth, seeing that brother and sister were engrossed in some silent communication, rose and made her way to the writing desk, where she took a fresh sheet of paper and began to write rapidly.

"Elizabeth?" Darcy's gaze turned on her.

"I understand the desire to protect a sister, Fitzwilliam," she replied, continuing to write. "I suspect Lady Catherine will not spare any around her from her current wrath, and Mary and Mr Collins are often summoned for her amusement. I shall send this by express immediately. I hope it will reach them in time to forewarn them, at least, for a horse can travel faster than a carriage."

She finished her note in silence and arranged rapidly for it to be dispatched, then turned to the others. Darcy had not succeeded in encouraging his sister to speak, and was watching her with mingled concern and sorrow. He looked pleadingly at Elizabeth, and she moved to join them.

"Lady Catherine's opinions are not shared by any of the people who love you, Georgiana," she said emphatically. "Do not take them to heart."

Georgiana shook her head. "It is not that."

"Then what? Will you tell us?"

The younger woman set down her empty glass, and rising, crossed to the window again. Darcy shifted in his seat, as if he would follow her, but Elizabeth took the vacated seat and placed a hand on his arm to stay his movement.

Georgiana did not turn around as she replied. "Lady Catherine would erase my marriage and all association with it. She did not even acknowledge that my unhappy past had produced two very happy results. When she entered, I felt like the child I was when I saw her last, but as she spoke, I came to realise that I am no longer that child. I am a woman, and a mother, and have already seen too much of life, yet I have not yet lived."

Her voice had grown stronger as she spoke, and she now turned resolutely to face them. "Brother, you have done so much to care for me, even so much as to stoop to concealment to protect me and my children when I feared what their father might do. You have always been my protector, and I am deeply grateful. But you, too, in your own way, seek to sweep my marriage away as though it never happened. Oh, not as Lady Catherine did," she said firmly, seeing he made as if to protest, "but you would take me back to Pemberley to be your Georgie once again and to forget I was ever married. You do not deny my sons, at least, but you would forget everything else if you could.

"My past has shaped me, and changed me from the girl I was three years ago. I know we are dependent on you, that

George made no provision for our future and that any remainder of my portion will need to be put to his debts. But I do not wish to lose everything I have become. I never came out into society and have never learnt to live amongst people. It is time I came out from under your wing, Fitzwilliam."

She cast her brother a pleading glance. He sat almost motionless apart from a small gesture to show she should continue. Elizabeth could feel his tension from her seat at his side, and she ached for him, admiring his determination to hear his sister out, however painful it must be for him.

"Your marriage has been founded on mine," Georgiana continued, "and I am inexpressibly happy for you both. I believe you and Lizzy are capable of that rarity, a truly equal and happy marriage, and I wish you every blessing. But if I return to Pemberley with you, as you assume I wish to, you will both forever be caring for me above yourselves, and I fear you will never learn what you might be to one another." She crossed the room now and knelt at her brother's feet. His face was a mask, and remained unmoving as she took both of his hands in hers, although his eyes gazed longingly at her.

"You must let me go. I shall come with you to London after the wedding, for it will be a pleasure to see our uncle and aunt again. When you return to Pemberley, however, I shall not join you."

"Where do you intend to live?" he asked hoarsely. His voice was defeated and anguished rather than angry or reproachful. He had fought Lady Catherine, Elizabeth thought sadly, but could not bring himself to fight his sister. He was too honourable to deny the truth of her words, however much he might wish to keep her close under his protection.

"I do not know yet. Perhaps I ought to return here, where

I have friends. Or perhaps it will be better to go somewhere with no unhappy associations. Bath, perhaps. Somewhere I might learn to live in society as myself, and not merely as George's widow or your sister. I shall live with a companion, but I will not live with you."

"Never?"

"I do not know. Perhaps in time, when you have children, I could return and be of service to you. I am not inexperienced in that, at least." She smiled a watery smile. Mr Darcy could not return it but continued to look earnestly at her. Georgiana carefully prised her hands from his and turned to Elizabeth.

"Do not think I am rejecting you, my dearest friend. It will be my greatest joy to see you assume your position as mistress of Pemberley, and I shall certainly visit. I have more trust in you than in anyone else I know, other than Fitzwilliam, and I know you will care for him as he deserves. But you both need the time to be together without always looking to see that I am safe and well."

With this, Georgiana took the hand of each and solemnly joined them. "This is for the best," she said. Abruptly she rose to her feet and stepped away, rapidly leaving the room before either could move to prevent it. The two sat stunned, each battling a barrage of emotions.

"Fitzwilliam?" It felt as though an age had passed before Elizabeth ventured to speak. Neither had released the other's hand. Mr Darcy had turned his face away from her.

"I did not mean to enclose or oppress her." His ragged voice betrayed his emotion. "I only ever sought her safety and her happiness."

"Fitzwilliam, look at me." He slowly did as he was bid, showing her a face aged by doubt and sorrow. Elizabeth lifted a hand to his cheek. "You have done everything you could do to help and protect her. She is a grown woman, despite her youth, and must be allowed to choose her own path. She does not act lightly or foolishly. She knows better than either of us the cost of a wrong choice. She asks for her freedom not only for herself, but for you—for us, and for the sake of our marriage. You have cared for her for so long now. Allow her to look after you."

"You support her choice then?"

Elizabeth looked him full in the eyes. "I do."

His shoulders dropped slightly as he let out an inaudible sigh. "We must seek out a companion for her. It will be hard to find another I can trust with her care after Mrs Younge."

"Yes," Elizabeth agreed, "we must. But do not rush and start advertising all at once. She would like a say in that too, I think."

With a defeated air, Darcy nodded. Elizabeth squeezed his hand. "It will not seem so awful soon, I promise. You are not losing a sister. This step may separate our daily lives, but it will tie her heart closer to yours than ever. Her freedom to live as she chooses is the greatest gift you could give her."

"Thank you, my love," he murmured, bringing a flush to her cheeks. "What is it?" he asked.

Elizabeth paused before answering. "Your words recalled your defence of me to your aunt."

"Do not call her that. She is Lady Catherine, and nothing else to me."

"Do not close that door entirely. Perhaps in time some common ground could be found."

"At this moment, I care not. What was it that came to mind?"

She blushed, but her reply was playful. "Only that I rather liked being defended so vigorously as the woman you love."

A small smile graced his lips at last, and he lifted his

hand to lightly brush her cheek. "I hope I would defend you to anyone, Elizabeth. I do love you, dearly."

Elizabeth smiled in return, before a laughing glimmer appeared in her eye. "I am pleased to hear it," she replied. "I would not have thought I had any cause for thanking Lady Catherine, but for that declaration, I shall confess I am entirely grateful to her."

CHAPTER THIRTY-NINE

W hen Georgiana returned to the room, she had lost some of the confidence with which she left it and appeared abashed. She entered cautiously, looking to her brother for reassurance that her outburst had not been taken amiss. He and Elizabeth had been talking quietly, but he stood at once and opened his arms to his sister, who ran forward like a child into his embrace. Elizabeth watched the two quietly, until Georgiana broke away and came towards her, reaching for her hands. Elizabeth did not take them, but stood and matched Mr Darcy's action, and Georgiana fell just as willingly into her arms.

They were none of them much inclined to talk, but they sat in companionable silence. After a full quarter of an hour of contemplative companionship, Georgiana returned to the subject on each of their minds.

"We shall need to seek a companion. Will you prepare an advertisement, Fitzwilliam?"

"If you wish me to," he replied, moving to the desk at once.

Before he could take up his pen, however, Elizabeth spoke. "It may not be necessary to advertise."

"Whyever not? Do you know of someone who might prove suitable?"

Elizabeth smiled. "We would need to speak to her, but I do have someone in mind."

"Who?" Georgiana asked, brow furrowed. "Is it someone I am not yet acquainted with?"

"No," Elizabeth laughed, enjoying her friend's confusion. "It is someone you know well, and I am surprised you have not yet thought of her. Let me see whether you can guess. She is an unmarried lady and of respectable birth. I believe she would benefit from some time spent away from her childhood neighbourhood, particularly since one of her dearest friends is soon to be married, and I think she might be very lonely."

Mr Darcy reached a conclusion first. "And do you believe Miss Lucas would be willing to become a companion? I would not want to insult her with any such offer."

"She will be pleased to help her friend. And," her smile grew a little fiendish, "since she is unmarried, I think the roles might be reversed. She would benefit from the companionship of a widow of independent means who would be able to chaperon her in Bath society."

Georgiana laughed a welcome laugh at this. "I am not sure I would make a successful chaperon! I shall be too shy to speak to anyone I do not already know."

"Charlotte would have no such doubts, particularly if you are able to furnish her with some suitable letters of introduction, Fitzwilliam."

"I do still have some connexions in Bath. Undoubtedly, I could arrange something of the sort."

Smiling, Elizabeth looked at Georgiana. "What do you think of my plan?"

"If Charlotte is willing, I think it would be an excellent arrangement," she replied at once, clapping her hands. "I would be glad to not need to introduce someone new into the children's lives. Yes, I think it would make me very happy."

"What say you both to a walk?" Elizabeth asked briskly. "I think your plan for a quiet afternoon has already been successfully ruined, Fitzwilliam. Why do we not seize the moment and call on Charlotte today?"

"Are you sure she would welcome us appearing all together to put the plan to her?" Georgiana asked doubtfully.

"In truth, my design is to encourage Charlotte to join us, and for you to put the plan to her whilst I steal a few moments to enjoy the sole attention of your brother," Elizabeth replied mischievously. "Then, if she is agreeable, I shall swap one Darcy for the other and enjoy your company whilst he resolves any concerns she may have around the business side of the matter. Finally, Fitzwilliam will be able to call for the carriage and escort you home whilst I make my abject apologies to Charlotte for having formed such a notion without consulting her."

Georgiana laughed again. "How could I refuse such a plan? I have not walked so far in ever so long, but I am sure it will do me good to be out in the air."

The three set out along the lane. When Elizabeth made an abrupt turn through a gap in the trees to one side that her companions had not noticed, Mr Darcy pulled up short.

"So, this is where you disappeared to that day! I followed after you, but I never strayed from the lane."

"It may have been for the best that you did not catch me.

I am not sure I would have been receptive to anything you had to say at that time."

He gave her a rueful look. "I regret that your uncertainty lasted as long as it did. I was grateful in the end that Bingley was able to speak to your sister about it."

"I wish I had known sooner. But all is well, now." Elizabeth smiled as his eyes softened and he drew closer to her.

"It is. And soon, very soon, it will be even better."

"Fitzwilliam!" Georgiana interjected playfully. He pulled back with a guilty air. "I think I would enjoy being a chaperon after all," she said sweetly, as she ushered them both along in front of her.

Charlotte met them with a great deal of surprise, for she knew their plan had been to not see guests that day. She readily joined them for a walk, however. Elizabeth had every intention of watching her closely to examine her reaction, but Mr Darcy had taken her assertion that she would have his sole attention to heart, and demanded she returned the same to him.

As they strolled, Mr Darcy cleared his throat slightly and said, "Lady Catherine's behaviour earlier was abominable."

"It was certainly unexpected," Elizabeth said calmly, following it immediately with a short laugh. "But it has made it somewhat clearer why Mama's manner has never caused you undue concern."

"With such examples in my own family, how could I disdain yours?"

"I am glad you do not, despite all the grandeur of your wealth and connexions. I do not think I could marry a man who despised my circumstances or refused to acknowledge my dear aunt and uncle Gardiner."

"I look forward to meeting them. On the subject of the

grandeur of my wealth, I have been meaning to speak to you regarding my finances."

Elizabeth was perplexed. "You have?"

"Indeed. In settling Wickham's affairs, it has become clear there are a great many debts left unpaid, some of which have been made in my name."

"And which you intend to honour," Elizabeth continued for him with a smile. Mr Darcy bowed his head in agreement.

"I could not in all good conscience leave the tradesmen of England to suffer from his behaviour any more than they have."

"And his other debtors? Surely they are not all tradesmen?"

"Forgive me if I keep the handling of those to myself and my cousin."

"I am sure you will do all that is necessary," Elizabeth replied. "But why did you need to speak to me on the subject?"

"Wickham's debts are substantial, and I shall be supporting Georgiana in Bath, as well as honouring the lease on Purvis Lodge. My income is adequate to support it, but you know already the rate at which he spent Georgiana's portion, and it will take some time to clear the more considerable debts. I intend to retrench. Nothing so very substantial," he added hastily, "but it might disappoint your mother. No ball at Pemberley to welcome our marriage, and shorter Seasons in town. I would not reduce your personal allowance, of course, but we may make a less grand showing than your mother expects. It would allow the debt to be cleared more rapidly."

Elizabeth laughed aloud. "Oh, I feared you were about to tell me you would have to sell half of your land or some such! I think I can bear not having a ball, and whilst I enjoy being in town, from all I have heard of Pemberley, I believe it will take me at least three years to explore it in its entirety."

"Then you do not mind economising?"

She laughed again. "I believe we may have different ideas of what the word means. I do not mind that you see fit to take these measures, and I heartily approve that you took the time to discuss them with me."

She accompanied these words with a light squeeze of his arm and a bright smile. He stopped in his tracks and turned to take both her hands in his and lift them to his lips. They were unconscious of all around them, and therefore it was with some surprise that they found themselves interrupted by a loud cough. Starting, they turned to find themselves confronted by Charlotte, arms folded and with a stern expression.

"Lizzy, how could you suggest this plan without even consulting me?" she asked reproachfully. Elizabeth flushed and began marshalling her arguments for why this would be an excellent plan for Charlotte as well as for Georgiana, when she noticed a twitch at the corner of her friend's mouth and a gleam in her eye.

She pulled herself up and boldly answered, in imitation of her mother, "Oh! Charlotte, to be able to go to Bath! To take the waters, and to visit the theatres—oh, the balls and parties one can attend! Oh Charlotte, what a kind thing it is of Miss Darcy to suggest it for you."

Charlotte could no longer keep a straight face and laughed along with Elizabeth. "If it were anyone else, I would be exceedingly cross for not having been consulted first," she said. "But I am inclined to forgive you for it. I cannot deny it is an excellent plan."

Georgiana came then and took Elizabeth's arm. "Come, I would like to talk to you."

Elizabeth smiled. "Let us talk, then," she replied, and set out walking at a good pace, leaving Charlotte with Darcy.

It did not take long for the others to catch up, and Charlotte called, "It is all right, Lizzy. Everything is arranged, bar a discussion with my parents, and you need not hide from me."

"I am glad to hear it," her friend replied, stopping and turning to wait for them. The four walked along comfortably, discussing what needed to be done to set the two ladies up together in Bath. When Georgiana began to grow tired, they returned to Lucas Lodge and sent for the carriage. Mr Darcy would have taken Elizabeth back to Longbourn, but she demurred, insisting she would remain with Charlotte. Knowing they would soon be parted, she wished to make the most of her time with her friend before she became Mrs Darcy.

CHAPTER FORTY

Longbourn was a hive of activity, for Mrs Bennet was determined that Elizabeth's wedding to a man of such consequence as Mr Darcy would outshine any other in the living memory of the people of Meryton. Jane, unwilling to be excluded from the delights of the preparations, was at Longbourn daily, and Mr Darcy also called every morning to steal Elizabeth for a walk when the weather permitted. He did not often linger amidst the tumult, but mentioned he was counting down the days until he might whisk her off to the quiet of his own home. Neither Charlotte nor Georgiana neglected their friend, although they were each busy at their own preparations for removing to Bath, and Elizabeth found herself much in demand.

The day before the wedding, after all the visitors except Jane had departed to prepare for the morrow, their activity was abruptly interrupted by another arrival, no less welcome than Jane's but entirely less expected.

"Mrs Collins!" Mrs Bennet greeted her middle daughter, her already high spirits overcoming her. "Oh, my dear Mary, you are here! And not a word to anyone! What a good joke, to come to us with no warning. Oh! I shall have to find you a seat at the wedding breakfast! You do delight in vexing me! Is it any wonder my nerves trouble me so?"

As this entire speech was made with a broad smile and was concluded with Mrs Bennet bustling out to herald the arrival of Mary and young William to her husband, no one was unduly concerned that Mrs Bennet's nerves would interfere with her happiness. Jane, however, had noticed her sister looked pale and wan, and quickly drew her to a seat.

"What brings you here so unexpectedly, Mary? Why did you not tell us you were coming? There is no trouble at Hunsford, I hope? You have not quarrelled with Mr Collins?"

This was, from Jane, a torrent of questions, and Mary hesitated before replying, looking nervously at Elizabeth. Her sister caught her gaze. "Lady Catherine," she said flatly.

Mary nodded. "She has been exceedingly vexed since her visit to Hertfordshire, and has insisted Mr Collins attend her at every opportunity."

"Lady Catherine was in Hertfordshire?" Kitty interrupted. "Was she in Meryton?"

"She called at Purvis Lodge," Elizabeth replied mildly, "to inform Mr Darcy that he did not have her blessing for our marriage. He, not being beholden to her, chose to follow his own wishes, rather than hers."

Lydia laughed. "I would have liked to have seen that. Did he frown menacingly at her? Or did he storm and rage and threaten to duel her, although she is a woman? I wish I could watch a duel."

"Nothing so thrilling, I am afraid, but Lady Catherine will not have been happy since then. Have you been much subject to her displeasure, Mary?"

"Not directly. I have not been invited to Rosings Park

since her return, although as I said, Mr Collins is summoned to attend her almost daily. When we received your letter, I suggested to him that I might be better visiting Longbourn, so that he can devote more of his attention to her. He had not wanted me to travel because—well, that matters not. Yesterday, when he called at Rosings Park, she expressed some sentiments that quite astonished him, after which he agreed it might be better if little William and I were not at Hunsford for a few weeks. I had meant to write, but we left in a hurry, and there was no time."

The reactions to this speech were all that might be expected. Lydia exclaimed, "You ought to have come earlier, Mary, whatever he thought!"

Kitty agreed, adding, "It is good that Mr Collins saw sense, if Lady Catherine is so very fearsome at Mr Darcy marrying Lizzy."

Elizabeth felt some sorrow at her sister's situation, although it was tempered with her good spirits and general inclination towards joy. "I am sorry that my happiness has caused you any distress. I am glad you are here for my wedding, even under such circumstances."

Jane, having watched Mary carefully as she spoke, merely took her hand and murmured, "I am very happy for you!"

Mary blushed at Jane's quick comprehension. "I had not meant to reveal it," she replied. "It is still so new."

Jane merely smiled and shooed away their younger sisters. "Mary will need to refresh herself," she announced, leading her middle sister away.

Longbourn had not seen such a harmonious gathering of the family in many years. Mrs Bennet, of course, could not be subdued; she fidgeted and exclaimed, alternately praising Elizabeth for making such a grand match and berating her for the lack of lace on her wedding clothes. Mary was content to sit peacefully in the drawing room, playing with young William. When she opened the pianoforte, she found it had begun to lose its tuning, and scolded Elizabeth. "None of the others play. I would have thought you would keep up your practice, for surely when you are married you will wish to be a credit to Mr Darcy."

Elizabeth laughed. "I am certain he did not propose to me for my musical talents, Mary. Especially not given how exquisitely his sister plays. But you are right, I ought to practise more, or I shall lose what little skill I have."

"I do not practise as often as I should, now that I am married, but I still set aside time for it," Mary said piously.

"And you are very good to do so," Elizabeth averred, before turning aside so that Mary would not see the twitch of her lips.

The Bennet family party was completed by Lydia and Kitty, who giggled, whispered, and bickered just a little, and Jane, who smiled benignly, smoothing ruffled tempers. Elizabeth was grateful for her calming presence, but found she was less troubled by her family's exuberance than she might once have been. She resolved to enjoy the relative harmony, and to not trouble herself over whether it would be a permanent change or not.

The morning of Elizabeth's wedding day dawned, inauspiciously enough, with a light but steady rain of a kind that promised to last for several days. Elizabeth, however, was in too great a state of happiness to notice. Mr Bennet was torn between wry amusement and concern when she brushed off her inability to escape the house for a walk with nothing more than a serene smile. He settled on amusement when he caught her after breakfast, humming to herself and dancing alone in the upstairs passage, thus proving herself as silly as any of her sisters.

Jane arrived shortly after breakfast, unwilling to miss the opportunity to share in Elizabeth's preparations. Mr Bennet, however, was very willing to do so, and promptly withdrew to his study. The women set about all their tasks with a will, and the house soon rang with the sound of their voices. Eventually, all was ready, and the ladies departed for church, leaving Elizabeth to be accompanied there by Mr Bennet, who had expressed a wish for a private interview before the ceremony.

In the carriage, he smiled benignly at her.

"I need not ask whether you are happy, child. Even my old eyes can see you are radiant. Nor do I need to say that I hope Mr Darcy will take good care of you. He has proved he takes his responsibility seriously. I shall miss you, Lizzy, very much, for without you here, there will be hardly a word of sense to be had. How shall I know what occurs at all the assemblies and dinners that your mother will insist on taking your sisters to?"

"Dear Papa," Elizabeth replied with laughing admonishment, "I believe you will find yourself quite comfortable with only two daughters to disturb your peace. Perhaps you might ask Lydia to become your informant. I am sure her accounts of an evening would be entertaining."

Mr Bennet appeared unconvinced. "I shall miss you, nevertheless. You will not forget your poor old Papa?"

"I promise to write to you twice as often as you will write to me," Elizabeth smiled.

"Then I shall have to be a less desultory correspondent," he replied, patting her hand complacently as she laughed again, "to ensure I hear from you frequently."

Elizabeth's merriment subsided as she approached the church. Not that she was anything less than happy at the prospect of her marriage, but as she stepped inside, she could not help but recall the first time she had seen Mr Darcy, in that same building, and of all that had happened since. How much had changed since then! She fought an impulse to grow sentimental at the prospect of marrying with all of her four sisters in attendance—nay, all five of them.

Georgiana was dressed in her customary black, but could not disguise her joy at the occasion, and her face was wreathed with smiles. She sat alongside Charlotte, who looked on with calm pleasure at the proceedings, sharing a quiet smile with Elizabeth when she caught her eye. After smiling fondly at them both as she passed, Elizabeth turned her full attention to the tall man at her side, whose eyes had been fixed on her from the moment she entered the church.

Elizabeth had not doubted the sincerity of Mr Darcy's intentions in their marriage, but there was a steadiness in his gaze that, had she been unsure, would have settled her concerns at once. His regard for her may have grown from his desire to see his sister well supported, but she felt certain it had taken root and would flourish for its own sake.

The wedding service passed as such things do. Mrs Bennet, unexpectedly enough, curbed her tendency to exclamation, silenced by the happy state induced by the knowledge of a third daughter married, and to a man with ten thousand a year! If Mr Bennet found he was in need of a handkerchief, his family were kinder to him than he might have been had the situation been reversed, and did not mention it. The only notice it received was from Mary who, accustomed to carrying spare handkerchiefs since her marriage, quietly passed him one of hers, in case he should require it.

The wedding breakfast was merry and created such a cacophony of noise and laughter that Longbourn might have been the assembly hall itself. Elizabeth found she was as often apart from Mr Darcy as she was beside him, and it felt as though half the population of Hertfordshire wished to bid her goodbye and offer their heartfelt congratulations. She was not reluctant to give time and attention to the friends and acquaintances she would be leaving behind. She was no longer Elizabeth Bennet of Longbourn, Hertfordshire, but Elizabeth Darcy, soon to be of Pemberley in Derbyshire. She was grateful, however, to see that Mr and Mrs Bingley had quietly taken command of her husband and kept him company when they had greeted all the well-wishers once, and she found herself pulled into conversation with some of them for a second time. She was pleased to see he did not confine himself to their company, but spoke readily with Sir William Lucas and politely enough with others who greeted him.

Georgiana, too, had retired to their quiet corner and, although fewer of the people of Meryton approached her, was not alone. Elizabeth saw Colonel Fitzwilliam, Charlotte, and Mary all speaking to her at different times, and more surprisingly on one occasion, Mrs Bennet. Elizabeth caught only a glimpse of her mother, and hoped she was not saying aught that would make Georgiana uncomfortable. As Georgiana seemed nothing more than mildly alarmed at the onslaught of conversation, however, and as Jane and Charlotte were both close enough to partake in the discussion if required, Elizabeth resisted the temptation to interfere.

Elizabeth delighted in the warmth of the wedding guests, but she was not sorry when the time came for their party to depart Longbourn for London. She glanced at Georgiana and Charlotte as they settled into the second carriage, set to ride no great distance behind them; the two boys had been sent ahead with their nursemaid and the luggage that morning.

As her husband helped her into the carriage, Elizabeth smiled at him gently. "I hope you do not think it too inauspicious a beginning that we have been kept apart so frequently today."

"On the contrary, I think it highly promising," he replied with a broad smile as he settled beside her. "From what I overheard of your conversation, and from what I know of your storytelling abilities, I am anticipating a highly entertaining journey to London as you regale me with your observations of all your neighbours."

"Ah, so now we have the truth of it! You have married me so I might keep you entertained on long journeys!"

"Yes," he replied solemnly as an arm wound around her waist, "that is exactly why I have married you, Mrs Darcy." He drew her closer until she leant against him, and looked down to meet her laughing eyes. "I married you to entertain me on long journeys, and over breakfast, and at interminable balls, and on walks in the grounds at Pemberley, and—if we must be apart—so that I am always assured of an excellent correspondent."

"Shall I tell you why I married you?"

"I suspect it will not have been because of the romance of my proposal."

"'Tis all in the past," she said with a wave of her hand, which he caught quickly in his. "And you corrected your error as soon as you perceived it. No, I married you because I find in you a man who takes his duty and his responsibilities so very seriously, and who I could see was concealing a deep well of compassion under a burden of care. I married you because I could not bear to see you carrying that weight alone when I could help you with it. I married you because I could see there was a man who desperately wanted to laugh but had forgotten how. I married you because I love you."

If Elizabeth had been expecting a similar speech in response to her assertions, she was disappointed, but could not complain when she found herself gathered up in his arms, in the closest embrace she had ever enjoyed. Her shriek of surprise was abruptly cut off by the warmth of his lips pressed to hers. She succumbed willingly, if breathlessly, and could not have accounted for how long it was before they broke apart.

"Do you need me to tell you honestly why I married you, lovely Elizabeth?" he asked, running his thumb across her cheek.

"At least once a day, dear."

"I think I can do better than that," he said with half a smile, kissing her again softly.

The End

ACKNOWLEDGMENTS

This book stands on the shoulders of two literary giants. In *Pride and Prejudice*, Jane Austen created a thought-provoking, entertaining, fascinating story and such rich characters that they transcend the novel and continue to inspire people today. Thirty-five years later, Anne Brontë published the radical and thought-provoking *The Tenant of Wildfell Hall*, exploring a situation that is very much of its time and yet has themes that continue to resonate today. I feel immensely privileged to have been inspired by both books in the creation of this one.

I am indebted to the online communities of *Archive of Our Own* and *A Happy Assembly*. They have inspired and challenged, supported and encouraged me. I am particularly grateful to the people who read and commented on the story as it grew, for being so warm, enthusiastic and thoughtful. There are too many of you to name, but you are wonderful and had you not been there, this book would never have existed.

This book was a constant learning experience, and I am also grateful to the people who devote their time and energy to maintaining sources of information—particularly the Regency Encyclopaedia and the Etymological Dictionary—which allowed me to explore and develop my understanding of Regency England.

I am of course indebted to everyone at Quills & Quartos,

particularly Jan Ashton, for reaching out and helping me turn my story into a real book, and for making the experience so enjoyable. Jan and Jo Abbott were both professional and supportive editors who guided me expertly and kindly through the entire process, and I am grateful for their patience with my many questions.

Finally, thank you to all my family, for the words and the stories. Most importantly, I would like to thank R for loving, supporting, and encouraging me in this and in so many things. We are my favourite story.

ABOUT THE AUTHOR

Elsie Fulbrook loves stories; whether a book, song, dance or drawing—if it tells a story, it has her hooked. She has always been a reader of anything she can get her hands on, from books to the backs of cereal packets. She loves words and is fond of reading the dictionary. Although a long-time Austen fan, she only discovered the world of Austenesque variations during the Covid-19 pandemic, where it provided a welcome source of distraction and delight, and she quickly took to writing it herself. She has a degree in English Literature, and lives in London.

Made in the USA
Las Vegas, NV
02 March 2024

86617319R00225